**Advance Praise for**

# *Made of Honor*

"*Made of Honor* is most definitely sassy, cynical,
humorous chick lit. But in Mary's inspired hands, her
book is also custom-made with love, faith and a
huge dollop of aromatic tenderness."
—Sharon Ewell Foster, Christy Award-winning
author of *Ain't No Valley*

"With a voice that begs you to relax, sit down
and put your feet up, Marilynn Griffith writes of the
complexities of love, family, friendship and what it
means to be the bride of Christ, and does so with
honesty, humor and grace. Don't miss
*Made of Honor* or Marilynn—both welcome
additions to Christian fiction!"
—Lisa Samson, Christy Award-winning author of
*Club Sandwich*

"Marilynn Griffith's voice just sings! Watch out, world,
*Made of Honor* will make you laugh out loud and
welcome you into the Sassy Sistahood."
—Kristin Billerbeck, bestselling author of
*She's All That*

"Fun! Fresh! Full of faith! A merry heart does
good like a medicine, and Marilynn Griffith's
writing is just what the doctor ordered."
—Annie Jones, bestselling author of *Mom Over Miami*

# Made of Honor
# MARILYNN GRIFFITH

Steeple
Hill
Café™

Published by Steeple Hill Books™

STEEPLE HILL BOOKS

ISBN 0-373-78554-2

MADE OF HONOR

www.SteepleHill.com

**Printed in U.S.A.**

For my parents, Donna Lee McElrath and Michael Onyedika. Thank you for giving me life. Because of your love I was created, fearfully and wonderfully made.

# Chapter One

I'm turning into a Chia Pet.

With legs.

Little children are starting to toss dandelions when they see me. The brides of Leverhill, Illinois, have taught the kiddies well. One little darling wants to grow up and be just like me—a big flower girl. She nailed it, especially about the big part, but we're not going there. Not today, with my formerly fat friend looking like Twiggy-goes-bridal, while I gasp for breath in a dress fit for a train wreck. My only consolation is not having to worry about Tracey aiming a floral missile—known to some as a bouquet—at me later on.

She wouldn't do me like that, would she? Nah. At least that's what I tell myself, but then I thought this wedding wouldn't happen, either. Still, this bride is one of my closest friends and my roommate for the past three years. Tracey Cox—well, Tracey Blackman now—has picked enough baby's breath out of my teeth to know better.

Just in case though, a pint of Chunky Monkey and a pedicure appointment await me after this reception. Who knows? Tracey just might snap and throw long. Marriage does things to people.

One day they're normal and the next they're inviting total strangers to wear ugly dresses in their weddings, and then after the ceremony, said brides proceed to cut off all communication with members of the wedding party except for goofy Christmas photos of the newlyweds cradling an ugly dog, signed "from all of us." And don't let them actually get pregnant. Have you ever seen an entire album of birth photos? Not cute.

Do I sound bitter?

I'm not. I have friends. And trying to keep up with them, keep my job and stay right with God occupies most of my time. Like now. I need to find Rochelle, my other best friend—yes, I have two—and founder of the Sassy Sistahood e-mail list. If I don't catch up to her soon, she might make a fool of herself.

Or me.

Though my girlfriend is a paragon of virtue most days, weddings turn Rochelle into a gelatinous pool of desperation. Remember the birth photo album I mentioned? It's worse. Okay, so nothing's worse than that, but it's bad. Even the sight of me, tangled in tulips after a bouquet toss, is easier on the eyes.

Using my emergency X-ray vision, activated by squinting so hard I almost fused my contacts to my eyeballs, I glimpsed a pink satin horror similar to my own, but a set of three-inch shoulder pads blocked my view. Who would wear a power suit to a wedding—?

My boss. There she was, looking just as angry as when I'd left her at work last night. I ducked before she saw me, recovering from my shock that she'd even shown up. The bride, who left our office to start her own graphic design firm six months ago, insisted on inviting Naomi, her former and my current employer, and Renee, my assistant, who was probably somewhere taking pictures of me for later blackmail. She'd be giggling in my ear for the next month. At least.

My next few weeks of torture aside, I was proud of Naomi for actually leaving the office—I think she secretly lives there. For her to show up at her own funeral would be the height of etiquette. Some people just don't grasp interaction, you know? And having "interacted" with Naomi daily for the past six years, I could do without her today. Besides, I needed to find Sassy Sistah #1 before she melted down and kissed somebody.

With that thought as fuel, I forced my satin shoes that were dyed to match the gown—the dye was free, I guess Tracey couldn't resist—across the sprinkle of autumn leaves on the ground. Rochelle tiptoed up beside me, fanning her face, despite the growing chill. Man Mania was in full swing.

"Did you see Ryan's brother?" she said breathlessly. "From the looks of things, Tracey should have picked him."

From the reality of things, anyone seemed a better choice. I mentally squashed the nagging doubt about my friend's hour-old marriage. Thoughts like that were getting me nowhere. It was done. God would have to take it from here. Me worrying myself to an ulcer before I got back to work on Monday was definitely a waste of resources.

I shook my head at Rochelle and considered reaching out and shaking hers. This time she was really in the zone. I spoke right into her ear, hoping it would jar her brain. "I wasn't really paying attention to the brother of the groom." Or any other man around here. What would be the point? The last guy I dated had just married my best friend.

Rochelle made a clucking sound. "You should have been paying attention. His brother is fiiine." She rolled her neck for effect, but didn't quite pull it off. I just stared. She'd been watching too much UPN again.

"Come on." I tugged at her arm and started back across the smattering of red-gold leaves, away from Mr. Fiiine. She'd hate me tomorrow if I didn't. If a man showed up later on in response to Rochelle's flirting, she would run for her life while dictating a restraining order into her recorder.

Usually, her wedding trance would have been long since broken. But this was Tracey's wedding. And whether Rochelle and

I were willing to admit it or not, we'd both thought that if any-one got married, it'd be us, not the cute, fat, geek of the group. Not that Tracey was fat anymore. Plump-but-cute girl was cur-rently being played by *moi*, my midsection pressed against the strangling fabric of my dress as if in agreement.

Rochelle made a shrill sound, almost like a whistle. The weary-in-well-doing sigh. Not a good sign. Her pink leather t-strap shoes, designed by her own hand and much prettier than my prom knockoffs, peeked from underneath her Pepto-pink frock, several sizes smaller than my own. Our skirts skimmed the lawn every few steps. This was downright antebellum.

Rochelle's words cut through my thoughts. "I can't help feel-ing romantic on days like this. Lately, I even wonder if—"

"If what?" My body stiffened. I'd heard this speech before. All my die-hard single friends give this little talk before crossing over into the sea of wanna-be wives. Tracey's little rant three months ago was still fresh in my mind. Rochelle? Despite her wedding breakdowns, I never thought I'd hear it from her. Well, not this soon anyway.

"I'm just talking," she said, moving faster. "It's nothing, really."

More like a big something, but I decided to leave it. This day had enough mess going without adding to it. Time for a detour. "I hope the punch is good."

Rochelle nodded, gathering her skirt to gain a little speed. Good punch could cover a multitude of sins. Even Tracey mar-rying Ryan. Okay, he's not so bad. He's rich, handsome and loves her to pieces. But there's just something creepy about the guy. I don't know. Forget I said anything.

While I pondered the groom's strangeness, Rochelle grabbed my wrist, digging her natural-length nails into my flesh. With-out looking at her, I knew it was already too late. And we'd al-most made it to punchdom.

Tracey wouldn't, couldn't throw that bouquet at me.

But she did.

A few inches ahead, a group of women floated onto the green in front of us, forming a frightening pastel cloud. The bride broke through, holding her weapon of choice—peach hybrid roses from the Leverhill Botanical Gardens.

"Run!" Rochelle screamed with the concern of a fire marshal at a brewing blaze.

Obeying her command was my first mistake. The stop-drop-and-roll technique is always best to achieve my goals: avoid head trauma, keep the contacts in and keep the dress covering my backside.

As previously stated, I deviated from this method.

When nothing tagged the back of my head—seriously, they stopped aiming for my hands two summers ago—I did a dumb thing and turned around. The bouquet slapped against my forehead like a Jackie Chan sound effect. I tripped on my skirt trying to escape—she'd already nailed me, of course, but it was instinct. My dress ballooned around my waist like a giant boat made of Bubble Yum.

Then…the pain burned beneath my eye. What was that? I dropped to one knee, jerking the whole pink mess of me back into place, while peeking through my fingers. Something I mistook for tears trickled into my mouth. Blood.

I wobbled to my feet. "What in the world?" I'd been hit with a lot of flowers, a few small shrubs even, but no one had ever drawn blood. This was past wrong.

Rochelle hovered over me, panting and picking greenery from between my braids. Satisfied with her job on that, she peeled back my fingers and surveyed the scratch under my eye. "The thorns. Tracey forgot to have them removed. It was the only thing on her list…sorry."

I took my hand off my eye. Rochelle's tone let me know that she hadn't been in on this but she had been aware of the possibility. Not for the first time, the Sassy Sistahs made me mad. Tracey approached slowly, waving like she always does after doing something crazy. I felt my anger wash away at the sight of her silly grin. Still, this was a bit much. "Thorns? You've got to be kidding."

"Wish I was." Rochelle dabbed my face with a napkin from her clutch. No doubt there was a first-aid kit, needle and thread, makeup bag and two shades of pantyhose crammed in that tiny thing. How she'd even managed to hold on to it while trying to drag me to safety was beyond me, but I'd long given up on trying to figure out Chelle's superhuman womanhood. She just has skills like that. I'm lucky to keep my shoes on. Although I did manage to keep my contacts in. A new accomplishment.

Just before Tracey reached us, someone from the groom's family intercepted and wheeled her away. The beginning of the end. She was no longer my roommate, my best friend. She was someone's wife. We walked past Tracey, giving us the "be right there" signals.

Rochelle smiled.

I sulked. "Knowing Tracey, she probably thought it was more Christlike to leave the thorns on." Mock disgust sounded in my voice. I was trying to be mad and couldn't.

"Hush you," Rochelle said, using our code phrase for when one started in on another of the three. It was the standard defense, but right now I felt like pushing past it.

Tracey joined us and slipped an arm around—well, almost around—my waist. "Got you, didn't I? Sorry about your eye though."

"You'd better be glad I love y'all," I whispered as people packed in around us. Pain seared my scalp where Rochelle had raked a stem through my hair.

"Maybe if you'd helped with the wedding errands, you could have taken care of those thorns," Rochelle said, reaching back in her purse for her dabbing cloth.

Ouch. That hurt way more than my eye. The truth always does. I pushed away Rochelle's hand, preferring to blink my own way back to health. In a minute, there'd be no skin left on the right side of my face. That girl was dangerous with a Kleenex.

Tracey started to say something, but was called away…again. I took a deep breath, watching her walk to the punch table with her mother-in-law. Where was the groom? Why was I the one getting jealous instead of him? Shouldn't her husband have been the one hunting her down?

Like I said, he's a little weird. This whole deal was. But there was no use trying to explain that to Rochelle. She wasn't trying to hear it. So I did what I always do—tried to explain it anyway. "Look, Rochelle, I already regret not helping out with the wedding. But I just wasn't sure about this. When I dated Ryan—"

She tried the neck thing again. With success this time. "Dated? Is that what you call it? That mess was so boring he just stopped calling and came back to the singles group. So he wasn't for you. No reason he can't be the one for Tracey." In a deft motion, she grabbed a napkin from the table next to us, wadded it quickly and removed several layers of my epidermis. "There's just one last spot…."

She reached out again, but I shook my head, thinking I should have thrown in some cookies with the Ben and Jerry's waiting for me at home. The line we'd joined without meaning to inched toward the punch and some gruesome-looking cake with what appeared to be bubble gum toothpaste for filling. I definitely should have helped with the wedding plans. At least the punch looked good. It would have to be.

The line crept on. So did the conversation, though I was reluctant to respond. "Just to be clear. I do not want Ryan. Never did. I don't want anybody. And I don't appreciate the insinuation." My lips barely moved as we spoke through our smiles so no one would hear. Only a ventriloquist could do better.

Rochelle nodded. "Okay, so that was a bit much."

"Quite a bit. I'm just not feeling Ryan, okay? I know you've got a chapter and verse for why I shouldn't think that, but I'm just being real. Tracey is like a piece of me. How can Ryan be totally wrong for me and totally right for her? I'm having a hard time understanding that." I glanced toward the punch bowl at Tracey. She looked happy. So why did I doubt she'd stay that way? "I'm surprised Ryan put down his cell phone long enough to get married, actually."

"Me, too," Rochelle whispered, in a moment of weakness. "But he married her," she said, regaining strength. "Now we have to keep them lifted up in prayer." She squeezed my hand.

I squeezed back, knowing she'd prayed for me just that quick. She was right. I needed to let this go. "I can't believe you thought I was jealous though."

I wasn't, was I?

Rochelle smiled. A knowing smile. "The real problem is that with Tracey gone, you'll be alone like the rest of us."

My neck craned forward, as if to catch the truth of her words before they hit the ground. The punch bowl was almost close enough to touch now. I needed a cup. Bad. When my friends nail me, I get thirsty. And this time, Rochelle had me. Since my mother's death, I'd only lived with Trevor years ago, the boyfriend I almost married, and Tracey. There were always Dad's sporadic visits when he wasn't drunk, but not frequent enough to count. Going it alone with God was frightening, but exciting, too.

An older man, the color of ripe peaches and scented with Old Spice, lingered over the cups. I slid my feet back into my shoes—I wanted to kick them off so bad—and tried to be patient. I couldn't help thinking that a drive-thru would have been faster than this.

I rubbed my arms. Between the tight sleeves and the cold air, it was a wonder my blood was still circulating. "You got me about the living alone thing. In my defense though, I did suck it up—with the help of a Lane Bryant cheetah girdle no less—and put on this dress. There has to be some points for that. Do I look like Miss Piggy with cornrows or what?"

Rochelle's eyes turned into brown, wet suns. She covered her face in anticipation of wild laughter.

I shook my head. Rochelle could be so silly. Tracey, too. And I was being serious here. When I actually went for funny they just looked confused. "For real, though, did you see anything when my dress flew up?"

She choked back a giggle. "Not a thing. It looked like a pink sailboat…covered with roses."

I pinched her arm. Hard.

When I turned back, there was Tracey. And the punch bowl. Perhaps I should have taken more time with my cup selection. When would this awkwardness go away?

*Lord, let me be wrong. Let them live happily ever after. Somebody around here needs to.*

Hard to believe the svelte beauty was once chubby, innocent Tracey, whose first experience with men was the warm touch of our personal trainer. Well, her personal trainer. I fired him after the fourth session. Why pay somebody to call you a failure? That's what friends are for.

I should know.

Tracey gave me a "be good" look as her mother-in-law filled my cup halfway. She never did like me and probably never would. No cause to be stingy with the punch though. It was a wedding, after all.

Ignoring the full serving plus a napkin that Rochelle received, and observing that the mother of the groom had somehow managed to pick a cute dress for herself while uglying up the rest of us, I headed for the nearest chair, tied back neatly in ivory linen. I had picked those chair covers, way back at the beginning, but nobody seemed to remember that. I sat down and brought the cup to my lips, and then froze, half sitting, half standing. Sure the liquid had been yellow instead of red, but I never thought…. The secret punch. She didn't forget me.

Rochelle's hand pressed into my shoulder. I eased down into the chair. Tears stung my eyes. "Tracey used my favorite punch for her wedding?"

We sat quickly, pretending strangers didn't flank us on all sides. Rochelle took a long sip, almost longer than my first. "Another drink was planned, but when you never showed up to any of the wedding functions, she thought you were upset and fought with Ryan's mother to serve your favorite, Pineapple Passion Fruit."

I dried my already raw eye. "But how? Daddy doesn't give anybody the recipe—"

"He made it himself. Ten gallons. And the ice sculpture, too."

That dolphin. I knew it looked familiar. A sob stalled in my throat. That old man. Just when I want to give up on him, on myself, he does something like this. And Tracey, too.

"Yoo-hoo!" My assistant Renee called to me from where she sat squeezed in between my boss and one of Ryan's big bosomed aunts, in a dress barely zipped up. They were two tables away, but still too close. Naomi nodded slightly, wearing her game face, permanently plastered on, no matter the occasion.

And so she should after the way we'd both been kicked out the conference room a few days ago. I'd recovered—with the help of a few bear claws—but Naomi was still sulking over the cancellation of the Java Lava scent project. Apparently, people liked to drink coffee, but weren't too crazy about smelling like it. I'd have to absorb Naomi's whirlwind anger on Monday at Scents and Savings, but there was no sense rushing into a tongue-lashing from her now. I stayed put, despite Rochelle's elbows, also known as hospitality prompts, digging into my ribs—well, the fat covering my ribs.

"Good to see you two. Some wedding, huh?" Despite my attempt to sound casual, even businesslike, my desire to run screaming to my car was apparent.

The deejay's bellowing voice swallowed Naomi's terse reply, leaving me free to shrug and turn away, savoring the deliciousness of my last sip of punch. The tangy sweetness reminded me of Daddy's Sunday afternoon dinners and lazy summers. Reminded me of a man who smelled like this punch tasted.

My first love.

It's official. I'm losing it. Can't even give me wedding punch now. I'm turning into Rochelle.

I pressed my wrist to my nose, as if trying to exorcise the memory of Adrian Norrell, the man never spoken of in the Sassy Sistahood. The original heartbreaker. Though my sister and ex-boyfriend did a pretty good job following up behind him. Still, that fiasco didn't compare to me losing Adrian, who seemed always to be at the edge of me on days like this, even though he was long gone. Vanilla Smella, the bestselling scent in my line of homemade bath and beauty products and Tracey's favorite, met my nose with notes of honey and crème brûlée, a warm blend that seemed to remove the chill starting to nip at my skin. At times like this, my I-don't-have-a-man-but-I-can-make-stuff tendencies came in handy.

If only I could get Rochelle to stop trying to make me quit my job and open a shop when she wouldn't even use my products. Maybe by the time I was making her honeymoon basket, she'd want to do more than decorate her bathroom with my stuff. As uptight as she could be sometimes, she'd still be married before me. Naomi would probably even beat me to the altar with her mean self.

I'd long since stopped trying to make sense of it. It's just the nature of things. Some girls get married and some girls get…

Flowers in their hair.

The reception dragged on, though I never felt received. People from BASIC, our church singles group—it stands for Brothers and Sisters in Christ, but it I secretly call it Brothahs and Sistahs in Crisis—stopped to speak to Rochelle and me, dropping not-so-subtle hints about who might wed next. My name was never mentioned. In the present company, that was a relief. Alone again, Rochelle and I indulged in girl talk, something we hadn't had time for in a while. Not face-to-face anyway, though we volleyed e-mails like Venus and Serena.

Rochelle saw me peeking at her punch and poured some into my cup. She wasn't into the sharing of food or drink, even when we were growing up ("disgusting") but she knew how badly I wanted more punch. And how much I didn't want to face Ryan's mother to get it. What happened to having a hostess pour the punch anyway? Some folks just have to control everything.

Rochelle tugged at one of my cap sleeves and, seeing how tight it was, went for another sore spot instead. "Have you used that half-off coupon for the body wrap yet?"

"Nope." I stared into my cup but didn't drink. Years of Rochelle's germ speeches had worn off on me. I just couldn't do it. Who knew I was actually listening? "Rochelle, the only thing that body wrap melted was my wallet." Fifty percent of a hundred bucks was no sale in my book.

She pinched her eyes shut. "You are certifiable."

No use disputing that one. We were all a little crazy. Isn't anybody who's worth knowing? "If you know of a cure for these red lines spidering up my sides, then we'll talk. Because if I get in an accident on the way home, I'll have to tell the paramedics I was clawed by tigers."

Or thorns.

Rochelle let punch ribbon from her mouth back into her cup instead of spewing it everywhere like I might have done. Not one drop got onto her dress. Oh, well, at least my contacts were still in. Rochelle made a face that let me know not to say anything more if I wanted to avoid a scene. For all her ladylikeness, that woman laughed like a farm animal when I got her going. Tracey, who was walking towards us now, was no better.

Ryan, the mysteriously absent groom, intercepted Tracey inches short of my chair. "Give me the garter, babe. The men await." His voice, the standard Fortune 500-speak, mixed with love talk, gave me the willies. It was like hearing Ralph Nader sing a Barry White song. Just wrong.

So wrong that when they started fumbling with the garter, I tossed back Rochelle's possibly-riddled-with-E. coli punch and turned to Rochelle. "Why do men get to fight over satin while I have to defend myself against thorns? It just doesn't seem fair."

Rochelle didn't respond, but her cheeks inflated like a blow-fish's. If I didn't stop, she was going to have an all-out fit, but at this point, I didn't care. I pressed on. "Throwing lingerie at a bunch of guys from BASIC, who have either never seen a woman's thigh or at best haven't seen one in a very long time, is just cruel, don't you think? Why raise a guy's hopes?"

I certainly didn't raise mine at these things. Probably because it was at a wedding that I was crushed, swallowed whole, watching while the love of my life married someone else, someone I'd thought to be a friend. The upside is, when my sister betrayed me with Trevor—minus the marriage, you fill in the blanks—a few years later, I ran into the arms of Jesus once and for all. And Rochelle even got to say, "I told you so." Or the quasi-Christian version of that—"Jesus told you so."

While Rochelle scrambled to compose herself, I fingered the scratch below my eye. For such an intelligent person, Tracey had terrible aim. Her judgment, however, was much better than mine. In the last year, my friend had launched a new business, lost 100 pounds and snagged the biggest software developer in the Midwest. In a few days, Tracey would be settling into her gated housing community while I, don't-need-a-date Dana, would sleep fitfully, in apartment 202, my lifelong residence.

Rochelle went for more punch. Tracey, abandoned again, took her seat. And my hand. "Sorry I didn't send my devotionals to the list this past week."

With all our members marrying off at the speed of light, there was only Rochelle, Tracey and I on the Sassy Sistahood e-mail list now, unless you counted my assistant, who read all but never posted so much as a semicolon. She saved her comments for my ears.

I patted Tracey's hand. "It's okay, Rochelle had something ready." She always did. It was easy for Tracey and me to get lazy and just let Rochelle write every day. She liked to expound on the daily need for holiness and modesty instead of enduring my "flippant irreverence" or Tracey's "greasy grace." So we let her do her thing and talked about our real stuff at home. Only now, Tracey wouldn't be home. The thought of my new phone bill made me shiver.

Tracey smiled now, knowing she'd be leaving soon for Hawaii. If she could find the groom again.

"Seriously, Tracey. I'll take your turn. And mine. I'm sure you'll be busy for a while." What she'd be busy doing, I didn't want to think about. Too bad I couldn't be like Rochelle and act like I didn't remember it—I did. Especially today. Why was that?

Pineapple passion fruit punch.

Thank goodness the hurt and anguish that followed such things was as vivid as the pleasure.

Tracey wouldn't hear of skipping her turn. "I'll do my spot. And after the, uh, honeymoon, I'll probably need some extra time in the Word."

I'll bet.

I hugged her. "I'll miss you. I do already. Especially at work. Naomi is all over me. I never realized how much you calmed her." Or me.

"You guys can be pretty volatile."

I laughed, loving, as always, the way Tracey can make a word like "volatile" sound so common. Once in an argument, she'd chided me about my *vernacular* and I couldn't do anything but laugh. Today though, our laughter was bittersweet. Things had changed forever.

"You looked beautiful today. So skinny. I had to blink a few times to be sure that was you," I blurted out. To a stranger they might have sounded mean, but Tracey understood. We were tight like that. Big changes are hard for me to get used to, even when I make them. And Tracey's weight loss, and the butterfly effect that followed it, was a big change. Sometimes, she even looked a little sick compared to the full, sunny face I was used to. The old Tracey, who knew how to pick the best ice cream and crush potato chips to perfection for the tops of her tuna casseroles, seemed to have sunk into the collarbones of this new person. My friend was still in this new body, but her light seemed dimmer.

Tracey ran a hand down her washboard abs, discernible even under her dress. "It's strange for me. I can imagine it's hard for you, too."

I managed a one-sided smile. Hard for me? I couldn't have her worried about me on her day. Time to stop and act grown up. I could always have a fit later. "You did good, girl. Got slim and got married." Not that I cared about either anymore. Aside from the somewhat formidable danger of cannoli cream bursting out of my arteries, I'd live. I didn't care beyond that.

She tilted her head again. "Yes, you do," her eyes seemed to say.

Maybe I did. A little. Not as much as Tracey, but maybe about two clothes sizes worth. "I'll probably rejoin Weight Watchers for the umpteenth time, if that woman's car isn't in the parking lot."

Tracey shook her head. "The receptionist? I told you, she still looks at me crazy even though I'm at goal. It's just her personality. She's like Naomi. Just overlook her."

Yeah right. Overlook someone staring at you and saying, "You? Again?" Easy for Tracey. Difficult for me.

Rochelle sat down across from us and slid a full cup of punch toward me—complete with napkin—but her eyes were fastened on her son, talking with a too-old girl in a too-little dress.

Tracey focused the same look on Ryan, the tallest in a circle of tuxedos a few feet away. "Weight Watchers was definitely a big part of my success. But Ryan helped, too. He loved it off me, what can I say?"

Tracey was joking, of course, but it still rubbed me wrong. I gave her my funkiest look. "No loving was allowed until tonight, so you'd better rephrase." Immediately, I regretted my tone and my "countenance," as Tracey would say. Being overbearing was Rochelle's job, wasn't it? What was wrong with me today?

The bride laughed nervously. "That's not what I meant, silly. You know, I lost that first bit with the trainer, and then more when we rejoined Weight Watchers. By the time I got to Ryan, well, we just talked and walked and walked and talked.... Somewhere in there, I wasn't hungry anymore."

How convenient. "Must be nice. He should open a woman-walking service. I'd sign up. At a discount, of course."

She laid her hand on mine. "Hush, you."

I did hush, wishing I'd been silent all along. Ryan was part of us now. An uninvited member of the hush-you club. He was a good guy and Tracey really loved him. Why couldn't I accept him, too? Sometimes I could be such a bum.

Rochelle's son, Jericho, sauntered to the table, bringing the eyes of every female from seven to seventy with him. I prayed he'd sit next to his mother today. I'd pay for it later if he didn't. It was at weddings that Rochelle felt the loss of her own love most. Sometimes I wanted to remind her that at least she'd gotten a kid out of it, that at least she had somebody, but we'd had that conversation once before. It didn't go well.

Not missing a beat, Jericho dropped wide-legged into the seat beside me, his seventeen-year-old knees and forever legs pressing against my shorter, softer ones. He picked up the remains of my bouquet and sniffed, then dropped it again.

"I don't know why they always throwing them flowers at you, Aunt Dana. You ain't never getting married. Mama, neither."

"Jericho!" Rochelle straightened in her chair. Her eyelids peeled back like only a mother's can.

I bit back a smile. I loved that kid, but he had a habit of saying just what came to his mind.

Wonder who taught him that?

"It's okay." I turned toward Jericho, not quite face on, but at an angle. If I turned more, I'd laugh and he would, too. Then we'd both be in trouble. "You're right. Marriage probably isn't in my future."

Why did just saying that bring me a strange comfort? A relief even? Maybe that's why I was eating myself silly, so I wouldn't have to deal with it at all. I took one of Jericho's ball-palming hands into mine.

He smiled at me, ignoring his mother's look that said he should apologize, that his comment had surely hurt me more than Tracey's thorns. Jericho knew better. He knew, as I did, following his eyes to the pink satin behind he'd left at the punch bowl, that it was his future that concerned me, not my own. I pressed his knee with mine until his legs knocked together. He smiled once more, then tossed back a cup of punch. "Oooh. The pineapple stuff." He squinted. "Y'all mad at each other about something?"

I kissed his fingers. Even at this age, he made me want to cry. "Something."

He nodded. "Is it over, or do I get baklava, too?"

"It's over." His poor wife, I thought. He's going to read her like a worn paperback. She'll never see it coming.

Holding his hand, I stared up at the sky—blue, lazy and slipping on a thin coat of afternoon. The unspoiled haze reminded me of the treasure I'd lost, the gift I could never regain.

The gift only God could restore.

I smiled at the thought that God was restoring me, verse-by-verse, piece-by-piece, but oh, how it hurt. Why did rebuilding seem so much harder than building? Perhaps because now I knew it could all be knocked down again. And so easily.

A throng of girls waved in our direction. Jericho's leg pressed against my knee. The look in his eyes as he took in each one of them iced my veins. I swallowed the rest of my punch. And my speech. He had a mother for that. Prayer was my job.

And pray I would, for Jericho and for myself. I usually skipped out on weddings long before this point and always limited myself to two cups of punch, even the nasty red kind they were serving now that Daddy's stash was depleted. I was currently working on cup number four and the sugar was making me dizzy.

Random thoughts and pictures did enter my mind, slipping back to when Rochelle and I—well, really her, but I watched— founded the Sassy Sistahood, boasting over 2000 members, the largest group of African-American women on the Internet back then. Then one of the members befriended us in real life, met my best friend Adrian at my house and somehow convinced him to marry her. I'd dropped offline and out of sight for a long time after that and when I came back, Rochelle was Bible-thumping so hard people dropped out of the group like crazy. When I returned for good after my mess with Trevor, our fun little social group had morphed into a tribe of prayer warriors sharing daily thoughts about the Lord. We considered changing the title, but never got around to it. Besides, with everyone else married off, it was just the three of us and we liked to think we had a little sass left in us. I was beginning to wonder.

Already assuming his role as absent husband, Ryan disappeared across the green with his business partner. Tracey looked longingly in his direction, and then hugged me. I knew from her grip that she'd had enough and was going after him.

It begins.

Tracey tugged at her gown, which for some reason, she hadn't changed out of. "All right then," she said with finality. "I've got to get back to my huzz-band, but I thank you for coming. For understanding." Her gaze rested on me. "It all happened so fast."

Too fast if you asked me, but nobody did. Though I was the junior oracle of singleness—at seventeen years and counting, Rochelle held the senior position—once my friends had more than a conversation with a man, I became persona non grata.

No kids? No man? Know nothing. I ought to make bumper stickers.

Rochelle, at least, had experienced being abandoned while giving birth to Jericho. This memory was somehow considered valuable. Too bad I didn't get credit for being in that hospital room, too. Or finding my sister in that bed with Trevor. Or watching my Adrian marry someone else. My pain, having no offspring or alimony to show for itself, didn't seem to count.

*I've caught all your tears in a bottle, marked them all in My book.*

God had done that, hadn't He? Oh, well. I hadn't meant to get all soppy like this today anyway. I'd promised myself I wouldn't.

"Aunt Dane, you're squeezing the blood out of my arm."

Dana Dane. My nickname. Adrian had given me that, too. Gave so much and took away even more.

"Sorry," I muttered, turning Jericho loose, remembering the last time I felt like this. Two months ago, the end of July. Sarah from human resources. A tangerine satin gown that actually fit. Overcooked chicken. Decent music. Escorted down the aisle by her eighty-year-old uncle.

Wedding party number nine.

# Chapter Two

She got him. I don't know how, but Tracey managed to get Ryan back to the table and keep him there. After a few minutes, we were all laughing and I wondered why I'd ever been worried. Things would be fine. Tracey was a big girl—well, not physically anymore—and could take care of herself.

And if not, there was always Rochelle. She'd try and take care of us all. A slip of humidity, orphaned by Fall, thickened the air. Afternoon, now fully clothed, burned away any memory of morning. I swiped my forehead as Rochelle held a piece of wedding cake up to her mouth, surveying the white icing, white cake and red filling. Strawberry or cherry, I couldn't tell, but that stuff looked seriously nasty.

Tracey's cake remained uneaten on her plate. "I'm full from that piece I shared with Ryan."

Yeah, right. I shook my head. My mother would have perished at the sight of this cake, if she weren't already dead. As it was, Mama had reminded me about how much sage to add to the Thanksgiving stuffing on her deathbed. She didn't do things fancy, but she did them right.

Jericho arrived with two pieces on his plate. "It looks good to me." With youthful abandon, the boy bit into a mammoth slice, pausing only to give a thumbs-up and shove more into his mouth.

Rochelle shrugged. "Remember that black fruitcake with the white icing a few years ago?"

Boy, did I. "How could I forget?" Wedding number four. Institutional green dress. Nice jazz. Horrible cake. Nightmare bad. I winced at the thought of it.

Tracey did, too. "Come on, ladies. Stop fronting on the cake. It's good. Right, Jericho?"

He nodded, licking his fingers.

As if a teenager's opinion about food could be trusted. I frowned. "That boy would eat the paint off my car."

Jericho paused, considering the possibility. "Not your car. Maybe Adrian's…"

Everyone except Ryan and Jericho froze.

Adrian. The taboo was broken. Someone had mentioned his name.

"Hush, Jericho." Rochelle looked away. Tracey's eyes avoided mine, too. I'd made it all day without saying it, though his name was ready on my lips. I didn't dare speak it any more than I dared open the letters and e-mails he'd sent me over the past year. I hoped I was being selfish and silly, denying him because of what he'd denied me, but I couldn't be sure. All I knew was that Adrian meant trouble. Good-looking, good-smelling trouble, but trouble all the same.

Jericho smiled, oblivious to my pain. "Adrian's Benz-o. Now, that thing is pretty enough to eat."

And so is he.

I pressed my eyes shut. "I'll have some cake after all." Rochelle's mouth was already white with icing.

My fork picked between the layers.

Tracey elbowed me. "It's good. His mother made it."

His mother? All that money and his mother made the cake? How could Tracey be so bourgeoisie and so cheap at the same time? I was no wedding planner, but you didn't drop twenty grand on a wedding just to let the mother of the groom whip up the cake in the church basement. I could see the telltale grooves from our fellowship hall baking pans now that I looked closer. "The swirls are pretty—"

"Eat it!" The cry was collective.

I jumped, banging my knees against the table legs. "All right, already."

Please don't let this taste as nasty as it looks, I prayed, then shut my eyes and slid the fork into my mouth. Strawberry filling, cherry icing and light-as-air white cake melted on my tongue. "Wow." Both hands flew to my mouth, a crazy thing I do when something tastes extraordinary. The food swing, as Rochelle calls it.

I moved a little too fast, evidently, but not fast enough for anyone to miss the hum of satin ripping up my sides. My chest tightened. Further inspection revealed two inch-high slits, hardly identifiable if I kept my arms down, but humiliating nonetheless.

"Now that was funny," Jericho said, choking down the rest of his second piece of cake.

Rochelle crossed her arms, trying to look serious. I sighed. Those quiet ones. They keep their emotions corked and when they blow, it's a total explosion of stupidity.

"Don't even start," I said, smashing my arms against me like sausage casings.

Tracey sputtered on the other side of me, making the sound my car does on winter mornings. I rolled my eyes, knowing that once the bride let that laugh go, it'd be at least ten minutes of uncontrollable giggling. Considering the stress of the day, she might go longer. That was a real concern. Rochelle's busting a gut was one thing, but Tracey rolling on the ground in her wedding dress was more humiliation than even I could bear. Not that I thought she'd go that far, but there was that time she'd giggled herself into the salsa at the junior prom.

"You people are sad, you know that?" I shook my head.

As if that had been the punch line for a sitcom, Rochelle reached across the table, yanked up one of my arms and then collapsed in her chair, her body contorting like James Brown. Her mouth opened and closed in the this-is-so-funny-no-sound-will-come-out laughter. Not one of her spritzed hairs dared leave its place.

"This is what happens when people don't get out much. Too easily amused." I secured my arms at my sides again.

My attempt to diffuse the humor had no effect. Rochelle turned from the table, holding her stomach. One look at Tracey, with both hands clasped over her mouth, told me this could get ugly. Ryan sat stunned for a second and then…escaped. No surprise there. Jericho reached for Tracey's cake. He'd seen all this before. And more. That left me to save Tracey from baying like a wolf at the moon. I lifted my cup of punch and extended it to the cackling newlywed. "Drink this. Now."

Tracey shook her head, waving me off with a pained expression.

Jericho smiled at a girl a few tables away, as if a trio of satin-clad crazy women was an everyday occurrence. It was, for us, of course, but he wasn't supposed to act like it. He turned back to me and pointed at Tracey. "She's gonna blow."

I agreed. "No doubt." A laughing fit was imminent and there wasn't a thing I could do about it…but drink punch. With a shrug, I lifted the cup to my lips, and then frowned at the luke-warm taste. How hard would it be to break a fin off Daddy's dolphin? No sense in me not having any fun.

"Dana?"

It was a man's voice. The voice of a man I'd once loved.

A man I still loved.

Suddenly, shaving the ice sculptures looked very inviting.

Maybe it wasn't him. "Adrian?" I turned, hoping I wasn't purple due to the oxygen that had sudden left my body. It couldn't be him, but it was. How could this be?

I was going to put Tracey out of her skinny misery.

The flower thing was negotiable, but Adrian's absence from anywhere that I am is an unspoken, understood request. I'd have to put these things in writing in the future. "How are you?"

"Fine." He took my hand and pulled me up from the chair.

A little too fine. He touched the corner of my eye. I drew back in pain.

"Bouquet?"

"You know it." My head started to throb. How silly must I look with this scratch and my melted makeup and chewed off lipstick?

He didn't seem to notice as he pulled me close. Too close. His signature scent, a pineapple coconut blend cut with orange essential oil, overtook me. I melted in his arms like a Hershey bar on a car hood.

Adrian pulled me back for another look at my face, by now negating all standards of beauty. "Man, it's good to see you. I'd planned to slip in and out, but I saw Tracey jerking around over here and I knew she was about to go into her act—"

As if on cue, laughter howled behind us.

The plastic cup in my hand cracked, spurting red liquid down the seam between us. I jumped back. Adrian's glasses hit the ground. I reached behind me, grabbed some napkins and wiped his chest, which was much more muscular than I remembered. "Sorry."

"It's okay." He rescued his tortoiseshell frames and shoved them on his face.

Clark Kent, move over.

He took off his suit jacket and shook it, smiling as rivers of red punch drained off it onto my feet. That same gorgeous smile, a little crooked from where I'd jumped over him at the skating rink in the fourth grade. Punch continued to rain from the edges of his suit jacket, a perfect fit over his broad body just moments before. I dabbed at my own front with what remained of my napkin pile, wondering if I'd end up with "Tracey and Ryan, The Real Thing" imprinted on the front of me. It would be an improvement.

Adrian tossed his jacket over a chair, knowing he'd be able to have what remained of the stain removed at the dry cleaners. He'd get rid of the shirt. That much I knew for sure and I hated that I knew it. He'd been so polite about my crazy appearance. Now I had him looking half as bad. I dropped my eyes to the ground.

Ugh. Ugly shoes.

He grabbed my chin in that mind-numbing way of his and lifted it. "Don't worry about it. Seriously." Then he kissed my forehead. Any remaining oxygen left my brain for good.

I rocked over onto one heel. "Well, I'll let you talk to Tracey now. That was nice of you to come all the way from Chicago."

He crossed his arms. "I came from across town. I'm back in Leverhill now. Didn't Tracey tell you?"

I pressed my lips tighter so the scream wouldn't escape. "Tell me what?"

Adrian squinted at me, despite his glasses, something he did when very nervous. More useless data I wish I didn't know.

Surprise plus embarrassment blurred Adrian's features. "So you didn't know anything? Not even that I'd be here today?"

I looked over at my two friends, who'd long since stopped laughing. "They wouldn't have told me about this wedding if they could've gotten away with it." My voice trembled, trying to conceal the truth of the statement.

Adrian didn't speak. Instead, he gave me what I needed. Another hug. "It'll be okay. I prom..." He let the word drift away, along with the pain that must have rimmed my eyes at his mention of promises. "It'll work out."

I dared look up at him, dared feel his embrace around me, knowing all that had gone between us, all that had been broken.

There was something still there, a shadow of a time when his face alone had been a promise. When his hugs had been a vow. How I'd missed those times.

Missed him.

I reached up to hug him back, only to hear that terrible sound of fabric going wrong again, this time not so softly.

As a swatch of animal print emerged from the pink satin, I suddenly questioned Lane Bryant's decision to sell cheetah girdles. And my decision to buy one. Adrian pulled me into his pineapple-orange chest as Tracey and Rochelle's laughter resumed behind us. He didn't laugh. He knew me too well. "I am sorry," he whispered into my hair.

"It's not your fault." I took a deep breath, knowing it wasn't my dress he was apologizing for.

"Where's your car?" he whispered.

I nodded to a gravel lot about a hundred feet away from the tent.

"Don't worry. We can do this." With that, Adrian swept me into his arms and calmly passed my table, where Rochelle sat on the edge of her seat, now devoid of mirth and ready to spring to my aid. I reached back for the bouquet and gave both Rochelle and Tracey a don't-move-don't-say-a-word look. I needn't have bothered. They both knew better.

Jericho obviously did not.

"You riding in the Benz-o, Aunt Dane? Save me a seat!" He cupped his hands around his mouth for volume. No one missed the message or its implication.

To think that I diapered that child.

Adrian squeezed me closer and set off for my Mercury Cougar. Adrian somehow managed to get me into the passenger's seat. He tossed his jacket across me before shutting me in. He rounded the car and got in.

I considered crying, but this was so far beyond that. "Now what?"

He reached in the ashtray for my keys. My mind reeled. He

remembered. "Now, I take you home, Miss." The salutation hung in the air. The ignition revved. Adrian looked over his shoulder and backed out slowly. "Or is it Mrs.?"

The sun glinted off his wedding band as he spun the steering wheel.

I turned to the window. A rose petal Rochelle had somehow missed slid into my lap. "I'm still Miss. Miss Dana Rose."

He carried me upstairs. I tried to protest, but Adrian wouldn't hear it. By the time we topped the first landing, sweat trickled of his bald head and onto my shoulder.

"I can walk," I whispered, suddenly feeling worse than before.

Adrian kept climbing. "You don't have to."

I slipped through his grasp and stood. "I know. Thank you." I gathered my skirts, careful not to scratch him with the thorny bouquet I'd snatched off the table as we went by. Why I'd kept it, I had no clue.

"Just like old times, huh?" I said, as we topped the landing of the stairs to my apartment. The apartment I'd stayed up nights in dreaming of this very moment. Only in my dreams, I wasn't dressed as an animal trainer/ballerina in need of a Band-Aid and Adrian wasn't wearing another woman's wedding band.

She's gone.

That was true. But where did that leave him and me?

Adrian nodded toward the door across the hall from mine, the place where he'd spent a few minutes of his childhood. The rest of the time, he'd been at my house. His grin faded into a pained expression. I knew he was thinking of his mother. I was, too.

"Your mother's funeral was beautiful. I loved that song you sang. She would have loved that." The service was a year ago, the last time we'd seen each other.

Adrian nodded. "I thought she would have liked it. Nothing else seemed appropriate. Thank you for coming, Dane."

I leaned back against my door, happy for the thorns pricking my hand. Their pricks muted the tearing of my heart. "If I'd known about it, I would have come to Sandy's funeral, too. Really." How long had I waited to say that? Two, three years?

He stiffened at the mention of his late wife, then fingered his ring, probably out of habit. "Sorry for not inviting you." He pulled off his glasses, pinched the bridge of his nose. "I needed some time."

Me, too. Still do.

I tried not to imagine what a mess we might have made of things if I'd responded to his phone call after his wife died. Without looking at the caller ID, I'd known it was him. Felt that it was.

Sandy had called me herself the night before and expressed regret for pursuing Adrian while she was supposed to be my friend. With labored breaths, she'd asked me to take care of him. I'd assured her, like I really had the power to do so, that she would recover and take care of him herself. When the phone rang again, it was Adrian, with all that pain in his voice.

"I called you once. When it happened." He ran a palm over his sweaty head. "I'm glad you didn't say anything." He reached out and pressed against the door, as if trying to hold himself up.

Staring up at him, I remembered that anguished hello. My phone outlet was still chipped from where I'd yanked out the cord, not trusting myself. His tone had reeked of need: emotional and physical. I'd known I wasn't the one to fill either category. Only Jesus could.

Both then and now, I feared one word might escape his lips. *Please.*

So I kept running, not giving him, or me, a chance to say it. Though Adrian loved God, I didn't fool myself about his humanity.

Or mine.

I smoothed my hairline, raking a broken nail between my braids. When did that happen? "I'd better let you get back to the reception. Again, I'm sorry."

"No more apologies." He paused. "Please."

There it was, filling the hall like a fog. Time for me to exit, or in this case enter.

Adrian's fingers brushed my hand as I fumbled with my keys. I pulled away. I'd already broken a nail because I wasn't paying attention. If I wasn't careful, my heart would be broken, too. Why had Daddy made that stupid punch filled with childhood memories? Why had God allowed Adrian to come here, waking love I thought long dead?

*I sleep, but my heart waketh: it is the voice of my beloved that knocketh, saying, Open to me, my sister, my love, my dove, my undefiled: for my head is filled with dew, and my locks with the drops of the night.*

The Song of Solomon. I avoided that book of the Bible, but Rochelle had included this verse in yesterday's devotional. I'd laughed at it, not knowing it would haunt me so soon. I hugged my middle and slipped out from under Adrian's outstretched arm. "Well, thanks again. I'd invite you in but—"

"That wouldn't be a good idea." His shirt eased across the rapid rise and fall of his chest, releasing more of that intoxicating tropical scent. He turned and headed for the stairs.

I brought my hand to my throat and slid my key into the lock. "Exactly."

I'd known Adrian would come back one day, and that it would hurt when he did, but I had no idea how badly. And Rochelle showing up at my door before I could lick my wounds didn't help a thing.

"You've got to admit it was funny."

What was funny? Rochelle racing over here like a maniac? "Not really." I kicked off my torturous shoes and started off across my living room, shoving an industrial-size tub of cocoa butter out of my path. My next destination was my room, to take off this wretched dress.

Rochelle kicked her pumps off. Her bare feet echoed mine against the hardwood floor. She paused at the tub I'd pushed aside. "That's a lot of cocoa butter. What are you making with it?"

Here we go with the interrogation. "Body balm, soap and lotion. For Renee's cousin's wedding. Spa party for the bridesmaids. More stuff that I can't think of right now."

"Wedding favors. Now that idea is a winner, Dane. You could build a business off weddings alone."

And feel like this every day?

I rubbed my eyes and leaned against the sofa, eager to end the chitchat. "I don't think so." I ignored Rochelle's attempt to cheer me up and hobbled to my bedroom, shutting the oak door before she could enter, but knowing she'd come in anyway.

My room, still darkened by my closed blinds, allowed a few strips of afternoon to leak through. Tracey had always jerked them up every morning. I missed her sunshine already. I yanked at my zipper for a few seconds, and then padded to the door. "Rochelle, can you come here a minute? Help me?"

She arrived all too quickly. "Sure." The zipper gave way and the dress with it. I maneuvered over the skirt and buried myself beneath my comforter. I turned to the wall. "Thanks."

Daytime flooded the room as Rochelle whisked my blinds up.

A pillow over my head solved that.

Pointy fingernails, Rochelle's version of tickling, jabbed at my middle. "Oh, come on. Get over it. It wasn't that bad. Probably broke the ice between you two."

I snickered. "It broke the ice all right. More like unplugged the dam."

My friend's hands went still. "But he didn't come in, right? I came right over—"

"No, Mother May I, he did not come in. Thanks for trying to block though. I see now what you really think of me." I lifted my head a little and gave her a smile, just enough to clear the concern in her eyes.

Rochelle slapped at the pansy-covered blanket. "I trust you, girl. Him, too. It's the enemy I don't trust. Know what I'm saying?"

I eased upright, resting my back against the headboard. "I do know. And I'm thankful you're looking out for me. You could have done one better though and warned me he would be there."

She held up both hands. "I'm innocent on that one. I figured she'd throw the flowers, but Tracey and I both agreed not to tell you about Adrian's move until after the wedding and not to invite him. Seems she couldn't go through with the second part. Probably knew you wanted to see him. Thought she was doing you a favor."

"Traitors."

She shrugged. "Just because you can't deal with him doesn't mean the rest of us can't love him. Adrian is like a brother to me."

A frosty pause ensued, probably at the mention of the word *brother,* as mine was still missing in action.

"So what did happen?" She slid under the covers, too.

"He carried me up the stairs."

Rochelle's jaw went slack. "Is that straight out of a fairy tale or what?"

Straight out of my nightmares more like it. "I got down on the second flight."

Rochelle nodded. "Brothah fell down, didn't he? I told you to stop eating all that pizza."

I punched her shoulder, for real this time. "He didn't say a word. I thought that holding my breath was making me lighter, until he started sweating."

She held her stomach. "Don't make me scream."

"Make you scream? You weren't the one standing there in *that* thing." I pointed to the rumpled dress on the floor.

Rochelle patted my arm, looking down at her own dress, a smaller, yet just as terrible version of the one I'd removed. "I tried to talk some sense into Ryan's mother about these dresses, but you know everyone thinks I'm too conservative. If you had—"

"I know. I know. I dropped the ball. I don't know why I let my feelings—or lack thereof—about Ryan get to me. I regret it already."

Rochelle pushed back the covers and stood. "No regrets, missy. Get up out of that bed and get dressed. We've got BASIC tonight, a special meeting and elections for officers. You're going."

I groaned and flopped back onto the bed. BASIC. Our sham of a singles group. A certified freak show if I'd ever seen one.

There goes my pedicure. And I'll never get to that ice cream with Rochelle here.

"Please. I just had to put a block on my phone because of Deacon Rivers calling me from the retirement home. And Tad-the-Harvard-Grad? If he starts in with why he can't seem to find a woman who is at his spiritual and intellectual level, I think I'll throw up. Watching him do the weather is punishment enough."

Rochelle leaned over my bureau and started her assault on my top drawer, no doubt looking for something suitable for me to wear.

"Don't start throwing stuff out of that closet, okay? Last time it took me half an hour to refold all those clothes. You know there isn't anything in there you like. Not one thing."

She waved her free hand. Her other five fingers remained buried in my drawer.

"Don't pay Tad any mind. He's already in love—with himself. And I'm encouraging Deacon Rivers to join the Seniors Bible Study, but he's still not convinced he belongs there."

"Neither am I. He chased me to my car so fast a few Sundays ago that I thought he was Jericho."

Rochelle harrumphed at the mention of her son. "That boy wishes he could run that fast. Maybe if he was chasing a girl. His coach called me all last year about his sluggish playing. I hope the summer AAU league helped some."

I considered telling her that summer league ball hadn't helped and that Jericho ran slow because he hated basketball, but some secrets were best kept. If Rochelle knew how much her son confided in me, our friendship wouldn't be the same. That Rochelle was head over heels for her kid was obvious, but sometimes she could only hear what she needed for him to say.

My amateur wardrobe professional slung a pair of jeans on the bed with a turquoise short-sleeved sweater. I narrowed my eyes. The shade was too close to teal, Adrian's favorite color. "Did you invite him? To church tonight, I mean?"

Rochelle stopped and stared at the ceiling. "I may have mentioned it, but I doubt he'll show. He's going to another church. That Messianic fellowship we went to last year."

Wow. "The place we went for the Feast of Tabernacles display? That was awesome." I'd wanted to visit again, once this work project was over. So much for that. The Nehemiah Group, comprised of a mix of believers—those Jewish by blood and those made Jewish by His blood—had intrigued me, both with the breathtaking outdoor display and open, vibrant worship.

Some of the detailed historical teaching had flown right over my head, but Rochelle had broken it down for me afterward. Such a place of scholarship and praise would be right up Adrian's alley, given his late father's Jewish background and his love of learning. I smiled, remembering his joy when I gave him his first Hebrew lexicon on a long-forgotten Christmas. Even when it came to the Bible, he was a nerd at heart. "I doubt he'll show after this morning anyway."

Rochelle picked up the pair of jeans and held them up? "A Velcro zipper? Dana, you've got to stop. This is crazy."

I pouted a little. "They're comfortable. And just for holidays and church potlucks, thank you."

She grabbed another pair off the hanger, clucking her tongue. "And look at these. Elastic in the waist."

"But they have a zipper. Look." I pointed to the front of the pants with satisfaction. Rochelle looked at me with pity, which made me laugh harder. I couldn't live her lacquered life for anything. The hairspray alone would do me in.

"Okay. Put these on. And no sneakers, either. I really don't think that Adrian will show, but now that he's back, you need to—"

"I'm not going to change myself in hopes that some man is going to react to me in some way. This is it. Me. All you get. All he gets." The *he* came out with a little venom. The growl of my voice even surprised me.

Rochelle leaned over and picked up a pair of moccasins with turquoise stones. A gift from one of my customers. I loved them, but never wore them out. She placed them between us on the bed.

"You're both my friends and I'm sick of you two botching this up. You may not see him for another month, I don't care, but tonight, we practice." She crossed her arms with finality.

We'll see about that.

I stood and started out of the room, both hurt and happy when Rochelle didn't follow.

It had nothing to do with anything that had happened today. The anger in my tone had been simmering for years. Sure, Sandy was gone, but was I just supposed to forget how he'd cut me off after our time together, my first time no less?

The painful memory drove me to the kitchen, hoping there would be a spoonful of ginger spice chai caked in the container. The way Adrian had played me then, so true to the Biblical account of Tamar and Amnon… It seemed that after we were together he'd hated me more than he had loved me. Understandably so, as he was the Christian then and I, the pagan soul. How could I blame him for running when I'd wrecked his faith?

I fell for that until Sandy took the distance between Adrian and I as separation and went for him, full throttle. And he went along for the ride, all the way to the altar, dragging my mother, my friends and even me.

"The first thing he asked me was if you'd started your business yet. He so believes in you. That's hard to find in a man." Rochelle's voice startled me.

I stopped short, my hand on the cabinet. "I doubt it's support. He just wants me to do something so he can come and steal my ideas…again." Adrian's business credibility wasn't the best with me, either.

Rochelle banged the chai container on the counter while I heated water. "Are we back on that? Adrian's store? Dana, you know that he didn't deliberately steal ideas from you. Whatever you told him a zillion years ago was just brainstorming. People do that. It's part of business." She blew out a breath. "It's not like you were going to do anything with those ideas anyway."

Was that the point? What I did with them? No. The point was the ideas were mine, something I could never seem to get Rochelle to understand. Let somebody come in there and "brainstorm" a pair of those shoes. It'd be all over. "We weren't in business, Chelle. We were in love. Even more, we were friends. Two friends on the stoop with big dreams…and he stole mine."

Even as I said it, Adrian's store, Kick! Candles, flashed through my mind. It was a woman's refuge, intimate and relaxing, swathed with tulle and fresh flowers: roses in summer, amaryllis and poinsettias in winter, anything from daffodils to handpicked wildflowers in spring, when like a garden, the place buzzed with color.

It was October now. In a few weeks, his store back in Chicago would be decked in velvet, from the tapestries dripping off the walls onto the small couches beneath them. Ladies' boots would line the edge of the deep shag as tired shoppers soaked their toes into its depths and bored husbands sipped cocoa and watched cable sports in massaging chairs. Overhead lanterns and die-cut sconces lined the walls, filling the store with a new scent every hour. A few times a year, Rochelle and I snuck up there and bought all the stuff we could on Adrian's days off. I always wanted to kick off my shoes and stay longer, but never dared.

It was a place girlfriends loved, boyfriends needed and husbands feared. A place I'd described to Adrian on a rainy Sunday while he rubbed my feet after one of Daddy's Sunday dinners. Our place.

Only he'd built it with Sandy instead of me.

And now Chelle wanted me to brush that away and jump into his arms, the very act that drove him away in the first place. "You know, this is why Adrian is off-limits. Of all people, you should be able to appreciate that some things just don't need to be discussed."

Not with people anyway. God and I would have a long chat about this tonight.

Rochelle added a swirl of milk to the already weak chai and walked into my dining room, taking a zigzag pattern to get around the boxes of bath and body supplies strewn around the space, chosen for its disuse and out-of-the-way location. All the time Tracey had lived with me, I don't remember her messing with my supplies, except to clean around them.

Leave it to Chelle.

"What's all this?" Rochelle demanded, taking inventory with her eyes. I looked, too, a bit ashamed at my excess, but it had all seemed necessary at the time. Shea butter, rose petals, calendula, chamomile, lye for soap along with coconut and olive oil…and then there were those boxes under my bed.

"Just some supplies." I shrugged. "My clicker-finger went a little mad."

She rolled her eyes. "A lot mad, I'd say. I know you think you're getting a deal from those online companies, but the shipping is killing you and there's always something better locally if you talk to people face-to-face—"

"Don't start." One-track mind, that one. If she wasn't trying to marry me off, she was trying to motivate me into the marketplace.

I took a closer look at the receipt dangling from Rochelle's fingers. Four hundred and thirty-eight dollars. An order I'd obviously made while rapt in the buzz of my promised-but-never-delivered promotion at Scents and Savings. Rochelle did have a bit of a point. I was going to have to get a little more mileage out of that small business license or forget this stuff altogether.

"Far better it is to dare mighty things, to win glorious triumphs, though checkered with failure, than to take rank with those poor souls who neither enjoy much nor suffer much, because they live in the gray twilight that knows neither victory nor defeat."

I grimaced. "Uh, Marcus Garvey?"

She shook her head.

"Winston Churchill?"

"Theodore Roosevelt. It's at the bottom of all my e-mails. Just goes to show how much attention you pay me."

She had me there. "Sorry. I sort of glaze over all that stuff."

"Whatever. Look, you can say whatever you want about Adrian, but at least the guy stepped out and took a risk."

My teeth set on edge. "Risk? What would you know about it? If you're not at work or church, you're home hiding behind that computer."

Rochelle flinched, then pressed the receipt back onto one of the boxes. "At least I can afford to. You don't hear me complaining about not being able to pay my bills. I'm not afraid to charge what I'm worth. If you come to Shoes of Peace, you won't find any pumps hidden in my back room. They're in the display window, where they belong."

I hunched a little, like a crazed kitten driven into a corner. "Complaining? I haven't asked you for a dime. You're always the one pushing, trying to make me something I'm not. Don't you know this isn't about money to me? This is something I can predict, something I can control. I can throw it out and start over if it doesn't work out."

Clutching my chai, I tried to get a grip. Why couldn't Rochelle understand? Tracey never bothered me about this stuff. I took a sip of the tea. Tepid. Ugh. I set it aside, ready to try once more to express my muddled feelings.

"Soap can't lie to me or—or show up smelling like oranges and daydreams, waiting to break my heart—"

"Oh, honey." Rochelle touched my shoulder.

"All these years you've waited, surely you know. Surely." I shrugged off her touch, realizing I'd crossed her boundary by mentioning Jericho's father. For once, I didn't care. I had to get it out.

"This is my risk…and my safety." My teeth nipped my bottom lip as if my subconscious were trying to shut me up. A staple gun would have been more appropriate. Why had I shared so much with Rochelle, shown her so much of my heart? She'd just use it against me in some subtle way, some devotional about the mouth showing the condition of the heart. Maybe if I actually talked to her about it instead of complaining to Tracey, she might realize what she's doing and how it hurts me. If she only knew, I'm usually well aware of my heart's condition before saying a word. "Now let's just let it go."

"Fine." She sounded wounded.

I stormed into the living room, slowing with each step. Normally, I would have taken Rochelle's dishing because I knew she had it hard being a single mom and sometimes needed to let go on somebody. But today, I just couldn't take it. Was it because I'd used Tracey for the same purpose?

I didn't want to think about it. As I dropped onto my leather sectional, a bulletin board framed with orders stared back at me. My bread store soap rack leaned against the wall like a gas tank at the middle of a long trip, half empty and half full. Just like my week. Just like my life.

"If you get your clothes on, we can grab some dinner before we go."

The apple cobbler soap I'd made two weeks before filled the room with scent as I rotated the bars so air could hit every side. The tart sweetness settled down around my shoulders like an old sweater. Or an old friend.

I turned. "I'll go, but I'm not voting and if Tad uses the words *spiritual intimacy* more than once, I'm out of there."

"Deal." Rochelle wiped her eyes and walked toward me, the skirt of her dress swaying with each step.

Knowing that she needed a hug, but wouldn't offer one, I opened my arms to her. She accepted my affection, but more stiffly than usual. My gut wrenched. Letting off steam had seemed right at the time, but now it seemed foolish. I hugged her closer, bending her rigid fear into my soft shoulder. Fear of loving again, fear of what would happen to our friendship without Tracey to blur our sharp edges, to make us laugh in the right places.

I patted Rochelle's back. "It's okay. I'm scared, too."

# Chapter Three

Deal. I should have known better than to say that to Rochelle, to agree to drag myself to the singles group. Such things never work in my favor. When I heard Kirk Franklin playing and saw the disco ball, well, all hope of escaping unscathed went out of me.

"What on Earth is this, Chelle?" I tugged at her sleeve, my feet poking around in those moccasins I'd vowed to save for a special occasion. This definitely wasn't it.

Waving to the DJ and other thirtysomethings trying desperately to look cool, she patted my hand. "Lighten up, Dane. It's just a little fellowship to go with the elections."

Fellowship? Maybe on an alien planet. Though a few hairs short of thirty myself, I knew I'd long since ceased to be cool. Somehow, these people hadn't been given the you-are-out-of-date memo. I'd been duped again. "Whatever."

I slumped into a chair for the first half hour, dreaming of my Chunky Monkey ice cream and my comfortable bed, and wondering whether the salon where I'd cancelled my pedicure took walk-ins. Today had been draining and tomorrow I'd have to be singing in the choir, serving dinner after church and probably back again in the evening. Coming along for the ride was one thing, but this added too much onto an already heavy day.

Rochelle's elbow, pressed to her side like a broken wing, jabbed me once again. "Are you asleep? Come on, we're counting the ballots."

I formed a lengthy reply, but telling Rochelle that I'd thrown my ballot in the trash with my last plate of chips would hurt her, so why bother? "Okay."

"Seriously. You should come on over. Talk. Some people are picking prayer partners and discussing ideas for next quarter's activities."

A look in the direction she pointed revealed all the reasons why I dare not leave my seat: Tad admired himself in the punch bowl, while next to him, Deacon Rivers checked for nose hairs. Near the door, the did-I-tell-you-about-my-divorce-yet group gathered in the corner. Normally, I'd suck it up and participate, but my tolerance for the ridiculous had run dry, expended on Tracey's wedding.

"Chelle, I don't think I can—"

"Wait! Hold that thought. They're here!" She whirled around and paced to the front of the general-purpose room…its general purpose tonight was to torture me. She had the DJ stop the music.

I drank in the quiet, trying to remember which scary movie this scene was edited out of.

"Well, everybody, I wasn't sure if they could make it, but I invited a few friends from the regional singles' conference. They're from Agape Worship Center, over by the mall."

I watched in disbelief as a line of balding, bulging fellows trailed into the room. They slapped hands with Tad, who promptly marched off to sanitize himself in the bathroom. For once, I had to agree with him. These gentleman just looked…wrong. Like a bunch of football players who'd been squished into a time machine and had the plug pulled midway through the trip. Those jeans definitely didn't make it to the new millennium. Not attractive. And to think that Rochelle tried to give me a makeover to come here.

Even if the room had been filled with male models, this church basement happy hour just didn't work for me. Rochelle, Bible guru that she was, seemed to be having a wonderful time, flitting from person to person, and just like earlier, not spilling a single drop of punch.

I'd already stained my jeans. With Sprite.

Why didn't I drive?

As I pondered the distance home, one of the once-upon-a-time tight ends from the other church reached for Rochelle's hand and proceeded to a chair at the side of the room, where he opened a Bible and began speaking intensely, no doubt trying to cultivate "spiritual intimacy." Too bad Tad was still in the bathroom. That subject was his specialty.

As the anger and the confusion of the day detonated within my mind, I knew I was going to lose it. I mean really lose it, like say something all of us might regret. I'm still not sure how I got that microphone...

"What are you people? Crazy?" I asked through the blaring sound system. "Hell-ooo, this is a church, not some pathetic nightclub. The singles group is not about getting with somebody, it's about being single!"

I raised both my hands and quickly dropped them to my sides as cheetah memories flashed through my mind. No time to think of that nightmare. I was on a roll.

Rochelle looked up from her deep conversation as if she'd swallowed a fly.

"I've come here week after week and listened to you people tell your little pity party stories about your ex-spouses and your baby Mama drama and—"

"I don't have any out of wedlock children, thank you—" Tad dried his hands.

Thank God there's only one of you.

"Anyway. I came here for you to pray for *me,* to study the Bible with *me,* not have you all tell me I'll be a real person when I get a man."

My voice quivered. "This should be a place where it's okay to be alone. Instead, you all act like it's some sort of crime. The real issue is, if none of us ever gets a mate, is God enough…or isn't He?"

A wall of silence crept up between me and the rest of the room. Rochelle stared at me, her eyes searching mine. The music stopped. Everyone took their seats. I remained standing, not knowing what else to do.

Tad brushed past me and took the mike. He started a slow, but mounting handclap. "Well, that was dramatic, now wasn't it?" He paused with his eighty-percent-chance-of-rain smile and I remembered why I never watched the weather anymore. The thought of what a blizzard might do to his lips was too frightening to consider.

Don't be mean.

As if they'd been taped for a laugh track, the whole room burst into guffaws.

Deacon Rivers tapped his cane against the floor. "Was that a skit, sugar? It was good. Shore 'nuff good."

By the time everyone got through hemming and hawing, I was mad. Shore 'nuff mad. Not that it mattered. I managed to slip off into the sanctuary just as Tad suggested a verse-by-verse study on Song of Solomon.

"To prepare our hearts for intimacy," he said as the door shut behind me. I took the steps two at time and collapsed on a back pew.

"Lord, what are You doing? You told me to be at peace in my singleness, and I am. Please, just let me be." The words rushed from me, more desperation than anything. I gathered my flailing braids into a ponytail and laughed at myself. Maybe Tad was the sane one after all.

"You said a mouthful in there." A deep, mellow voice spoke above my head, articulating each syllable.

At the sound of his voice, I sat upright, took one look at Adrian and began estimating the distance I'd have to walk home. Not too far probably, but considering my speed was about .5 miles per hour, it could get ugly.

He came close enough for me to smell him, but walked past me and took a seat in the next pew while I digested the fact that he'd heard my little tirade.

"The music started up when I was just outside the door. I saw some weird-looking guys when I was parking. Do you all have a football team?"

That cracked me up. I slung an arm over my eyes. "We do now."

"Well, anyway, I was headed back to the car when I heard you in there. Good stuff."

I peeked at him, with that big, crooked grin. My toes curled in my moccasins.

He leaned over and pinched one of my toes, my pinky. "Nice shoes. The real thing?"

I nodded. "Always."

He pulled his hand up onto the back of the pew. "You're the genuine article. I'll give you that."

No, you gave her that.

Where did that come from? Was I losing my mind? Probably. If not, I would soon if he kept staring at me like that. By the time I remembered I could look away, that this wasn't one of the stare-down competitions from our playground days, I could almost hear the bionic music in my head.

He nodded. "Definitely a Six-Million-Dollar moment."

My eyes fluttered shut, my brain flashed to us running down the avenue making our bionic noises, our way to break the mood after a long day at school. Later, it became the cover for tense moments, as well. Me falling down the stairs in the civic center with my name on my back or Adrian blowing up the chemistry lab were never, as our teachers termed them, "painful experiences" or "embarrassing times." Just Six-Million-Dollar moments. Like now.

*God, are you trying to kill me?*

The tears ran sideways down my face. Into my ears. My hair. I didn't bother to wipe them away. Resistance was futile.

He leaned over that pew somehow because I could see the blur of him above me, but he didn't leave his row. For that I was thankful.

"Just cut it out, okay? Please. Go home," I said.

His fingers, long and slender, and always smelling like something good, touched the corner of my good eye. He didn't try to wipe the tear away. He just touched it. His touch felt like a poker searing through my brain. Jasmine, my favorite scent, escaped his fingertips to torture me further.

"I am so proud of you, Dane. I'm sorry I didn't say that this morning. It's true though. When I heard you in there tonight, I couldn't help but think that. How proud I am of you." He traced the path of my tears to the top of my ear and then leaned back on his knees, safely restricted to his pew.

I lifted my head, more to let the tears drain out of my ears than to face him, but there he was. "I wish you hadn't come in on that. It's just—"

"I think you explained it very well." He stacked his fists on the edge of the pew and rested his chin on top. "I get it. Trust me."

Trust him? Hadn't I tried that program before? "I guess I'll have to. Trust that you understand, that is. It's been so long that my mind plays tricks. We're grown up now. Changed. I don't know you anymore, not the man you are."

That should get rid of him.

Adrian sighed. He pulled off his glasses, pinched the bridge of his nose.

Uh-oh.

"Don't try that with me, okay? I'm not your Dad or Jordan. Or even Dahlia. I know I messed up. I should have called. I should have tried harder to connect with you, even when you wouldn't respond. Still, it wouldn't have been any easier than this."

I stiffened at the mention of my brother and sister and at his quick deflection of the isolation tactics that worked so well with others. I sat up slowly, estimating the miles back to my apartment again. Couldn't be more than six, maybe seven…

"She told me that she called you. Sandy, I mean."

That struck me like a punch. Had she told him what she'd said, too? Had he come here for that? For me to "take care of him?" I hoped not. I could barely take care of myself. "She did call. I had hoped we'd talk again." I paused to mop my eyes. "Tell me what happened with her exactly? I never could get the story straight from Rochelle. She said lupus, but I told her people don't die from that."

"Sandy did." He stared off in front of us, to the cross suspended overhead. "Some women do. Black women mostly. They don't always know why." He whispered the last of it, as though he'd told me a secret, the way I'm sure I sounded when I talked about Mama's stroke or other senseless things. My mother's death had shattered me, and though God had healed so much of the hurt, made a mosaic out of my broken pieces, the jagged edges poked me still. Of course they cut Adrian, too, losing as he had: his father, his mother, his wife…

"You can stop rubbing your head," I said as he started on his temples again. "The trouble won't go back into your brain, no matter how big your mind is."

He glanced up at me, then nodded with a chuckle. "I suppose it never did much good. Not then or now." He reached for my hand. "Or maybe it does. Sometimes you think something's a habit, but later you realize it was more."

"Or less." I pulled away, taking a second to focus on the cross myself. One day back and we were doing it already. Playing games.

"Right. Well, I'm going to get out of here. Need a ride?"

I considered it, but no Bible passages came to mind regarding rational interactions with sweet-smelling widowers. "I'll pass," I said, nodding toward the downstairs door. "They have to come up sometime. Thanks for asking though."

Adrian shook his head. Laughter creaked through his lips. "You sound sincerely afraid of me."

I didn't crack a smile. "I am."

"I'll take two vanilla lotions, a shower tower of soap…lavender, a fruit cocktail mask and—"

I stared up at Renee, my assistant and default member of the Sassy Sistahood. Times like this I regretted indulging her request to join the loop. Too much information for coworkers. Well, then there was Tracey, who I'd worked with and lived with, but that didn't count.

It was too Monday for this, especially after the weekend I'd had. Sure I was flattered that Renee wanted to order everything on my little product menu, but how many times had I told her to keep that stuff out of the office?

My desktop rebooted. "Renee, you'll have to e-mail your order to me or leave it on my answering machine at home." I dropped my voice to a whisper. "I'm on company time now."

Raking a long purple nail across her chin, Renee nodded. "Naomi is gone. I made sure of that before I came over. Don't worry. I got your back."

Had my back? This wasn't sixth grade. I turned back to my computer. "I appreciate that, Renee, but it's not just about Naomi. It's me, too. I don't want any confusion. While I'm here, my mind is on S&S products, not mine."

In theory, anyway. I could harness my transactions, but truth be told, my mind did wander back to my dining room and all my new supplies every half hour or so. At least.

Renee pursed her blue-black lips and ran a hand through her brunette hair, laced with skunk stripes of blond. "Oh. Trying to be Miss Clean, are we? Well, I won't bother to close all those files you leave open every night with all your notes and recipes then."

I opened my mouth to say something and shut it again.

"Gotcha," she said, extending her index finger.

What could I do but smile? I didn't mean to do that, scribble in those digital notepads, but when an idea came to me, I needed to write it down…didn't I?

*Do not work unto man, but as unto the Lord.*

My chest tightened. Wasn't it enough that I'd stopped taking home all the pens and folders? This Christian thing. There was always something else to work on. So far, I'd only mastered pants up, man out and a few other basics.

"You're right, Renee. I'll have to try and hold those thoughts until my break or—" As I pulled up my e-mail and scanned the first one, my breath slipped away.

From: SassySistah3
To:thesassysistahood
Subject: Whose turn is it?/Devotional
I know you guys said I could skip because of the honeymoon, but I needed to do it. Here goes. This should tell you where my head is. I've been a wreck since we got here. He's been on the phone or on the computer since the first night. I walked the beach today with a bunch of strangers. Did I marry the wrong guy? (Dana, don't answer that.) Please pray for me.
Tracey,
The Loveless Laptopper
"And a voice came out of the heavens: "Thou art my beloved Son, in Thee I am well-pleased." And immediately the Spirit impelled Him to go out into the wilderness." (Mark 1:11,12, NASB)
God confirmed Jesus' identity as the Son of God. What has God promised you? What are you waiting for Him to shout

to the world on your behalf? Who does God say you are? Think over these questions and post to the list. And if you're really struggling, you know what to do, pick up the phone and call one of your sistahs!

(Rochelle and Dana, be ready for a call from me. Things are NOT going well.)

PS. Hi Renee. Thanks for coming to the wedding.

Renee popped a bubble. "Ooh, yeah. I read that one. Real messed up, huh? She should cut him some slack, though. Everybody's got to work. It paid for that fancy wedding, didn't it?"

"I suppose it did." But was it worth it? Could a price tag be put on love, or as Tad put it, "spiritual intimacy?" I sighed, wishing my bad feelings about Ryan hadn't proved true, at least not this soon. I stared at the clock, figuring the time until I'd be able to call Rochelle.

Renee fluffed her hair with her fingertips. "You could learn something from that Tracey and her husband. Start your own business. For real, like in the mall or somethin'. Your stuff smells way better than the sorry mess we sell here. Why do you think Naomi stays on you so tough?" She smoothed her hairspray-soaked fingertips down her sweater.

Yuck.

"Shoot girl, your stuff is better than Fingerhut. And Lord knows I loves me some Fingerhut—"

The phone rang and I smiled, praying it was for me. Renee was my girl and all, but I just wasn't up for a two-hour discourse on the merits of Fingerhut. Contrary to popular opinion, being compared to the illustrious catalog company wasn't my idea of a compliment.

I held my breath, hoping I'd say the right words to Tracey. "Hello?"

"Hey." Wrong friend. Rochelle sounded tired, like her after-hours self. "Did you get that e-mail?"

"Just got it." Tracey's e-mail made me sad, too, but nothing usually taxed Rochelle's pep during working hours. She was on until the door swung shut at six. Right now she sounded like roadkill. "Ryan will have a lot of making up to do, but I'm sure they can work it out."

That or I'd be flying to Hawaii to get her somehow. Was cocoa butter returnable? Why didn't these things ever happen on a weekend?

I turned to Renee. "I'm going to take this in the break room, okay? Mark me for thirty minutes. If anybody needs me, I'll be in there." The "break room" was actually just Tracey's empty cubicle, but it sounded good.

Filing at her nails as if trying to free herself from a glittery purple prison, Renee nodded.

A few steps and a punch of buttons brought me back to Rochelle. "Hang that up for me, please?"

"Done," she shouted over the partition, reminding of just how little privacy I had. I'd have to concentrate on being quiet, or not saying anything incriminating. My assistant played dumb, but she was far from it. She had the sense to turn down my job and forgo the pleasure of working closely with my boss, not to mention the ingenuity to hang around until now she knew so much about me I could never get rid of her. She probably had one ear glued to the other side of this partition. This time, I didn't care.

I clutched the phone to my ear. "So what's going on with you? You sound as bad as Tracey." Worse.

"Jordan's back."

My head shook in disbelief. This shot the Tracey thing right out of the water. Off the planet, even. Jordan. Back. We'd prayed for it, but what would we do now? Jordan was a lot easier to pray for than deal with. "Since when? Are you sure?"

"He called. Talked to Jericho." Her voice trembled. I shivered at the fear streaming through her words. Even when Rochelle went into labor and Jordan went to the water fountain and never returned, she hadn't sounded like this. With every contraction, a tear had trailed her cheek. Nothing more.

"Out of the *blue?* Where's he been? Does he think he can just waltz in here and—" I paced the minuscule break room, squeezing my forehead, hoping Adrian was right and the movement had some power after all. "Is he married? Does he want you back?"

Rochelle paused before answering. "He's not married and… It's so crazy you'd never believe it. He's been in Mexico…in a coma."

I gulped for breath. *How convenient.* "If he didn't want to say what happened, he didn't have to. But to make up a story like that? I mean, come on…"

More heavy breathing. "It's true."

The cord twisted around my elbow as I turned in circles. "True? You've got to be kidding. That's straight out of *The Guiding Light.* Don't go back to being stupid just because he's—" I caught myself but too late.

"So that's what I was, huh? Stupid? You're right. I was stupid to help you through school, to help take care of your mother, to raise Jericho alone…I was stupid." A sob blared through the line. "Still am."

Man, I'd done it now. "No, you're smart. And strong. That was a mean thing to say. I'm just…confused. I don't know what to think. There's so much going on."

"Tell me about it."

"So what does this mean? Everything is just hunky-dory? He still abandoned you. Didn't call for how many years? I don't know when this other stuff happened, but he was still playing ball on TV for a long time."

"Right. There's still no excuse. He didn't try and make any." She laughed a little hysterically. "He didn't need to. Jericho was ready to jump through the phone into his lap."

Whoa. This was bad. Really bad. Rochelle didn't mean to be, but she was a little greedy about her son. I couldn't blame her. Jericho was all she had.

*She has God.*

God had me there. I tried to put a positive spin on things. "Isn't this what you wanted, for Jericho to know his father? For Jordan to want a place in his son's life?"

Another sob exploded through the phone. "Not like this. Jericho wants to *live* with him. Can you believe it? After everything I've done for that boy? Jordan didn't even sign his birth certificate. He's never even met him…." The tears strangled her words.

"I know." I fumbled for something else to say, but nothing seemed right. For once, I let silence suffice.

She paused to catch her breath. I took a breath, too, figuring I'd need it before we were done. "I should have known when I got that letter from the people taking care of him a month ago—"

"A month? What letter? And why didn't you tell me?"

She sniffed. "Tracey was getting married. You had that project at work. Adrian was coming…it didn't matter."

"Didn't matter? Rochelle, what are you talking about? It's been years. Long years. I've been going through this, too." I grimaced. No wonder she'd been acting so strange. Why hadn't I picked up on the signs? I thought she'd just finally cracked and gone man crazy with the rest of the world. Now I wondered if that wouldn't have been better. That I could fix.

*Is my arm too short to save? I can fix this, too.*

"Can you talk to Jordan? Get him to understand that this isn't a good idea?" I said the words and regretted them as the passed my lips. It was like asking if she could take a ride on the sun.

"Talk to him? Dana, come on. You know him. Better than anybody."

The truth of it hit me like a brick. I knew him all too well. And I wasn't proud of it. I rubbed my forehead and cradled the phone with my shoulder.

"How is it that I ended up with Jordan as a brother and you as a friend? It doesn't seem fair."

A dance of unsteady breaths was Rochelle's only response.

# Chapter Four

Thirty-one minutes. I'd tried to be careful, to watch the clock, to count my time, but the thought of my brother, calling after all this time, taking Rochelle through the pain of losing him all over again... As always, I'd be left to clean up the mess.

Renee appeared in the doorway. "I can't believe him. Coming back now? And that Mexico thing? That's rich. Really rich." She picked her teeth with a miniature plastic sword, no doubt salvaged from her weekend.

Had she actually clicked in on the line this time or what? I didn't even have the strength to ask. Her ears were like fine-tuned receivers anyway. "I really don't want to talk about this, okay?"

As usual, she ignored me, this time stabbing at her lip with those ridiculous nails. "Do you think they'll get back together? Now that would be a wedding. We could call it in for one of those reunion shows on TV. Keep me posted."

My hands smoothed across my denim skirt. "Uh, I'll try. I hardly know what's going on myself. I haven't even talked to him." Why suddenly did that seem important, that no one had called or written me when I was Jordan's sister?

She lingered, her hands on the doorknob. "Yeah, that's pretty messed up. That he'd call them and not call you. Especially him being your only brother and all."

I took a deep breath. Renee wasn't going to get me stirred up today. "He'll call me when he's ready. But since we're discussing family, how is your brother?"

My assistant's eyes flickered, a bleak hopelessness replacing her haughty gaze. "He's okay, they're moving him to federal next week. I can visit him there. It's closer."

Why did I say that? Sometimes I could be bone cold. "Right. Well, if you need time, just let me know." I hadn't meant to go there, to remind her of her own problems, but I needed to get back to my desk before Naomi emerged with a stun gun or something. She popped up at the most unlikely times.

I paced through the maze of cubicles hoping my boss would be too busy plotting her next scheme to be promoted to know about my phone call. As bad as the call went, I could have hung up and made it back to my desk on time. Bad enough I'd wasted my lunch on it. Another starving trip through the drive-thru tonight…and then straight to Rochelle's. Maybe I'd do better then. The one thing I could have done to help Rochelle—pray—had totally eluded me on the phone. The shocking news of my brother's mysterious re-appearance and the shaky story behind his absence had blown my mind. Had he really been in another country all this time? And all alone?

Renee's question about Rochelle and Jordan's relationship bothered me as well. The two of them getting back together had never occurred to me. Surely she wouldn't be that stupid. He was my flesh and blood, but he'd left her before. What would make Rochelle think he'd stick around now? Or was that really my heart talking…about Adrian? Both of them had given Rochelle and I something to hang our disappointment on, something to shield us, warn us about giving our hearts away again.

Shuffling back to my cubicle, I prayed for Jordan, wherever he was, asked God to give me grace when I saw him, to keep from exploding like I'd done on Rochelle this weekend. I'd have to drive around to the racetrack tonight and find Daddy and give him the news. That'd sober him up. Quick.

I pushed back my chair and sat down at my desk, grabbing the Cool Cucumber file from my inbox, where I'd shoved it this morning. And then that call... It'd be time for my meeting with Naomi soon. I'd probably have to skip lunch and just—

"So there you are." Naomi's voice grated like cat claws on a kitchen sink.

Smile. No matter what she says, smile.

I swallowed hard before turning to face Naomi Titan, a thirty-eight-year-old barracuda in heels, recently overlooked for a promotion she'd worked three years for. She'd been hunting heads ever since, and from her tone, it was my braids she wanted on her platter today.

"Hello, Naomi." I used my best conflict-management voice.

She puckered her lips and yanked her blazer closed. "It's nice of you to come back to work. Sorry to break up your little phone call—"

"I was—"

"I know exactly what you were doing. We had a phone monitoring system installed last month. Didn't you get the memo?"

Monitoring? She had to be kidding. Was that even legal?

Her nostril—yes, nostril, very scary—flared. "Don't even think about it. All legit. The whole team signed off on it at the quality assurance symposium."

My eyes bulged. "That was over a year ago. How am I supposed to remember that? And I definitely don't remember anything about monitoring being mentioned."

"I believe it was called productivity banking, a consultant-based analysis of how we spend our time." She grinned wickedly. "And I've been assigned as the consultant conducting the analysis."

I blinked. It was a first, this smile of Naomi's, and a much more hideous sight than I'd imagined. It looked as though her adult teeth had staged a sit-in and her baby teeth hung around to watch. There had to be fifty-two on the top alone. With shoes like that, you'd think she could afford an orthodontist. People were weird that way.

Naomi lingered on each word to let the implication soak in, twirling one of her frizzy curls. I stared at her hair, trying to figure out, once again, what nationality she was. She had Jennifer Lopez hips, Barbara Streisand hair, Angela Davis rage and a nose that curved like the photo of my Cherokee great-grandmother's. Today I didn't ponder the question long. Whatever she was, she wasn't happy.

Neither was I.

"So I talked on the phone a minute over, Naomi—"

"Ms. Parker."

Back to the maiden name, were we? This could get ugly. "All right…Ms. Parker, I'm sorry for my infraction. Now if you'll let me get back to work so I can prepare for our meeting this afternoon—"

Another sinister smile zipped across Naomi's lips. If her lipstick had been a few shades redder she'd have been a dead ringer for the Joker.

"You won't be meeting with anyone today, Dana. Not here anyway."

The stale Cheerios I'd eaten for breakfast knotted in my stomach. I suddenly wished I'd downed a few bear claws, too, so I could offer them up on Naomi's precious shoes.

*We wrestle not with flesh and blood, but with principalities and powers….*

I rolled my eyes to the ceiling. God was right, of course. Naomi wasn't my real problem…but she sure did a good acting job. Very convincing.

"What do you mean?"

Like a super villain in a very cute skirt, she snatched a sheet of paper from her clipboard. A Fingerhut receipt. Naomi turned the paper over to reveal a massive order from Renee, now gone to lunch, scrawled in blue eyeliner.

I grabbed my throat. My hand rose to the healing cut beneath my eye. It burned as though it'd been sliced afresh. "I told her I couldn't take orders here—"

"And yet she did it anyway. Perhaps because of the allure of your products? Products which, interestingly enough, I've never seen or been offered any samples of."

Huh? Now she sounded like the Abominable Snowman from one of the Rudolph Christmas specials, attacking the world just to get a little love. "I didn't think you wanted any. I'd be glad to make you a basket—"

She snorted. "I'm kidding. I don't want any of your kitchen sink cosmetics. It'd probably eat my sensitive skin right through."

One could only hope.

*Lord, forgive me.*

Triumphant, Naomi dropped into the seat beside me—Tracey's old desk. How I missed her right now. I never realized how much of a buffer she had been between me and, well, everyone.

"I've talked to Steve and we decided that this whole enterprise of yours is a conflict of interest. You're probably using our connections with fragrance suppliers for your own personal gain and who knows what else."

As if I'd want to use that wretched smelling stuff? It was bad enough to have to sample it.

"On top of that, our productivity inventory has shown the decrease in your work product over the past year. A direct result of your outside enterprise in our estimation. So…go home and talk to your little buddies all you want." She leaned over and clapped her palms like a seal. "You're fired."

With that, she strode toward her office, never bothering to look back.

I sat frozen for a few seconds and then mashed three numbers on the phone before I remembered that the line was monitored for "productivity assurance" or whatever she'd called it. I shrugged and punched the remaining digits. What did it matter now?

"Shoes of Peace." Rochelle still sounded like someone had shot her with a tranquilizer.

"You'll never believe it."

"What? Is it Tracey?" I could hear her scrambling around the register. "Don't tell me. Jordan called you, too—?"

My stupid brother was the least of my worries. Visa was going to come and repossess my teeth if I didn't figure a way out of this one. And just when I was considering that saving-up-for-a-rainy-day thing. "She fired me, Rochelle. What am I going to do now?"

"Fired you? Naomi?" A cheerleader's voice replaced her melancholy tone. "Get over here as fast as you can!"

I stared at the receiver. My friend had sprung to life at the news of my financial demise. Was I missing something here?

"Come over there? Now? No, I'm going home. I've got a date with some ice cream."

"No, little sis. You come by here. I've got something better than ice cream."

Better than ice cream? Now we were talking. "Whaddya got? Baklava? I knew you weren't serious about starting our food program today. Baklava is in the points book, but—"

"No, Dane, no baklava. What I'm going to feed you will keep you full for a long time. We're going to cook up some dreams."

The dream was almost done. A little raw in the center, overdone around the edges, but the details for my closet-hobby-turned-business were falling into place. The past few weeks had been a flurry of paperwork and planning—two things I'm not too good with. First, burning the midnight oil with a business plan had kept me busy. Then came the fun stuff—market research, product line development, price points and displays—all the stuff I'd dreamed about.

Only the reality turned out to be more like a nightmare. The insurance? Forget it. I came home from that meeting sweating like I'd been to spinning class. For extra fun, add in ordering bacteria challenge tests for my products, designing labels, obtaining UPC codes. All sorts of madness. But somehow, I felt more alive than ever. I'd thought Rochelle was nuts to push me into this, but I had to admit being excited. More excited than I'd been about anything in a long time, except maybe when Adrian showed up again. But now he'd disappeared just as quickly.

*Mind your business. I've got him.*

*And you.*

I smiled, easing my hand over the almost unrecognizable scar under my eye. My cocoa butter soap and lotion had done wonders. Renee, who'd volunteered to help me unload boxes, peeked around the corner of my Thanksgiving display, a burst of orange, gold, copper and green draped the shelves in layers. A cornucopia full of pumpkin pie bath bombs would soon grace the top for effect.

An emerald nail cradled Renee's cheek. "I know this wasn't easy, but I'm so glad it worked out. This is so…you. I can't believe Rochelle gave you the rest of the money though. I knew she did well over there with those shoes, but this well?" She swept a hand around the upscale retail unit.

I snapped on my latex gloves and a pair of goggles before heaving a tub of sodium hydroxide, a necessary and lethal ingredient in all soap, toward the back. Why was it Renee always voiced my thoughts?

"I don't know the details, Renee. I didn't ask. I'm thinking she took out a loan. She said it's a gift, but I'm going to pay her back. Somehow."

The empty shelves stared back at me mockingly as I tried to imagine them full of jars and bottles sporting the funky fuchsia and tangerine labels Tracey had designed.

"Don't worry. You'll do it. Wonderfully Made is going to be a hit."

"I hope so." Besides Rochelle's gift, I'd secured a small loan for women-owned businesses and cashed in my pitiful retirement fund. The cheery flowers on my foaming bath oil caught my attention, the product's title hugged the curve of the bright petals in a swirling script on the label.

*Hope floats.*

I sighed. Hoping. Helping. That's what this was about, helping women relax and rediscover their God-given beauty instead of cutting and peeling themselves into an early grave. It'd work out somehow.

Renee stood back as I passed by, as if the lye could escape the container and harm her somehow. Her posture humored me, but I was glad she took the safety concerns seriously. I'd been reluctant to let her come today, knowing the lye shipment needed to be stored properly. "I'll be back in a sec."

Tired of dragging the fifty-pound-double-garbage-bagged lump across the floor, I pushed it with my boot, hoping no stray lye crystals would jump onto my shoe somehow. Toe burns were no fun. Smelling a velvety bar of lavender oatmeal, six weeks old and smooth to the cut, made tasks like this bearable. Though I'd made hundreds of batches, there was still nothing quite like bathing with soap I'd made. It seemed the longer it cured the better it felt.

Getting to the point where I had supplies to shove around hadn't been easy. To pull it off, my life had become an express business seminar. My days had been laced with acronyms from dawn to dusk—IRS, SBA and SCORE—all which basically illuminated the fact that I was BROKE. But God did it anyway.

In spite of the odds, Wonderfully Made, my soon-to-be-opened bath and body shop, was a reality. I scanned the back room of this freshly painted strip mall unit. With boxes every-where, the place didn't look much different than my dining room at first sight, but the stucco lining the walls and the chandelier in the main area hinted at the possibilities.

I hoped this place would live up to its name. Adrian had cer-tainly lived up to the title of his business, heart kicker in the first degree.

*Easy come, easy go.*

He'd no doubt returned to Chicago by now. Though it hurt that he hadn't said goodbye, I was thankful. With him around, my mind had played tricks on me. Dangerous tricks.

I looked down at my bare wedding finger. Maybe I needed to take my relationship with Jesus as seriously as Adrian had taken being with Sandy. And Jesus was still alive…

That's deep.

Lugging the bag of chemicals into the hazardous materials cab-inet, I strained to remember a thought that could be food for the devotionals I owed the Sistahood. Especially Tracey, whose new husband had not only declined to apologize for his physical and emotional absence on their honeymoon, but scheduled a series of out-of-town trips in the weeks following. And she was not in-vited to tag along.

A chime rang at the front as I emerged from the storage area. It'd taken Rochelle long enough to get the food. The deli was only a block away. She'd rejoined Weight Watchers with me enough times to know how cranky I could be on Week One, even if we were trying to do it on our own this time. I'd seen the I-can't-believe-your-fat-self-is-here-again receptionist's car on Saturday and peeled out like a wimp.

I pushed back my gloves and grabbed the drawstring handles of another bag of lye. I'd have to wash down the floor with vin-egar before leaving tonight. Next time, I'd have the guy deliver to the back. I gathered my determination as the weight taxed my strength. At least I'd have some food now, I thought, heaving with all my might. "What'd you get? Not plain turkey, I hope. Some honey mustard at least—"

"I didn't bring any food, but I could go get some if you'd like."

Adrian's voice stopped me cold. Only my safety phobia allowed for how that lye bucket made it back to the floor without spilling. I looked down at my sweatshirt and holey jeans in horror. Renee's laughter whispered from behind the display behind me. What was he doing *here?*

He stepped around a stack of boxes. "Hey."

I stumbled over my former burden, suddenly unconcerned with the danger of its contents. He looked like a dream. A beige turtleneck sweater smoothed against his chocolate throat. His jeans fit, but were slack enough for comfort. A gold stud he'd abandoned when he got saved ten years before sparkled in his left lobe. Tapered loafers and a hip-length leather jacket the same color as his skin finished off the ensemble. He held a small Kick! bag in his hand.

"You look like dinner." Renee snickered.

No, she didn't say that. Bad enough that I was thinking it. When Adrian left, I was going to get Renee good. I cut her a scathing look. She raised an eyebrow, knowing that she'd voiced my true thoughts as usual.

Adrian doubled over with laughter, shaking his head as he straightened. "And you two look like businesswomen. Congratulations." He slipped out of his jacket. His muscular shoulders strained against the knit shirt as he sat the bag on the floor. As his graceful fingers intertwined around the garbage bag handles, his wedding ring was notably absent.

"No busineswoman here. I'm just helping out, though I've always been part of the vision." Renee walked to the front of the store and started cleaning the windows. I'd have to give her double vision if she didn't hush.

He picked up an hourglass-shaped vial of shower gel—Peachy Kleen. "Nice logo and trade dress. Tracey?"

I nodded. Most people wouldn't recognize Tracey's signature curls and swirls, but as her friends, we recognized her work easily. "Yes, she did an excellent job."

Adrian nodded, lowering his voice. "When were you going to tell me?"

I stared into the empty display case, then took a seat on the floor, Indian style. "I don't know. I didn't know where you were. I figured you'd gone back to Chicago."

He didn't look convinced. "I have a cell phone. E-mail. Not that I'm one to give advice on communication."

"True." I leaned over and opened a box of body butter and started loading it on a low shelf. As hard as it'd been to get these products made and labeled, making the display looked like it would be just as difficult. Especially with Adrian around. He pushed up his sleeves and squatted down beside me. Right beside me.

"I went to do management training for the Chicago warehouse and manufacturing plant, but now I'm here." His lips brushed my forehead. "Where I belong."

I adjusted the bandanna on my head, using all my willpower to keep from wrestling him to the ground. Why did he say such things? I dragged another box toward me.

"How'd you find me anyway?" I asked, back to the task at hand.

"Not the way you think."

I ran my tongue over my teeth. Rochelle, of course.

"I told him!" Renee shouted from the front, sounding particularly proud of herself. She was definitely full of surprises.

"I called your job and she filled me in." He stroked his bald head, then picked up a package of latex gloves from on the floor beside me. He pulled on each elbow-length glove carefully, smoothing it up to the crook of his arm, then buttoning his cuffs carefully around his wrists. He lifted the chemicals I'd abandoned with ease and started for the back.

I tried to get up. Didn't quite make it. "Hey that's—"

"Lye. Sodium hydroxide. Fatal if swallowed. You'd wish it were fatal if it gets on your skin. You forget I was a chemist before I turned candlemaker?"

True. In fact, it was Adrian who'd helped Tracey and I get on at Scents and Savings during his tenure there as a fragrance formulator, back in the good years before they starting ordering stuff that smelled like fumes. "Just being careful."

He paused. "Haz-Mat cabinet?"

I nodded. "It's just as you go in. The red one. And watch yourself, even with those gloves…" Chemist or not, Adrian's days in the lab were long gone, and sodium hydroxide was no child's play. In the eyes it could blind, in the belly it could kill, and on the skin? Trust me, not fun.

"Got vinegar?" His shoulders flexed as he lifted the tub out of my line of sight.

I pointed to a gallon of white vinegar a few feet away. "Yeah."

"We're good then," he said, his body disappearing, too.

"Should we lock him up back there?" Renee called out from the front.

Void of any energy to deal with another moment of this day, I dissolved in laughter. "You're a mess, you know that?"

Renee smiled. "I know it. My husband knows it, too. Now if I can just get you two nitwits together. Maybe I'll just leave and see what—"

"Don't." The alarm in my voice surprised me. "Please."

The thought of me alone with Illinois' Businessman of the Year in a poorly lit retail unit scared me senseless. Sure we'd spent a lot of time alone together growing up, but then he was a virgin chemist, not a sexy widower with an earring.

Before I could compose myself, Adrian returned. Renee whizzed her way back to the front as quickly as she'd come. He made two more trips, each faster than the last, moving the remainder of my lye shipment. He held out his wrists in front of me. If lye was on his gloves, he couldn't risk touching his clothes.

I opened the pearl snaps on his sleeves and took my seat on the floor. He peeled off the gloves and tossed them into a paint bucket nearby. He grimaced, then dashed his forearm with vinegar. He smiled at me. The bionic music mounted in my head. Where was Rochelle with that food?

"What should I do next?"

Drive back to Chicago? "We've got things under control here. Thanks for asking though." I held my breath, waiting for some crazed announcement to the contrary by Renee, who was now wiping the stainless steel interior of our facial cart. She made a squeak with the rag, but said nothing.

Adrian narrowed his eyes at the metal kiosk Renee was polishing. "What is that?"

"Facial bar. Fresh fruit. Veggies, too."

He nodded, walking to the front for a closer look. "This is ingenious, Dane. You could take it to the mall, outdoor shows, anywhere with power. I could formulate a natural preservative—"

"Stop. I'm over my head just being here. If it gets to that point, I'll call you." Or the local firing squad.

Adrian slipped across the room for that bag, the one I'd amazingly forgotten about after one look at him. He reached inside and pulled out a small, stuffed animal. A cheetah. I dropped the ice scoop.

He approached cautiously and placed it in my hands. "I know that Tracey's wedding was hard for you, for a lot of reasons."

I listened, but didn't look up from the toy. It got to me, this gift, even though I'd chucked my stuffed animal collection long ago—a zoo of elephants, tigers and bears, most won by Adrian at fairs and amusement parks over the years. Then there were those two wedding gorillas Jordan won for Rochelle. She couldn't bear to look at them after he left. One ratty bunny with the beans falling out that Daddy had given me many Christmases ago. And a life-size cheetah, identical in looks to the tiny one in my hands, that I'd won myself.

"I also stopped by to share a little news of my own." Adrian dragged one of his shoes across the floor.

The cheetah squished in my fingers. Don't tell me. He's getting married. I should have known.

Instead of proclaiming his undying love for another woman, Adrian nodded toward the partially covered front window, where I watched in horror as two men lifted a sign onto the marquis on the shop across the street. I read the teal and fuchsia sign with wide eyes.

Kick! Candles.

Adrian shrugged. "We're neighbors."

# Chapter Five

"You've got to be kidding." Rochelle looked at me like I was crazy, and then plopped a bag of food on the counter. Never one to be caught without cute shoes, even for painting and scrubbing, she sported a pair of peach Reeboks. And matching socks, of course.

"I wish I was kidding. How did you miss that? Kick! across the street? There's no hope for me…he's got the best candles in the state. Probably the Midwest. How much did we spend when we went last year? A couple hundred between us?"

As if starting my own business wasn't scary enough, having the man I'd spent most of my life loving across the street terrified me. Having Renee jump for joy at the sight of Adrian's sign hadn't helped things, either. She'd offered to stay, but I'd been all to glad to send her home when Rochelle showed up. We'd needed to be alone for this, for Rochelle to tell me that my stuff was just as good as Adrian's and to rebuke me for my negativity.

Not.

"We spent three hundred at least. We bought gifts, too, remember? To think, I wasn't even into candles then. I burn his raspberry honeysuckle every night."

But you won't touch my stuff. "Same here. Lemon pound cake. The soy one." I rubbed my chin, remembering all our undercover trips to Adrian's store over the past couple of years. The candlelight lent an eerie effect and I'd often thought we might all go up in flames, but it worked somehow.

Tension drained out of me when I walked in there—after I made sure he or Sandy weren't around, of course. I'd always want to stay for the next scent, but the thought of running into either of them made me run through the store grabbing stuff like a crazy person and then ducking into Rochelle's car.

I stared across the street at the men struggling with the sign and Adrian giving directions from the sidewalk. The candles were the least of my worries. How would I ever avoid him?

A soft punch landed on my shoulder. I definitely couldn't avoid Rochelle's clutches. Should I show her the cheetah? I'd told the story up to his store moving across the street and stopped there. Maybe later. Rochelle didn't know how to stay calm in these situations. She'd be having me fitted for a wedding gown…just in case. Not that I could fit much of anything right now. Maybe if I skipped the fries… But there was always Flex Points.

And Velcro jeans.

Rochelle turned on her heel, her paisley headscarf bobbing with her words. "I didn't tell him anything about this." She discarded the bun and wrapped her turkey in a leaf of lettuce. "He didn't do this on purpose, Dane, if that's what you think. He wouldn't."

"I know. He called the office. Renee told him. But he'd paid on this place already."

She touched my arm in reassurance. "It will only help you to have Kick! here. That place is special and he's drawing in your target customer."

My point exactly.

My handsome nemesis dangled from a ladder across the street, straightening his new sign. He waved, leaning back almost far enough to fall. I waved back, and prayed he wouldn't plummet to the ground. Although, admittedly, it might make this all a bit simpler.

*Lord, forgive me.*

I sure was saying that a lot lately. All Adrian's fault. "Still, this shop looks half the size of the one he had in Chicago. He'll probably go back once he gets this going."

Rochelle shook her head. "Don't you read that Black Enterprise subscription I pay for every month? He franchised a few months ago. All the new stores are smaller."

A few months ago? All the new stores? How many were there?

I frowned. "Is there any other good news you'd like to share, Rochelle?" Is that where she'd been running off to those weekends she said she was busy? To every Kick! shop she could find? Not that I could blame her. I looked outside again. Neighbors. He had said that, right? Not competitors or partners or any other such thing? Suddenly I wasn't so sure. Rochelle carries a tape recorder at all times. Today it would have come in handy.

"Nothing else I can think of to tell you."

Cool. I had nothing else to tell her, either. It'd take a week of sleepless nights to figure out what I was thinking, let alone trying to decipher Adrian's thoughts. "There's just one thing." I retrieved the cheetah from behind the counter. "He bought me this." What happened to keeping my mouth shut?

"I knew it! You'd better act right, Dane. This is it."

"This is something, that's for sure."

Rochelle counted out six French fries and nibbled them one at a time, like carrots. Though I'd seen her do it before, I watched in amazement, wondering how long it had taken her to get that down to a system. More time than I had, I decided, shoving a handful of fries into my starving mouth. My taste buds sang in my head.

My joy must have reflected on my face.

"You are pitiful, you know that? A few fries and you light up like a Christmas tree. A handsome man comes in here, hauls some stuff to your back room and gives you a gift and all you can think about is how it's going to affect your business."

I shrugged, licking the salt off my fingers. They usually didn't put enough salt on, but someone had known just how bad I needed it. "What else am I supposed to be concerned about? Everybody can't go from Singleville to becoming the Bachelorette of the Year in one swoop—"

"I resent that."

"Really? I'm glad to hear it. I know this stuff with Jordan is weirding you out, but you're really scaring me. That dress you wore Sunday was down right obscene…" I scooped a spoonful of chocolate shake to my lips, glad to have something to shove in my mouth besides my foot. Why was I discussing this with Rochelle? I knew she was going through something, but hey, so was I. Several somethings, in fact.

The fact that no ring had appeared on her finger or that my brother had neglected to surface hadn't been lost on me. Neither had her sudden surge of desire for a relationship. What I couldn't understand was why? Did she need someone to want her now? To make her feel pretty again? All she had to do was look into the mirror.

I stared at the cheetah on top of the cash register. It went deeper than wanting to be pretty. That much I knew. "Have you heard anything else from him?"

Rochelle turned her back to me, continuing her fry nibbling in silence.

"I'm sorry. I shouldn't have—"

"Don't worry about it, okay? I don't expect you to understand. There are some things even you can't get."

On the outside again. "So I can't 'get it,' huh? Why, because I'm not a mother? Because I've never been almost-married or whatever you and Jordan were?" I guess Trevor's proposal didn't give me any points.

She shoved a box of Coconut Lime body lotions over to the display case. "That about sums it up."

Six containers of Banana Berry Mint mask lined the facial cart, all as fresh as when I'd pureed them this morning. Though I'd sell the fruit products as good for twenty-four hours with refrigeration, I wanted to give the cooler a trial run and do some bacteria challenge tests for my own information—now that I knew how to do such things. I should have given my comments to Rochelle a trial run, too. This conversation had taken a turn into the abyss of famous last words.

And of course, I started it.

Where is Tracey when I need her?

Off fighting with her husband instead of fighting with us. Leaving me on the outside of the circle of the wed and/or childbearing. How long would it be before Tracey entered the Mom Club, too? Her bumpy beginning with Ryan didn't fool me. Tracey was too stubborn to give up on anybody. She was still my friend, wasn't she? Lord willing, they'd stick, Rochelle and Jordan—or somebody, the way she was acting—would work things out and here I'd be, as always, the last Sistah standing.

How would I ever survive without them? Really bad, considering how I was cutting up right now. Rochelle stacked on in silence, her perfect placement showing the tangerine-colored bottles from every angle. Her rapid breathing meant she was fuming but too loyal to leave.

*Humble yourself in the sight of the Lord, and He will lift you up in due time.*

I shoved another mouthful of shake down my throat to cool my burning thoughts. Humility? Again? People who thought Christians were wimps had another thing coming. It was hard. Crazy hard.

Rochelle caught me staring off into space. "Are you just going to sit there? Or are you going to do some work? There's a lot to do here and I have to go get Jericho from basketball in a couple hours. I don't have to be here." Rochelle sniffed and righted the last bottle of lotion on the top shelf of the three-tiered display. I'd wanted them down on the table, but she'd insisted everything be eye level or above. And she was right.

As usual.

I opened my mouth again, but not for chocolate this time. Rather for a heaping dose of humble pie. I was determined to swallow, no matter how bad it tasted. Hopefully, she'd go easy on me. "I know you don't have to be here." I walked over and put my hands on her shoulders, careful not to touch her skin in case some lye from earlier might have snuck under my fingernails. I'd gone to scratch my back after a batch once and almost killed myself.

"I appreciate everything you've done for me the past few months. You're always here for everybody. Me. Tracey. Jericho. Tracey's wedding totally rocked and it wouldn't even have happened if not for you. Shoot, Tracey probably would have forgotten to show up. But you made it possible, because that's what you do—look out for people and it's okay for you to look out for yourself, too. I guess I'm—well, I guess I'm just a little left out, you know?"

Rochelle nodded. "Yeah. We've all done everything together for a long time. It feels real weird that Tracey isn't here today. Opening this shop…"

I laughed. "Yeah. I knew there was too many fries for some reason."

"You two are some eating fools." She shook her head. "But I know what you mean about feeling left out. Right now, my son has locked me out of his life while he waits for his 'Dad' to arrive. Tracey has moved on…and you—"

Me? "What? I'm still the same. Nothing's changed."

Rochelle swallowed hard and looked up at the chandelier, then around at the slowly filling shelves. "Everything's changed, baby girl. You just don't know it yet."

* * *

The grand opening wasn't exactly grand, probably because I was comparing Wonderfully Made's one little, two little, three little customers with the line of giggling women spilling onto Adrian's sidewalk. I did manage to snag a few browsers who wanted to buy everything in the store—at a discount.

Brides. Mothers-of-the-Bride. Wedding planners. Even a few grooms. They'd come in small but steady numbers looking for favors for their weddings. I could just imagine the possible impetus of this phenomenon—Renee waving one of my baskets and comparing the prices with her latest Fingerhut catalog.

"Can I get this in lavender? This salt scrub?"

I gritted my teeth at the silver-haired matriarch, so much like my mother would have been. "No. That's the bottle for the Plumeria products. The lavender is a much lighter shade. If you'd—"

"This is lavender. That's lilac. Brook's wedding colors are not lilac. Can't you just pour that into some of these bottles and put her name on this cute label?"

Oh, fun. "I'm really not set up to do personalized favors. My printer—"

"I'll pay extra and we'll take all that you have here for the spa party with the bridesmaids." She fumbled with a large Mount Blanc pen. "What do you say?"

What could I say? To have any hope of paying Rochelle back, I needed to sell as much as possible. "Sold. Let's step over here to work out the details. Can you spell Brook's last name here…"

The morning continued like that, bargains struck and checks written, all for projects I hadn't planned on. As much as I appreciated the business, the glee and glow of the soon-to-be-wed, and their uptight family members, was doing damage to my nerves. Could anybody be that happy? And for how long? Tracey had smiled like that, too.

\* \* \*

Days turned in my devotional Bible, each one dotted with little sleep and much stress as the exacting wedding planners and haggling mothers-in-law flooded my shelves.

As much as I wanted to go berserk over Jordan and confront Rochelle, I didn't have time. I'd seen her at church last Wednesday night, tripping up the step in a new pair of shoes—lime green. Her guilty color. Though she waved and ran on, I figured Rochelle had probably seen Jordan and didn't want to feel bad because he still hadn't bothered to contact me. Her contrition was thoughtful, but unnecessary. My brother and I hadn't been close. Though I'd prayed for this time to be different, there was no use breaking the rules now.

Adrian had been a curiosity, too, working hard outselling me, and spending the rest of his time trying to hook up with me and talk business. Though I knew we needed to be getting together, strategizing, I knew that neither of us would be thinking of marketing if we were within a foot of each other. What I didn't know was where I wanted those feelings to go. But like I said, such things would have to wait for when I had time to think about them.

For now, I went to work and to church—on slow days, I slipped off to noonday prayer. Those retirees know how to pray. I hadn't had time to touch the phone outside of business…or the computer, thanks to Tracey handling my Web site and covering my devotionals. Being out of touch was great, in a way. I'd forgotten what it was like to just pray and sing all by myself. Like it was when I first got saved and Rochelle was busy with her business and Tracey was in school for the tenth time, before finally hitting upon her call in life, graphic design.

I took a deep breath and took my church dress out of the closet, hoping it would be looser since the last time I wore it. I slipped it over my head, noticing at once the grip the sleeves had on my shoulders.

Tighter, not looser.

I frowned, thinking of Tracey, who'd given me this outfit when she'd abandoned her flab. Amazing what affect Ryan had on her. When I'd dated him, he'd driven me so nuts, I was on a first-name basis with the pizza man. Tracey, on the other hand, was so in love she'd forgotten to eat…or so she said. Whatever the case, she'd sure looked good in that wedding gown. And here I was about to explode out of another dress.

I'd been doing okay with my eating, but couldn't seem to squeeze in time to get to the gym. The blistering cold kept me from my summer walks and work seemed to beckon from every corner. Gone were the days where excess pounds dropped off in a week or a month. Less than a year shy of thirty, I had to fight to lose even an ounce. And at this time of the month, it was pretty much a lost cause.

Shoving back my closet door, I stared at the satin cemetery of bridesmaids gowns in the back—ten dresses in a rainbow of pastels, peach, lavender and robin's egg blue. A lovely canary yellow that had actually looked good on me. The last, a shocking pink with a ruffled skirt, sported two slits down the sides.

Remembering it was the third Sunday and the choir needed to dress the same, I reached for a black wrap-around skirt and white blouse, both in a size I'd vowed never to wear again.

Why'd you keep them, then?

Just in case, the same reason I still had my hope chest full of dishes that Mama had given to Adrian and me. The thought made me a little queasy. I'd have to get rid of that. It was just weird.

I stared at the clock. Six-thirty. At noonday prayer on Friday, I'd promised Mother Holly I'd pick her up for church this morning. Did she go to the early service? I'd forgotten to ask. I'd been too busy soaking up her powerful prayers for my situation with Jordan and Rochelle. I didn't give the details, but having been my mother's friend, she knew enough to read between the lines.

"Don't worry about it, baby," she'd said in that singsong voice of hers. "You just do your thing. Keep your eyes on Jesus. He's got this."

I smiled at the thought, both knowing and wondering if she was right. He did have this thing, didn't He? 'Cause I didn't.

Peeling off the tight-sleeved dress, I smoothed my skirt down over my stockings, then tucked my blouse into the flexible waistband.

Ahh…much better.

Nothing like elastic when you bloat up like the Good Ship Lollipop.

The phone rang, interrupting my silly thoughts. I walked toward it, put my hand on the receiver, but didn't pick up. Surely Rochelle wouldn't choose now to try and "get things straight" as she had on many other Sunday mornings. Nah. Maybe later, after her solo, when she felt especially holy.

What about Adrian? Besides our inopportune run-ins in the business owners' parking lot and my constant glances across the street, e-mail had been our only contact. And even that proved more than I could deal with. Three messages from him awaited my reply.

"You have reached Dana Rose. You are fearfully and wonderfully made. Leave a message and have a blessed day."

"Dane! It's Tracey. I know you're there. Probably standing up in your stockings talking to yourself. Pick up! I—"

She knew me so well. "What is it, silly? And I'm not talking to myself. I'm thinking, thank you."

"Mmm-hmm. In your stockings."

I shrugged, staring down at my toes peeking through the black sheer. No sense arguing the obvious. "How've you been? Things any better?"

Tracey didn't respond. I slipped my foot in one shoe and waited, growing concerned with the lengthening silence. When there was something big to tell, Tracey went quiet on you. Surely their marriage hadn't gone totally sour in two months? "Tracey? Is everything okay?"

Sobs poured through the phone. "No…it's not…okay."

I stared at the clock. Six forty-two. Mother Holly wasn't going to make it to the early service. Neither was I. "Take your time, hon. Whatever it is, we can work it out. God can work it out."

"Mmm-hmm."

I could imagine Tracey nodding, tears trailing under her chin. Besides her laughing capabilities, she was a great crier, too. Should have been an actress. Only these tears were all too real.

"Just say it. I'm here."

"I'm…I'm…"

My neck rotated in circles as if I could make her spit it out. "Yes?"

"I'm pregnant!"

I let out a long breath. "Wow."

"Is that all you have to say?"

Oh, no, there's a lot more I could say, but I'll hold my tongue for now.

Rochelle is going to blow.

"I'm so happy for you, Tracey." And I meant it. I think. A baby. I *so* did not see that coming.

"Are you, really? Happy for me, I mean?" Another sniff.

"Really." I sat down on the edge of the bed, staring into my closet. Who knew? Maybe this would be the thing to help them get closer. I doubted it, but maybe. "Aren't you happy, too? I know it's not the best time, but you both want children."

Her voice turned to a whisper. "I know. It's just—I'm scared, Dana. Ryan seems happy about it and everything, but I feel the munchies coming on and you know how fast I can gain—"

Boy did I. Nobody could gain or lose weight like Tracey. I maintained a steady up creep to keep things interesting, but over the years, Trace had earned stock in everything from Deal-A-Meal to Jenny Craig, only to drop it all when she finally fell in love. Still, I was surprised that weight was her main concern.

"You'll be fine. Just walk the block. Eat some fruit and veggies every day and don't overdo." Good advice. Why didn't I take it?

"That's easy for you to say, Dane. You always look good."

I tapped the receiver. Was this thing on, or had my just-married-now-pregnant friend lost the last bit of her mind? "You called Dana, not Rochelle. Dana."

"I know who I'm talking to. Rochelle is too skinny to live. You're a great size. You just insist on buying clothes that don't fit and make you look bigger than you are. You're beautiful. And those eyes? Man. I was so afraid Ryan still liked you. Really afraid."

Whoa. What was this, Black Confessions? I could only take so much. "Afraid? Of me? Trace, you're like a genius, you dress like a goddess and you're so nice. Everybody loves you. Everybody."

She sniffed again. "Not everybody. It's horrible out here. Everybody at church has kids. All the women are perfect. Just perfect. A bunch of stay-at-home moms—"

I rubbed my eyes, suddenly feeling very sleepy. "But that's what you want to be, remember? You'll be perfect, too. The best mom ever. Now go back to sleep."

"Sleep? Ha. I can't. I have to run to the bathroom every ten minutes and then I get thirsty. Then I'm hungry, then I get sleepy and right when I nod off, and it starts all over again. I—"

"Tracey." For all my friend's bubbliness, she had a manic side, too, the side I'd considered dousing with punch at her reception. Getting her to stop this hysteria wouldn't be easy. "Let's pray."

"Okay. You go."

Of course. "Lord, You said that children are a blessing from You. Thank You for giving Tracey and Ryan this gift. Help her to stay calm to trust You and do the things she knows to do. Give her the peace that passes all understanding."

She sighed through the receiver. "That was soo-oo-o good. Peace that passes all understanding. You always know just what to say."

I groaned. "It's in the Bible, Tracey." She always made it sound like I'd made some Shakespearian performance every time I prayed. Her kid would have disgustingly high self-esteem. She'd probably cheer every time she changed a diaper.

"I know, but you just say it so well."

"Whatever. Look, I've got to go. Your church doesn't start until eleven, right?"

"Ten-thirty."

"Okay. Take a nap and have a great worship—"

"Rochelle is going to have a fit."

I smiled. "A honeymoon baby? Oh, yeah. She'll go nuts. But don't worry about her, she's busy being mad at me."

"What's up with you two? Is it—"

"More than I have time to tell."

"E-mail me."

"I will."

The phone beeped indicating another call. Who was it now? Rochelle would be on the way to the seven o'clock service by now. Had I given Mother Holly my number? Maybe she'd looked it up in the church directory.

"Look. I've got to go. Someone's calling."

"At this time of the morning? Who is it? Should I hold—"

"No. I love you. And it will be okay. It really will. Bye."

I pressed the button, collecting my apologies.

"Mother Holly?"

A man's voice, still and calm, answered my greeting. "No, sorry to disappoint. It's Adrian."

I stumbled, trying to jab my foot into my other shoe, now overturned beside the bed. "Uh, hi. Coming to Broken Bread today?" My ankle wobbled. I flopped onto the chair. "Or are you going to the Messianic place?"

"I'm coming with you today. Are you okay?"

Probably sounds like a dogfight over here. "I'm fine." I watched in horror as an inch-wide run tore up my leg like a flame. My last pair of hose.

"I just figured that since we're going out after service to talk business…"

"We are?" I clutched the closet door.

He sounded hurt. "I think that's what your last e-mail said. Me coming to Broken Bread. Us going to lunch to discuss the joint coupon promotion idea?"

Somehow I'd missed that part of the e-mail. Honestly, I'd forgotten the whole thing until he called. I'd have to read these electronic communications from him more closely. Us girls just sent stuff back and forth, knowing we'd have to follow up with a reminder or a call. Guys actually scheduled things based on a "sure." Me, I'm a skimmer. There was always some fine print to our interactions that I never got around to. "Right. Lunch. No problem."

"Great. I'll pick you up," Adrian said calmly, while I tried not to panic.

I stared down at my bare leg peeking through my torn hose. "On second thought, today's probably not the best day. I have to pick up one of the elders this morning."

"Even better. I'd be honored to help. My car's got plenty of room."

I'll bet, I thought, trying to keep my mind off my last image of him—long, strong legs, packed into a pair of jeans. What would he wear today? I gulped, thinking of how he'd looked in that gray suit at Tracey's wedding. Those square-toed shoes…

That's one fine bald-headed somebody.

As I realized that I had just had "man feelings" without realizing or authorizing them, Adrian's voice creaked through the receiver, tangled in a ball of static.

"So…I'll be there in a minute…I'm losing the signal."

"Huh? Wait!" Too late. He was gone.

# Chapter Six

When the doorbell rang, I'd peeled off my ruined stockings, buzzed the downstairs door and ran to my own door, my legs bobbing like skinless drumsticks. I reached for the knob, thanking God that I did at least have good calves. Probably from riding a motorcycle through high school and college. It was hard for me to imagine doing something like that now.

I pulled back the door, hoping Adrian wouldn't notice my fancy-free legs.

My concern was unwarranted. Adrian wasn't the one at the door. The face that met me on the other side, eyes so much like my own, stared back at me, draining any remaining resolve I had.

My brother Jordan. The last person I expected to find at my door. A month ago, I'd been dying to see him. Now, I was late, my legs were bare and I had no idea what to say.

"Hey, sis."

"Come in." It was all I could think of.

We never were close. He was always running, jumping, shooting, dribbling… Moving past me, away from me. Away from the women trailing behind him—Rochelle, Mama, my sister Dahlia.

They pounced on him every chance they got, cornering him, demanding he confess his unrequited love.

And he did, on cue, like a battery-operated action figure, while Daddy and I looked on, both in awe…and disgust. In awe of Jordan's muscles, his magnetism, his power to make the women in our house love him so readily, so greedily. In disgust of the same things. How could he be so cavalier about being, well…himself?

It seemed arrogant in the rudest way then, but looking back, I guess he was just a kid after all. Nineteen. A few years older than Jericho was now. What a switch between those two. If Jordan was so mature and did what he did, what hope was there for Jericho?

*Jesus is the only hope for anyone.*

I sighed, looking over at my brother, now seated on my sofa, silent after all these years. Where did he stand with Jesus? Was it even appropriate to ask? Most Bible thumpers would have said yes, but I'm more of a relationship witness and right now whatever relationship we might have had seemed nonexistent. Or was there something left?

He'd come to my door today, with not so much as a phone call of warning and knocked softly, as was his way. He'd never needed to pound. Somebody always ran before he could knock twice. He could turn Mama's head just by breathing in her direction. Even now, with his long legs crossed and his Dudley Do-Right dimpled chin perched on his fist, he was Jordan. The one.

"I saw Dad at the airport." His voice surprised me. I'd forgotten the rumble of it, low and warm like those hot toddies Mama used to make us when we had colds. A winter voice.

"Was he drunk?"

Jordan shook his head, his eyes dancing with alarm.

I chuckled. If Dad being drunk worried Jordan, he'd be in for a lot of sleepless nights. Like the ones I'd had worrying about him.

"What did Dad say?" Besides bumming money of course. That was a given.

"Not much. He said I looked good and that Mama had—had missed me. And I should have called or come to the funeral."

Wow. Dad said all that? He must have been really drunk. Or really sober. The sight of Jordan probably freaked him out. I thought back, trying to remember if he'd ever said that much to my brother…nope. In fact, he'd avoided Jordan like a flu bug once he grew past six feet.

I grabbed a pillow from behind me and clutched to my chest, as if to hold my heart in. I hadn't planned to hurt today. Not that the men in my life seemed to notice. Suddenly, the shop, Rochelle, even Adrian paled in comparison to this moment, this pain I hadn't even realized I had.

A memory invaded my head. "Do you remember payday, J.?"

My brother shrugged his shoulders. Why would he remember? I'd always been the one clinging to Daddy's heels.

"Friday, four o'clock. Dad would toss that money on the table and smile at me. I'd smile back, but Mama didn't. She'd count it, tuck it in her bra and turn back to the stove. Or the sink. Or the refrigerator. But she never smiled. Or said thank you, or even kissed him like those happy blond women on TV. She just kept chopping, scrubbing, cooking…" A tear trailed my cheek.

"Dane…"

I choked up at the image of my mother in the kitchen, her dress bulging with that wad of Daddy's money, her brown eyes glossy and vacant, her lips silent and unkissed.

"'Curse you woman,' Dad would say and march off to the back door, the front door, the window, any way he could get out."

"Yeah. He always was a runner. Always going somewhere."

I guess you got it honest.

"And you know why, J.? Because he couldn't stand to stay and see her eyes light up when her real man came home. Her true love." I turned to face him. "Jordan Kennedy Rose, her only son and gift to the world. The rest of us, well, we'd do in a pinch."

Before, he would have said, "It's not like that." But not today. Today, Mama was dead and we were grown and things just were what they were. There was no use trying to sugarcoat it. I drank in the silence, wondering where Adrian was. The last thing I needed was for him to walk in on me like this. A few swipes with the back of my hand cleared my eyes, but soon they flooded again. Adrian or no Adrian, we had to talk this through.

"I wish it would have been you, Dane. You don't know how it was. So much pressure. I could never just…be, you know. I had to do. Something. Everything. Mama. Rochelle. Even Dahlia."

I winced at the mention of our little sister. He frowned in confusion, but continued. I hugged the pillow harder. If Rochelle hadn't told him about me and Dahlia, then I wasn't going to, either. Not now, anyway.

"Everybody was depending on me to make it to the NBA, to bring us out. Even Daddy. He might not have said anything, but he didn't pay for those sneakers for nothing. The message was clear. Make it or don't come back."

I tossed the pillow on the floor. It wasn't helping. "But you did make it." I stood, trying to run before I lost it. Too late. "And you didn't come back!" The scream came up from my toes.

Sobs wracked my body. Jordan caught my wrist, pulling me down onto his lap. "I'm sorry."

"Mama waited for you! They all did. They sat by the phone every night. Watched your games on TV. Tried to call the team…" My fists pummeled his chest. His face. He didn't try to shield himself, only held me tight by my waist. Finally, I collapsed on his shoulder.

"She died waiting for you. That morning, before she had the stroke, she said, 'Did he call?' 'No, Mama,' I told her. 'He'll call tomorrow.' Tomorrow. She said that every day. But you…never… came!"

Jordan pulled me closer and lifted my hands, inspecting each of my fingers, like a father to a baby. He let me cry until I fell silent.

He looked down at me. "Are you done?"

I slumped against his chest. "No. But I'm tired."

He reached for a tissue from the table behind us. I took it and dabbed my face, trying not to think about what I'd look like when Adrian arrived. Right now, I just wanted him to knock on the door. I needed him.

"You don't have anything to say about Rochelle, Dana? About the baby?"

Baby? Jericho? The boy was almost six foot three. If he qualified as a baby, Tracey was in big trouble. "I don't even want to get into that. I'm just going to say that since Mama died, Rochelle has been there for me every step of the way. We raised your son—Rochelle, Tracey and I. Only now, he doesn't want—or need—any of us. He needs a man. Something you obviously know nothing about being."

He lowered me back to the couch, talking in that Nat King Cole voice again. "Now we're getting somewhere. Let it out."

"No."

"Why not?"

"Well, first of all, it's no fun screaming at someone who isn't screaming back and second of all it doesn't matter. It's done. Forgiven. Over."

Jordan bridged his fingers under his chin, then sat back on my sectional. He still had the same dark curls, though it looked as if someone had cut out a perfect circle in the top with a rotary cutter. Still tall, but not as tall as I'd remembered him. He was a giant to me back then. Now for all his height, he looked small. Old, as if this whole mess had hurt him just as bad. Only his eyes held that same twinkle.

Mama's twinkle.

"Forgiven, huh? It sure doesn't sound like it. Say what you need to say. I can take it. I just wanted to come here to see you—"

"See me? Didn't you see me waiting scared to death in the hospital room with Rochelle? You didn't just leave her…or Jericho. You left me." Though I screamed the words in my head, they came out as a whisper, like ashes of all the love I'd once had for him. Love? Yes, in spite of myself, I had loved my brother. And loved him still.

Where was that pillow? I reached behind me and dug my fingers into another one. Why couldn't Jordan have come here after church? I stiffened. Had he gone to Rochelle's with this same calm speech? I remembered his unscratched face and knife sharp pleats when he'd come inside. Nope. He'd come here first.

"Dad says he's handsome. Tall."

"Jericho?" My face crumpled, realizing he hadn't seen Jericho since…well, ever. Just those baby pictures Mama had sent everywhere. Most of them returned.

"Yeah. He's gorgeous. Your spitting image with Rochelle's eyelashes, Mama's legs and Dahlia's mouth. Oh, yeah, and Daddy's ears."

"That's quite a picture."

I nodded in agreement. "It is. Wait 'til you see him…." My voice faded. How could he do it? All these years and show up now, calm, like nothing ever happened? To never even call? What kind of man does that?

What kind of Christian tells someone they're forgiven but refuses to forget?

*There's a lot on this tab, Lord. A lot.*

I took a deep breath. "Did Dad ask you for money?"

"I gave him three hundred. He rode home with me in the taxi."

Home? What on Earth did that mean? Jordan's apartment? Or did he think this shell of a place as his home? He'd taken the home from here long ago.

*Don't judge before the time.*

The time was years ago! I dropped my head back against the sofa. "Don't give him so much money. He'll kill himself."

Jordan stared at me like I was speaking Russian. To him, I suppose I was. When he'd left, Dad only got tipsy at a wedding or barbeque now and then. Now he stayed drunk. With three hundred dollars, he could wreck himself for sure.

"Okay. I didn't know—"

"There's a lot you don't know, J. Like paying Dad's rent, putting food in his fridge once a week, taking him to the doctor, making him take a bath—" All of which I hadn't done with any regularity lately.

"I'm sorry." My brother's words came out sweet and syrupy, like the gooey insides of a pecan pie. The scratch kind. "I never meant for you to have to become the man of the family." He hung his head. "I'll try and make it up. When I find Dahlia—"

I pulled away. "Good luck with that."

"What happened between the two of you? You were so close. You had her. I didn't think you needed me. Well, maybe she did, but not you. Never you."

He left off what Mama would have said. Dana, she's the strong one. What a joke. I was strong all right, but only because I didn't have a choice. All the "weak" ones did the choosing for me.

"When you find her, ask her yourself. But don't look for her to help you. She won't." I swallowed. Would helping Jordan fall to me, too? "You can stay here if you want, but I warn you, Rochelle is welcome. Jericho, too. They always—"

He shook his head. "I've got a place. I didn't come here to take anything from them. Or from you."

There's nothing left to take. "That brings me to the real question, J. Why are you here? Mama's not waiting anymore. And I'm worn out from covering for you…and praying for you—"

He stiffened. "Praying? You?"

I guess that forgiveness bit had gone right over his head. I tried not to be offended by his surprise, remembering what a pistol I'd been growing up. Judging from the way I was acting today, I still had a few bullets left in me.

"Yes, me. Who else?" I paused. "Well, Rochelle prayed, too, of course." Probably not lately. "Maybe Dad, too. He gets real holy when he's drunk. Prays for everybody on the globe."

I wiped my tear-streaked face. "Me, I've been praying for your sorry behind every day since you left, though none of those prayers probably made it past the ceiling until the past three years."

Crow's feet creased the corners of my brother's eyes. "Three years? Are you sure?"

I snorted. "Oh, believe me, I'm sure. I'll never forget the day. June—"

"Ninth?"

We stared at each other. What had happened to him on that day? The day I was born again.

"Those prayers got somewhere all right, sis. In fact, they made it a long way." He patted the sofa beside him. "This is going to sound crazy…"

I braced myself. "Okay."

"You know I played a few years for the Celtics. Then got into some trouble…"

Yeah, I knew. Drugs, fighting, all sorts of madness. And plastered on the news for Mama to see. "She really thought you'd come home then."

He shook his head. "Don't say anything until I'm done." His jaw set into a line. "For real."

I closed my eyes, prayed, and then opened them before nodding in agreement.

"Well, after I got kicked out of the league, I went to Europe, then wherever would have me. I met a woman…."

While we were teaching Jericho how to color inside the lines, he was traveling with a girlfriend? Was this what Rochelle didn't want to tell me? And why did I feel both pity and anger toward this stranger, this woman who'd changed all of our lives? Maybe because I'd tasted the wrath that led her to such violence and only the sweetness of Christ has washed the bitterness from my mouth.

"Anyway, we were at a tournament in Mexico and things went bad between us. Real bad." He wrung his hands, then lifted his sport shirt. A mishmash of scars cluttered his chest. I gasped, both at the wounds and the outline they made—a crooked cross. "She left me for dead then killed herself. I spent ten years in a coma." He dropped his shirt. "Three years ago, on June ninth, I heard somebody calling my name, telling me to wake up...." His lip trembled. "That it was time for breakfast."

Tears streamed down my face. I gripped the leather so hard it squeaked. The bacon call. I could hear it just like yesterday. "Mama."

Jordan shook his head. "No, Dane. It was you."

I looked at my brother in disbelief. Me? He'd heard me calling him? I tried to think of a sensible response. "Let me get this straight. You heard my voice and woke up?" My hands dropped to my lap. I stared at the clock. Thirty minutes had passed since I'd opened the door. Forty since I'd hung up the phone. Where was Adrian? This was more than even I could handle alone. But then I wasn't alone, was I?

*Lord, please. Is Jordan serious?*

He sure looked it, with that solemn face, now etched with time. "Yes, Dane. I know it sounds crazy. How do you think I feel? It happened to me. I've spent the last few years learning everything—walking, talking— all over again."

"But who paid for you to be there? Did the team know you where you were?"

He shook his head. "The team thought I'd split town and quit. I don't know who paid the bill. Who knows? I'm just glad to be alive."

I scratched my head. All these years, I'd envisioned my reunion with Jordan, this wasn't the way I thought it'd happen. "Well, I guess this changes things, but you still could have done for Jericho the years you were around."

He frowned. "Do for him? I was a kid, Dane. I sent him money. What else could I do back then?"

The sound of a needle screeching across a record tore across my mind. I skipped over my brother's warped sense of responsibility, and landed on one word—*money*. "What money?"

He snorted. "The green kind. I sent it to Chelle. Mama, too. While I had it anyway."

Confusion bubbled inside me, giving way to understanding. I paused, then exhaled slowly, to delay spontaneous combustion. My eyes watered remembering Rochelle's mysterious "settlement" so many years before—the money that had sent her to Fashion Institute of Technology. Jordan's money?

Had Rochelle, my friend, my mentor, my sister in the faith lied to me?

You've lied to her, too. And a lot more recently than that.

"Dana? What's wrong? You didn't know? You thought—"

"I thought you never called. Never wrote. Never sent a dime." Wrong was still wrong, but it did give things a little different spin.

"Money wasn't enough. I know that now. But back then, I thought money could do anything, you know. Especially that much money."

That much? My brow furrowed. Did I dare ask the sum? Would Back-To-Life man even remember? "Do you remember how much? The money, I mean?"

Jordan stared up at the ceiling. "Let's see… A couple hundred grand to Chelle and fifty or sixty to Mom. Might have been more, but somewhere around—"

"Three hundred thousand?" My throat closed. So that's where Mom got the money to buy this apartment. When the co-op offered the place for sale, I'd offered my pennies, too, but the bulk of the money had been a mystery.

He nodded. "Sure. I'd planned to give more, but then I got drunk that night and didn't wake up—"

I held up my hand. "Whoa. I can't take anymore. We're going to have to weed through this information a little at a time." I took a deep breath. My brother was home after almost losing his life. He'd heard my voice, but had he heard the voice of Christ?

"How about Sunday dinner...after church. I'd love it if you'd—"

"I don't know if I'm ready for that, Dana. I have a lot of people here to apologize to before I go prancing up in church."

"God is the only one you need to worry about and He's always ready to forgive."

Jordan smiled. "People are a little more difficult, believe me."

Dahlia's teary-eyed face flickered across my mind. "Forgive me, Dane. Please," she'd said.

My teeth ground together. *Don't start, Lord. This isn't about me. It's about him.*

The doorbell dinged. I jerked upright at the sound of the doorbell. *Thank God.*

Jordan stood.

"Rochelle?" he asked softly.

I shook my head. "Adrian, most likely. I can tell them to come back—"

*Ding.*

He shook his head. "No, you go on to church. You took this much better than I thought. I considered wearing a football helmet in here."

"You should have."

*Dong.*

Jordan followed me to the front door. "Church must be doing something for you. You used to be something else."

I sighed. I was still "something else," but I was trying to make it a good something. Jordan hugged me one last time and at his nod, I pulled back the door.

Before I could say a word, Jordan dived across me and gathered Adrian, already in midair, into an embrace worthy of a greeting card—a regular sweater fest.

Adrian's keys hit the ground. Were those tears in his eyes? "J.? Is that really you? I can't…" He choked up and looked at me with such tenderness that my tears flowed, too.

Jordan chuckled. "It's me. But, is it you? Look at you, man! You all thick. And here I've whittled away to nothing." He hit his chest. "Dana's cooking, huh? She always could throw down. Just like Daddy."

My mouth hung open. Jordan had always teased me about my cooking tasting horrible. Adrian's eyes got just as wide. "We, uh, aren't married—"

Jordan swiped at his eyes. I paused to consider that he hadn't shed one tear with me. Since when were he and Adrian that close? My brother's voice cracked. "I have so many regrets. Missing Jericho's life. Mama's funeral. Dane's graduation… At least I didn't miss the big event with you two…" He stared into the hall at the door of apartment 203 where Adrian's family had lived. "I'm sorry about your mother, too. I promised her that I'd look out for both of you."

Adrian kneeled down and picked up his keys, then cast a quick glance over his shoulder at his old place. "Well J., that's one promise I hope you can keep." He stood and patted my brother's shoulder and reached for my trembling hand before I could say anything I'd regret. "C'mon, Dane, or we'll be late."

# Chapter Seven

We didn't say much, Adrian and I, as we drove to pick up Mother Holly. Jordan's arrival had sucked the words out of both of us. That and trying to make the second service on time. There was an hour to spare, but Mother Holly could be counted on for two things-loose change and surprises. Most times I loved that about her, but today my surprise-o-meter read "full."

Every now and then, Adrian looked across the front seat at me and took a breath. "Jordan. Home. After all this time," he'd say, or "Who'd have thought?"

I smiled foolishly, allowing the impact of the whole thing to settle. Sure, I'd known about my brother's reappearance for weeks, but to see him... It brought back so many old thoughts, old hopes. I'd known in my head, that nothing was impossible with God. Now, I knew it in my heart. When Adrian's fingers locked with mine, I knew he believed it, too. But hadn't he always? I looked up at him at a red light. Searched his eyes. Hope flickered there, dancing amid the steady gaze of faith shining from behind his glasses. Sandy's death had taken from him but it had given him something new, too. I nibbled my lip as he held my hand tighter. Losing was curious that way. Getting something back that you thought was lost was even more strange.

He kissed the top of my hand. "Is this the house?"

I nodded toward the small ranch home with Holly spelled out in sticker letters on the mailbox. Getting our passenger in the car proved more difficult than I'd anticipated. She almost fell out at the sight of my shiny, hoseless legs—I marveled at them, too, but for another reason. Under my dress, the rest of me resembled an alligator. Amazing what a little shea butter lotion could do for the skin. I'd have to make another batch of that lotion for myself pronto—taking a bottle from the store was an absolute last resort.

Adrian carried Mother Holly's coffee table-size Bible while I struggled with her suitcase-shaped purse. Was it full of dumbbells? By the time we'd tucked Mother Holly into the backseat beside me, I'd broken a light sweat despite the freezing winter air—a sheen, as Rochelle calls it.

"So nice of you two young folks to come after me this morning. Even so late and all…." She turned to look out the window as Adrian's Mercedes pulled out of her drive. I stared at the bars on her windows, feeling just as imprisoned as she probably did every day. "I guess we'll have just one more stop and then move on to the church—"

"Uh, Mother Holly, Adrian was nice enough to do me-us-this favor. Let's not trouble him. I can take you back to the grocery store after service."

Adrian's ears twitched. I stared at his face in the rearview. I'd insisted on sitting in the back. It made him feel like a chauffeur, but I didn't want to give the older woman any room for gossip. I was beginning to see that she might not need any room, for gossip or anything else.

This was getting too complicated. "We were going to lunch after service, Mother Holly."

Adrian cleared his throat. "But we could take you out later, after the evening service."

I rubbed my nose with the heel of my hand. Planning to make a day of it, was he?

The old woman shook her head. "No, baby. What we need is a 'right now' thing." She ran a wrinkled hand over my smooth calves. "We got to cover them hams real quick like. You get up there with them big brown legs out and every man in the house will be lusting instead of worshipping."

I tried to think of something to say. Anything.

Adrian chuckled quietly in the front seat. "We definitely can't have that, can we, Mother?"

"No, sir. Menfolk try hard, you understand, but some are easy to stumble."

Stumble? I stared down at my ankles, searching for the power to throw all mankind into the pit. Somehow, I just didn't see it. But I knew when to go along and when to fight. This was a time to go along.

Adrian laughed a little louder.

I jabbed the back of his seat.

"Go easy, baby. Don't be rough with the man yet. Save up something. Save up." She nodded slightly, the silk orchids on her hat vibrating like a tuning fork.

I bit the inside of my cheek. Save up something. Wasn't that what I'd told my nephew all those weeks back, the day that Adrian crashed back into my world? I shook my head, wondering if the shards of myself I'd gathered on the altar almost four years ago were enough to offer anybody. Even me.

With a shrug, I settled back into my seat. What a morning. First, my brother shows up and now the few inches on my body that weren't riddled with cottage cheese were going to be a stimulant for our aging, or should I say aged, congregation.

Adrian pulled into a convenience store. "Will this work?"

Mother Holly smiled. "It'll do fine. Hope it wasn't any trouble."

I rolled my eyes. Trouble? This old woman was the embodiment of trouble. She'd seemed so sweet inside the church…Mama was like that. No wonder they'd been friends.

"No trouble," Adrian said. "It's on the way."

A slap hit my thigh. "Give the man some money, hon."

My head began to throb. "I was just going to—get out and get them myself."

Already outside of the car, Adrian pressed himself against my door, sporting a smile sure to be my undoing. "Pantyhose, right? I got it." He bit his lip and stared inside the car. "Queen, off black?" He rubbed his chin. "I guess nude could go with that, too."

*Queen?* Did I have a sign on my forehead that read, "I am a *big* girl. I wear *queen*-size pantyhose. In case you hadn't guessed already?"

"Uh, no. Size B, coffee."

Adrian choked. Well, no, more like chortled. "O-kay. Coming right up."

I spent the next few minutes listening to Mother Holly's tips on getting a man. When I tried to assure her that Adrian and I were just friends—were we?—and that I was not looking in the market for a mate, her response…?

"Anybody who comes out for church with naked legs is looking for a man."

At that, I crossed my ankles and shut my mouth, trying to figure out how I was going to sing in a pair of off-color pantyhose a size too small. How did I get myself into these things?

With a poker face, Adrian emerged from the store and tossed me a bag, then backed out of the parking lot slowly, his arm behind the seat and his eyes more on me than the road.

I opened the bag only to find three pairs of pantyhose—coffee B, nude queen and off-black queen plus.

"I think that'll do it." I bristled. Sandy had trained him too well.

"One more thing, young man. Can you turn left here and pick up my grandbaby, around the corner from me, on MLK?"

I opened a channel to God with the quickness. But not quick enough.

Adrian wrenched the steering wheel in a sharp left. "Uh, sure."

"Stop here," she said pointing over Adrian's shoulder at an aging townhouse. She reached around his shoulder and mashed the horn. And I was the one being fast by forgetting my hose?

I froze, watching as the matriarch settled back into her seat, then dug in her purse for a mint. "Have one?" she asked in a sweet voice. I shook my head, steeling myself for further humiliation.

Adrian shrugged and I went back to staring, this time across the street at a house with snow-covered bushes trimmed into the shape of horses. Now that was just sad. Here I was working seventy hours a week to break even and somebody had time to make equestrian scenes in their front yard? Even in winter? Something was seriously—

"I thought you weren't coming, Nana."

A buxom teen with blond highlights somehow matted to her head jumped into the car. Literally. I thought I'd imagined the car bouncing, but the way Mother Holly gripped the back of Adrian's seat, I knew it was for real. "Hi," the girl said, turning to Adrian. "What took you so long?"

He stared at me, then answered our latest passenger, so familiar with people she'd never met. "Pantyhose. From Russell's."

Sporting a pink purse Bible and matching lipstick, the girl turned and shoved her pudgy hand in my direction.

"The Ebony Mama line? Those things are horrible. They don't have anything for all this." She ran her French manicured nails down the full-figured body that matched her face.

Adrian gunned the gas pedal while Mother Holly sat beside me smiling the maddeningly innocent smile she'd displayed all those times in church. She was definitely back in Grandma mode. Was this a bad dream? I shook myself, but that only left me dizzy.

Mother Holly struggled to get her skirt up, revealing a lump of nylon around her more than ample thigh. "Knee-highs are good enough. When them other hose tear up, just cut them off and tie a knot—"

"Uh-huh," her granddaughter said. "We get the picture." And what a horrible picture it was. No wonder she was against showing skin. Whew! I checked the time. Ten twenty. In ten minutes I'd be singing…in size B hose.

The chunky young chatterbox kept going as we rolled into the church parking lot. I wondered if Adrian's ear would catch on fire. "Did you get queen plus? You have to go one up. You know those things are made to fit a midget."

A curious smile broke out across Adrian's face. "She got size B."

The girl's head jerked around as she scrutinized me. "B? Oh, my. Whatever floats your boat."

Her hair poked me in the eye, but I decided against mentioning it. Mother Holly tapped the back of her granddaughter's seat. "Watch that wig now, sweetie. You like to have blinded her."

Shemika, Jamaica or whatever she'd just said her crazy name was, went on to explain that she wasn't wearing a wig, but a stocking cap with human hair glued to it that she'd designed herself. I could fit B hose if I walked real slow, but she was stuck with that hair hat for the entire service. It looked like a dead animal.

The church loomed on our right like a safe haven. At this point, I'd do just about anything to get out of this car. Adrian must have felt the same way, because he set a world record for parking in our church lot, where no spaces can ever be found. From the look on his face, Adrian might have just driven on top of someone's car if someone who'd stayed behind at the early service to chat hadn't pulled out and provided a spot.

The girl pried herself out of the passenger door. Mother Holly's purse had blocked my view when the girl got in the car, but now I saw it all. Some of her rolls had rolls.

I am so going back to Weight Watchers.

"Thanks for the ride. It was nice meeting y'all." She turned to me. "If you squeeze into those hose, make sure you soak when you get home, 'cause that's gonna hurt."

"Watch it now. My knees ain't that good, you know. I might fall right off this pew." Mother Holly fidgeted beside me as if I'd been the one grinding my knees into her for the past hour. I mustered a smile and received a note from the older woman's granddaughter.

Your boyfriend is cute. And you're not that fat. Do you think y'all will get married? He smells good and looks like he's got bling. No hair though. Can you work with that?

I sighed, thankful when Mother Holly snatched the paper and tucked it into her purse. Money or hair wasn't the issue. There were other things to consider....

Like being scared to death? Confused? Unsure?

All of the above. As Mother Holly pinched her granddaughter into submission, I took a deep breath, avoiding Rochelle's gaze in the choir stand. This morning was so jacked up I was going to have to call and tell Rochelle about it even though we weren't speaking.

The pastor's voice cut in again. "Sometimes things just don't make no sense. No how. Can I get an amen?"

"Amen." I couldn't restrain from joining in. Nothing was making sense. Not my business. Not my family.

Adrian winked in my direction. I fought off a chill tickling up my back. Nothing made sense but Jesus, and the man sitting next to me. How I'd missed his friendship.

My eyes wandered back to Rochelle, above us, and my empty seat beside her. We'd arrived too late for me to sing and I wasn't sad about it. I could have made a fuss and gone on up, but I'd leave that to grandstanders. There are certainly enough of them, I thought, staring at the hats blooming across the front row like a wayward garden.

I read the sermon text again, this time really considering it's meaning.

"You have shown Your people hard things; You have made us drink the wine of confusion."

That was in the Bible? I checked the verse again. Psalm 60:3. How had I missed that in all these years? Even when I was doing my thing, I'd read the Psalms, and this one was a zinger. Not only had I been sipping the drink described in this Scripture, but everyone in my life was, too.

The pastor's collarless suit bulged around his neck in defiance of his attempt to keep up with style. "When things get rough, saints, when you're swirling around, drunk with the wine of confusion, you got to cry out to the Lord for direction."

"Yes, sir," Mother Holly half shouted, nearly scaring me to death.

Confusion? What did the old woman know about it? I looked over at Shemika—or was it Jemicka?—who was filing her nails and brushing the dust on to the floor. Well, perhaps Mother Holly had problems, too.

Didn't we all? Rochelle lifted her hands in the choir stand behind the pulpit, looking first toward heaven and then toward me, with that we've-really-got-to-talk look I've always dreaded.

"We cry out, Lord. Tell us where we have we made wrong turns. Did we go into battle without guidance as David did in this passage? Or is something stumbling us? Stopping us up? Meet us where we're at, Jesus. Show us the way out of our mess."

I closed my eyes. Had I done that? Gone up without God's guidance? Sure I'd prayed about my business, given it a scriptural name, gone to a Christian accountant, talked to the pastor…but had I really put myself in God's hands? Asked Him what He wanted?

Adrian grabbed my hand and gripped it with the kind of force serious praying required. I squeezed back, just as hard.

*Lord, if I've taken a wrong turn, lead me back to where I went wrong so I can fix it or better yet, You fix it for me. I'm fresh out of solutions.*

The pastor was praying, too. Everybody was. In whispers and in shouts. The building was filled with prayers and praise. Then someone gasped from the choir stand. A hush fell over the congregation and I got that knot in my stomach I always felt when people stare at me. Someone shuffled into the aisle behind me. Two someones, from the sound of it. I dared not open my eyes, but knew I had to.

Jordan. He'd made it to church after all…and he'd brought a friend, a woman who looked like she'd been painted by number and greased into her dress, bright orange with matching heels.

*This is so trifling.*

Before I could say anything, Jericho fought his way out of his aisle, past the couple and out the back door. His charcoal suit whizzed past me like smoke.

After smoke came fire, that much I knew. I grabbed my purse and pushed through the aisle, while Rochelle sat frozen in the alto section.

Mother Holly, having already twisted herself into a pretzel to see the action, grabbed my wrist as I shoved past her. "No wonder you came out with naked legs. Y'all got trouble."

It'd taken considerable effort to tackle Jericho in the parking lot—well, more like grab his waist and let him drag me a few feet—but somehow I'd managed it, even with my circulation constricted by the waistband of my too small undergarments. Once I got him to stop running, things got complicated. I had no explanation for why his father decided to turn up at church with a scantily clad stranger or why his mother chose to ignore it. Well, I had some clues on that one, but still…

The scary thing was that it was probably my words that had encouraged Jordan to show up. How was I to know he had yet another surprise up his sleeve? Now here we all sat, minus Jordan, at our regular Sunday buffet restaurant, as though nothing—and yet everything—had happened.

Rochelle sat next to me in her usual seat, with one of the men from the singles party. I wondered how he'd come to be present, but any explanation she could provide would be more information than I could handle.

"They got some steak up there. Tender, too. Go get you some." Her guest misted a fine spray into the air as he spoke. If I'd considered a steak, the thought was gone.

"Maybe next time."

"Suit yourself." He took a little hop with his chair, leaving him to belly up to the table.

Had Rochelle hijacked this character after service in case Jordan showed up here, too? I shuddered at the thought.

Rochelle turned toward me, as if she'd read my mind. "Your brother isn't coming here. I talked to him." She paused. "It's you and I who need to talk, Dane." She gave me a harried look from behind her mascara-blurred eyes—a never-before-seen event, by the way.

The ring of mascara around her eyes held me captive. Why hadn't I bought that photo cell phone when I had the money? Tracey would never believe it. What was she saying again? Oh, yeah. That she and I needed to talk. Talk, shmalk. It seemed to me Jordan was the one who needed to do the talking. Although there was that business about the money…

"Leave Aunt Dane alone, Mom." Jericho reached over and grabbed my hand. I squeezed his mammoth fingers lightly enough for him to sense but not hard enough for Rochelle to notice. She was getting on my nerves, but her relationship with her son had been threatened enough lately. All I knew was that we hadn't given enough consideration to the effect this reunion might have on Jericho.

Or on me.

Adrian sat next to me eating quietly. He smiled every couple of bites, even gave me a keep-your-chin-up nod.

Stabbing my salad, I tried to do just that. My chin, sliding into my chest, had other plans. The last hour was a blur. It seemed that one minute I was comforting Jericho in the church parking lot and my next coherent thought came sandwiched between Adrian and Rochelle at Golden Corral. An aptly named restaurant, from the way Rochelle's guest attacked his plate. Maybe we should drop him off at a barn on the way home.

And I thought I was greedy.

"Ooh, the meat cutter is here. I'm getting some roast beef. Y'all want some?" Rochelle's guest asked half-heartedly, before leaping from his seat. He was gone before any of us had a chance to reply. Unreal.

"Seriously. We have to talk." With her friend absent, Rochelle spoke in her normal tone. Loud.

My head hurt. Which thing were we supposed to be talking about? My ridiculous brother and that skin-tight woman, her son's mental health, or the pants her date was wearing?

Before I could decide, Adrian wiped his mouth and stood, pausing to give me a weary smile. "Come on, Jericho, let's you and I get some dessert."

The boy looked wildly from me to his mother. "I'm not hungry."

"Sure you are." Adrian somehow swung around the table and "helped" my nephew out of his chair. He nodded to Rochelle. "You ladies have your little chat while we're gone. Dana and I are supposed to be discussing business today and in spite of everything, I mean to do it."

His tone was less than convincing and I knew he was just trying to lighten the mood. Still, I appreciated the gesture. Jericho skulked off beside him, looking like an overgrown boy in man's clothes. I sighed, remembering the sound of Jericho's teeth grinding as I hugged him on the church steps. "It was supposed to be about me. Not my daddy," he'd said.

Tell me about it.

Rochelle had ignored the whole thing, never leaving the choir stand. After service, I watched her and Jordan exchange a few clipped words, but for the past hour, she'd acted as if my brother's stunt hadn't happened. Until now. Now, she wanted to talk. Well, I didn't, and I kept silent to prove it.

Rochelle pushed celery and chicken around her low-carb plate—she never ate from the buffet, even though single entrées cost more. Until watching her pseudo love interest chase every server that came out of the kitchen, I hadn't understood Rochelle's buffet ban. Now I did. Sometimes, too much was just too much.

Like now.

For once, I didn't have an appetite, not even for the wings Mama used to shove in her purse like a crazy woman. Right now, even the tastiest wing couldn't compel me to chew. There's a first for everything.

"Dana." Rochelle's voice was quiet as her friend guided his food-laden plate to the table. She spoke just above a whisper. "Would you come to the bathroom with me?" She paused when I didn't respond. "Please?"

I nodded, but moved cautiously, scrolling my chair along the carpet as I pulled it back. Maybe I should have eaten something.

"Come on," Rochelle whispered into my shoulder, tugging my hand.

My eyes rested on the sundae bar. Adrian stood patiently in line, flashing that aggravating smile. Jericho stood behind him, holding a small bowl like it was glued to his hand. Rochelle was right. I had to deal with her now—there were too many other folks waiting in line to mess with me.

The bathroom was a typical buffet restaurant sort, reeking of Pine-Sol, a trick I now employed in Tracey's absence to fool myself and any visitors. It was nice to smell something, I guess. I'd certainly never sniffed today coming. Tracey pregnant? Jordan back. And whatever this was with Rochelle.

Best to get it over with. "Aren't you going to say anything?"

Rochelle checked her lipstick in the mirror. It was actually smudged. A piece of skin hung off her bottom lip. Amazing. "You start."

Me start? I didn't call me in here. "I don't know where to start, Rochelle. It's all a mess to me."

"You've got that much right. Let's begin with you getting up and chasing my son out of the church for one thing. That wasn't your place. I know you're his aunt, but this is a family matter—"

"Oh, I see. And just who is Jericho's family? Jordan, who has just met the boy? Or you, who've spent your whole life with him, but still don't know him?"

"Don't know my son? I know him better than he knows himself." She clutched at the lime-and-purple scarf around her neck. I wanted to choke her with it.

*Lord, help me.*

"You've held that child for ransom, hoping that Jordan would come back and want him. Want you. Now it's all blown up in your face and you're mad because I wanted to comfort Jericho? I didn't see you doing anything—"

"I was ministering—" She rolled her eyes.

A snort rattled in my throat. "Ministering, huh? Well so was I. Sometimes the most powerful ministry is to your own. Now are you done? 'Cause I've got some discussion items, too."

Rochelle frowned. "Wh-what?"

Obviously, this hadn't gone down the way she planned. Usually, I sat quietly while she put me in check, allowing her to bleed. Well, today I had a gusher of my own. "Let's see…Jordan sending you money? You lying to me about it?"

She hung her head. "I never told you where I got it. I wanted to, but your mother asked me not to…and when she died, I didn't know what to say. I am so sorry—"

"You should be. You and Mama both made Jordan into a monster. Now I find out he paid for my home? For your shop?"

"And yours, too."

My muscles tensed. I tucked a braid behind my ear. My pantyhose slid over my calves and settled into two black silky pools just above my shoes.

She shook her head, going back into mother mode. "So that's why you were walking like that?" She kneeled down and tugged at one of my pumps, pausing to express concern over the bad fit. "Step out."

I lifted one foot from my shoe while she pulled off my hose, and then the other, careful to be sure my feet never hit the less-than-clean floor. Goose bumps pimpled my legs, but I was glad to be free. That Shemika was right. I'd have to soak for sure.

Rochelle stared at the tag before tossing them into the trash. "Size B?" She paused, then nodded toward the door, and the man on the other side of it. "You can be so ridiculous."

My thoughts snapped to the human disposal back at our table. "I can be ridiculous? What about the Purple People Eater out there? Those pants should be banned from public wear."

She stifled a chuckle. "Don't, okay? I know he's a little different, but he's nice. Really. And right now I just need someone to be nice to me."

There it was, the bottom of the bucket, what this talk was really about. "I'm sorry Jordan pulled that stunt today. I know how you must feel."

"You can't know." Rochelle stared at the floor, drawing my eyes to black-and-white tiles.

My heart skipped a beat. Anger shrilled in Rochelle's voice, but jealousy echoed just underneath it, mixed with something else. Love? No wonder she'd stayed in the choir stand. My brother had humiliated her all over again. I swallowed. "I hate to ask this, but do you still have feelings for Jordan? Now, I mean?"

Her head snapped my way, but she didn't answer.

I didn't need her to. She loved him. While Mama had stirred a daily brew of resentment for us girls to drink, Rochelle had managed to hold on to her love? "How could you?"

It wasn't what I meant to say. I meant to speak of grace and forgiveness. To tell her I loved her, that I understood… But my inner madness reared its head. It was okay for me to love my brother, but Rochelle loving him seemed another slap in the face. Another betrayal.

"This is not about you, Dane. It's about us."

Us? Where was "us" when the diapers had to be changed and the bottles warmed? Where was us when I stayed up all night with Jericho and went to school all day? "It's about me, too." What "us" was she talking about anyway? The guy had shown up this morning with another woman and she didn't look like a friend.

"Just stay out of it, okay? The last of the money went to help-ing you with your shop. I invested some, used some for design school and to start the shoe shop."

"I'll bet. I can't even afford an ankle strap in that place. I love how that Italian leather smells though…."

"Oh, Dana. You know I'll make you a pair whenever. I just hate making them and then you never wear them. It's a waste."

"I don't wear them because you make them for you, not me." Sort of like my life. Save her favorite lime strappies, Rochelle's idea of a cute shoe was chunky-heeled mules. No toes showing. I paid good money for my pedicures and I meant to make my toesies earn out every dime.

We stood quietly, contemplating following this safer tangent of conversation or diving back into the unexplored depths of our relationship—both with each other and with my brother. Neither option looked promising.

"Be right back." I stumbled into one of the stalls behind us, trying to digest it all. Mama's place in the whole plot would require my singular attention later.

"Come out, will you? I know you're just standing in there."

"So," I whispered over the door, wishing for once that she and Tracey didn't know me so well. My lifelong fear of public bathrooms wasn't exactly a secret, but only those two knew to what extremes my phobia ran.

"I truly am sorry. I have nothing to say for myself," she said. Another stall clanged shut beside me, just the barrier between us, the walls around our hearts seemed to come down. "Forgive me?"

"Of course I do." I pulled back the stall door, wondering whether it was best to come out of this little truth booth. *Can't hide forever.* I stepped forward. "So that's it? Nothing else you aren't telling me?"

Rochelle turned and walked to the sink. I followed, choosing the basin beside her. "There's more." Her words were close, almost brushing my face.

*God, You're really pulling out the stops, huh?*

Tracey's presence would have been wonderful right now. The baby thing brushed against my mind, but I pushed it back into the box where I'd locked it. This was no time to trade secrets.

I turned to my sink and rolled her words over in my head. It hit me, like the roar of the ocean in a seashell. The truth had always been there, I just hadn't been listening. My fingers clutched Rochelle's shoulder. "It was you, wasn't it? You sent the money to Mexico. You…kept him alive. Why wouldn't you tell me?" I paused as this wave of new truth crested in me. "Why didn't you tell Mama?"

Two old ladies behind us leaned in closer, no longer concerned with their turn in the stall. A six-year-old joined us at the sink, pushing me aside to take advantage of the still-running water.

Rochelle stepped away from the counter. From me.

"I didn't tell you because I was ashamed." She touched the doorknob. With a paper towel of course. "I didn't tell your mother because she would have brought him home. While he was in that coma, I could dream…even hope."

I took two steps in her direction, then stopped. How could she? The question raced through my veins, my mind, demanding an answer, yet my heart remained silent knowing exactly how Rochelle had deceived my family…and herself.

She'd done it the same way I had two years ago when I hung up with Sandy. Though my mouth had said all the Christian things, my heart had spoken another language, asked another question—if she does die, what might that mean for me? Was Rochelle so wrong for asking the opposite, what would happen to her if Jordan lived?

*She who has sinned not, throw the first stone.*

My hands wilted to my sides. "What were you ashamed of? The money? Lying to me?"

Rochelle shook her head. "I was ashamed of still loving him. I shouldn't have then." She pulled back the knob. "I shouldn't now."

# Chapter Eight

It was only a matter of time. My mother had it and her mother before her, but after years of keeping watch for the facial hair that had marred my forebears, I figured I was safe until menopause.

I awoke that morning to two hairs curling out of my chin like something from an off-Broadway production of *Cats*. On another woman's chin—a woman who wasn't working too much and spending her leisure time with senior citizens—it might have been cute. Humorous even.

On this woman, it was not. In fact, when the screaming and plucking subsided, I called Tracey long distance.

"It's just a hair, Dana," she said in a groggy voice. Pregnancy didn't sound good on her. Rochelle had sounded like the tooth fairy all nine—in her case, ten—months. But that was Rochelle.

"Hairs-s-s-s. Plural. As in more than one. You don't understand. This is it—"

"What?"

"The hormone surge. I'm not ready for it. No wonder the UPS man looked so cute yesterday. What if I cave to the biology and do something stupid?"

"Like get married and get pregnant?"

I jumped on top of my bed as though rats covered the floor. "Yeah!" I screamed at the top of my lungs, only to realize what I'd just said and who I'd said it to—a married pregnant woman. I eased down on to the side of the bed. "I didn't mean it like that."

Tracey giggled. "You meant it just like that. That's what I love about you. I never have to guess what you're thinking." She sighed. "I just wish I could make one friend here half as honest. Or as funny."

Funny? I stroked my chin. There was nothing funny about this situation. Not one thing. "You've still got me. And Rochelle." I supposed the last part. Rochelle and I spoke at church, and made polite remarks behind each other's backs, but something between us was broken. And I didn't know how to fix it.

I heard a swishing sound through the phone. "You're on that pink stool, aren't you? Twirling the phone cord back and forth?"

Tracey choked up. "See, that's what I mean. No one here would know that. No one here knows me…."

Ryan knew her, didn't he? Better not go there. "They'll get to know you. Give them a chance. How's the baby?"

"Good."

"And the mommy?"

"Not so good."

A sigh from my end. Tracey had done an awesome job on the graphics and logo for my latest project—Figgy body pudding. Quick turnaround, no mistakes. Great for me, but it didn't bode well for her. Like me, work was Tracey's outlet when things were less than perfect in her personal life. The whole time she'd dated Ryan, she'd missed every deadline. "Want to talk about it?"

"Yes," she said in a purring tone. "But I won't."

Not with me anyway. She'd probably been giving Rochelle a daily earful. Manless me was only good for other secrets. Had Rochelle told Tracey about all the lies she'd told me? I didn't ask.

As if reading my mind, Tracey jumped to the one absent from our threesome. "You should call her, you know."

Rochelle's fingers weren't broken, either. "I know. I've tried a few times. I wave at church…."

"Uh-huh. I heard. She really needs you. She's hurting."

Aren't we all? "Does she still love him?"

A pause stilled the line. "No, not the man he is now. But she's still in love with the idea of him, a father who would come home looking for his son, looking for her…"

Prince Charming again. Somebody should shoot that guy. "And then he waltzes back into town not too interested in her or her son."

"Exactly."

After a gulp of air to still my nerves, I dove in for the real info. "Did she mention anything to you…?"

"Like what?"

Leave it alone. "Nothing."

"It's more than nothing. I know that."

Good. "Pray for us. I'll call her soon. I know you've got to get going. Any new clients?"

"Some site updates, a couple brochures and a new client interview today at three. Nothing much on that end. It's making it to the bathroom and keeping food down that keeps me busy." She laughed wistfully. "I'll e-mail you later."

Nodding as though she could see me, I stroked the throbbing splotches where my megahairs had been. "Okay then, see you." The phone was almost to the cradle when I snatched it back, knowing she never hung up first. "Tracey? Did you tell Rochelle? About the baby, I mean?"

More silence. Finally, Tracey responded. "Didn't you tell her? She was acting funny, so I just thought—I guess with all this Jordan stuff. Oh, well. I figured telling you got me off the hook."

Suddenly I forgot about my chin. "Since when?"

Tracey made that swishing noise again. "Since ever. You never could hold a secret. You're all surprises these days."

"I guess so." I whispered into the receiver and slammed it down into the base. Getting fired. Starting a business. Jordan. Rochelle's lies. This crazy whatsit with Adrian—relationship was too strong, friendship no longer fit. And now finding out that Tracey didn't trust me.

I stared up at the ceiling, grazing my swollen chin and wishing I could reach my heart to give it a few strokes, as well.

A prayer escaped me like a dying breath. *"I know You're shaking things, Lord, but leave me something. I'm losing them all."*

There were people outside despite the subzero temperature. I arrived at the shop ten minutes late because of the plucking and talking to Tracey, but they were there waiting, seven women, each with a Kick! bag and a smile.

"The candle guy sent us." A perky blonde, who had a bob so razor-sharp I almost ducked as she turned to point across the street, stood first in line.

"That was kind of him." I fumbled with my keys, thankful that I'd come by at 3:00 a.m. to do the new holiday displays. "Come on in."

Maybe I needed Adrian's help after all. I shook off the thought and flung the door wide. Maybe not.

From the collective gasps of the women, they must have liked what they saw.

I stumbled behind the counter, trying to muster a smile.

"Wow," one woman murmured. "He was right. This stuff is faboo. Never would have known it looking at her though…." The woman's voice dipped in tandem with my self-esteem as the other women nodded, adjusting the Kick! bags on their arms.

I looked down out my Wonderfully Made sweatshirt, jeans and loafers, trying not to imagine how my still blotchy chin was looking about now. To say I'd seen better days was putting it mildly.

A smile forced its way across my mouth. It was a better day. For the first time in the past week, I had new customers and Adrian had sent them. He hadn't called. He hadn't e-mailed. He'd done one better and brought me business. And based on my November sales numbers, I was lucky to get it.

I joined the group at the facial bar and gave a little demo, pur-eeing mangoes, grapes and yogurt for an eager volunteer.

"I add a touch of rose petals to soften," I said, whirring with my hand mixer. "And some irises to cleanse."

The ladies oohed and aahed at the results, but I watched pain-fully as, one by one, they trickled out the door without buying. Others sniffed and talked, smiled and waved, only to disappear minutes later.

When I thought I was alone again, I freshened ornaments and runners, praying as I went. Though it was great having my own business, the impending sense of doom was a bit overwhelming. Was I going to fail at this, too?

"I'd like a quart of everything on the bar—and add the rose petals, please."

I twirled around. "Are you sure?" So much for the confident saleswoman.

The customer, sporting a cutting-edge bob and the authentic version of the knockoff loafers I had on, nodded. "I'm positive. I'm doing a spa party for my bridesmaids tonight. This will be perfect."

Bridesmaids. Bless their hearts. I'd try to really make this nice. I grabbed ten containers and started dropping fruit, clay, oatmeal and yogurt into the appropriate slots and churning the blender like a madwoman. "I've been a bridesmaid more times than I'd like to admit. I'm sure they'll appreciate it."

She took the thinker's pose. "I think so, too. What else do you have?"

Those words began my biggest sale. While the mixer whirred, I talked the bride-to-be—her name was Austin I soon found out—through everything in the store. She walked her credit card right behind me, buying one of everything. My prayers of gratitude followed her, rejoicing at each product she added to the list. I hadn't sold any big-ticket items in months.

"Can you make me smell like Christmas? For my wedding, I mean?"

Okay, so maybe this wasn't going to be so easy. I cleared my throat. "I can try, but Christmas probably smells a little different to everyone."

She didn't bat an eye. "I'm going for a cookies-in-the-oven-mistletoe-overhead-with-a-dash-of-pine sort of thing. Can you do that?"

Unfortunately. "I think so."

She grinned. "Great," she whispered, looking both ways to see if anyone had entered the store. "I'm planning to wrap myself as a present on the honeymoon."

Too much information. "Interesting." I moved to the register, reminding myself why I was enduring this. "Would you like anything else before I total? A facial for yourself perhaps?" That last pitch smacked of a "would you like fries with that" suggestive sell, but I couldn't think of anything else.

"Nope. That'll do me."

I swallowed, going down the list: six lavender oatmeal soaps, three quarts plumeria lotion, two pounds of apple cobbler body butters, twelve honey butter lip balms, six cups of peppermint foot soak, twelve peachy clean bath bombs, four quarts of brown sugar scrub, a gallon of my 3-in-1 Vanilla Smella shampoo, shower gel and conditioner, a sample kit of everything in stock…and *ten* quarts of apple-iris facial. I got tired just ringing it up. "That'll be four hundred dollars and ninety-seven cents."

She handed over her card without a thought. I held it, wondering if this was a scam—credit card fraud or something. She looked the part, but this was a big purchase. "Can I see your identification, please?"

"Sure," she said, unleashing her wallet, armed with more plastic than a Rubbermaid factory. When I saw her KRSV-TV ID, I realized where I'd seen her friendly face.

"It's you! Austin Falls, from the news." She was the one who saved me from Tad's weather report.

She nodded. "Soon to be Austin Shapiro. And because of you, it'll be so much better."

I thanked her, gave her a receipt and walked her to the door.

"This is a wonderful place. I'm going to recommend it. Do you have a price list for your wedding packages?"

Wedding packages? "I…uh—"

"You know, like what I just bought. A head-to-toe trousseau sort of thing. All the boutiques have them, but they're nothing like this. Feet, hands, face, hair, skin or the whole bod. That's the kind of info I need."

I just stared. After all that work I'd tried to do coming up with a million different product lines, this stranger had boiled down my business into a few sentences.

She patted my hand and handed me her card. "Fax it to me at the station when you get the list together. You'll have to ditch the denim for some silk, but it'll be worth it. Oh, yeah, and only take appointments. Women pay more when they make appointments. Especially brides."

Brides? Appointments? Silk? I had a price list, but I hadn't been trying to focus on the bridal products. They just sort of sprouted up by themselves. But money was money and I needed it. A lot of it. Dad's rent was two months overdue. And though I didn't use Italian leather like Rochelle or anything, the fruit and vegetables alone bore a hefty price tag, especially in the winter. The rent on my space had gone up, probably due to Adrian's success. There was that Visa ball and chain, dangling around my neck accruing interest by the second.

A smile worked across my mouth at the thought of that particular debt. "Thank you."

"Don't mention it. I know something good when I see it." She adjusted the almost fist-size diamond on her finger before leaning over and whispering in my ear…I'm not sure why, we were still alone in the store. "Besides, I like finding things first. It's the huntress in me. I have a few friends working on Valentine's Day weddings. They're way behind in their planning, but I'll send them over."

Do tell… I nodded, emerging from behind the counter to hold the door open for her. "Well, thanks for everything. The encouragement, the word of mouth—"

She winked and pointed to the small fish sticker on my door. "Don't mention it. Us sistahs have to stick together. God has a big family. Don't forget it." And with that she was gone, leaving me with my mouth wide open and my mind in an uproar.

Sistahs? And she'd said it with such conviction, her slim fingers snapping and her blonde hair tilting like something out of a *Saturday Night Live* skit. I bent over with laughter. God knew just what I needed today. A good laugh. But now what?

I mean I was grateful for heaven's provision and all…but weddings? Tofu, spandex and Tracey's Barry Manilow albums all rubbed me wrong, but weddings really grated on my nerves.

As the door clanged shut with finality, I contemplated the aversion to matrimony. Did it revolt me because of Adrian? Because Rochelle had waited her whole life for a church ceremony and never gotten one? Or maybe because Tracey had jumped into a wedding without realizing who was she marrying?

Making a note to make more Peachy Kleen bath bombs, I realized that my wedding phobia went back to my own parent's wedding—or lack of one. Whether bitter because of her courthouse union or genuinely in earnest, my mother had spent her life decrying the frivolity of weddings, all the while secretly planning one for me. Instead, it was Adrian's ceremony with another woman she'd helped arrange, a horrible act that I thought then was just to spite me.

I think it was just closure. My mother had imagined a wedding with Adrian for so long that when it became apparent I wouldn't be the bride, she couldn't let go. And after all, it was her last chance, wasn't it? Jordan wasn't coming back, I was hopeless and Dahlia, well, she was giving up the milk a little too readily for anybody to want to buy the cow.

The thought of my sister made me shiver. I wondered what had become of her. Though my estranged Aunt Cheryl, on my father's side, and others heard from her now and then and said she was well, I couldn't help wondering as much as she'd hurt me. Maybe through these weddings, healing could begin. With me.

At the computer, I pulled up my regular brochure and cut and pasted it into a new document, changing the information to my new bridal line. What would I call it?

*Beloved.*

Yes. That was it. Nine of my luscious products in one custom package. It wouldn't be easy work, but nothing worth having was. Maybe I could even make a difference, praying over these ditzy women and their husbands before things went bad. Maybe when these couples smelled my stuff, they'd catch a whiff of the smell that had filled my imagination growing up when tempers grew hot and patience grew thin. A scent that said to my mind, "God is here…and He's got flowers."

I smiled and ripped off a poinsettia from the planter next to me. I tucked it behind my ear. Weren't those things poisonous? I couldn't remember and at the moment it didn't seem to matter. I might not ever be any man's bride, but I had Christ's love and that was more than enough.

It would have to be.


Three days later, after my first full night's sleep since I don't know when, the absurdity of my life struck me while stacking Mimosa body butter on my display. What was my life coming to? I spent my social time with the ladies of the Noon Day Prayer group, of which Mother Holly was president. Those old women were too much for me. I might have to go back to hanging out with the boring singles.

Rochelle wasn't talking to me and Adrian was trying to fix it without talking to any of us by sending stupid "Peace on Earth" e-mails and buying us off with gifts. I didn't mind that part.

I got an Iron Diva catalog from Harley-Davidson with a five-hundred-dollar line of credit and a note not to discuss my gift with the others. I didn't have the heart to tell him that I really needed the money more than the gear. It sure was fun picking out some stuff though. I definitely need to ride again. As soon as I could afford to I'd buy my bike back from the guy at Scents and Savings who bought it from me, and left it to rust in his garage. I tried to tell him his wife wouldn't go for it, but he thought he could talk to her. Men.

Then this morning, my father, whom I hadn't seen in weeks, showed up clean-shaven with creased pants and groceries in hand. Just stopped by to check on me, he'd explained while cooking eggs as though this were routine and normal. I managed not to scream—and to scarf down an omelet—but I'm not buying the everything-is-okay act. This is madness and I'm afraid more is to come.

Not that I haven't always thrived on a little insanity. I have. But I'm a low impact type of girl. Endurance is my game. This stuff was bouncing a little hard for my liking. When things start turning too fast, I unravel. The main reason I'd fired my personal trainer was his annoying habit of changing my treadmill program without warning. I think he enjoyed watching me fly off the back of that thing. Anything more than three miles an hour and I was a goner.

I stacked the last jar on my pyramid. As close to perfect as I'd ever dared go. Until lately, that was Rochelle's position. I rubbed one leg against the other, watching a muscled figure emerge from the shop across the street. Adrian. God had come pretty close to perfection there, too.

At least I had my calves. A girl couldn't have it all. The bell chimed and Adrian came into the shop with a picnic basket and notebook. He hunkered down at the register.

"Hungry?" His smile lit up the room.

I nodded and dimmed the open sign, though it wasn't really necessary. Besides my fresh influx of brides, which were now by appointment only, nobody was stopping by. I turned back to him and caught him staring.

He didn't turn away, unwrapping one of the sandwiches instead.

"Is it good?" I asked, eying one of the ham and cheese bagels with glee.

"Very." He held out one to me.

I took the warm bundle of silver foil and opened it curiously, staring at the melted cheese hanging over the edge. Excellent. One bite told a different story, however. Far from melted, the cheese in the middle seemed cold. Frozen even. They must have only zapped it in the microwave. Too hungry to care, I took another bite, trying to ignore the frosty middle. "It's ice-cold in the center."

Adrian nodded, his eyes penetrating mine. "Disappointing, isn't it?"

"Very," I said, picking up on his real meaning. My sandwich disappeared into my mouth, icy middle and all, lest either of us say something we couldn't take back.

# Chapter Nine

She had to be kidding.

At least I hoped so. But when I opened my eyes and swallowed the rock in my throat, Tangela Daniels, one of my brattiest brides yet, was still standing there with that stupid smile and all ten diamond-studded fingers holding my calloused ones. She had that look that all brides had when they popped the question to me. Only the others had been people I could tolerate for more than sixty seconds.

"Will you be in my wedding?"

I blinked in disbelief. Maybe I should close down my bath and body shop and become Dana Rose, professional wedding attendant. The money would be steadier for sure. "Don't you have somebody else? A cousin? Neighbor? Paper girl?"

Tangela laughed in that fingernails-on-steel way of hers, but I didn't crack a smile. I was too scared. And rightly so. Nothing good ever came of my bridesmaid experiences. And that was with people I liked.

She exhausted her high-pitched whining.

It's a good thing she's cute. That noise could kill someone.

"Oh, Dana, you are just so funny. The other girls will just eat you right up. There's no one else. Bristol had the nerve to get pregnant and get too big for her gown and everyone is too…well, you know…"

I didn't know, nor did I want to. For once, I was actually jealous of the pregnant woman who got to ditch this assignment. Formulating a bridal fragrance for Tangela had been hard enough, but being in her wedding? Well, I was tired just thinking about it. The woman had driven fifty miles on four different occasions to get just the right scent for her wedding night.

I usually put a little of my Vanilla Smella in all the brides' scents to hook the husbands into coming back for more. Not this time. I didn't want to see this woman—or her NBA-round-one-draft-pick fiancé—ever again. Now I was considering guiding them down the aisle. I closed my eyes.

"Come on, you've got to do it. There's another girl, but she's trying to get pregnant, too, and she just refuses to put it off until after the wedding. And I was her maid of honor. Can you imagine?"

My eyes opened, but I wished I'd kept them shut. The hydrangeas on the new wallpaper behind Tangela's foot-high French roll started to swim. Could I imagine that a woman and her husband didn't want to put off the conception of their first offspring for this nutty buddy's three-hour, hundred-thousand-dollar sideshow? I could imagine. Too bad making babies was the only way out of this madness.

I raked a hand over my not-so-flat stomach. Some days, I could pass for gestating, but everybody knew pregnant was one thing I'd never be. That would require a man, a bad habit I'd laid at the altar of Broken Bread three years, five months and six days ago. I refused to pick up that particular package from God's hands even if Adrian was looking so good lately that it was criminal.

"The nerve of her, putting her family before you," I said in a mock tone of insult.

The whole thing flew over Tangela's head. Big-time.

"You understand just how important all this is." She pursed her lips and reached out to touch my hair. "And fixing you up will be fun, too. Like a life-size black Barbie."

Okay, that's when I almost lost it. I had to turn and look at my purse and let my eyes burn through the leather to that negative balance in my checkbook. Though it was December, the month Adrian promised I'd be living off of for the rest of the year, I was going to have to play Barbie with this fool.

*Lord, I know I prayed for patience, but I think I prayed too hard. Cut me some slack here, will You?*

"Well, Tange, here at Wonderfully Made we aim to please. I'd be glad to help out at your wedding. A hostess perhaps. Give me a call later in the week. Let me just take that check for you—"

I almost had the money, but girlfriend pulled back. She shook her head. "Ah, ah, ah, Dana. I see your game. You're trying to get rid of me."

She really wasn't as dumb as she looked. "Well, I do have a big order of masks to make for the spa party tomorrow, choir practice is soon and another bride is coming by this after—"

"Shh." Tangela dropped her humongous bag on the counter and scrambled for a pen.

Having daydreamed through most of the pages in the Coach catalogue, I wondered how I'd missed this pink monster. How many cows full of strawberry milk had bit the dust for that one? It could level a small nation.

"If you do this, I'll add another zero to your fee for my favors. Today's check is just a start."

A zero? As in the ten-thousands place? I was no beauty queen, but when it came to math and money, I could run with the best of 'em. I felt like doing the robot to make sure I could move my new doll arms and doll legs. I did a mental inventory of what I'd order the minute Sweet Pea left the shop—ten buckets of cocoa butter, a few drums of olive oil, jojoba, a good bit of shea…Bulgarian lavender, some organic chamomile…

Even with the bridal accounts, the bills were mounting faster than I could open them. Two days ago, I'd been praying to stay in business after the New Year. Just as quick as I'd been knocked down, I was back in the game. And all for the small price of my usual yearly humiliation—joining the supporting cast in someone's fairy tale.

Tangela extended the check to me. I smiled and tried to count to ten and look professional. You know, not too eager and all that. I made it to about four before I snatched the note and scanned for all the pertinent information—social security number, phone, that sort of thing. My eyes skipped across the single line at the top. Sheldon Manson. No numbers. No address. No nothing. The groom's name said it all.

Cash money.

More than I'd ever make in a lifetime, which wouldn't amount to much if things had kept on at their current pace—in addition to the new rent, my essential oil supplier shut down and moved to Miami, tripling my shipping costs. I folded the check and slipped it into the register, grateful for this timely payment and the promised installment. All those zeros were honey to a sistah's heart—even if it did come with a price.

"Now we're even," Tangela said. "And if…uh, when you ever get married, I promise to not be pregnant, fat or otherwise indisposed. I understand just how stressful this all is."

I almost laughed then, staring at homegirl's bejeweled and designer exterior. Stressful? What did she know about it? Whatever problem Tangela's man didn't pick up, her daddy would. Though he'd taken to wearing clean shirts and cooking me breakfast, my father was no doubt on the casino boat, at the racetrack or on his way to the shop to borrow a few dollars to "tide him over."

Next, Renee would come for her weekly fill-up, and then my no-good cousins, who stopped by on weekends to see if I wasn't being "stingy"—meaning whether I'd let them plunder the soap bins and slather lotion from head to toe, filling their purses with goodies for their friends.

No, ole Tange didn't know a thing about stress. My Daddy in Heaven had my back, as Renee so deftly put it. I'd never join the ranks of my once-intelligent, college-educated former friends who'd morphed into breastfeeding, baby-talking soccer moms with sippy cups and minivans. Tangela would become one, too— in the off season, of course. She and Tracey could keep it. There'd be none of that for me.

What about Adrian?

I shrugged off the thought. Things between us were strange but bearable. His sporadic visits and communications kept things they way I wanted them, under control. Church, work, books, bills. Those were my world. And not necessarily in that order.

The cash drawer clicked shut. There wasn't any turning back now. Unless…I wasn't pregnant, but I still had my childbearing hips. They'd gotten me out of worse jams than this. "Are you sure the dress will fit?"

"Perfectly. She spread at the bottom first…if her belly had held on another two months, we could have made it."

"Right." Great. I was a perfect match for a pregnant woman. Next, I'd be a stunt double for a linebacker or something.

Tangela lunged forward to give me a hug. I stumbled from the stench of her perfume. Estée Lauder's Beautiful. Half a bottle at least. Not a bad choice, but with all that money, I'd expected Chanel, but considering her rate of use, cheaper was probably better. Woke my sniffer right up.

She dug in her purse of mass destruction and pulled out a pamphlet. *Tangie's Bridesmaid's Handbook.* It actually said handbook. Some people have way too much time on their hands.

"The dress will be delivered tomorrow."

"On Sunday?"

Her grin said it all. "FedEx."

Some intense brides-to-be had passed through my door in the past few months, but this one was not to be believed. "You already sent it?"

The hyena laugh again. "I knew you'd say yes. Why wouldn't you?"

I could think of one tall, brown reason and it stood across from me, reeking of SD 40 alcohol. That wet cement settled in my throat again—God's way of reminding me that sometimes it's best to just hush. I shrugged. Why not, indeed.

"The schedule of events is on page twelve. But in case you don't get around to reading it today, the bachelorette luncheon is next Saturday. Semicasual—"

Was this a wedding or an inauguration? "Don't you mean bachelorette party?" Not that it mattered. I'd be working.

"Oh, no. That's not until after the slumber party, the sisterhood tea and the spa cruise."

I stared. First at her, then at my purse and finally at the ceiling. A girl had to watch out what she prayed for to be sure. I didn't know what God was up to, but this sounded like a doozy. I tried to focus on all the lovely soap I'd be able to make. And bath bombs, lotion, maybe even launch the natural hair care line— especially the twist and lock butter and the roll-on scalp shampoo I'd been playing with.

"Sounds like a riot." The damp sand taste in my mouth traveled to my gut....

"You're so cute. It's all in the book. Read it over. I'll get back with you." She waved like a little brown puppy. "This is going to be so fun...and wait until you see your escort. If I hadn't met Sheldon first...well, you know."

I did know. Girls like Tangela went for the dollars, not the dude. I had to laugh though, considering how much of a jerk Sheldon had been the one time he'd come to the store with her. Girls had come out of every store on the block, flocking behind his Lincoln Navigator limo like it emitted the last oxygen on Earth. He'd stepped out of the car with a cell phone plastered to his cheek and pushed them all aside…including Jericho and my silly cousins, who were too old to be out there anyway. Besides his cornrows, that man was a total loss.

At least Miss Black America hadn't mentioned her gift registries. Purchasing one more crystal candleholder would send me and my credit card over the edge. What did people want those things for anyway? Staging their own murder mystery party? Whatever happened to a Crock-Pot? I held my handbook shut, not daring to look at the index page.

Tangela waved stiffly, like a beauty queen with arthritis. "See you next weekend, okay? And don't worry. You'll do fine. How many weddings did you say you'd been in?"

Mama always said chitchat comes back to haunt you. "Ten." I whispered it, wishing that even I couldn't hear.

"How many?" Tangela's forehead crinkled. Just as quickly, the supple cocoa skin eased back into its normal place.

"Ten!" In my best you've-made-me-mad loud voice, I prayed for forgiveness as the sound echoed off the bottles of peach cobbler conditioner stacked nearby.

Crinkled forehead again. I hoped she'd save that look for the other side of the altar. "Ten weddings and you're still single?" She floated toward the door, almost knocking the chocolate body mousse off its display. "Well, if three is a charm, I guess ten is a chance, huh? With Austin spreading the word about you, you're bound to land somebody. Ciao."

Yeah. I'd have to drop Austin a note on this one. Everyone else had only been half-batty. Trying to fix me up with one of her groomsmen. Puleeze. I released my clenched abdominals remembering the one man I'd met at a wedding—Adrian's wedding. The best man, Trevor Ice. He'd lived up to his name. Just plain cold. I pushed away her insult and focused on the big picture. I could stay in business.

Though I'd never get married or have a man to protect me, God had come through for me…again. This money could mean a trip to the Illinois gift show next year—the first step between breaking even and national distribution. In spite of her attitude—and mine—I grabbed Tangela and gave her a quick hug. "It might be fun playing bridesmaid one last time." I doubted it, but stranger things had happened.

Tangela added a squint to her expression. "Bridesmaid? Did I say that? I have enough of those." She bumped the door open with her hip. "You're going to be the maid of honor."

"Somebody has to tell her."

I looked at Rochelle and turned my head. True enough, choir rehearsal had been a painful sound, but I wasn't going to be the one to tell Sister Wells that her gifts might be better served at the hospitality counter than the soprano section. Or in her case, the soprano-alto-tenor section. The woman couldn't even hold a pitch through the chorus. "It's not going to be me. Mother Holly is still cutting her eyes at me after I took her solo. It's your turn."

I could tell from the look on Rochelle's face that she was close to total meltdown. Choir practice and taking turns driving Jericho around—his driver's license had been suspended one week after he got it—were about the only communications we had left, but she was here and I needed to talk about Tangela's wedding with somebody.

I leaned in closer to look at Rochelle's shoes, her feel-good strappies in lime leather with chunky heels. My eyes rested on the polka-dotted scarf at her slim neck in contrasting orange and turquoise, both brilliant against her dark velvet skin. Where did she get those wild, wonderful color combinations?

She started arranging the sheet music on the stands. Ours was a little choir, though when the Minister of Music put on his robe and took us to the heights of the scale, the sound would fill the house from front to back. Being so small though, one person singing out of key changed the melody.

In Sister Wells's case, she changed the whole song. The choir leader was out of town, but if he had to deal with this situation when he returned, he wouldn't be pleased, nor would he deal with it tactfully. God was still working on Simon in that area, and I didn't hold it against him. I had my own struggles to focus on.

"So are you done with that basketball guy's girlfriend? Angela?"

I knew she'd work her way around to it. "Tangela. And no, I'm not done. She asked me to be in the wedding—"

"That might be a good thing."

Huh? Just when I was about to go into my tirade about how ridiculous the whole thing was, my best bud—well, former at the moment, but we'd get back—says that this nightmare is a good thing? I bit the inside of my cheek. The only explanation for her behavior was something I didn't want to think about—a man. She'd been absent from Golden Corral the past few Sundays, but I hadn't seen her with Bad Pants, either.

My eyes widened as we walked silently from the church to our cars parked side by side in the gravel lot, which looked big without Sunday's cars spilling out of it. We stopped at her Lexus, facing my eight-year-old Cougar. Shoes were an easier sell than soap. Our vehicles reflected that.

"Since when is being a stand-in a good thing, Rochelle? And for Tangela, no less? You know…how people treat us singles. Always a fix-up—"

A sheepish grin crept across my friend's face. A grin I'd missed. "Speaking of single, I'm seeing somebody…"

My breath caught in my chest. My girl. My partner. The last single Christian woman in my world holding it down on the job and holding out in the bedroom. Even if we weren't speaking outside of e-mail, knowing Rochelle was going through the same things had helped me stand strong. What was next, Daddy getting a job? "Somebody? Not that guy from Golden Corral? Please, tell me it's not."

She didn't say a word.

I turned back toward the church. Had I somehow driven her to this by not participating in BASIC?

Let's not start the blame game.

"Why not Deacon Rivers instead?" At sixty-two, he hitched his pants up to his armpits, but he wasn't bad-looking and could sing a mean hymn. He was too old for her, but if she was going to settle, why not sell out all the way?

Rochelle walked around her car, opened the door and sat inside. She motioned for me to get in too. Car talk.

"Why now?" I asked again, slamming the car door. "What's changed? Just tell me that."

I am the same yesterday, today and forever.

Rochelle tapped her foot on the gas pedal. "I'm not sure myself. This stuff with Jordan, I guess. It's time for me to move on. I've known it a long time, but I didn't want to let you down."

Let *me* down? I'd always thought it would be the other way around. "Okay…why that guy then? Not to be funny, but I didn't take him for your type." Or anybody's type for that matter. Even Tad would have been better than this.

She shrugged. "Because he wanted me, I guess."

A pause whistled across the space between us. I blew it away, trying to catch my breath. Had it come to this? "You're scaring me."

She turned to face me, her shiny black curls reflecting in the rearview mirror. "He's a chauffeur."

I blinked. "A who?"

"You heard me."

"I thought I did." This was too much. All the times I'd let a fine blue-collar brothah get away because of Rochelle's needling about having something in common? And now she was going to run off with someone's driver?

"He owns the limo and rents it out, but he does the driving himself." Her voice dipped in pitch. "He does well. It's not serious yet, but if it doesn't work out, I might try one of those dating things."

I leaned all the way against the passenger door so I could get a look at my friend's face. A good look. "A dating thing? What exactly does that mean?"

She smoothed her scarf against her neck. "It means that a few like-minded people get together and have dinner, exchange business cards...that kind of thing."

My chin hit my chest. Had everyone lost their minds? "I can't believe you, Rochelle. You're not only dating, but planning for it not to work out?"

She sucked her teeth. "See why I didn't tell you? Because I knew you'd act just like this—foolish." She put the key in the ignition and started her car. "I know I blocked you from good men plenty of times and I thought I was right, that we didn't need anybody...now I'm not so sure. For the first time I think someone good has come into my life. I'd like to find out."

I cut my act. "Does Jericho like him?"

"His name is Shawn and Jericho likes him okay. It's different. We're taking it slow."

Poor kid. Both his parents had lost it. At least she had that much sense to do it slowly. I opened the passenger door to get out. Quickly.

"Be happy for me and be good in the wedding. We're not getting any younger," she whispered behind me.

Too stunned to respond, I shoved my purse up on my shoulder and focused on getting to my car. What this conversation, this day, meant was more than I was ready to consider. The only thing I knew for sure was that I was hurting.

Bad.

# Chapter Ten

Unfortunately, Tangela was a woman of her word. When she said the dress was coming tomorrow, she meant it. After church, I stopped by the store where the Federal Express box awaited me. After an exhausting morning of trying to sing over Sister Wells and trying to soothe our Music Minister's frustration at our off-tone melody, I had little energy left to deal with Tangela's dress. And let's not even talk about me and Rochelle. We'd been the dueling soloists this morning.

I'm ashamed of us both.

Rochelle thought I was jealous of her little man-fling. She couldn't have been more wrong. In a weird sort of way, I was happy for her. The thing that bothered me was the numbness, the deadness in my own heart. A year ago, I might have listened to her little speech and thought, "She's right. I'm not getting any younger. Maybe I'll give it one last shot."

Now, nothing of the sort came to mind. Whatever love had remained in me, was only for Jesus.

I held the red satin slip of a dress in my hands. What kind of woman chose red for a wedding? And strapless at that. I didn't have the nerve to try it on. Just holding it up to me was bad enough. The silhouette of that soft fabric against me, made me think of a part of myself I'd buried long ago in ratty T-shirts and baggy clothes.

My secret woman-self.

The part of me that had always caused me the most trouble in the past, the part of me that I'd surrendered to God and accepted His love in return for. Was He now trying to reopen that hidden chamber?

Today at church, a nice-looking man had sat on my pew and given me all the usual signals, but I didn't bother to return any of them. A quick once-over gave me all the info I needed about him—too good to be true—probably living with his mama, driving some other woman's car, "in between" jobs. Not to mention that he probably came to the Lord last week. I smiled at the guy, shot up a few prayers and pointed him to the singles' group after service. It was the least—and the most—I could do.

And now I had the rest of the day to myself, since Rochelle was too caught up with her new man for our usual after-church lunch and hang-out. I could go to Jordan's, but then I'd have to hear about his girlfriend and a whole lot of other stuff I'd rather not know. So I guess I'll just be still…as long as I can stand it anyway. Probably go down to the shop and get a little work done.

A knock boomed at the door. "Dana! You in there?"

I dropped the flaming dress back in its box and kicked it in the closet. I'd deal with that later.

Lips pursed, I set out toward Rochelle's voice, not bothering to put on my shoes. "Coming."

As I pulled the door open, she almost tumbled in, with Jericho and the new boyfriend following close behind. While she gathered her breath from running up the stairs, I surveyed Mr. Car-and-Driver. He looked the same, wearing his pants tighter than I was comfortable with, but he had a kind smile.

"Girl, I tried to call you. Why didn't you answer?"

I shrugged, shutting the door behind them.

"Don't know if you remember me, but I'm Shawn. Nice seeing you again." The new guy shoved his beefy hand in front of me. I shook it and peeked at Jericho, already across the room and seated at my computer.

"Same here." I extended my hand.

Rochelle gave us both a little shove. "Later for all that. Listen. Since you were too rude to hang out with us, I took Shawn over to the health food store so he could see some of your stuff." She paused for effect.

It worked. "And? What?"

"It wasn't there, that's what!"

"That's impossible. I just gave them a new display last month."

My nephew dropped onto my leather sectional. "The display is still there, but it's full of Adrian's candles. And that's not all…"

What else could there be? "Spill it." I wasn't in the mood for a tease.

"I figured I'd have to go way to the mall then and show him your stuff at Smelly Chick. Your stuff was gone there, too."

"Don't tell me. Candles again." My chin hit my chest.

"Yep. I checked all your accounts in town and I couldn't find a thing. Not one bar of soap. Not one bottle of lotion, shampoo, nothing. Even the Vanilla Smella display at High Life was gone."

I dropped to the couch, wondering how I could have missed the signs—the unreturned phone calls, the lack of interest in my new lines, no requests to restock the displays—it'd been so long since I'd been dumped by a guy, I'd forgotten the signals. A few new stores had sprouted up since I'd opened, but I'd managed to have a presence in all of them. Until now.

Now I remembered the signs of being jilted, and even though it wasn't Trevor or some other man this time, it hurt the same. And it was all Adrian's fault.

* * *

He was sleeping, but I didn't care. When Adrian came to the door wearing his pajamas, I stormed right in, with Rochelle and her boyfriend behind me.

"What are you trying to do, wreck me? First you steal my idea and now you take my wholesale accounts? I thought you were my friend." Or something.

He woke up real quick. Slammed the door. "Hold up. First off, how are you just going to bust in here talking to me like I'm a child? And stealing? I haven't stolen anything from you. The stores came to me. I tried to ask you who you had accounts with months ago to keep this from happening, but as always, you wouldn't respond."

"And stealing ideas?" He turned to Rochelle. "Is she talking about Kick!?"

Rochelle nodded.

Adrian paused and offered Shawn a seat. "Hey, man, sorry they put you in the middle of this."

"No problem. Anything to eat?"

Still playing it cool, Adrian nodded toward the kitchen. He wasn't fooling me. Any second now, his entire face would squish into a ball of anger. And then…fireworks. This time I didn't care.

"So you think that Kick! was your idea, Dane? The actual store itself?"

What did he think I was talking about? I crossed my arms. "If the candle fits."

He raked a palm over his sweaty dome. "It was my idea. Mine. Don't you remember?" His voice climbed in volume.

Shawn returned from the kitchen with a sandwich worthy of Dagwood, but quickly sensed the mounting tension. "Maybe we should go."

Adrian didn't even turn around. "Sit."

I squared my shoulders. I remembered all right.

He shook his head. "That last night on the stoop…after they took—" his voice faltered "—my mother to the institution. It was raining and your feet hurt because we'd walked up the hill to get ice cream for the apple pie."

I hadn't recalled the specifics until now. It made no difference though. I remembered the big stuff.

"I was rubbing your feet and you asked me if I thought anything could help her—Mama, I mean. All I could think of was the way she smiled when we lit candles. And how one time Daddy had lit them all over the house and she'd laughed and laughed. For a few minutes it was like before she got so bad." He turned away. "I wanted to make a place that captured that laughter forever. A place where she would know I was always burning a candle for her, waiting for her to come home."

I scratched my chin, trying to grab at a response. That wasn't how it went, was it? It couldn't be. I was so sure, but he seemed so sure, too. And my mind is bad sometimes. What if I was wrong? How would I talk myself out of this one? "That's not how I remember it, Adrian. I told you about my dream place."

He sighed and strode away from me, sinking into his sectional. "No, Dane. You told me you like to swim your toes in carpet and that too many smells at once gave you a headache. So I only burn one scent an hour and the shag is as long as they could make it. So there, that's what I stole from you—barefeet and a headache. Anything else you want to scream at me about?"

Why did you marry Sandy in the first place? Let's start with that? I cleared my throat. "Not that I can think of."

"Good. Now sit down and listen to me for a second."

"I'll stand."

"Whatever, Dane." He stretched up to the ceiling, working the anger out of his muscles.

Goodness.

I needed to get out of here. My confidence and my ability to keep from either slapping or kissing Adrian was waning. "I guess we should let you get back to your nap. We can talk about this later."

Adrian shook his head. "I'm up now. Maybe you'll think twice next time you go banging on people's doors like the police, accusing them of things."

He dropped to the couch, still simmering. "Did you get that business plan revised for the bridal line?"

I groaned. "I don't have time, okay?"

"See? You have time to berate me for doing my job, but don't have time to do yours. I see you over there all times of the day and night. Working yourself to death. Streamline it, Dane. You'll kill yourself."

He'd been talking to Rochelle, no doubt. "You do it like you do it and I do it like I do it, okay? All that organizational stuff just doesn't work for me."

"How do you know? You don't even try."

For a reason I'll never understand, I walked to the couch and plopped. I guess everything just caught up to me. Tears streamed down my face. "I'm tired of trying. I'm just plain tired."

Adrian leaned close. His arms circled me. His lips brushed my head. "I know. Me, too."

"And I feel like a fool. I really believed—"

"I know. I've always known there was a problem about it. I thought it was just because of Sandy…." His words drowned between my braids.

I looked up at him slowly as if seeing him for the first time in many days, his eyes brown and clear. Everything Adrian had said about his mother ringing in my head. Sometimes, like today, he looked like her. Beautiful.

My eyes fluttered shut, oiled by fresh tears. I had to admit, there was a lot of his daddy in him, too. Especially around the mouth…. I reached for his hand. He pulled away.

"I went to see my mother at the mental health center before she died."

Shawn coughed. I prayed. Adrian always used terms like "institution" or "hospital," but never had I heard him use the words *mental* and *health* in a sentence together.

"You know who she asked for?"

Uh-oh. I'd gone to Sunnyside once a week until the day she died. I read her the Bible and let her beat me at cards. She never asked about Adrian except to tell me to feed him more carrots. "That child's eyes are just bad," she would say, then shudder at the horror of it.

"You, Dane. She shouted it. 'Dana, tell him to leave. Dana…'"

I tried to swallow, but I couldn't get the knot down this time. Why were crazy folks always calling for me? I couldn't even help myself.

"It's because I went there sometimes. Prayed with her." He glared and turned his head. I clutched his shirt. "Listen to me. Please."

"No. I won't listen. You're always crying about what somebody took from you. What you don't have. You have everything. Always have had it. She always loved you."

No use arguing that. I'd often thought growing up that Adrian and I had been switched at birth. His mother, with that mole on her face and that big red afro… She looked like sunshine to me.

When I came over, we didn't talk. She'd grip her cigarette and grab a Jimi Hendrix eight-track and a sketch pad. Blues, greens and yellows on Monday, Wednesday and Friday and red, orange and purple on Tuesday and Thursday. She'd sneak me into the Bid Whist game on Sundays if my parents didn't catch it. Adrian was always somewhere reading, playing with his chemistry set or…something. I'd never considered that I'd stolen her from him.

"I'm sorry," I whispered.

He looked away. "Me, too."

I've always been the same pretty much. The same friends, same places. Right down to still living in the apartment I grew up in. Tracey, Rochelle, Adrian—we'd all lived here once, on the second floor. One by one, they moved away. Tracey's parents' divorce, Adrian's mother's nervous breakdown and his too-tired father's too-soon heart attack had plucked them away.

Only Rochelle had stayed, abandoned by her mother when she learned of her pregnancy. The woman had come to our apartment and asked my mother to look after Rochelle, saying that she was moving to Arizona with her new husband. I'd often wondered what Rochelle really thought of that whole thing, but what did it matter? She would have done anything to be with Jordan then, and anything to be rid of him now.

Maybe she regretted it. Not Jericho, but loving Jordan so hard. She would have died for him then. In truth, she had died for him. We all did. I'd just pretended to live so as not to hurt my mother's feelings. Wasn't losing one child enough? And he wasn't any ordinary child.

Neither was I, I realize now, but survival clouded my greatness in a haze of coping routines—prayer with Rochelle, cooking with Daddy, hanging with Adrian, talking to Tracey, staying out of Mama's way, babysitting Jericho and when I could, riding like the wind on my motorcycle. Our place was one big pile of crazy, a place that only my true friends understood.

And of all my friends, Adrian was the truest. Even once he was staying with his grandfather across town, he could pick up my vibe on the phone and jet right over on his moped or even take the dreaded Leverhill transit bus if that's what rescuing me required. He told me years later that he'd been saving himself, too. Our family, our fireworks of emotions, was a welcome change to the sterility of his uptown world.

Now standing here on the landing outside his apartment, I wondered who would save him this time? I'd had my chance and fumbled the ball. Tracey was the next natural choice, but from her e-mails, she could use a little salvation herself. Not that she and Ryan didn't love each other.

But was love alone enough? Even in the best of matches, you're still marrying a stranger. And sometimes they're stranger than you thought. I hadn't tied the knot myself, but I'd watched it choke plenty of folks, all the while wondering if it would have been like that between me and Adrian.

Today, I realized that no matter how close people are to one another, there's always a place—a secret place—that only God can see. A place that folks don't know exists until it's too late. Some people know about it, but they stuff it with all the wrong things and when they open it, like Pandora's box, it unleashes devastation on their relationships. I now know my box was stuffed with fear. And Adrian's? Chock full of memories of his mother's schizophrenic screams and his father's powerlessness. All the words he'd never said, tears he'd never cried. They were there waiting….

And Sandy? The years he'd spent mourning her were just the beginning. She'd always be a part of him and though it was hard for me to admit sometimes, she'd made Adrian a better man and me a better woman. The question was, where did I fit in now?

Not in Tangela's wedding dress to be sure. Spring was a few months away. The usual post-wedding rings around my waist and hips would be permanent after a few hours in that thing.

Maybe she won't go through with it.

With Tracey's wedding, I'd thought the same silly thing. But she had gone through with it, just like she kept going to the personal trainer after I quit, met her Weight Watchers goal while I was at home staring at "come back and see us" coupons. She'd even turned Ryan into marriage material with her quiet diligence.

"Are you going to sit out here or what? We're freezing in the car." Rochelle held the banister of Adrian's stairwell.

I shrugged, then started the journey down. Tracey was definitely the one to help Adrian.

It was a finisher he needed.

* * *

The bell over the door at Wonderfully Made shrilled the announcement of a visitor, but I didn't even raise my head. It'd been a long day of intermittent chimes, signaling a trail of sniffers and lookie-loos, but no buyers.

Not one.

The day Rochelle had come to report the loss of my local accounts had been the beginning of what I'd chosen to call "The New Year Slump", for lack of a better name. Christmas had been a blur of all-night basket sessions and last-minute super sales, but since then, my customers seemed to have disappeared. As bad as it'd been though, I'd never had a day like today. A no-sale day.

Well stop complaining and make a sale, girl.

I snapped erect, realizing I'd bought into the thought of striking out. "Welcome to Wonderfully Made," I said to a man's leather-clad back, trying to combat images of a guy from my past who wore similar gear. Trevor. It had suited him.

His broad shoulders turned in my direction. "Wonderfully Made," he said, letting the syllables slide off his tongue. "Very appropriate."

I tried to smile, but those haunting brown eyes and that painfully familiar voice wouldn't allow for smiles. I could barely breathe. The guy didn't just look like Trevor. It was him. What was with the old boyfriends turning up? It was like a nightmare episode of *This is Your Life*. A no-sale day suddenly seemed like a good thing. "What are you doing here?"

He grabbed my left hand and massaged my fingers, as had once been his habit, stopping at my ring finger. Bare. He smiled. I shuddered and pulled back. How dare he touch me, after what he had done?

"I'm looking for you. What else?" He ran a finger up the inside of my arm.

My stomach tightened. After all this man had taken me through, how dare my body, my emotions, betray me in his presence? He moved closer, stepping inside my fortress of womanhood, painfully chiseled by years of solid Christian living. Years that seemed to fade with each inch closer he came.

And I'd thought my biggest worries this year were fitting into that ridiculous dress or trying to keep the shop going.

This was something ten times worse. This was like a recovered alcoholic at a wine tasting. This was me, alone, with Trevor Ice, the worst habit I ever had.

*For this, I have Jesus.*

"So how's Dahlia?" My sister's name tasted bitter in my mouth.

He froze, an inch from my face. I stored the effect in my memory for future use. Man repellent couldn't have worked any better.

"Fine, I guess. You know how she is. It's always something." He shrugged, waiting for my agreement.

He wasn't going to get it. I crossed my arms, shielding myself from the horrible memory of the last time I'd seen him in her arms. The hurt that sent me screaming into Broken Bread Christian Fellowship, where I'd played church for years, singing solos on Sunday while living a torrid duet during the week. I had one prayer that day—that Jesus would forgive me for the mess I'd let Trevor talk me into and that He'd make me strong enough not to do it again.

Watching Trev's muscles ripple under his usual skin tight black T-shirt and knowing without looking he had on black Timberland boots and Levi's button fly jeans, I felt a deep, low ache in my gut. Not for Trev, but for what I'd once felt for him. Love. Would I ever have it again?

From the look on his face, he certainly thought so, but his brain lay far south of the usual location. As if reading my mind, he shrugged out of his leather jacket and tossed it on the counter. I held my breath, hoping he wouldn't sing to me. Hearing him on the radio was bad enough. How convenient that he'd finally made a hit after those years I'd supported him. He pulled up one sleeve, revealing a fist-size rose with four letters arched around it.

*Dana.*

"Remember this?" he asked, with a raised eyebrow.

I pinched my eyes shut at the sight of the tattoo. I remembered it, and a lot more. All things I was ashamed of now. My knuckles gripped the display case as I tried to wash away the recollections with my raggedy prayers. Though God had forgiven it all, I hadn't forgotten it. And that was a punishment in itself.

"Yeah, Trev. I remember it. Are you buying today? Because if not, I'm going to have to ask you to leave."

I stared at the door, praying for Dad to stop by for a loan, for Tangela to call about that stupid wedding, anything…

"So it's like that, Dane?" Minty breath warmed my neck, he leaned over so far.

I swallowed hard, my mind skipping over the scriptures so often on my tongue, trying to get one of them to speak up against this madness. My mind and mouth remained silent. Only the wall of muscle hovering over me spoke in the language I knew best, where sentences were formed with scents and smells. This aroma, a precise mix of patchouli and sandalwood, almost toppled me off my trainers.

Man in a bag. My next best seller after Vanilla Smella. Surely he hadn't kept his bottle after all this time? His lips brushed against my cheek, ripping me from my reverie.

I recoiled as if I'd been bit by a snake. In a manner of sorts, I had.

*You are all together lovely. And you're mine. Resist the devil and He will flee from you…*

It was nice to know that God was still there cheering for me, as suddenly that spiritual undergirding I'd been skittering for flooded my being.

I pulled my mind together, past my shame and hurt, past Trevor's fine body and intoxicating scent, and stepped toward the front door to escort him out. Before I could, the bell chimed. In walked a woman wearing skintight white leather, trimmed in fur. And if I knew her like I thought I did, not much underneath.

Dahlia. And she wasn't alone. A little girl with pigtails sticking up like donkey's ears held to my sister's hand. The child had eyes like saucers.

Trevor's eyes.

Tears threatened as I estimated her age. Just when I thought nobody could hurt me any worse, Dahlia had to prove me wrong.

"Nice store, Dane," she said, purring like a cat, with that usual fake diva tone.

My chest heaved as I tried to think, to see past that little girl's eyes.

My sister picked up a bottle of coconut verbena lotion, and took a long sniff. "Not bad." Her eyes focused on me instead of the bottle.

I turned away. I'd drowned in her gaze enough times to know there wasn't any water at the bottom of those sable pools. Those eyes were just glass windows…to a rock-hard heart. Those two were perfect for each other.

Trevor took the lotion. "It's great, isn't it? Look how she's got the bar going for the masks, and the bath bombs stacked up like that—"

"It's just grand," Dahlia said, tossing the lotion back on the pile. "But you always were grand, weren't you, *Aunt* Dana?" She smiled down at the little girl, who eyed the strawberries with longing.

I swallowed back years of pain, thankful when no bitterness washed up in my throat. What was done was done. I walked over and grabbed a few strawberries I'd cleaned this morning and handed them to the little girl. My niece. She gobbled it happily as I turned back to her mother, the sister I'd spent the last few years trying to forget.

"Thanks, Dahlia. But trying to be grand—" I righted the lotion in the display "—is your job."

* * *

"Why did you let her see you looking like this? Man, Dana, you just don't care, do you?"

It was my cousin Lynn talking. My no-job-having-always-borrowing-something-even-though-she-has-money cousin. I looked down at my soap-splashed shoes and my Wonderfully Made sweatshirt, pitted from a fragrance oil spill this morning. My smock had taken the brunt of it.

Not that any of the women in my family would understand, especially Dahlia, the fair flower who'd just left with the man she stole from me—though he was never really mine—three hundred dollars worth of product and their love child. The word *free* had never passed her lips. When it came to Dahlia, your money was always safe. Your man? Well… My premature birth allowed Dahlia to be conceived and she took that as a cue to help herself to the rest of my goods.

I watched as my three cousins and my aunt, all on my father's side, rummaged through my shelves. After Jordan skipped town all those years ago, this crew had made themselves scarce, but since my grand opening, they were becoming a weekly effect. I pinched my eyes shut, hoping Dahlia didn't plan to adopt that trend.

No. She and Trevor would never stay in Leverhill. I had that at least on my side.

I might not look perfect, like Lynn and Page in their cute seventies outfits, or sophisticated, like Aunt Cheryl in her sharp pantsuits, but at least I paid my own way. And I cleaned up good when I had the time. "Dahlia saw me like she saw me. I wasn't expecting her." Or him. "This is my uniform—"

"That tired outfit? Dana, please. You need to—"

"Let's not tell each other what we need to do, okay? We could all do to make some better choices." So my little sweatshirt with the store logo wasn't the hottest thing going. Good enough for me. Being good enough for them was out of the question.

"You could use a little makeover yourself," I said. She was look-ing a little thicker around the middle than usual. Even thicker than me. Maybe middle age had finally caught up to her.

My aunt decided to step in here. Telling Lynn the truth about anything is specifically off-limits, her being the special child and all. As I kid playing with these two, I'd been convinced I was abandoned by some other species, but a trip to the courthouse for my birth certificate told the torturous truth—I was related to these people.

"Dana, don't talk to your cousin that way. And don't be so de-fensive about your appearance. You're both beautiful girls."

I looked down at my hips and over at Lynn's widening form. Booty-full was more like it. Now with Dahlia back in town, look-ing like my twin minus forty pounds, I felt especially unhungry. Looking at Lynn quieted my growling stomach, too. Ole girl was looking straight plump. And a little ill maybe? Her eyes looked glassy, yellow. Best to leave it and pray for her later, I thought, mentally adding her to the list of my own problems. Like a store full of folks racking my brain without buying anything.

"Well, what do you lovely ladies need this morning? I have choir rehearsal and then I have to come back and open up at noon."

Page, my next oldest cousin, who'd sat at the facial bar silently through all the conversation, cleared her throat. "Can you hook me up with a mask? Strawberry-banana. And a Vanilla Smella pack for tonight. We're going out."

She checked her face in the mirror, smiled and turned to me with those pretty lips of hers, covered as usual in 3-D shine. Sometimes I wondered if that was gloss or Crisco. Rubber ce-ment, maybe? I'd tried to get her on my natural lip balm, but she always went back to an inch of that goo.

"I'll take a gift pack, too," Lynn said. "But I still want to know about Dahlia. Did she tell you—"

"Look. I've got to go." I grabbed up my keys and covered down the containers of fruit on the face bar and checked the level of the ice. It would keep fine until I returned to replenish it. "Here, Aunt Cheryl." I handed my aunt a gift pack of Vanilla Smella—lotion, shower gel and body mist. "Share if you want to. The two of you, if you're not buying, you're not getting. I told you last time, freebies are over."

Page tooted her lips out like when we were kids. Never could take no, that one. "Uh-huh. Look at her. Running off to church and won't even see to her family. Some Christian you are. Just like Rochelle. You're all alike."

At the mention of my friend, I spun around. The cousins had always blamed Rochelle for scaring Jordan off with all her talk of marriage. Why couldn't Rochelle just be a lifetime girl-friend like everyone else? Wasn't getting paid good enough for her? The problem was all of them were looking for their own cut of the pie. "Look. I've been giving you guys stuff for years. I can't do it anymore. I've got to make this place work. Do I ask you to do my nails for free, Page? Or give me a free hairdo?"

"I wish you would. I'd be glad to—"

"Just answer the question."

Lynn cut in. "That's not the point, Dana. You can't compare that with, well—" she looked around "—this."

There it was again. No respect. Everybody wanted to use my stuff, but nobody wanted to admit that it took any effort or thought to do it. "This is what I do. Not much to you, I'm sure, Miss Lawyer who works when she wants to, but I don't have any big cases to live off of, no rich husbands to pay my—"

"Girls!" Aunt Cheryl stood between us like a pygmy, extending her hands. "That's enough. Let's go. We'll stop by the mall and get some things. Nothing to argue about. Let Dana go on."

My shoulders slumped. "Stop by the mall? So y'all can pay Bath and Body Works, but you can't buy from me? That's cold. Page, when I came to your shop, I always paid, even when I didn't have it. Even tipped you."

Lynn held up her hands, the back of her arms swinging like turkey gobbles. "See how she is? Always an argument. It's not like we never do anything for you. We try, but you won't let us. You just want to be some miserable martyr, working all the time and going to the church the rest, trying to make somebody feel sorry for you." She put down her arms and turned for the door. "Well, I don't feel sorry. You're smarter than all of us. Prettier, too. That's why I didn't want that—that sister of yours to see you like this."

Usually I have the fast comeback, but Lynn stumped me this time. Sure I'd cut myself off since I got saved, but that was what you were supposed to do, wasn't it? Sanctification and all that stuff. I lowered my tone. "I don't want you to feel sorry for me. And don't worry about Dahlia. I'm not. I've got other troubles, like this wedding I'm in—"

Page dropped back onto the barstool. "What wedding? Ooh, is it the basketball player's girlfriend?"

I nodded. These people were so predictable. The "she might get a man" shuffle was coming next.

A shiny smile appeared on Lynn's face. "Hostess?"

Even my aunt looked with anticipation for my answer.

"Maid of honor," I said, trying not to think about how crazy it sounded. I'd met Tangela four times in my life and that had been four times too many. Being her maid of honor was like giving a eulogy for the butcher—awkward at best.

"Yes!" Aunt Cheryl pulled her little arm down like a fan at a football game. Only it was my life and to hear them tell it, I was losing. "See, girls, I told you prayer works. I may not be a Holy Roller like Dana here, but we're going to get this girl married—"

Would anything ever change? Ever? "I don't want a man, and it's just another wedding, something I've been in many times before. Don't get too excited. It's no big deal." I pulled the tops off the strawberry and banana and dumped a scoop of each along with a spoon of mask mix into the blender labeled "mask 2." I tossed a couple gift packs at Page and Lynn.

They were too excited to comment on the products, staring at me in that crazy what-are-we-going-to-do-with-her look. "What's the dress look like?"

I shrugged and hit blend. "Ridiculous. It's in here somewhere." I fumbled for the handbook behind the register. As if playing Barbie for one madwoman wasn't enough.

Lynn stared at the cover. "A handbook? And I thought I was crazy."

Aunt Cheryl snatched it from Lynn. "You are. Don't try it when you get married again, either." She flipped to the table of contents. "Dress basics, page twenty-three. This child needs help. Major help."

I poured Page's mask into a container and capped it with a bow. "We all need some help, don't we?"

No one responded. I guess that was a nice way of saying I should speak for myself.

"Shooo…" My aunt whistled and turned the book around for us to see. A strapless Mermaid gown—the long, tight kind. My eyes widened in horror, though I had the real thing in my closet. Those two words weren't in my vocabulary anymore. Strapless and tight.

"Oh, yeah. It's on." Lynn reached up for my shaggy bob of braids, picking her fingers through my tousled mop. "Page, you're on hair and nails. I'll do shoes and makeup. Wait, are the shoes in the book, too?"

Aunt Cheryl shook her head. "Uh-huh. Stilettos. And a list of preferred stylists."

We all looked at each other.

Over the top. Way over.

"Well, I'd love to sit here with you all and chat about this crazy wedding, but I'm late for choir rehearsal. Lock up when you leave." I handed Lynn the keys.

She handed them back and reached over and gave me a squeeze. "We're going now, cuz. I'll call you later. And if your daddy comes by…"

I rolled my eyes. "I know, I know, don't give him any money."

She smiled. "I was just going to say don't treat him like you treat us."

Ouch. What had I done to them so terrible? Torture them with free stuff? "Gotcha."

Page kissed my cheek. "Thanks for the goodies, Dane. And congrats on the nailing the wedding." She tugged the bell sleeves of her blouse. "I guess we worried about Dahlia and Trevor's wedding for nothing—"

I dropped my keys. "Wedding? Is that why they're here?"

Lynn punched Page's shoulder. "You have a big mouth, you know that?"

"His mother sent over an invitation. I thought you knew." Aunt Cheryl dug in her purse and pulled out a piece of parchment, pausing to interject a diplomatic smile. I scanned the cover and handed it back to her, breathing easier than minutes before. Though I knew anything I'd felt for Trev was dead, this still hurt.

"What did his mother say when you said you couldn't come?"

Aunt Cheryl squinted. My cousins looked away.

They were traitors, all of them. "You're not."

Lynn groaned. "She's our cousin, too. It's been a long time—"

Page cut in. "I'm just going for the food. Them Ice's can cook up a meal now. I'll probably just go to the reception."

Aunt Cheryl cleared her throat. "I'm just going so no one will get the wrong idea. I wouldn't want it to hurt your business. Rumors, you know." Ever the diplomat, my aunt. Who cared?

I forced back my tears. As if Trevor hadn't humiliated me enough. Now my whole family was going to his wedding. And hers. Would their pretty little daughter be the flower girl? Why did that hurt worse? I didn't want kids, did I?

Not until I saw my beautiful little niece. What was her name? Sierra. A cough choked in my throat. "At least I don't have to worry about Daddy going."

Lynn gave me that sickening "uh-oh" look.

"You've got to be kidding. Dad, too?"

Aunt Cheryl wrung her hands. "Well, even your father thought it'd be best if we showed a united front on this one, considering—"

"Considering what? That this guy made a fool out of both his daughters? Did you think I was going to go the wedding and do a cheesy '80s Vesta video?" I cringed at the thought of myself crooning sadly outside the church while the once love of my life ambled toward the altar with my little sister. They needn't have worried. Sure Trev had driven me to do some stupid things, but those days were over.

Lynn grabbed my arm. "It wasn't like that. We just thought—"

"You didn't think at all. Y'all never do." I pushed the door open and waited while they left the store, ignoring my aunt's pleading eyes. With my back to them, I turned the lock, determined not to let them see my tears.

"For this I have Jesus," I whispered to myself.

# Chapter Eleven

You can tell a lot about a person from their furniture. Mama said that. Who could argue with a thirty-year-old living room set? I'd reupholstered our living room set, but it was all still there, even the three-leaf table everyone used to crowd around on Sunday afternoons after church, when the real service started. When people cried into their coleslaw and huddled in clumps of prayer over ribs and potato salad. It was our living room where secrets were whispered, babies announced, trouble exposed.

The way our pastor led the morning service, Daddy had once served as our dinnertime priest. It was during these hours of the week that he had shined—cooking hush puppies crispy and sweet, fried fish and cheese grits, his tribute to the Georgia he'd left behind at age fifteen. Mama would sit beside him and peel potatoes, her bitterness draining away with each slice. Then somehow, as if by magic, a laugh would ring out of her mouth, followed by the low rumbling of Daddy's trash-talking voice.

"Don't make me have to stop cooking and come over there and get some sugar from you." When he talked like that it was better than hummingbird cake. Sweet. Airy. And Mama ate it right up, all the while playing hard-to-get.

"Don't you come over here. You're burning that food as it is...."

I would stop just short of the kitchen, soaking in their once-a-week love ritual of bartered kisses and flirty words. "Honey," he'd call her. "Baby," she'd answered. "Sweetheart." Daddy usually whispered that one. All those nicknames choked out by everyday life. For me, it tasted better than the food, their love talk. And considering the offered fare, that was saying a lot.

The doorbell would start singing then, each note filling our home with friends and family. Even my father's sister, Aunt Cheryl, and her horrid daughters would come, though they'd never speak to us on the street during the week. Stuck-up though they were, nobody with good sense could turn down Daddy's fish. And those ribs? I get dizzy just thinking about them.

Right before we'd line up with our plates, there would come a knock at the door. Adrian's mother. She said only strangers rang the bell. She always tumbled in like a bouquet of daisies, laughing and swaying with those spidery lashes spilling onto her cheeks. When we were small, Jordan swore they were fake. I dared him to prove it. He tried to pull them off and almost blinded the woman. Took him months to look her way again.

I always gawked at her when she came in, knowing I'd get a licking for it later. I couldn't help myself though. Her face called to me and so I went, looking over every inch of it, memorizing every pore, wondering how someone so perfect-looking could walk around like normal people and let barbeque sauce drip on her dress. Even after I realized she wasn't perfect, I couldn't stop looking at her. Her smile was like a slow song after a long day. It just hit the spot.

Adrian didn't mind me looking at his mother. He was used to people staring. She wasn't. She'd always turn to me and say, "Baby, is my slip showing?" Adrian was proud of her beauty because it meant so much to me.

I was proud, too. Of Daddy, who never stared at Adrian's mother like all the other men. It would have been easy and nobody would have thought bad of him for it—Mama stared at her, too—but he kept his eyes glued on Mama until the last dish was washed and the last chair emptied. Only when we took the middle leaf out of the table and shoved it back to its normal size, did his heart scamper away from us.

I sometimes wondered if Daddy didn't stick around because of those Sundays, if he didn't swallow each Sabbath evening like a pill, gulping every second, hoping that some morsel of that love would protect him from the war to be fought in the same kitchen over the next week. If Jordan hadn't left, the Sundays may have kept things going. Tided us all over with a little hope.

But Jordan did leave, and when he did, Mama took the middle leaf out of the table and covered it with a white plastic cloth and stuffed letters under it. Letters marked "Return to Sender." I'd tied them all up and set them in a box in case Jericho ever wanted them. Until today, the table had graced my foyer, cherry wood gleaming under a burgundy linen cloth and mats of forest green. I never found the middle leaf. That Daddy had known where it was all along had never occurred to me.

Until now.

The scent of hot fish caught me on the stairs. I'd stopped at first, my heart galloping, trying to make sure I wasn't hallucinating. The coconut oil Daddy used to cook it—his secret ingredient—floated into the hall and lingered around my head. I stepped cautiously to my door. Laughter and music greeted me from the other side.

He didn't. Surely not.

Before I could turn the knob, the door swung open. Jordan's girlfriend, whatever her name was, opened the door. "It's her!" she squealed, her makeup bunching up into a blur of beiges, greens and blues.

"Yes, it's me. At my own house. What a surprise," I mumbled.

Licking his fingers, Jordan appeared behind Miss Tammy Faye. "Surprise!" he shouted as I stumbled into the foyer. The spot where the leaf table used to be, waiting quietly, burdened with flowers, too afraid to remember what wonders it had once beheld, was now bare. The old table, bold and full of memories adorned the living room. All twelve original chairs circled the oval of cherry wood.

I swallowed hard and forced my feet toward the smell of hush puppies rolling in a vat of olive oil, taken from my soap supplies, no doubt. He'd probably borrowed the coconut oil, too. I ignored Trevor and Dahlia, intertwined on the couch. My couch.

It's her house, too. Let it go.

Sure she'd grown up here, but I'd redone the place, helped Mom buy it from the co-op. And here Daddy had gone and done this? Just as I was about to melt down, my niece bounded out of the bathroom with those antenna pigtails and Trevor's chocolate-drop eyes. She was beautiful, like Adrian's mother. I could hardly take my eyes off her.

The little girl matched my steps and took my hand. "Hey," is all she said, as if she'd been waiting for me.

"Hey yourself." I saddled her on my hip—though I hadn't planned on it—and considered how I'd fix her hair so that gravity could do its work. We shuffled past Rochelle and her driver friend. I tried to smile, but I'm sure it came out more like one of those Gary Payton smirks from the NBA finals. You know, the "How you doing? Well, I hope you're well because I'm about to kick your behind" look? That one.

Sierra clung to my neck. "You have a pretty house," she said. "It's happy."

Happy? My house? What kind of life was this child living? "Thank you. You have pretty hair. Will you let me do it for you?"

We'd reached the kitchen now and were leaning up against the door frame, watching as Adrian dropped the balls of cornmeal into the oil and my father fished them out. At the sight of them together, I took a sharp breath.

If my niece noticed my alarm, she didn't show it.

"Would you do my hair?" she whispered. "Mommy makes it scary. I want happy hair. Like this house."

A tear trailed my cheek and wet her braid, standing on end like a curly exclamation point. She felt my tears. I knew because she squeezed me tighter, but she didn't say a word. I cried harder, sorry that someone so young was so accustomed to being cried on. "I'll make your hair as happy as I can," I said in a creaking voice.

She nodded and the hush puppy team turned at the sound of my voice. Adrian smiled. Daddy turned away.

"So what's all this about?" I reached for a hush puppy and blew on it before handing it to Sierra. From another heaping plate of fried fish fillets, catfish from the looks of it, I pinched off a piece.

Daddy shoved the mustard down the counter. "This is about family. About the family we were and the family we can still be. It ain't nothing easy, but good food can make it go down a whole lot better."

"Yum-mo," Sierra said, her face bright as the sun. "Does it have twansfat? I can't eat that."

All three of us paused and stared at the little girl. Dahlia surely hadn't changed. "No transfats, baby. Here." I blew off another and turned back to Daddy. "But did you have to do it here? Bring them…here?"

Adrian straightened, rolling a grainy ball between his palms. Another smile. "Chill," he mouthed without making a sound.

He'd been away far too long. For me, this was chill, as chill as I could be on a day I'd come home and found the whole block partying in my living room. I stared at the layout—paper plates, cups, condiments, food. At least they hadn't used any of my stuff.

Watching my expression, Daddy let out a hearty laugh. "No, I didn't use nothing of yours besides the oil. Wasn't nothing to use. No wonder you so evil, living on old cereal."

More like the drive-thru. The cereal was just for Monday mornings when I started my "program" for the nth time only to quit by the end of the day. I decided not to explain.

"As for the 'them,' where else could I bring 'em? You ain't paid my rent." He tasted a hush puppy and licked his lips.

The heel of my free hand smacked my forehead. Dad's rent. Hadn't I paid that? I'd called…. "I'm so sorry, Dad."

Daddy shrugged. "Sorry? Don't be. I'm a grown man. It's about time I started acting like one again."

Wow. "Where are you staying?"

His eyes bore into me. "With my son."

Jordan? Talk about two who deserved each other. How long would that arrangement last? I clamped my mouth shut.

He frowned and motioned to Adrian. "Put another egg in that, son." He took another bite. "And a splash of milk." Nodding as if agreeing with himself, he turned back to me. "What was I saying?"

Sierra looked up from licking every finger. "Had to bring 'em here."

Daddy wiped his hands on his apron and kissed her chubby cheek. "That's right, baby. Thank you."

She smiled at me and whispered, "He's nice. My gwanpa." I nodded in agreement. No sense confusing her by explaining that he was my Daddy, too. When I'd finally figured out that my grandmother was my mother's mother, I had a headache for days. I was four, but they told the story forever. I hoped Daddy wouldn't make the connection and recite the tale now.

He opened the oven and checked something delicious-smelling but blocked my view so I couldn't see. I closed my eyes. I didn't need to see. I could smell. Carrots, raisins, butter, eggs… Hummingbird cake. My favorite.

"Stop peeking, girl. Anyway, the child is right. I had to bring them here. You had the table."

My eye started leaking again, remembering Mama standing here, laughing and teasing as they took the platters out to sit them on the table. "You knew where the middle leaf was? I couldn't find it anywhere."

Daddy scowled a little. Well, he tried anyway. "You never asked me. It was in the attic where Nella wrapped it. You know we kept it. Your mother made me keep it."

"For this?" My eyes stared over the bar in the kitchen at the people singing, talking, laughing... They shot up out of my floor like thirsty plants and this place was the oasis. Even I had forgotten how wonderful it was.

"No, honey, not for this." He nodded toward Adrian. "For your wedding."

I hung my head. For my wedding. Even in her pain, Mama had hoped for it. How had she felt when Adrian married someone else? Better yet, why hadn't she told Daddy to do something else with that stupid piece of the table? I smiled down at Sierra, snoring like a little haystack, her head against my shoulder. I would have thought that Dahlia might have come for her by now—I would have if it were my kid—but no doubt she was still plastered to the couch, looking beautiful. "Well, at least Dahlia can use it for her reception."

Patting Adrian on the back, Daddy moved to the sink and washed his hands. "Never know. You might use it first. These folks are just warming it up for you."

Adrian's eyed me with a glance of caution. He didn't need to say it this time. I got the message. Chill.

I tried. "I guess it's okay. But just for today. Don't ever do this again."

A squiggly line eased across Daddy's forehead. His white hairline lowered an inch. "Never?"

I glared at him. "Never."

He clanged the bottom of my Wolfgang Puck pasta pot with a wooden spoon. "Your attention, please!"

The clamor subsided and everyone turned toward the kitchen. "Dana has been so gracious as to extend her house to us for the rest of the year. So be here next Sunday and every Sunday after that."

He kissed my cheek and gave me a stern look as everyone cheered. "Don't ever tell me never, girl. That's where your Mama went wrong."

I stood there with my mouth open, wondering if Mama hadn't gone wrong a few other times, like on the day she said, "I do." I didn't mean that of course, but I thought it. I turned and walked to my bedroom, to lay Sierra down between the mountains of coats and jackets. When I tried to get up, she clutched my neck. "Sleep wif me?" she asked in a desperate voice.

An explanation of why I couldn't rose to my mouth, but suddenly none of it made sense. The slow sleepiness of the old Sundays settled over me and I sank down next her, throwing Aunt Cheryl's mink over both of us. Something told me we could both use a few hugs and a bit of shut-eye. "I'll sleep with you, Sierra."

"Fank you…" she said, drifting off to sleep. My heart echoed her words, sending off one last prayer before sliding off to the land of dreams.

Red satin stilettos. My eyes bulged as Tangela held them up in one hand, all the while referring to the proper page in her handbook with the other. I knuckled the sleep from my eyes. Though I'd been awake since 4:00 a.m., this little "chat" was putting me to sleep.

"Boring, isn't it?"

I turned toward the voice, to find a pudgy brown face, with maroon smudged over each eye and an immaculate layer of blue fingernail polish on every finger. I looked down. And toe. Shemika, was it? She looked a little different, cuter actually, but it was definitely Mother Holly's granddaughter. How had she managed to become part of Tangela's wedding party?

Tangela's voice broke in again, just as the shrimp cocktail was served. "Now be sure you have the right bra for your dress." She stared at me, before rolling her eyes at Shemika. "And a girdle if you need one. I don't want anything hanging out. That's nasty."

All the similarly coiffed Tangela look-alikes nodded in agreement. They all wore different shades of the same outfit—a wool skirt, silk shell and cardigan, all with the same pumps that I'd seen when flipping through *Vogue.* If not for the different shades of skin, I'd have thought that Tangela cloned herself into an army of bridesmaids. Little Bit (well Big Bit) and I were the last bastions of normalcy.

That's a frightening thought.

"What are you doing here anyway?" I whispered to the teen, watching in amazement as she slurped down one shrimp after another.

"She didn't want me, that's for sure. But grandma wasn't having it. She tries to act all high and mighty, but you can't dog your peeps, you know?"

Peeps? Tangela was related to Mother Holly? I felt faint. After taking me through all this drama like she was a blue blood of black nobility, Tangela was just a wanna-be from down the way.

Figures.

"The question is," the girl whispered, licking cocktail sauce off her fingertips, "did you get your man?" She shook her head.

I gulped down my glass of water to keep from choking. This girl was a t-r-i-p. Reminded me of Jericho. I smiled while she continued.

"My boyfriend? He ain't nothing but a dog. I've got one for him though." She lifted up her shirt a little—higher than I wanted. "I'm four weeks gone."

My arm shot forward as I resisted the urge to slap her. *Lord help me. I'm turning into Mama.* All the nights trying to study and babysit Jericho while Rochelle was at work buzzed through my mind. What was this girl thinking? What were any of us think-ing? I sighed, thinking of Sierra. She wasn't much better off.

"Are you insane? Did you plan that? Your grandmother will—" All my cool auntie talk left me like air hissing out of a balloon.

*Lord, make a way for this baby, and the one she's carrying. Help me not to judge her because in all my sin and foolishness I could've been caught out there the same way.*

The girl smiled, creasing the shiny plum dots of lipstick on her cheeks. I squinted at the identical smears above her eyes.

"Don't be jealous, okay? I know you're old and don't have a man or no children. I didn't expect you to understand." She leaned a little closer. "But could you hook me up a little sumpin-sumpin for my wedding? I saw that white girl on the news talk-ing about your shop."

I sat stunned, listening to Tangela drone on about elbow ex-foliation and kneecap lubrication or some other nonsense, while Shemika talked joyfully about throwing her life away to win some silly boy's love. A boy who might not even acknowledge her, much less marry her. The wind drained out of me in slurping gasps, remembering how hard it had been for Rochelle.

*Don't give up. Step up.*

My mind switched gears. Could I somehow make a difference in this situation? Had God planned for me to be here? I sure wasn't batting a thousand with any of the other relationships in my life. Tangela stood at the front showing bridal accessories like an airline stewardess—in the event of an emergency, this will turn into a flotation device and buoy you right out of the church….

Though my ears heard Tangela's craziness, my eyes rested on the little girl—that's what she was to me—sitting beside me painted like a castoff doll head. Her natural twists hung below her shoulders. Earrings marched up her lobes like golden moun-tain climbers. Her lips, lined in red and filled with the same lip-stick smeared on her eyes and cheeks, twisted into a frown. Her eyes looked past me.

What was she thinking so hard about? Being pregnant didn't seem to faze her. I decided for a change of direction. "You know a lot about makeup, huh?" I was careful not to say whether she knew anything about applying it.

The girl squirmed in her chair, then took a sip of the pop in front of her, topped with a cherry. "It's not so hard. You have to know how to pick the colors." She nodded, staring at my plain face. "You'd look good in some of the neutrals. Warm colors would look nice, too. Come to think of it—"

"Uh-huh." My lips twisted to the side then. Why did it always have to come back to me? "I was just thinking that maybe you could spend the night with me this Saturday and we could go to church together in the morning. What do you say?"

Shemika stuck out her tongue and made a gagging motion. "Church, church, church. You bad as Grandma. It's so boring. And so fake. All those girls up there singing in the choir like they all holy." She folded her arms. "I see half of 'em in the club the night before. Some of them don't even change they clothes."

I made a sour face, knowing it was the truth. How many times in years past had I done it myself?

"And those guys? Please. All dogs. Maybe when I'm old and lonely like you and candle man I'll go to church, but I get more out of just praying to God myself. We got a thing, me and Him."

Tangela cleared her throat and looked in our direction. I ignored her.

"A thing, huh? An understanding do you mean?"

She pounded the table. "Yeah, girl! An understanding. And now you understand, too."

Sadness clouded around me as I heard the words I'd said so often in my younger years. My distorted belief system. I had one, of course. No atheism or anything like that for me. Jesus died, was buried and rose on the third day. John 3:16 and all that. And I'd get to the rest of it later, say when I was approaching thirty or so? Until then, I did my thing and God understood. People in the church were phony. It would turn out fine.

It hadn't. And it wouldn't for Shemika, either. How could I reach this girl without turning her off? Did I dare speak the truth to this stranger when I couldn't have this conversation with some of my own family?

*God, who reconciled us to Himself through Christ, and gave us the ministry of reconciliation....*

There it was, Tracey's devotional verse. It wasn't the pastor's job to help this girl, or even the church's job. God had sent her to me, a minister of reconciliation.

I turned my chair her way. "If you knew a couple who were perfect for each other and truly in love but someone came along and lied to one of them and convinced her to leave the other, would you try to get them back together?"

She waved her hand like waxing a car. "Oh, yeah. I had some friends like that. Josefina and Ricky. I could not let them stay apart—"

My hand covered Shemika's. "So you understand how I feel right now. God has loved you from the foundation of the world. He loved you when you were born, when you did right and you did wrong. He's watched you give up your treasure to this boy because you thought you had to do that to be loved...."

She squeezed my hand.

"I thought that, too. I gave myself away, hoping that would be enough to keep a man by my side. It never was. I was trying to fill myself with human, failing love when what I needed was the love of God."

Shemika nodded. "I just wanted him to love me, you know? I thought that if I gave him a baby—" She choked back a sob. "It works for some of the other girls."

I shook my head. "No it doesn't, sweetheart." My sister's sad eyes at Sunday's dinner flashed through my mind. "It never works to try and win a man's love. But God can fix it. Jesus can put the pieces back together. He did that for me. He'll do it for you, too. Spend the night with me this Saturday. We'll get pretty for church and go to your boyfriend's house after and talk to his—"

"No." The word hissed from between Shemika's teeth. "His mother will lose it. And I'm afraid he'll—"

"He won't. We'll pray and God will go before us. It'll be all right." In an Adrian-inspired moment, I kissed the top of her head.

As she returned my embrace, a round of soft applause filled the room, the kind produced by a lifetime of Junior League luncheons. I turned to see even Tangela wiping her eyes. Just as quickly the spark returned to her. "Well it's obvious that Dana isn't going to be quiet, so we're dismissed." She waved her hand toward my table. "Next time, keep all that at home."

I smiled through my tears as Shemika wrote down her phone number. We stood.

"Do you need a ride now?" I asked, hoping she didn't. I'd dived in over my head again and would need a day or two to recover.

"No, my boyfriend is picking me up," she said, wiping the black trails of mascara from her face. "He just got his license back."

My body tightened. "Oh, yeah. Him." I picked up the pen where her phone number was written. "What's his name again?"

She looked both ways. "Come on, Miss Dana, don't you know?" She forced herself between the tables, moving for the door. "It's your nephew. Jericho."

# Chapter Twelve

Saturday came before I was ready. In my mind, I was still back at the South Sails Country Club with Jericho's name echoing in my head. I hadn't gotten any sleep that night, between wanting to throttle my nephew, being sad for him and wondering how on Earth to tell Rochelle without her killing us all.

Add in Daddy popping over and eavesdropping—or playing close attention as he calls it—and the whole thing was a nightmare. For the first time ever, I was thankful Mama was dead. It's a horrible thing to say, but had she been alive, I might have been the stroke victim. Daddy wasn't happy about the pregnancy, but he took it in man-fashion, offering to cook for their wedding and let them take his bed at Jordan's after the ceremony. I squashed that until Rochelle found out, in hopes of keeping them from a bed at Saint Elizabeth Hospital.

So by the time Shemika showed up on my doorstep, clean-faced and somewhat sensible-acting, all my wonderful plans for girl-talks and makeovers had gone out the window. I had orders for two impromptu bridesmaid spa parties to get out by Monday and Daddy had taken over my kitchen with Sunday dinner preparations.

What a surprise when Shemika turned out to be a hard worker under all that Ebonics and lipstick? Without anyone saying a word, Shemika set to work, chopping and boiling the twenty pounds of potatoes for the potato salad, making a pot of the best baked beans I have ever tasted—I'd never admit it to Daddy—and helping me wrap and label 500 heart-shaped soaps and create the scented centerpieces for an upcoming Valentine's Day wedding.

Jericho managed to come over and help, too, looking happier than he should have been. When he'd arrived to pick up Shemika and I gave him the news, instead of being crushed as I expected, he seemed intrigued at the prospect of being a father. He smiled at me now, then scooped some of the potato salad into a bowl.

"Don't let Grandpa catch you. If you eat now, you might not eat tomorrow."

He didn't seem concerned about that, either. "Does the baby mean I don't get to play basketball? At college, I mean?"

"Probably not," I'd said, trying to let him down easy. He went to the refrigerator for an orange, peeled it and put it on a plate for Shemika. When he started grilling her on her milk intake, I got a little upset, but managed to keep from kicking him out until an hour or so later, when Rochelle called. I wasn't sorry to see him go. This whole situation would take some getting used to.

Dahlia showed up next, reminding me I'd promised to babysit while she went with Trevor to the recording studio. I'd managed to block the whole thing out of my mind, but as soon as she mentioned it I remembered. I'd agreed only because the all-night daycare she'd mentioned taking Sierra to was always in the news for child abuse. A regular avenger of the downtrodden I was these days. The question was, who would take of me?

*I will.*

*I am.*

And He was. Through all my bumbling the past few months, God continued to sustain me, to hold me up with His right hand. As I collapsed onto the couch with tears daring to flow, a knock came at the door. A knock, not the doorbell. Adrian. Daddy had managed to call him between the peach cobbler and the chocolate cake and I was glad to see him.

Without blinking an eye, he listened to all the problems as they tumbled out of my lips. He hugged me, put Sierra to sleep, and herded Shemika and Daddy out of the kitchen.

"I'm taking everyone to dinner and a movie," he said softly before tossing a fifty-dollar bill on the coffee table. As everyone happily filed out of the house, he kissed my hairline. "Take a nap. If you're too scared to mess with your Dad's food, order something. The Mexican Mama is doing takeout now. I can order for you on the cell if you want."

Why wasn't I married to this guy again? Issues. Issues. The undoing of us all. "You've done enough. I'll figure out something. Thanks so much."

I ate my delicious chimichanga, sanitized the kitchen for Daddy's next round in the kitchen—or mine—and watched a funny movie on cable before drifting off on the couch while considering whether or not to risk Daddy's wrath by sampling a little of his peach cobbler. When a knock sounded again, I stumbled still half-asleep, but crazy enough to decide on kissing my benefactor. The cheek would be best considering my salsa-dinner-and-a-nap breath.

Still groggy but eager to show my gratitude, I drew back the door, taking his cheeks in my hands and puckering before diving in, unfortunately before opening my eyes properly.

Only when lips met mine instead of stubble, did I realize that these cheeks were smooth and a few inches lower than they should have been.

"Well, hello to you, too." Trevor, in a shirt I'd bought him six Valentine's ago and a pair of jeans fitted in all the right places, stood just beyond my face, licking his lips.

I shut my eyes as if this would all go away. "I am so sorry. I thought you were— That wasn't supposed to happen."

Trevor stepped inside and kicked the door shut with one of his boots. "I'm glad it did. I've missed you, Dana. I mean really missed you."

*Run!*

Doing a football shimmy I once saw on a horrible exercise video, I got away the best I could, though Trevor closed the distance with two strides.

"What are you doing here anyway?" I said in a pitiful voice. My chest heaved from the short run. I *really* needed to get back to the gym.

"We wrapped up early. Came to pick up the baby."

I swallowed hard, trying to ignore his lingering scent. I stared at Sierra snoozing on the couch behind me. Good thing I didn't send her with Adrian or I'd have had to face Trevor alone. "Okay. Let me gather the baby's things. I had, uh, planned to take her to church in the morning."

As I dived into the hall closet for the baby bag, I decided to toss it to him on the way to the door.

Don't look at him, whatever you do.

When I got back to the living room, Trevor was half out of his shirt. Obviously, he had plans, too. Flipping him the child's bag in a pass worthy of the Super Bowl, I made for the door, jerked it open...and ran into Adrian's chest.

He wasn't smiling.

Trevor shrugged on his shirt and called to Sierra, now awake and blinking on the sofa. "Come on sweetie. Let's go home." He winked at Adrian. "Our work here is done."

What I wouldn't do for a quiet little Sunday.

Today was anything but. Instead of sunshine, angry clouds raged on outside my windows, clumps of cotton against the blue-gray sky. As freezing rain burst from the clouds, tears eased down my cheeks. I tiptoed past the couch where Adrian and Daddy slept. Shemika and Jericho were propped uncomfortably on two recliners. Holding hands. It'd been a long night for sure.

I paused and looked down on Adrian's smooth head. My hand rested on his, pinching the bridge of his nose even in his sleep. Remembering the confusion with Trevor, I pulled away, grateful he wasn't awake.

Or so I thought. He pulled my hand to his chest. I didn't resist. A tear splashed on his forehead.

"I believe you," he said, rising from the couch, and heading for the door. He pulled me along for the ride.

"I know how it must have looked." I didn't really. I know how it looked to me when Trevor had unbuttoned that shirt. I didn't dare think how it might have looked to another man. Especially not Adrian, who had so many times removed himself from my presence so as not to get either one of us into more than we could handle. I'd spent most of the night crying in my room after the look he'd given me. Even Shemika seemed disappointed. But somehow during the night, some way, Adrian had changed his mind.

I smiled as we reached the door, thinking of Sandy, his late wife. What must it have been like to be married to this man? I'd always thought of Adrian in superhero terms, much as a teenager I'd dreamed of El Debarge or Prince—until I realized he was less than five feet tall. This was different. Grown up. Real. Jesus had changed things so much between us. "Thank you. For taking everybody out. For believing me."

He nodded. "You met Trevor at my wedding, remember? I know his games." He squeezed my hand and reached for the doorknob. "And I know you."

How can you? I don't know me.

I nodded, thankful Adrian hadn't showed up any later. I'd learned early on in my walk with Christ that the place I felt strongest was often the place the enemy attacked first. I'd always expected war in my weaknesses, but it was my strengths that often brought me down.

Being single and celibate had come first on my list of Christian virtues. And allowing God to refine me had become my deepest prayer. Watching Adrian walk away from me, limping as though he'd been shot through the heart, I knew two birds had been killed with one stone this time. I could only hope that my faith in the rock of my salvation would prove stronger than the boulder of my past.

"Dana?" My father's slippers hit against the floor like a flyswatter against a screen door.

"Yes, Dad. It's me." I tensed, then walked to the kitchen, knowing that's where I'd find him. Watching as he started the Day Two recipes for the dinner—things that were best made on the day of eating, dough for rolls, salad and the pineapple passion fruit punch Tracey served for her reception—I marveled at the care with which he prepared this food and the disdain with which he lived his life. Though he'd cleaned up these past few months living with Jordan, he refused to get a job or go to church, a place he had once loved.

My heart raced at the memory of his baritone voice slipping over the sanctuary. I'd loved watching everyone's backs hit the pews as he sang the pain out of them, drawing out the sting of a long week with each honeyed note. And if any hurt was left, well, it was nothing a slab of ribs or a plate of hot fish couldn't cure. I sighed. Why were things so simple, but so complicated?

"You'd better get them young folks up and dressed if you all plan to get to church on time. Takes about thirty minutes just to find a parking spot over there. And don't you have to sing? You look like—"

"Daddy." I took another sip of tepid water and put the teakettle on the only available burner.

"Well, you do. Tea isn't going to help those bags under your eyes. Grab one of those cucumbers and go lay down. I'll set you out some clothes and get those children going." He paused, probably thinking of just how many children he was really referring to.

Set me out some clothes? I hadn't heard him say that in years. He'd once heard me complaining to Mama after service about being too old for the ruffled taffeta dress he'd chosen for me. The next Sunday he'd told me to go and put something on with my grown self and that had been that. What a fool I'd been. I needed somebody to lay my clothes out today. I needed somebody to lay out my life. "Thank you, Daddy," I said, slicing a bowl of cucumbers—after recovering from the shock of actually having cucumbers—and heading for my room.

"Thank you, moppet."

Moppet. My lips curled inward remembering the blowout Easter afro that had earned me the name. As the day went on, everyone else's hair got bigger. Mine shrank, flopping at my ears until I looked like a little brown rug, parted down the middle. Muppet they'd called me, until Daddy corrected them. "No. Moppet. She's so cute you could wipe up the floor with her."

It was corny and he was drunk when he'd said it, but that didn't lessen the hot, sappy feeling rising in my gut as he said it now. "Oh, Daddy." I hugged him with all the strength I could muster.

He squirmed and wiggled, waving me off as though I were a killer bee. "Go on now. Women. Never know when they're going to act crazy."

I giggled. Men. I always knew when they were going to act crazy. As long as they're breathing. I stretched and set out across the dining room, which had shaped up nicely without the cardboard boxes that had once filled it. I wondered what kind of crazy outfit Daddy would "set out" for me.

My front door exploded in a chorus of angry knocks before I could think on it further. I inched along with my head tilted back to keep the cucumbers on my eyes, but one fell off with a splat. In true teen boy form, Jericho jumped out of the recliner and ducked onto the balcony, choosing to weather the pouring rain and freezing temperatures rather than the impending storm in my apartment.

With a sigh, I stuffed the remaining cucumber in my pocket, then started for the door. Still Sundays, I used to call them. If God let me see one again, I'd never complain.

Shemika pulled her covers up around her neck as I passed her. I shook my head. "Tell him to get back in here before he catches pneumonia."

The girl looked torn. "He thinks it's his mother."

"Nah. This one's for me." I knew Dahlia's crazy knocking anywhere. No doubt, Trevor had gone home and shared his imaginary escapade with my sister. Or even worse, my sweet little niece had bumbled out the scene as only a toddler can.

Two more steps brought me to my door, now shaking like plywood instead of oak. Who knew Dahlia's skinny butt could hit so hard?

"I'm coming already. Cut it out. You're going to break it down." I shook my head. Only man-wrath could give that kind of strength.

I pulled the door back.

Rochelle stood, livid, on the other side. I swallowed, realizing the one thing more powerful than man-wrath was inches from me....

Mother love.

When I vowed to take Shemika to see "that boy" and his mother, I didn't know what I was getting into. Nothing had prepared me for seeing my strapping nephew cry like a baby trying to explain to his mother what he'd done. The rage flashing in my best friend's face shocked me just as much. I'd expected her to be disappointed, upset, but this? Every few seconds I wondered if she'd turn green and tear out of her dress. That it was purple didn't help.

Rochelle paced the floor, swinging both arms. "I saw it coming," she said, making an abrupt pivot at the end of my sectional. "I asked you again and again. But noo-oo-oo. 'Mama, I ain't doing that. Mama, why you always on my back. No,' you said. 'No!'"

"Rochelle." I touched her arm, lightly at first, then firmer when she didn't respond. "Calm down. We can talk later. Let's pray now and back off. Get to church."

Her head swung around what looked like three hundred and sixty degrees. "Church? *Church?*" Her tone made me feel as though the word itself was absurd. When I'd lost everything with Trevor, she'd been the one who prayed me through. Was I this bad? Would I be able to stand up to her and tell her the truth like she did for me? My shoulders slumped.

She sucked her teeth. "Church. Girl, what are you talking about? I've given God everything I have. And what did it get me?"

Jericho shook his head, pinching his eyes shut. "Mama, please. Don't say that. I'm sorry. I didn't mean it. It's just that—"

Rochelle threw her head back like she did on Sundays when the choir ended up on the floor with everybody else. When she threw her head back like that, there wasn't any use in fanning yourself, 'cause in a few minutes you'd be sweating for sure. This time though, the sway of her head scared me more than the sight of Trevor's smooth skin last night.

Almost.

"I have nothing," she cried in a haunting voice. "Nothing!" She turned to Shemika. "And here you are, running up behind me trying to get a piece of nothing, too."

It got still then, almost like the air had thinned. I tried to muster words, but it was all I could do to breathe. Shemika walked to the balcony and slid back the glass door, ushering in the roar of morning rain. Lightning danced on the downbeat, offering the only flash in the drab darkness. All seemed lost, until a precious sound sliced through our silence.

"Be still, my soul…the Lord is on thy side. Bear patiently the cross of grief or pain…"

Without thinking, I picked up the note, adding body to Daddy's low, sweet voice. "Leave to your God to order and provide…in every change, He faithful will remain."

He took my hand first, then Rochelle's. And we sang. To each other, to the rain, to God. My voice creaked on most notes, especially when I felt the current of my father's baritone holding me up. Hadn't he been singing this last night? He'd seen the storm coming long before it had broken forth.

After the last refrain, Daddy waved us to the dining room table. I followed, smiling through my tears. At each chair was an outfit for everyone, crisp and ironed. One of Jordan's old suits for Jericho—never underestimate the retro potential of ugly clothes—one of Mama's sweater sets for Shemika that must have been maternity. Was Mama ever that big? There was a royal blue wrap skirt and blouse for me, and for himself, a seersucker suit that I'd never remembered seeing before. My jaw swung open like a trap door.

Daddy tapped it shut. "That's what attics are for, baby. Rainy days."

We were all there. I hadn't been to church with Daddy in over ten years, and besides the fiasco a few months back when Jordan first arrived, I hadn't seen my brother there either. On any other day, I'd have rejoiced, but Rochelle looked as though she'd fling apart at the seams at any second. She was shaking her foot in the choir stands under her robe. Even when the music wasn't playing.

Rochelle stared right at us. No one else seemed to notice but me. I hated to say it, but I wished Jordan and his little honey had chosen the end of the pew instead of sitting next to me. My friend was looking like she had a poison peashooter under that choir robe. And we all know if somebody throws something, ain't nobody getting hit but me.

Daddy sat on the other side of me, with Dahlia and Trevor next to him. I didn't know what to think of Trevor's presence. How could someone act such a fool and traipse up in church the next morning with a Bible and a smile?

You did it for a long time.

True, but it's still scary. Adrian must have thought so, too. He'd walked toward us, but when he saw Trev, he dropped into the next seat he saw and buried his head in a hymnal. How I wished I could do the same, especially given the topic. Holiness. Talk about a doozy.

Pastor Galveston usually got the Word in, but he didn't like to hit it too hard. The old folks would call him at home afterward and the young folks wouldn't come back. Tracey, Rochelle and I had survived on Oswald Chambers, inductive Bible studies and a steady diet of tapes and Internet broadcasts from our favorite Bible teachers. But today, something was different. Even Daddy seemed to sense it, gripping the back of the pew.

"I've got to come clean with you church. Can I come clean with you?"

"Yes, sir," someone shouted from the choir stand.

The older man planted both fists at his sides. "Good. I've served the Word at the church for thirty years. I've seen some come and go. Married y'all, buried y'all and everything in between. But I have let you down."

The pianist hit the wrong key.

He mopped his mouth with a handkerchief and stepped down from the pulpit. "That's right. Play the off note. I said it. I've let you down. Every one of you."

Jericho leaned back so far I thought he was going to end up in the bosom of the lady in the pew behind us. Probably not, she was breaking her neck too. Where was Pastor going with this? I'd had my share of surprises for the year. I looked down at the front row, where the pastor's wife's eyes bulged. She'd looked scared, like a train was 'bout to hit her.

Pastor took off his robe and walked past his wife. He kept coming in our direction and Daddy and Jordan both stared at the door at the same time.

"I've let you all think you could come in here once or twice a week and get your praise on, then go live like you wanted to and everything thing would be okay." He shook his head, but kept stepping our way. "But that ain't true.

"God is mighty, He's loving, He's gracious. He's a way-maker, a pain-taker…" He stopped at the end of our row.

At Trevor.

"But He's holy y'all. And we've got to be holy, too. I've got to be." He nudged Trevor with his elbow. "Stand up, son." He whispered it, but it whistled through the mike.

I tried to swallow, but my throat wouldn't cooperate. Daddy looked at me as though he'd been trapped in a circus sideshow with no means of escape. I shook my head.

The one time my family comes to church, Pastor has to show out.

"What's your name, son?"

Trev looked at the floor, for once drained of his ever-ready confidence. "Trevor. Trevor Ice."

The pastor took a long breath. "Well, Trevor Ice, I have a confession to make. And the Lord told me that you're the man to tell it to." He turned and looked around the room. "And all y'all of course." Everyone laughed, but with nervous, tight laughter. The kind of laughing saved for jokes at funerals or times when you're not sure if funny is safe.

It wasn't safe now, that much I knew for sure. Trevor must have known it, too, because he didn't crack a smile as the pastor continued.

"Trevor, I've been having an affair."

A collective gasp fell over the church.

"See that woman up there?" He pointed to his wife, trembling on the front row. "For thirty years, I've been telling her I'd get to it later. We've lost our children to drugs, jail and hell because I put this place first."

He covered Trevor's hand with his. "Well, no more. I lay this church today back in the hands of the God who made it. It's His church, and nothing shall prevail against it."

The room blurred before me. All I could make out was the first lady's pink-suited form rocking several rows ahead. "Thank...You...Jesus," she said over and over to a rhythm that must have been ground out over many Saturday nights. Many Sunday mornings.

Pastor himself sobbed into the microphone. The whole church lost it then. But he silenced them. "Hold on, church. You'll get your turn. We're gonna clean house today. Starting with this young man."

"Me? Naw..." Trev tried to pull away.

"Yes, you. Ten years ago, the Lord told me to do this with someone but I didn't want to mess up the program. Didn't want to interrupt my pretty sermon and make a fool of myself. I'd pull him aside next Sunday, you know, real quietlike." He stared down the pew at Daddy.

My heart beat in my throat.

"What happened?" somebody called out.

"I never saw that man again...until today." He cleared his throat. "And I don't have another ten years to wait. So tell me son, what do you need to 'fess up this morning?"

Trevor looked up from the floor and then pivoted slowly...his eyes first on Dahlia, then his little girl, and finally resting on me. Why was he looking at me?

Don't say anything crazy.

Across the aisle, Adrian rose and started for the door. Trevor wiped his mouth and stared up at the ceiling. "My problem, pastor? It's real messed up. I'm in love with my baby's mama…"

My nails dug into my skirt at his pause.

Don't say it.

"And my baby's aunt."

# Chapter Thirteen

"Dahlia ran out of the church?" Tracey's voice echoed through the line.

I leaned against the cash register. "She did."

"And you ran after her?"

My head throbbed. "You know it." Wasn't that my job lately, to chase people out of the church? "I hadn't factored in having to squeeze past Trevor at the end of the pew. He held my hand when I tried to get by. Said he was sorry."

"He's sorry all right. What did you say when you caught up to her?"

I shook my head, remembering chasing Dahlia down the back stairs. "We cried. Me because I know what it's like to love somebody and have them unwilling or unable to return that love. Her because—"

"She sees now how wrong she was? That no man should ever have come between you two?"

"Not even all that. She was just ashamed, you know? You never think you're going to get played. It's always somebody else. But there was sorrow, too. The tears were cleansing for both of us." Repentant even. Whether it was Trevor, the pastor's words or just God reaching down and touching her, my sister seemed to have realized that she'd made a grave mistake. Though I'd forgiven it, the tears were cleansing for me, too.

"And what was the other thing you started to tell me? About Jericho?"

Better let Rochelle handle that one. "I'm sure Rochelle will bring you up to speed on that one. The question is what's up with you? You obviously called me for a reason other than hearing about my drama. Everything all right with the baby?"

"The baby's fine."

"So?"

"I'm not fine. In fact, I think I might need to come up for a while."

O-kay. "Come on. Bring Ryan, too. Daddy and Adrian would love the company. How about next weekend—"

"I'll be alone, and it might be for a little longer than a weekend."

I stared out my glass storefront into Kick!'s front window at Adrian, who was talking to someone behind his register. A new employee? And from here, though her back was to me, I could tell she looked cute. A little too cute.

Mind your business.

"You know you're welcome anytime, Tracey. I just don't want any trouble with Ryan. That's why I think a weekend—"

"I was thinking more like indefinitely."

What? "Now come on, nothing is that bad. Did he hit you? Cheat?"

She paused. "No, not literally."

"Well, we'll pray about the figurative. I'm always down to be your refuge if you're in danger, but I can't be your excuse. Besides, if you were here for more than a weekend, you'd run home. It's madness."

Marriage counseling would be a tight fit between the other recent developments. Not to mention the fact that I was totally un-qualified. "Have you talked to Rochelle about this?"

"Every time I call, that guy is around."

"Every time?" That surprised me. Rochelle barely let us come to her place, and we were her only friends.

"Pretty much."

Not good. Not good at all. "Hmm."

"My thoughts exactly."

Adrian stepped out of his shop, pausing to sweep the walk and then…

Is he coming over here?

I breathed into my hand to check my breath. My leftover cat-fish breakfast had left its mark. Ick.

The bell over the door jingled as Adrian stepped inside. I kept my back turned, fumbling in my pockets for a mint. Nothing but lint. As I grasped for freshness, I suddenly remembered the trio of goat hairs that had resprouted from my chin this morning. Did I really get that last one?

His hand rested on my shoulder

"What are you doing, Dane?" Tracey half screamed through the phone.

"Dying," I whispered. "Adrian's here. Call me later."

For once, she hung up before I did. My shoulders turned slowly as thoughts of the half inch of new growth fuzzing up from my scalp battled with my chin-hair nightmares. Since I'd started walking my two miles every morning again, I seemed to be sprouting. Chia Pet definitely seemed to be my destiny.

"Good morning," Adrian said, his hands tucked under each arm. A satisfied grin adorned his soft-looking lips.

"Morning," I mumbled, using as little fish breath as possible to form the word.

His eyes twinkled. What was that about? "The closed mouth treatment? Is that any way to greet a customer?"

I covered my mouth. "Catfish for breakfast." The words slipped through my parted fingers.

He leaned closer. "Huh?"

This was so humiliating. "Catfish for breakfast!" There, was he satisfied? My mouth smelled like Lake Michigan. "I wasn't thinking. I brushed my teeth this morning, but I grabbed some of Daddy's leftovers on the way out."

He grabbed his gut, unable to restrain his laughter. "Sure, you did. Tell me anything."

I drew in a sharp breath. "I did! You know I don't play that."

He nodded with another playful grin. "There's only one way to be sure." Rounding the counter faster than I could escape, he took my head in his hand, tickled me with the other and took a big whiff when I opened my mouth—after trying everything short of passing out to hold my breath. When I gusted him with my saltwater saliva, he fell back against the wall. "Oh, yeah. That's nasty." He reached in to the back pocket of his jeans for a tin of breath mints.

My breath quickened. Tangerine Altoids. What his kisses had always tasted like. I reached in and took a few, but he held up his hands in protest when I tried to give the tin back to him.

"Oh, no. Keep them. Your daddy isn't going to stop cooking fish anytime soon. And if you breathe on somebody with that, they'll sue. I'll write it off, business expense."

I punched his shoulder. "What do you want anyway? And did you hire someone? It looked like someone was behind your counter a minute ago."

He paused, giving me that look that always made me turn away. "About that—"

I didn't like his tone. The bad news voice. Was she his girlfriend? If so, how could I be mad? Hadn't I had the same chance? I wasn't ready to be with anybody—though my body kept sending signals to the contrary. "You don't need to explain. It's your store." And your life. I grabbed another handful of Altoids and stuffed them into my mouth.

That got a big laugh out of him. "Oh … so now it's my store? If I recall, I stole it from you." He tickled me again. The breath mints suddenly became an orange-flavored death knot in my throat.

"K-k-k." I was trying to say help, but that's how it came out. The letter *K*. Figures.

He tapped my back. "Are you okay?"

I shook my head as the purples and peaches on the shelves melted before me. My knees buckled. My last thought?

*Please, God, don't let me fall on him….*

Pain exploded across my back as he slapped me across my shoulder blades. The choker gob of candy hit the floor. Right before I did.

"Dana! You all right?" Adrian went down with me and cradled my head on his knee. His gold cross dangled from his neck, grazing my nose. I took a deep breath of him, evaluating Adrian's new scent, as I always did in crisis situations. Leather, lime and new money. He smelled just like he looked. Suddenly choking half to death on a ball of breath mints seemed a totally wonderful thing to do.

"I'm okay," I whispered, thinking how strange it was that I actually did feel okay. Better than I had in weeks. Maybe I needed to freefall on my head more often.

He took a deep breath and kissed my forehead, then my cheek, then…he stopped himself. To say that I was disappointed would be an understatement. "That's what I get for playing with you. Your breath smelled fine—"

My finger touched his lips. Another mistake. "Hush, you. I'm okay. Really." I sat up and smiled, just to prove it.

"Scaring a guy to death. Is that any way to treat a customer?"

I dusted off my pants and stood. "I don't know. You'll have to ask the guy across the street. He's got them all."

"All except the one I want." Adrian held my hand so I could balance.

If my head wasn't already throbbing, I'd have swooned. We both shared a goofy look, then Adrian turned his head sideways a little. "Did you fall on your chin, too?"

I bit my lip, remembering how I'd yanked at my chin one last time to be sure right when he'd walked in. "No. Why?"

"There's something…I thought it was a scratch before, but it's a…" He narrowed one eye.

I closed both of mine.

*God, please. If he just doesn't say it…*

"It's a hair!" He shouted it as though the *Candid Camera* team were going to shoot up from behind the displays and start taping. Before I could convey my embarrassment, he snatched it out and laid it on the counter. "Got to get 'em at the root." He pulled a handkerchief out of his pocket. "Here, get that blood."

I was still too stunned to speak.

He frowned. "What's wrong? Embarrassed?" He smiled. "Don't be." He rubbed the top of his bald head. "I'm happy to see hair any way I can. Brings back memories. Mom used to get them all the time."

His beautiful mother? That did me in, and I doubled over with laughter. "You are just crazy—"

His face went blank.

I covered my mouth. *Crazy* still wasn't a word he was fond of. "I mean silly. Silly."

"It's okay." His smile reemerged. "I'm kind of over that."

"Right."

Another awkward pause. The bell jingled at the door. Adrian tapped the Altoids on the counter. "Is it safe to leave these?" he asked, starting to leave.

"I'd say so. That's the most fun I've had in weeks."

The customer, an older Jewish woman who came in for my talcum-free powder every week—who could use a whole tube of powder every week?—entered the store.

Adrian chuckled, then paused. "The most fun you've had all week? Oh, Dane. Don't tell anybody that."

I snorted. He needn't worry. I didn't have time to tell anybody anything. Besides, wasn't he the one with something to tell me? "I won't. But hey, what were you going to tell me? About your, uh, employee?" I somehow felt ready to hear it now, whatever it was.

"There's nothing to tell really. Just that she's—"

The older woman turned and stared right with me.

Adrian moved a little closer to the door before finishing his sentence. "She's a single mom who came to me for a job. There's nothing between us. I just wanted you to know."

A sigh whistled through the older lady's lips and she wandered back to the lavender section. I stared at her for a second and did a little mental dance of my own. "No problem. That was nice of you."

He swung the door open. "Glad you think so. It's your sister."

"It's for my bedroom and master bath. The drawers, the sheets, the carpet. Lavender keeps everything fresh…and special, you know?" She tipped her head across the street and cleared her throat. "Have to keep things a little special, yes? That sister of yours, she knows that. But her eyes? Nothing good inside." She pinched my cheek and wagged it back and forth. *Ouch.* "You? You are a good girl. You eat too much and work too hard, but you're a good girl. And he's a good man. Don't be stupid, eh?"

And with that, she waddled down the avenue. I stared after her. How had things got like this? The week before Naomi fired me, I'd given away all my houseplants. The thought of a relationship with anything plant, mineral or animal, let alone human, was totally out of the question. Between making soap and stuff, church, work…there wasn't time for anything. And I'd liked it that way.

Or so I thought.

Now there was Daddy, Jordan, Dahlia, Sierra, Jericho and Shemika, Rochelle and her…whatever he was. Sprouting like weeds everywhere. Just like my chin hairs. Without me asking, here they had all come, trampling my safe little world to bits.

*God, oh God. Deliver me from myself.*

I stared across the street at Dahlia's slim form. She bent over to get something and then she laughed. I closed my eyes. It was a performance I'd seen so many times before. Why did she always have to take anything—everything—I had? And why did the men in my life always seem willing give it?

I could almost hear what Renee would say—"He believed in you. Why think the worst of him? He's just helping her."

Reentering the day's numbers in my computer accounting program, I shook the thought from my mind. As usual, the accounts receivables and the accounts due didn't match. For some reason, the bank was still holding Tangela's last check. I'd been trying to call her…no matter. I had another of her ridiculous bridal functions this weekend. I'd talk to her then.

I closed my eyes for a second, remembering Adrian's lime-leather-money scent so close to my face. The bell broke my reverie. I'd never been so thankful for a customer. I swallowed when I saw it was Adrian. Again.

"This trip, I'm a customer. Sorry about earlier. I know I didn't handle that too well. I told your sister to come to you—"

I'll bet. "You don't need to explain. How can I help you?" I couldn't afford to get tangled up with him anymore today. My sister, either. I had work to do. I'd hash it out with Tracey this weekend. All of it.

For the next twenty minutes, Adrian walked the floor, ordering a little of everything. My everything. All the stuff I really love and personally use. I stopped every few minutes to crack my knuckles. Who was he buying this stuff for? Surely not me or he would have said it. We're open about gifts. Was he that into

Dahlia already? Or was this to get back at me? Could he think Trevor and I really had something going on?

The possibilities alone made me tired. So I just didn't think about it, choosing instead to try to estimate the number of Weight Watchers points in a chocolate chip cannoli. Estimating got me in trouble, both with my waistline and my pocketbook, but guessing was always fun. Especially since it kept my mind off everything that was going on.

After emptying half my Fresh Facial cart, Adrian asked for gift wrapping. Okay, that sent me over the edge. I charged thirty-five bucks for gift wrapping a large purchase, because with only me here it's a pain to do. The brides get it free in their packages, and no one else ever wanted it. Except Adrian.

"If I do all this and you just hand it to me, I'm going to hit you," I said in a weak but hopeful tone.

All it earned me was a look of confusion. "You? Sorry, Dane." He cracked his wallet. "Do you want something?"

I shook my head. How stupid did that sound. I made the stuff!

"Some candles then?"

"No," I said, though my lemon pound cake votive stash was dangerously low. Dahlia had probably primed the wicks with gasoline in hopes of me buying some. I'd stick to choking on breath mints, thank you. I shook my head, wrapped the last gift and handed him his bag. I didn't know what he was up to, nor did I care. Well, a little.

He dropped the bag to the floor like an afterthought. Guys. Who could figure them out?

"Sorry I missed dinner Sunday. Did everything get straightened out?" He wiped away the sweat beading on his lip.

I stared at the thermostat. Seventy-three. Not hot enough for sweat. Did that mean he was asking about Dahlia and Trevor? How would I know if things were straightened out between them? He was the one working with her.

When I didn't answer, he clarified. "With Rochelle and Jericho, I mean."

"After you left church? It got a little ugly. Jericho got up and told everybody about Shemika and asked the church for forgiveness. Mother Holly fell out and started screaming."

He winced. "That bad, huh?"

Worse. "Pretty much. But once we got back to my house, somewhere between the catfish and the peach cobbler, people started acting civil again."

His lips formed a grim line. "Your Dad's food has that effect on people. Always has." I knew he meant the way his mom would chill out at those dinners, even when she was off her meds. I could still remember the fear in Adrian's face when the last song stopped and they all had to go home.

"Everything else got straightened out, too? For you, I mean."

For me? Which everything was he referring to? "As much as possible I guess. Some things just take time."

He looked away. "Tell me about it." With a smile, he leaned down for his bag and dug in his pocket as he straightened.

His handkerchief. Was he looking for it? "Your hanky is in the back. I washed it."

"Hanky? You are so cute." He took out his wallet. "This is what I was looking for." He tossed a hundred dollar bill on the counter. "Go get your hair done." Before I could comment, he added an identical bill to the pile. "Better yet, tell her to come to you. And get some rest. There's a lot going on."

A little too much going on if you asked me. I grabbed the bills without hesitation. If anyone else had done it, besides Rochelle and Tracey, I would have been insulted, but how could I argue the truth? My do had given up on the job long ago. I stuck my fingers in the bird's nest formerly known as my scalp, braving my personal safety to do so. "Microbraids, you think?"

He shrugged. "Whatever you want. Don't start trying to please me now." The smile he tried to hide escaped.

I snickered. "Try to please you? I'd never be so foolish."

He rolled his eyes.

"As if I'd know what you like anyway, mister."

He lifted the bag of his purchases onto the counter. "Oh, you know what I like."

My face got hot. I did know what he liked. Even with my hair. If he had his way, I'd take out my extensions altogether and get my real hair braided like I did all through high school. Mama hated it, but Adrian went wild over it. I always did, too, until two weeks later when it looked like … this. Hair just isn't my thing. I need to be free from dealing with it for months at a time.

He walked to the door for the second time in one day while I tried to ignore how good he looked from this view. And forget how bad I'd probably looked from his view. The sad thing? I felt even worse. For all my superwoman act, the trouble on the home front was getting me down.

"Adrian."

He stopped short of the door.

I needed to know something, something I didn't really have the courage to ask. Just say it. "Why did you leave the church on Sunday? Did you think Trevor was going to contradict what I'd told you?"

"Nope." He turned to me, the light gleaming off the lens of his glasses. "I knew exactly what Trevor was going to say." Adrian shoved a fist into his pants pockets. "I also knew what I'd do if I were there to hear it."

to: Soldoutsista1
From: Soldoutsista2
Subject: Tracey

Hey, Rochelle. It's me. I know it's cowardly to e-mail instead of call, but I need to be brief. I don't know if Tracey's told you yet, but she's pregnant. If she hasn't told you, please pick yourself up off the floor and keep reading. She's been calling me a bit down (and probably you, too) and wants to come up for a while. I'm going to put together a surprise baby shower for her this weekend. I need for you to be there. Saturday 2 o'clock. My place.

Agape,

Dana

I'd wanted to sign it with love or your friend or something, but only God's love seemed an appropriate closing. At this point, not much else seemed left between us.

When Rochelle showed up Saturday morning and started cooking and folding napkins without saying a word, the smile flashed between us said it all. This was bigger than both of us. This was what friends were for.

And we were friends. My brother's emergence reminded me that Rochelle wasn't always somebody's mother or big sister. That there was a time when she wasn't Rochelle much at all. She was just Chelle. Today, I saw under her watchful eye and reproving glance the girl who'd gotten knocked up by my brother at seventeen and knocked down by the world not much later. She'd worked long and hard, but there was still a fun-loving person inside there. Her part of "Chelle and Jordan" had somehow managed to survive.

Four hours later, when my apartment blared in pastels as if someone had dumped Easter onto the walls early, the first knock came at the door. I gasped when I opened it and saw Naomi, my former boss, looking as shrill as the day she fired me. "Come in."

She dragged on a cigarette. "Don't look so shocked. You invited me, didn't you?"

I nodded, thinking I had Renee to thank for that. What kind of gift would my former assistant bring? Definitely something from Fingerhut. "Can you, uh, put that out, Naomi? Tracey will be here soon and smoke isn't good for—"

"Whatever." She held up her hand and released another wisp of smoke as she stepped inside. "Where's the bathroom? I'll go in there."

Great. Now I'd have to gag for the rest of the weekend. I considered the possibility for a second and decided against it. She wasn't my boss anymore. This was my house.

With a light touch, I draped my arm over Naomi's shoulder and guided her back down the hall to the stoop. "This is a no smoking zone. House rules. I'm sure that you, of all people, can appreciate rules. Feel free to come in when you're done."

Her face scrunched like she'd sucked a lemon as she tottered onto the metal balcony. "I can't believe this—"

Believe it. "Have fun." Refusing the urge to slam the glass door, I slid it shut instead and sniffed my freshly done braids for smoke, while running for the air freshener. When Rochelle emerged from the kitchen choking, I figured the deed was done.

"What's with the death by Lysol?"

I nodded to the stoop. "Smoking. Naomi."

Even Chelle looked shocked. "Naomi? Here?" She stared at the glass door. "Wow. That's two in a row. Tracey's really got pull."

She got you here, didn't she?

"I've got pull, huh?"

We both spun to find Tracey behind us in a pink maternity dress. The light bounced off the butterfly clips in her newly cropped afro.

"Tracey!" Chelle and I cried in unison, racing to her side. For someone who was considering leaving their husband and upset about her pregnancy, she sure looked good to me. As we hugged her, my stomach lurched, looking at all the decorations.

"Oh, no! The surprise!"

Rochelle threw a hand across her mouth and let Tracey go. "You weren't supposed to get here until—how did you—"

"The door was open and Naomi's Saab was parked outside."

I took a deep breath. "Well, surprise anyway. Welcome to your baby shower. Have a seat."

Tracey shook her head. "I'm tired of having a seat. I came to work. Why do you think I'm early?"

Both my hands flew up. "So you knew?"

"Of course." Tracey grabbed a bag of mints and filled the last empty candy dish. "You were acting too fishy, girl. I know when y'all up to something. And I've been up to so much nothing, I couldn't stay away."

Rochelle shook her head and walked into the kitchen. "You can't even surprise folks these days."

Too happy to see Tracey to lament the ruined surprise, I took her hand and walked towards the front door to close it. Man, how I'd missed her. Seeing her made me realize how much. "Maybe we can't surprise you, but we're going to feed you good. Your hair is too cute."

She giggled a little and then drew a quick breath.

"What is it? Are you in pain? Should I call the doctor?"

Tracey didn't answer, but stared at the door instead.

My eyes followed hers. I dropped Tracey's hand. Not only should I have shut the door, but locked it, too. Dahlia stood in the hall, her coat open to reveal a celery-green minidress with matching pumps, one of which she rocked onto its side. In her hands was a small bag. A Kick! bag.

Adrian and his big mouth.

My sister's eyes darted back and forth between us. "I know I wasn't invited exactly, but I hadn't seen Tracey in a while—"

I shrugged. "It's okay. Come in."

Sierra emerged from behind her, toddled up to Tracey, put her face up to Tracey's belly and sniffed. "Smells like a gurrrl." With that, she made for the candy dish as though belly sniffing were an acceptable profession. Her mother followed.

We all stared behind them. I shut the door and flipped the lock. I wasn't sure who would walk in next, but I wasn't taking any chances. Tracey stared wide-eyed at nothing in particular, then took a deep breath.

"Forget what I said earlier," she said, turning again to look at my sister and niece, whose exact age I'd neglected to mention in all our conversations. "Color me surprised."

"So the pastor is really changing things, huh?" Tracey popped the last shrimp puff into her mouth and pushed aside the tower of gifts left by the throng of well-wishers who'd filed through my living room. Not many had time to stay, but everyone brought a present, a smile and plenty of well wishes. Even Renee, who'd graced the occasion with a limited edition porcelain doll from Fingerhut. Naomi? Well, she'd eventually come off the stoop where she'd spent most of the time sulking to give a beautiful card and a wad of cash. "Baby shopping just isn't my thing. But if it's a girl, call me when she's five. I'll buy her the world."

Too bad Naomi couldn't afford just a little kindness instead. Not that money wasn't nice. It was just easy for her to give. One day, she and I would have to sit down and talk about such things, since I had nothing left to lose with her. That someday, however, wouldn't be today. Today, it was just Rochelle, Tracey, me and—surprisingly enough—Dahlia and Sierra, who was curled up like a cat at the end of the couch with a fuzzy baby rattle one of the ladies from church had brought.

Rochelle answered first. "Yeah. Pastor is really shaking things up. Just what we'd always prayed for."

"Then why do you sound so sad about it?" It was Dahlia's voice. We all turned, stunned. Sure she was here, but we'd neither wanted nor expected any response from her. Well, let me correct that—*I* hadn't expected her to say anything. Tracey looked delighted.

"I was just thinking that myself, Dahlia," Tracey said, taking a sip of orange sherbet punch. Another of Daddy's recipes. "This stuff is so good."

At least something had turned out right. I sighed. Usually I added too much ice cream or not enough Sprite. This time it was just right and with a splash of guava juice. Good stuff. Better than the direction of this conversation to be sure.

"It's not that we're not happy about it, Dahlia. It's just that there's a lot going on now, you know? When we were really pressing in and praying for Pastor to hit things harder, we thought we had it going on. Thought that we were spiritual."

Tracey snorted. "I know that's right. I look back at my devotionals from last year and wonder who that was. I thought I was soo-oo holy. And look at me now."

I tried to cut her moaning off at the pass. It wasn't info I wanted to arm Dahlia with. "What do you mean look at you now?" I took her plate and cup and headed for the trash. "You're married, pregnant and serving God. Sure things aren't perfect, but you're hanging in there. You made it to the altar. That was the hard thing." I dropped the cute pansy plate into the trash and headed back to the couch.

A tear streamed down Tracey's face.

Oh, yeah. Definitely the hormones.

"That's just it, Dane. I didn't make it to the altar. And now I'm paying for it."

My eyes crinkled like they had when Naomi was smoking earlier. "Of course you made it. I was there."

Dahlia cleared her throat. "That's not what she means, Dana. Get a clue."

I got a clue. Quick. So that was the weird vibe I'd had about the whole Ryan thing. "So you lied to us the whole time?"

Rochelle hung her head. Tracey looked away.

Dahlia grabbed a handful of peanuts. "Sounds like she didn't lie to everybody. Just you."

I thought that was your job.

Tension knotted in my shoulders. "So you, too, Tracey? Looks like everybody here thinks I'm just someone to be lied to and played like a fool. Is there anything else I should know?"

Though it was a rhetorical question, I knew as soon as I'd asked it that it was a mistake. Concern clouded all their faces, especially Dahlia's. Anything the others had to say worried me, but another confession from her in this lifetime might just do me in.

Dahlia rubbed her cheek until her palm was covered in foundation. "I understand what Tracey said about doing things wrong and then maybe having bad things happen because of it." She bit a nail. "I mean, I've done a lot of things that I'm not proud of now, most of them to you, Dana. I know you don't think so, but I do believe in God. This is just all new to me, you know? I didn't really get it before."

I rolled my head in a circle. "That's okay," I said in a low voice. "I still don't get it sometimes myself. I just take it day by day."

"Yeah," Tracey said.

"It's all you can do." Rochelle poured herself some punch.

Dahlia nodded. "Still. I've done some pretty messed up stuff. Some of it, though, I didn't mean to happen. I mean the thing with Trevor—"

"Let's not go there." Rochelle's words trembled a little. She was probably remembering the lunatic I was for a while after the whole situation. Even after I was saved.

"It's okay, Chelle. Let her talk." For some reason, Dahlia's words didn't seem to bother me as much as what Tracey had said. I'd expected more from her. Dahlia had always hurt me. Well, maybe not always, but for a long time. I was getting used to it.

"Anyway, Trevor paid me back. No matter what I do, he still seems to want you—"

"Dahlia." I cringed, remembering her haunted look as she'd run from the church.

Another sniff. "We've got Sierra. She needs us. We'll work it out. He knows that you love Adrian anyway—"

Rochelle choked on her punch.

"It's not like that exactly," I whispered. My heart wrenched, refusing to acknowledge the admission in my tone. A baby shower. That was all this was supposed to be. Cake. Punch. Gifts. Fun. This was not fun.

Brown mascara blurred into the creases of Dahlia's eyes. "That's the thing I'm most sorry for. The thing I never meant to happen…" Her voice faded.

The room spun a little as words marched past my lips against my commands. "What *thing?*"

She gave me a puzzled look. "The thing with Adrian. He never told you?"


"You don't look so good."

I smiled at Austin. I didn't feel so good, either.

"Rough weekend?" She stabbed at her salad.

Rough didn't begin to describe it. "Nothing a few pounds of chocolate couldn't cure."

She giggled. "A few *pounds?* Oh, man. That must have been a doozy. Well, I'm glad you came to our lunch date anyway. Did you have girlfriends to console you?"

"You know it." I took a sip of water.

"Feel better?"

I shook my head.

"Will Dove bars help or is that overkill?"

Not for this. "I'm not turning down anything, but I don't want to get sick on you."

She flashed me her TV smile. "Right. No need to overdo." She maneuvered the fork again, bringing me face to face with her rock of a wedding ring once again. Talk about overdone. What archeological dig had unearthed that thing?

I knew she wanted to talk about my sister's untimely revelation, but as much as I liked her, we weren't that close. In truth, if Tracey and Rochelle hadn't been there to hear it, I don't know if I'd have told them. But they'd been there. I didn't want to speculate anymore or try to figure out the gory details. It was over. He'd ripped my heart out, roots and all. "Enough about me, Austin. How's married life treating you?"

She shrugged. "I can't complain. There's a lot to work out. Joshua has lived a sheltered, loving life. I haven't. Sometimes it's hard for me to understand how much family means to him and it's hard for him to understand how much my work means to me. But we both love the Lord. We'll work it out."

My eyes crinkled again. "The Lord? I thought he was Jewish?"

A ribbon of romaine hung out of Austin's mouth. She sucked it in like spaghetti. "Yes, the Lord. Yeshua. Josh is Jewish in heritage, but he's Christian by faith. Messianic. Haven't you heard of it?"

"Sort of." Like that Nehemiah thing Adrian went to. I'd surfed the Internet to learn more about it a few times when I couldn't sleep, but I'd delete those bookmarks now. I'd never be going anywhere near him again.

Austin munched on, oblivious. "Oh, yeah. It's a big thing. Jews for Jesus and all that. Wonderful services. A friend from work invited me. It blew me away."

"Sounds amazing. Did you meet Josh at the single's group there?" Duh. Did they even have such things?

Austin smiled. "Hardly. I didn't even give him a second glance. I was so into Jesus I didn't pay much attention to anyone else. His mother was paying attention though…"

"His mother? She hooked you guys up?"

"Oh, yeah. She's a little lady, but she knows what she wants. She irons her sheets. Powders her bathroom with lavender. She cracks me up."

I dropped my fork. "I think I've met her. She's a customer."

Austin threw back her head and laughed. "Figures. She doesn't talk much, but she knows everything. I thought that stuff had to be yours." She cupped her chin in her hands. "We're having Passover with them this weekend. Christian ceremony. Want to come and surprise her?"

I chewed my bland chicken, wishing we'd gone out like I'd suggested, that I'd ordered the ribs I really wanted right now. "Sure. Why not?" At this point, the thought of surprising anyone but myself sounded pretty good.

They called him by another name, but I recognized Him immediately.

Yeshua.

Emmanuel.

Jesus.

God.

In a dimly lit parlor scented with lamb, rosemary and honeyed apples, somewhere between the bitter herbs and the matzo ball soup, Jesus became alive to me again.

Though I'd taken many communions, read all the Gospels, sang all the songs, it wasn't until I sat around the table with a bunch of strangers that I realized that my life was not about me paying the price for my past or even making some holy tangle of rules and rituals, but rather an offering, much the same as the one made for me, however woefully inadequate it seemed.

As I envisioned the blood on the doorpost of those Hebrew slaves and the haste and hope with which they ate this meal, my anger, confusion and pain at recent events melted away, swirled into a burst of color and then ran together in one red line across my mind.

A bloodline.

"Most folks have the wine, you know. The real thing." Mrs. Shapiro's peppermint breath feathered across my cheek. "I had a bad time with the drink a long time ago." She pointed upward. "He delivered me from it, but no sense in forcing the issue, eh?"

I nodded, sliding the lamb off my fork. No sense in pressing the issue indeed. The music swirled around me as she patted my hand and moved on to the next person around the table, a colossal oval that reminded me of the conference room back at Scents and Savings. Only here, people smiled.

God had brought me so far since then. Out of the stress and pressure of that world into…my own stress and pressure? The absurdity of the thought startled me. So did the gentle rushing of the music, washing over me in waves of Hebrew. The men around the table echoed the words in throaty tones. I smiled at the underlying drumbeat, eerily reminiscent of a famous rap song.

Nothing new under the sun.

Austin winked at me from across the table. Her husband waved, then gripped her hand. She blushed and I laughed, both at her and myself. She'd seemed so savvy and cosmopolitan, but in the presence of the man she loved, she acted like a sixteen-year-old girl.

They moved in to kiss and I turned away, but not before a pounding at the door sliced through the beat of the music. Austin's stern but pleasant husband leapt from his seat and ran from the table with expectance. Austin shook her head. "Men," she mouthed, trying to regain her composure.

I nodded, narrowing my eyes in agreement, knowing she was trying to recover. She needn't have bothered. Her melting at the sight of her husband had only endeared me to her more. She was a sistah indeed.

Her husband returned to the table with a laughing mouth, pulling a leather-clad man behind him.

A man I knew all too well.

My fork clattered against the china. Grape juice splashed over the rim of my glass and seeped into the linen, purple raced across the table as if highlighting the path to the newcomer. "Adrian?" I choked out his name as I righted my glass.

He looked at me, first puzzled, then delighted as he grabbed a napkin to help sop up my mess. "Dana," he said like music. "I see you found my little Bible study after all."

# Chapter Fourteen

The grape juice came out of the tablecloth, but that night stained me forever. Though I'd spent many nights since Dahlia's confession wondering what I'd say to Adrian when we did talk again, only Christ mattered that night. We sang to Jesus. Prayed to Him. Drank Him in though worship and Word. We laughed and cried.

More intimate than any kiss or rendezvous was the simple sweetness of our Savior and one look across the table after the last prayer left me seeing Adrian as if for the first time. Seeing Jesus for the first time. As if knowing how much the night had meant and not wanting to spoil it, Adrian slipped away first with a simple wave.

"I promise not to stay away so long next time," he said to them, while looking at me.

His presence at Broken Bread every Sunday meant his absence here, I realized.

With that, Adrian left me there to deal with Jesus. And to deal with myself. I didn't do a good job with either.

Spring rolled in and the days peeled back, dry and scaly, ripping at old wounds. Daddy came to cook every Sunday, but he hadn't been to church since "the incident" as he referred to the Trevor's little confession some weeks prior. Jordan and his girlfriend remained scarce. Rochelle and I maintained our shaky peace, solidified through silence and distance. Tracey? Well, she went home to Ryan and called me more than was healthy for either of us.

Dahlia called regularly, her voice tinged with regret. I spoke lovingly to her, surprised to hear my pity in my voice, but it was there. Pity for her…and for me.

Sure it's nice to know that Jesus loves the little children and all, but there was also a one-of-a-kind crazy love, the love I'd felt at Austin's dinner. Song of Solomon love. Whether I'd been operating before out of duty or discipline I didn't know, but now there was a devotion, a bond that made me want to pull away and be touched by Him.

Filled.

My once clear-cut goals didn't even make sense anymore. I mean, yeah, I wanted the store, but I don't want it to own me. And this thing with Adrian…despite my vows to protect myself from him, somewhere in the worship, as God lavished His love upon me, I'd forgiven my old friend and acknowledged my love for him. Whether anything would ever change between us was up to God.

I'd loved him all my life, but how could I consider being in love with him, devoting my emotion to someone else when I wasn't sure how to love myself? There were no easy answers, but something had changed. I wanted Adrian, and I wanted to be the mother of his babies. Yes, that was plural.

Sierra proved to be the biggest eye-opener in that regard. Kids were something I wrote off my wish list a long time ago, mainly because I didn't think I had time enough, money enough, love enough for another human being. Being with her, I saw that God had enough love and so would I, whenever the time came.

And Trevor? I realize now what I didn't when we were together. No woman could fill his needs. Even Dahlia couldn't fill that pit.

Only Jesus could. The question was, what would I do with all my love now that I'd owned up to having some? Give it away again or give it all to God, where it would be safe?

*Love your neighbor as yourself.*

The only thing I'd been loving lately was this shop. And I couldn't even carry that anymore. I loved my business. It fulfilled me. But if it had to end, so be it. Really, how much was too much? Where does good stewardship leave off and idolatry take over? Seeing as it's 3:00 a.m. again—and I'm still here with sweaty braids and dirty jeans I tugged on out of my overflowing laundry basket, I've crossed the line somewhere.

My fast-food-littered apartment and the foot of junk on the floor of my car skipped through my mind. My gaze wandered, stopping at my belly partitioned distinctly by my belt. And my Bible, where was it again? Still in the car from church?

I sighed, skinning peaches for Tangela's last bridal event—the one-day spa cruise. She'd promised to have the second installment of my fee tomorrow, though I wondered now if I'd even stay awake long enough to collect it. Of everything going on, this maid of honor thing had been the first place I'd crossed the line for the wrong reasons.

And it hadn't been the last. The red numbers on my electronic balance sheet echoed the stark reality. Even with the money Tangela had owed me, only God could help me now.

Four hours of sleep managed to look good on me, or so I thought until I scrambled down the freezing boat dock in the midst of a pink army of DKNY-clad Tangela clones. There was something so ridiculous about their head-to-toe perfection that struck me as painfully funny.

Tangela didn't seem as amused. "Did you bring the stuff?"

I nodded, lifting the tubs toward her with my peach-stained fingers.

She grimaced. "Just take them inside. Everything is ready. What happened though? You were supposed to come and help me set up."

Hmm…true enough, I hadn't been reading the manual, but I certainly didn't remember any such agreement. "Well, uh, sorry, but I was working to get this stuff made and I had to get Chelle to cover the—"

"Save the sob story. The maid of honor always helps with the spa cruise. Haven't you ever read *Modern Bride?*"

Obviously not. I stared at her, waiting for her head to start revolving completely around.

She sniffed and stormed on to the boat. "Just come on."

Once inside, the cabin of the boat seemed much smaller than it looked from the outside. With all that pink in a cramped space it looked as if someone had dumped a vat of cotton candy on the room. As the boat swayed under my feet, I suddenly remembered where I'd left my seasickness pills.

On land.

As I struggled to find a seat next to Shemika, whom I was surprised hadn't been relieved of her wedding hostess duties already, Tangela slithered to the front—all she was capable of in such a tight skirt—while Shemika greeted me and offered to help carry the facial tubs. I declined, of course.

Tangela's nasal voice whined through the microphone. "I hope you have your handbooks everyone. We've got some great food and fun planned, but first things first. Turn to page seven and let's walk through the dress code again…."

I rolled my eyes. Somebody ought to be having fun. My stomach was rumbling, daring to roll down the waistband of my too tight skirt. My feet were pinched into a pair of "cute" shoes so uncomfortable I'd decided to take them back, but couldn't find the receipt. Catching my reflection in a porthole, I gasped. With my new "auburn" wash-in hair color and my bloodshot eyes, I looked like Raggedy Ann's sloppy sister.

I stared around the room at the princesses surrounding me. Not one of them looked capable of a smile, yet they had every hair, nail and toe in place. I unbuttoned my jacket and took a deep breath. I'd take a smile over perfection any day.

Shemika tapped my shoulder. "So how are you?"

I paused. What a simple, yet difficult question. I decided to go with the safe version. Pregnant or not, she was just a child. "God is really growing me right now in some areas. But overall, I'm blessed."

I really was starting to sound like Mother Holly.

In a much softer voice than our previous conversations, Shemika agreed. "God's growing me, too. In more ways than one." She lifted her head for a quick smile, then looked away. "I think she wants you, Dana."

Tangela motioned to me from the makeshift podium at the head of our table, littered with remains of spinach salads and picked-over trout, all except for our two plates at the end. I stood and approached the bride-to-be, remembering my plan this morning to pray instead of complain—no matter how crazy she acted. I bit my cheek. I could have waited a little longer on that one. With so much going on, the rocking motion of the boat was hardly noticeable. Okay, well more than hardly, but not that noticeable.

"Hey, Tangela. Great lunch. I must say I'm tired though. I'm going to leave the facials with you and if you don't mind, collect my check and go home—"

She cleared her throat. "About that." She held up a hand. "There's been some…changes. Minor changes of course, but changes just the same."

It was that same singsong voice that people used when they'd broke your favorite CD, eaten up the last of the ice cream or left your gas tank on empty. A closer look at the bags under Miss Moneybag's eyes signaled certain disaster. How had I missed those black moons? Probably too preoccupied with my own.

Definitely a leftover from a crying jag. More bad news. Rich girls only cried about one thing.

Money.

I dropped into the nearest chair as she prepared to share something I knew I didn't want to hear.

"You see, Sheldon's been cut from the Bulls, so I don't have the, er, finances that I'd planned on. I can still pay you for the favors, but let's reduce it to the original price we agreed on." Her lips curved upward into a tight smile. She patted my wrist as though I were her pet poodle. "You can keep the other four thousand. Consider it a tip. O-kay?"

A tip? My head went right. Left. Then right again. "Uh, no. It's not o-kay. Nor is it a tip. I ordered your supplies already. You said—"

Her smile disappeared. "I said what? I don't recall. And since we have no written agreement, perhaps I should just recall my business altogether."

I mumbled the chorus of one of the songs we'd sang at Passover under my breath. It was either me give thanks or Tangela meet her maker. I hadn't felt "aggressive" in a long time, but suddenly I felt capable of inflicting a great deal of bodily harm.

Chill.

"Ms. Daniels, if this is the way you do business then perhaps you should go elsewhere. You broke your word." I shoved my fists into my pockets and stood—to keep an unexpected swing from escaping me. She was doing that crinkled forehead thing and I wasn't sure how long I could hold it in. I rose. "Oh, and by the way, whoever you get to fill the order…let me know and I'll send her the maid of honor dress."

"You wouldn't," Tangela hissed.

*You shouldn't,* my heart whispered.

"I will!" I shouted, wishing the both of them would be quiet. Why was I the bad guy for making her stick to her word? I hadn't wanted any part in this in the first place. Now I was going to be stuck with a bunch of bills because she changed her mind? I was in hot water with my suppliers anyway. And without my local accounts...

A low moan, sort of like the sound of cattle waiting to be milked, pierced my eardrums. "I—I knew you'd be like this..." She sputtered and slobbed between the words. The boat eased back into the pier. Was that it? The spa cruise? A spin around a man-made inlet? She was broke.

Shemika emerged beside me with a box of tissue. I shook my head. Tangela had put me on the verge of crying many times with her careless words, but this was just plain ugly. With her lipstick half across her face, she looked like a clown.

And what did that make me, the evil ringmaster? Pretty much.

"You talked a-all about G-God and then you... Ohhhh!"

I took a deep breath. I'd try to witness to the girl one time and now she had to go and pull that card? I sighed. She'd only paid half. I was out five thousand bucks that I'd already spent to keep the store afloat. What on Earth was I going to do now?

Charge it to my account.

Come on, Lord. Sure I'll let You cover her arrogance and rudeness, but what about the money? What about me? Why must I always be the one to lay myself down? What about the bill for Rochelle and Tracey lying to me, for Mama dying and leaving me, for Jordan leaving me behind, for Daddy wanting to be his father all of the sudden as if I haven't been here all the time?

Tears blinded my eyes. Who was going to save me this time?

*I am. I'll take care of you, Dana. Just like always.*

I shrugged. "Don't worry about the money."

Tangela's eyes miraculously dried up. A moistened facial cloth appeared from her bag and whisked her face clean. Wow. She was actually pretty under all that paint.

A hand tugged at my arm. Shemika's. "Don't worry, Tangie. You, either, Dana. I'm sure your boyfriend will hook you up."

My head snapped in her direction. My boyfriend? "I don't have a—"

Shemika pointed out the window to a larger boat docked a few feet away. On top was a small group of people. I made out Austin's face, then her husband and Mrs. Shapiro. A tall, dark man with a guitar sat between them.

He started to strum.

Adrian's arms closed around me like a fortress. I had no strength or desire to get free. I was spent, plain and simple.

His face leaned in toward mine. "I know things didn't work out the way you planned. I'm sorry about that." He paused, pulling me farther down the boardwalk, his guitar banging against his back like some mariachi band member.

"You do know that I'm willing to help—"

Hadn't he helped enough? I groaned. "So you're my sugar daddy, now?"

He flinched, then smiled. "I'm only two years older than you so I don't think I quite qualify for that role. And in case you forgot, we're friends. Would you turn down help from Tracey? Didn't Rochelle loan you the money to open the shop?"

Hmm…he had me there. Although the loan had turned into more of a gift at this point. Even if I held on to Wonderfully Made, paying off that debt would take the next twenty years. Rochelle urged me to forget about it, probably because it was Jordan's money anyway. I wasn't sure if that was any better. Owing Visa was bad enough, but family? Not cool. I didn't want to add Adrian to my list of creditors. "Sure she loaned me the money, but I hate that I put her in that position."

I bit my lip before saying something that I'd been thinking for weeks, but didn't dare voice. "Maybe this is God's way of shutting the door on the business…."

Adrian came up short and looked overhead. He kissed my hand. A strange look passed over his face. What was he thinking of? Sandy? His mother? Other times when he had been "so sure," too? "Maybe. Maybe not. Maybe God is opening the door to something else."

My cheeks and forehead bunched up into an expression I'm sure resembled Tangela's Klingon look. "Something like what?"

He lifted his guitar over his shoulder. It dangled over his fingers by the strap for a second while we stared at each other, his eyes searching mine. He lowered it gently to the ground. As he moved in closer, the scent of figs, something I'd debuted a season before and he'd bought a ton on clearance for an unknown reason, opened my nose the way a good melody perks up my ears. It'd sold decently as a woman's scent, but on a man? Oh my.

*Stop working. Your business is probably over anyway.*

He leaned down, pressing his forehead against mine. My stubby fingers laced through his long, slender ones. I closed my eyes, waiting for a kiss.

The kiss.

I'd run from it all these months, since that day at Tracey's wedding when I'd wanted to lay one on him right there in that torn dress.

Tangerine-scented breath blew across my mouth instead. It sounded like someone had stabbed an over-inflated balloon.

He peeled his face away, then touched my face, traced my brows, my cheeks.

My eyes closed. This wasn't funny. "Please," I whispered. "Don't." Somehow kissing would have been so much easier to walk away from.

He traced his finger down the curve of my chin and kissed the spot where he'd extracted a hair not so long ago. The guitar crashed over but he kept his eyes on me.

My stomach did cartwheels.

"I love you, Dana. I always will."

Before I could reply, his lips marched back up my cheeks, my brows.... Each kiss as warm and steady as the next.

"Please don't." I whispered it this time.

With a pained look, he pulled back.

I took a deep breath and pointed to his cheek. "Are you trying to grow a beard? You know you almost slit your throat trying to shape up that pseudo-beard you had in eleventh grade…." My voice creaked. I hated to deflect him with a joke, but I couldn't do this. Not yet.

He tapped my shin with his foot. "The pirate beard? You were forbidden to mention that."

Forbidden. Wasn't that always the buzzword between us? Though I didn't welcome it, Dahlia's confession darkened the scape of my mind. My lips tightened into a line. "Yeah, well lots of things are forbidden, but that doesn't stop us, does it?"

His eyes sparkled with questions. "Sometimes, though, things aren't forbidden at all…just delayed."

I took a deep breath. Weren't we talking about my financial demise? Wasn't that my biggest problem? Why then couldn't I focus on it? Probably that figgy pudding lotion he was wearing. I'd made it, of course, but it hadn't smelled like that then. No, every person brought something to a fragrance, unlocked it. Owned it. And Adrian had surely just reinvented the fig.

I shrugged. "Delayed. Denied. Sometimes it's hard to tell. Especially when you're traveling a road with baggage in both hands."

He touched my face. Lighter this time. I fought the urge to bat his hand away. What was he trying to do, kill me?

Maybe I should just tell him that I know about Dahlia. Just put it out there.

As I considered it, he turned away, reaching down for his guitar, now with a loose wire and a scratch grooved on the side. When had he even learned to play? Another piece of the puzzle of this new person he'd become. He strapped the instrument on the front this time, creating a distance between us.

With a melancholy look, he patted my hand one last time. "You're right, sometimes the luggage is so heavy, the trip is impossible."

Remember that frozen hot dog bun that Oprah ate back in the eighties? Well, I think I topped that today, tackling a brick of God-only-knows-how-old raisin bread from the freezer. A Weight Watchers coupon had come in the mail the day before, just when even my Velcro jeans wouldn't pull up. Did they have spies or what? In preparation for the dreaded weigh-in, I was making an effort to eat better.

I hated the thought of facing that receptionist, but I was having my I'm-too-fat-to-live headaches and Rochelle, who hadn't said a word about my weight in a while—or much else—had expressed concern about my huffing and puffing up the stairs at church last Sunday. I'd been a little peeved at her weakly disguised intervention—I'd done enough of them for her and Tracey in years past to see one coming—but when I saw the fear in Chelle's eyes…I realized her sincerity.

Considering my mother's high blood pressure, I can see how it would scare her. And truthfully, after getting those pictures back from the baby shower and realizing it was my belly blocking the shot instead of Tracey's, I knew I had to do something.

Freezer-burnt raisin toast definitely wasn't the answer. I should have known by the thud of the bread against the counter when I took it out of the freezer. I pried the inch of ice off it and shoved it into the toaster, only to be shocked half to death while trying to retrieve the soggy wad of dough a few minutes later.

Not easily shaken, I tried the oven method. Well, after downing that rock of raisins—dry, of course—stroke or heart attack is the least of my worries.

I drove straight to Starbucks holding my throat and only felt my tongue again after three white chocolate lattes. Oh, well, so much for a new start. I think this time I'm going to have to approach this eating thing from another angle. A wider lens, too, to catch my hips.

I wanted to be balanced, but my lifestyle, the 60-hour work week, family dinners with more fat than the local butcher's, loving and hating my former best friend and business competitor, the revival of my church at a time when I was dying and just trying to survive, didn't bode well for my good health.

Driving to work, I stared up at the red light, burped a mouthful of raisins and prayed for the traffic light to change. Adrian's figgy pudding kisses, or maybe my sorrow at the thought of never experiencing another one, had inspired me to start a new men's line. It'd gone over like gangbusters. If I pushed a little harder, I might be able to save the store after all. Even pay Rochelle back. Or should I give it to Jordan? Too much to figure out.

With a deep breath, I eased into the store, staring at some of the half empty shelves. I'd needed to stay up last night making stock to replenish the shelves after my last wedding order, but my body had given out without my permission. And it was a good thing.

I dared to hope, to believe that somehow things would work out. They had to.

I shoved my purse in the safe and looked in the mirror, finally having the time to really pay attention and being lucid enough to process what I saw. I gasped. Who was that? I mean sure I'd been running ninety to nothing, babysitting Sierra, worrying as much as working...but that hag in the glass couldn't be me, could it?

Why didn't anybody tell me?

Rochelle's concern-filled face and Austin's frustrated voice— "What are you doing to yourself?" —skipped through my mind. Tracey chose to lead by example, looking slim and perky even though now quite pregnant. Daddy had been much less tactful— "You blew up like a hot air balloon. You sick?"

Even Mother Holly had made a few comments at the last noon day prayer about trying to cut back on her eating. Usually, having Dahlia around was enough to make me starve myself out of sheer vanity, but this time I just couldn't care less.

What was this fat to me? A wall? A place to hide from my womanhood, my past and my future? Was I using the weight to try and hide from Adrian? Or worse yet, from God?

I shook off the thought, noting the dangers of self-analysis. Calculating how much product I could make before the store opened in an hour, I measured out the ingredients for my shea-based products—body butter, lotion bars, lip balm and my new bestseller, Figgy Fella for men's hair, nails and skin. After measuring everything into my meticulously clean utensils—my lack of care for myself had been translated into my care for my shop and products—every dropper and beaker was twice cleaned and sanitized between batches.

As I capped the last jar and arranged the labels face out, though the first morning rush would mangle them all again, the phone rang. I paused, wondering who would call me here at this time of morning, then picked up, figuring it was Tracey, Austin or Rochelle. Perhaps even Adrian, whose shop across the street would remain dark until 10:00 a.m. when my beloved sister would trot up and unlock the door.

"Hello?"

"Good morning, Miss Rose. This is Bob, a Visa customer care representative. After many attempts to contact you—"

Oh, great. Now the bill collectors even knew I worked overtime. Guess they figured that should translate into a payment. "Well, Bob I—uh—cashavutomoo—"

"Huh?"

I stared at the receiver as confused as him. My "I do hope to make a cash payment tomorrow" had somehow come out garbled.

"Sowecanyoucallmesomeovatimo?"

Okay, I was definitely working too much. Sweat dripped onto the receiver. And working too hard. In fact, I felt a little dizzy....

"Miss Rose? Are you all right? You sound—"

Broke? That was my snappy comeback, of course, but my lips refused to deliver it. As if I'd applied Novocain lipstick, my mouth did a sort of saggy, draggy thing. As I tried to feel my tongue, a pain shot up my arm. I dropped the phone.

*"Miss Rose?"*

Bob definitely sounded upset, but not quite as angry as I was. As he spoke, I dropped to the floor like lead and heard the rip before I hit the ground. My new pantyhose. Eight dollars and seventy-five cents. A lot to pay for the pleasure of buying size B, but a girl's gotta do what a girl's gotta do. Oh, well, I could still make knee-highs out of them. Mother Holly would be proud of me.

Sprawled on the ground, I tried to smile at my witticism, but my lips wouldn't comply. My eyes refused to stay open, either. With sweat dripping into my mouth, I conceded to the pressure squeezing up my body and fell into a deep, blissful sleep.

Sight escaped me. Words defied me. But my nose refused to give up. The scent of Betadine and saline solution assaulted my senses, dragging me from the comfort of unconsciousness. My eyes slit open just enough for me to make out the street outside my shop, still dark with morning, but somehow crowded with people. Loud people.

"How long since the Visa guy made the call?"

"Ten minutes I think?"

"And he said she was lucid when she answered?"

I heard a shuffle of papers. "Right. Said hello with no problem, but it went down from there."

My body sped along suddenly, then went over a bump into the ambulance.

"Okay, so we've still got a window for the tPa to work. How old is she again?"

"Twenty-nine—no, thirty. Today's her birthday."

I tried to frown with no success. My birthday? What kind of person forgets her own birthday? I really was working too hard. No wonder my lips went on strike. My eyes ripped open. Strike. Stroke?

Though I'd never been present for Mama's three strokes, it didn't happen like this. On TV, it was more…dramatic. Maybe this was Bell's palsy, like Tracey had one summer in college. Her face drooped for a few weeks, but she recovered. Not that I had a few weeks to droop…. In fact, who would cover the store today?

I tried to sit up. "Ineedsomeverraimpor—"

Something pushed me back down as the ambulance pulled away. "Could you make that out?" Betadine asked.

"A little," said IV solution. "Let's just get her there." With that he proceeded to cut off my pantyhose.

Miraculously, I found my voice. "Noooo! Eightsebentyfive!"

Betadine scowled. "What'd she say?"

"Eight seventy-five?"

The first guy nodded. "The hose maybe? They look expensive."

"You would know, dude."

I lifted my lead lips and pushed through all the air I could muster as the last of the nylon was ripped away. "And they weren't on sale."

He looked like a cartoon character. As I'd spent my childhood Saturdays watching TV, a cartoon guy he was.

"You took us on quite a ride, Miss Rose." He smiled reassuringly in that way doctors do. Usually I found it aggravating, but not today. Today, I took it for the life raft it was. I mean, if he was smiling like that, surely I couldn't be totally dying. The Novocain lipstick seemed to have left my mouth. I could actually smile back at him. A pain shot up my arm, erasing my grin. And his.

"Pain in the arm?"

"Yes," I said, stunned at the sound of my own voice, garbled, as though I were chewing a mouthful of spaghetti and trying to talk at the same time.

He patted my arm with one hand and waved for the nurse with the other. "Don't be surprised about your speech. It may take some time to return to normal." He paused. "We'll do therapy during your recovery."

I swallowed hard. "So, it was a stroke?"

He nodded. "Yes. I don't know how much you owe Visa, but you might want to pay them. That bill collector saved your life. We got you here in time to administer tPa, which bursts the clots, and from what we can tell, there was no permanent damage to your brain tissues—"

A muffled sob escaped my lips. "Thank You, Jesus."

The doctor's eyebrows raised a half inch or so, making him look very surprised. He looked up at the nurse, who'd been quietly checking my blood pressure, pulse and other vitals on the computer screen and on my person.

She nodded. "Everything is normal. Her pain meds are probably just wearing off. Is the arm sore, hon?"

Her beehive hairdo and southern honey voice made me smile—or at least attempt to—again. "Yes. Sore."

"Okay, when the doc is done I'll come back and we'll work on that."

I nodded, wondering if she'd return with an omelet and some hash browns from the thanks-and-come-again rhythm in her speech. I guess this place served up its one recipe day after day— a menu of healing. "Thank you."

The doctor grabbed the side rail. "There are many things that we'll discuss with you in the next few days, but the most important ones I'll say to you now. You got away this time, but you'll have to make some changes. Fourteen percent of people who have a stroke, have another within the next year. Unfortunately, with African-Americans, the rate is even higher." He took off his glasses. "As nice as you seem to be, I do not want to see you in this unit again. I sent your family downstairs because I didn't want to alarm them until I'd talked to you...."

His words turned to fuzz. Family? How long had I been there? And who had come? Oh, goodness.

"However, when they come up, I'm going to explain to them as well about the need for lifestyle changes in diet, exercise and stress level. Your sister told me that you run a business alone. Is that right?"

Dahlia? I nodded, rubbing my arm.

"That will have to change. If you can't afford a staff, I'd suggest closing the store or even selling it. Your life isn't worth the risk."

Life? "I thought there was no damage."

"Not this time. The next time might not be so kind." He gathered my chart and slipped it back into the groove at the back of the door. "I treated your mother. That was the only time in my practice that I was relieved a patient didn't survive."

I jerked upright. "You were my mother's doctor?" Why didn't I remember his round face, button eyes? No, there was a taller man—

"I was called in to consult. There was nothing to be done, but after the brain scan, I was almost thankful. Even though she got to the hospital fairly quickly, her attack was a bad one." He reached for the doorknob. "And it wasn't her first. Bottom line? Change your life or you'll be disabled or dead."

My head fell back against the pillow. It was almost too much to take in. Dead? Disabled? I was barely thirty years old! No children. The shop was just getting off the ground. I was only beginning to live.

*I set before you life and death. Choose life.*

I couldn't help but smile as the scripture zinged through my mind. God gave open book tests. Simple questions. He even provided the answers. I pulled a hand over my eyes, to give my throbbing arm another position and shield my tears from my imminent "family." Pineapple and cilantro skipped along the bed rail like music. A chair screeched at my bedside. Though he didn't say a word, Adrian was there. Grateful, I closed my eyes.

# Chapter Fifteen

"So what are you going to do?"

My father moved like a dancer between the pots and pans—jambalaya with chicken breast and shrimp for me and fried calamari and garlic bread for the rest. Not that it was really helpful to smell all that, but I appreciated the thought, as well as his question. After over a month of speech and occupational therapy, plenty of praying and talking to family and friends, I still didn't have an answer.

"I don't know, Dad. I just don't know."

"*Hmph.* Just let it go. If you need money, we'll figure something out. I'm thinking about opening a restaurant—"

I choked on my water. "What?"

"It won't be for a while. I've been working at Smokey's and he really thinks I've got what it takes."

"Working? At the racetrack restaurant? I thought you were just—"

"Betting? Drinking? I know. I can't say I blame you for thinking that, but with my family back together I thought it was time I try to get myself together. Your mother would have wanted it this way." He paused as if wanted to say more, then tunneled his words down his arm and into his spoon, whizzing around a bowl of cake batter faster than any electric mixer ever could.

"It's angel food. The strawberries are in the fridge. I hope you like it. I made it for her—the first time." With halted words, Daddy turned to walk away, but I caught his arm. He pulled back, probably surprised at the strength of my touch—hey, weeks of biceps curls had to be good for something.

"Why didn't you all tell me about Mama's first stroke? I remember her going to the emergency room those times."

He shook his head. "It seemed so harmless. Like this thing with you. I know now that it wasn't." He wiped his eye. "Don't take a chance, moppet. Just don't take a chance."

Water trickled down my throat as I pulled my glass back to my mouth. I appreciated Daddy's concern, and truthfully, it matched my own, but what was I supposed to do, give up everything in my life and wait for death to come and claim me? Surely that wasn't the life God had for me. I needed change, the people at the hospital had made that clear.

In the four weeks I'd spent there, I'd lost twenty pounds and my blood pressure had plummeted. But what about now with work, church and all the drama of my family? Not to mention the shop, which Adrian and Dahlia were miraculously holding together.

I was ashamed to admit that Dahlia's appearance might have had some impact on the new sales figures, which she proudly called in each evening. And Adrian had even pulled in Jordan and Trevor to help in Dahlia's absence, which had to be a crazy mix. I could hardly imagine Trevor stacking jars with my name tattooed on his arm. Crazy. But somehow it was working.

And they'd make it work as long as I needed—or at least until Trevor needed to get to work on his next album. They loved me enough to pick up the slack. Even my evil cousins and Aunt Cheryl were said to be seen pitching in on the weekends. Austin, too, when she wasn't on the set.

But as for what I really wanted to do, I wasn't sure. I still lost my balance from time to time and had to slow down when speaking, but in many ways things seemed much like they'd been before. Yet, I couldn't forget that doctor's last phrase—disabled or dead.

Adrian sauntered into the kitchen with a slice of watermelon for himself and one for me. I took it, thanking him graciously. "Where'd you get this?"

"Bob brought it. The Visa man? The one who saved you by calling the ambulance?"

Saved my life. At the sound of those words, the backs of my ears prickled. Though I tried not to think about it most days, the fact that I'd almost died was unavoidable. But for some reason, God had chosen to let me live. And He'd used the Visa guy to do it. "He's here?"

Adrian pointed at a muscular fellow with raven hair and a cross earring. Sort of a Latin Fabio with a Bible. Adrian waved in Bob's direction and took my hand. "C'mon."

He didn't have to tell me. I was already half-across the room, watermelon in hand. I stopped just short of him. "Bob?"

He squinted at me. "Dana?"

Adrian grabbed the watermelon just in time, and we hugged like old friends. "Thanks so much for saving my life."

He smiled. "Thank God, not me. I wasn't trying to do anything that day but nail you. You were on my top ten most wanted list to actually talk to."

I shook my head thinking of how hard I'd been driving myself. "Well thanks for doing your job. And sorry about the bills and everything. I'm going to work that out."

Bob—who names a guy who looks like a movie star and smells like the ocean, Bob? I guess his mother couldn't have predicted it—winked at Adrian. "Don't sweat it. It's all been taken care of."

My eyes, now squinty, went from the Visa guy to Adrian. I knew that code. It was the shut-up-I-didn't-tell-her-yet look. I glared at my old friend. "What did you do?" Sure, I'd been sick, but he wasn't my husband. This was too much.

He grabbed my hand and tugged, then frowned at Bob. "Thanks, buddy! We'll see you later."

The guy laughed and went back to the cluster of people he'd been standing with before. People I'd seen at church, but didn't really know. Since when did the family gathering become the free-for-all hangout? While I was in the hospital, I suppose. I followed Adrian's tug into the dining room where we sat down at the table. He tucked my soggy slice of watermelon in to one of the linen napkins as though it were a rose.

He pulled out my chair, then quickly took a seat, raising one hand before I could go on my tirade.

"Look, before you say anything, hear me out, okay?"

"Okay."

His face went solemn. "I know you don't want my help. I know that you don't need it—"

"You're already helping at the store. Taking my appointments—"

He cocked his head sideways. I reached for another slice of watermelon from a bowl on the table. I bit into it and the juice squirted onto his face. He smiled. "Let me finish. I need to help you right now. There is no resource that I have that I won't use to keep you well." He dragged a clenched fist across his nose. "Even you can't deny me that."

"Deny you? I'm not trying to deny you anything, it's just that…" My voice trailed as I tried to slow down and get my lips to cooperate with my words.

Adrian took the opportunity to get a word in himself. "It is about denying me and everybody else. Why do you have to al-most kill yourself before we can help you? Have you thought about that? I've been begging you since I came back to town for us to work together, so you wouldn't have to work so hard." He buried his head in his hands. "I can't believe I let this happen."

My stomach knotted. "You?" I talked slow this time so the words would come out clear. "You've been nothing but kind. My hereditary put me on a path to this, but I charged up the road."

He kissed my cheek. "Yeah, but I let you go on, knowing it was too much. When we were just friends, it was so much easier. I could tell you what I thought and know that it was honest and for your best interest. Now…"

Dahlia slipped into view in a pink and red paisley off-one-shoulder sundress. She started toward us. Adrian held on to my hand and never looked her way. The rest of the room, though, took to her like a cactus to water, drinking her in and holding on.

"How are you feeling, sis?" she whispered into my mane of twists. Having a hairdresser who did house calls turned out to be a great idea.

"Better," I said. "Much better."

She nodded. "You look it. I guess having this guy around doesn't hurt, does it?"

When you're here it does.

Adrian looked up with a plastic smile. I eased out of his grip and stared at the placemats. Apples. Rochelle's motif. She'd wanted to ditch my pansies for years. Much the same way that I needed to ditch the pain of what had passed between Adrian and Dahlia. It rose again now, like a bronco, breaking through the barrier where I'd corralled it. Why didn't I just talk to him about it and get it over with? With her right here, too? "Speaking of Adrian, maybe we should…"

Dahlia turned. "What?"

I stared across at the empty seat where he'd been. "Nothing. Have a seat. Tell me all about the shop."

I tried not to be jealous, but I wasn't so sure if I pulled it off. While Dahlia rattled off the sales figures, slipped the digital camera out of her purse and showed me the new store arrangements, her sketches for new labels and logos for each line—how many lines did I have again?—I really had to stay calm. When she pulled out a spreadsheet of the top sellers over the last six weeks plus a graph for the trends for the month to come, my breath left me. Sure, I had the creative thing going on, but my sister was good at this business thing.

Really good.

"Don't look so surprised. I know you expect me to be stupid." She snapped her purse shut.

"It's not that, it's just that—"

She smiled. "I know. You weren't expecting it. Me, either. I mean sure, I'm good with shopping, and I got A's in business school, but this is really my thing."

You mean my thing. As usual.

I scratched my cheek.

"I mean your thing, of course. It's your business, but I'm— forget it. I can't make everything up to you, but I'm trying to do what I can." She stared at the ceiling. "Trying to make you proud of me."

I could almost hear that anonymous radio voice, saying, "This is a test. This is a test of the Christian response broadcast system." For a moment, I thought it was a test I would fail. This was what Dahlia had been seeking all those times that she hurt me. Recognition. Approval. Love. Now, when she was seeking it in constructive ways, did I have the strength, the faith, to build her up? I didn't. But Jesus did and He loaned me a little just before my little sister's eyes clouded over.

I gathered my sister into my arms. "I'm very proud of you." I stared across the room at Sierra, bouncing on Jordan's lap. "You are trying to pull your family together, you're working hard to help me and regardless of what's happened between us, you came back to try and make it right."

Her tears moistened my shoulder. "It was Trev who insisted we come back. But I'm glad we did. I need you." She looked around the room and whispered, "All of you." Just as quickly, Dahlia collected herself, wiped her tears, and nodded toward a handsome newcomer standing in the living room. "Who's the hunk?"

I giggled, then stopped, swallowing my laughter. She was crying one minute and scoping the next. I had to remember who I was dealing with. "That's Bob."

Her mouth opened just a bit. "Bob?"

"The Visa guy who called the hospital when I had the stroke. Turns out he goes to the Spanish church down the street from ours." I spoke the last words slowly, watching her watch him. Didn't we have enough trouble? "Don't get any ideas."

She looked hurt. "I was just curious, Dane. It's not like that. The last thing I need is another man. I realize now I've had too many. That's my problem. I just want more of Jesus." She stared over at Trevor, sitting on the couch between Adrian and Jericho. He looked tired. Drained.

Jesus had certainly been busy while I was away.

Sierra rubbed her eyes and started to whine, but Trevor crossed the room and picked her up before anyone else could. He walked her out, eying Dahlia as he went.

She ignored him, but moved to the edge of her seat when he disappeared down the hall. "One more thing. What's the deal with this Tangela chick stiffing you for all that money? Why didn't you tell me about that?"

Tangela? I covered my mouth then let my fingers slip away. "Oh, no. Her wedding. I forgot all about it."

Dahlia narrowed her eyes as if I'd said the stupidest thing ever. "You had a stroke and you're still worried about that woman? That's how you got to the hospital in the first place. I know you love God, but business is business. When she showed up, I showed her the door. And don't worry about the money she owed you. Lord willing, Trevor and I are still headed for the altar in a few weeks and you can be my maid of honor."

Maid of honor. If I was going to do it, it should be for family, but it'd be easy to say that and just be doing it for the money.

Despite the hugs and pie graphs, I knew Dahlia could easily hurt me again.

She pursed her lips. "Since you're taking so long to even say anything, I'm sorry for asking."

I took a deep breath. "I'm just surprised. You and Trevor don't even look like you're getting along, let alone getting married. Not that I wouldn't be happy for you. I just don't want you to feel like you're doing penance or making things up to me. If I'm going to do something like that, I want you to mean it."

And for me to mean it, too.

She nodded. "I do mean it. About Trevor and about you. I want you to stand up for me. As my sister."

"Are you serious?"

"Serious as that stroke you had."

That girl always did have an off sense of humor. She actually thought that was funny.

My throat tightened. Should I do it? Everything seemed all wonderful now, but what about when Dahlia pulled a fast one like she had so many times before? Sure I wanted her to grow into the woman God wanted her to be and I did love her, really I did. But I couldn't escape what felt like another flashing red light. It was probably just my fear, but it was flashing just the same. Sierra tumbled out of her uncle's lap and ran across the room to me, prying open my arms and snuggling her hair in mine. I smiled. "Let me pray about it and talk to the doctor." At least I could actually fit into a decent dress. Not that I'd recommend the brain trauma diet plan.

Dahlia plucked her baby from my arms. "Okay, whatever. We'll talk more about it later. It'll be a small ceremony anyway. Gotta run."

I'd hurt her, something that I'd tried to avoid, but I couldn't keep just going along. To Dahlia, standing up before God with Trevor might not mean more than a chance to buy a pretty dress. A glorified version of the prom. For me, the ceremony and its participants were a statement, parts of a covenant between a man and a woman and God who made them. To have me being a "maid" of honor and Dahlia just hooking up with her baby's daddy until their next breakup, wouldn't work for me. Maybe I wouldn't have a lasting marriage, but I wouldn't be offering my presence at the altar anymore for whoever happened to ask—not even for my sister.

Life, I'd learned recently, was too short and too sweet to waste on things I didn't mean.

They took good care of me. Dad kept me stocked in fruits and veggies and cooked dinner for me every night while the others came and went, calling and checking, dropping by. While the attention was nice, I craved the solitude and time with God I'd rediscovered at the hospital.

With no agenda driving my days, I woke each morning to fill myself with God's promises, prayer, walking the neighborhood I'd forgotten existed, waving to neighbors I'd long ignored. Tracey and I e-mailed often and talked on the phone daily, sharing recipes and tips for the online journaling program she'd suggested I sign up for. It suited me much better. After our food talk, next would come her pregnancy woes. Today was no different.

"Did you know that the average age for weaning is four years old worldwide? Isn't that amazing?"

More like gross. It was La Leche League day, so I could expect at least twenty minutes on the merits of breastmilk. The cost of friendship. "That's wild, Tracey."

"It really is. The body is just so awesome, you know? Like your shop. Fearfully and wonderfully made. Psalm 139, right?"

"Right." I'd read it this morning, in fact. Only the merits of the female design hadn't been on my mind then. When I read the passage, I reflected on how well God knew me. The intimacy He craved with me. I'd been wonderfully made to worship Him...to know Him in a way that only I could.

I closed my eyes and took a deep breath. Talking to Tracey was great, but I suddenly wanted to be alone again—with my Savior. Especially since the stock was running low at the store and I needed to start building inventory. Not with my usual intensity though. Just a batch of something each day.

"Dane, you there?"

I blinked. "Sure. Sorry."

Munching sounded through the receiver. "It's okay. It's time for me to have my snack anyway. Go and have yours."

Snack? "I just ate, Tracey."

"I didn't mean food. I meant spirit food. Treasure your single-ness, Dane. Love Jesus with all your heart…while you've got the time." She crunched one more time. "And send us a great devotional when you're done. I say take the whole month. You've been killing it."

"Well, near-death experiences do have the benefit of spiritual insight," I said in my most reverent church voice.

She fell out laughing. "Now I've got Kashi cereal on my keyboard. Stop it. Seriously, go. One day soon you'll be married and looking for all these deep Bible notes you once wrote."

Married? Me? It sounded strange, but the way things were going with Adrian and I, it could happen. We were closer than ever. "Whatever, girl. We'll talk soon. Are you still coming this week-end?" I held my breath, hoping Ryan had agreed to come, too.

"I'll be there."

I knew better than to respond. "Okay. I'm praying for you two."

Her voice flattened. "Good. That makes one of us."

Before I could say more, she hung up. I stared at the phone, deciding whether or not to call back. A knock at the door decided for me.

Trevor bounded in the door like a puppy fresh off the leash. "Is Adrian here?"

I shook my head. "I think he's coming for lunch. Want to leave him a message?"

He paced around the coffee table, his leather jacket pulled back over his shoulders. "Nope. No message. I just wanted to tell him something…" His face clouded. "I guess I can just tell you—"

Uh-oh. I looked around, thankful the door was still open. Easier for him to leave by. "Maybe you shouldn't tell me anything. I'm sure Adrian will be here soon."

Besides, I really wanted to sneak in some more time with the Lord before Adrian showed up. As intense as things had been between us lately, I had to be double prayed up when he came around.

Before he could say another word, Jericho appeared in the doorway, smiling first, then frowning when he saw Trevor. I nodded. "It's fine. Come on in. Shouldn't you be at school?"

He clapped hands with Trevor, but didn't verbally acknowledge him. "I signed myself out. I need to talk to you."

Take a number. "Okay. You hungry? There's hummus and whole wheat bread. Minestrone soup in the pot." Didn't you have to be eighteen to sign out? One more thing I'd have to tell Rochelle to check on.

He frowned again. "Aunt Dane, I'm glad you didn't die or anything, but all this weird food is messing with me."

"Try it. Hummus is all that." Trevor gave a quick nod of approval.

Jericho shrugged. "Okay," he said, then started for the kitchen.

I turned back to Trevor. "Hummus? What do you know about it?" Sure he'd done that tofu jag when we dated, but Trevor was a takeout junkie just like me.

"Since I've been helping Adrian out, me, him and Joshua go over to Garden of Eden for lunch every now and then. Hummus and tabouli. Falafel, too. I love it." His face lit up like a red disco bulb from the seventies.

Hilarity wasn't Trevor's usual motif. Something had really happened to him. Something with Dahlia, perhaps? If so, I'd do best not to be in the middle of it. A few feet away, Jericho clicked on the Cartoon Network.

"Not bad," he said, spooning a mouthful of minestrone. "Even that who-moo stuff is pretty good."

I smiled, not bothering to correct him. The boy had more to be concerned about than the acceptable pronunciation of chickpea paste. Shemika was showing…and Rochelle was showing out. She'd visited often during my hospital stay, but the pregnancy and the situation with Jordan had definitely taken a toll on her—and on our relationship. Things just weren't the same. Not to mention her lumbering boyfriend, who always seemed to end up sandwiched between us when we did try and talk. I'd accepted that things might not ever be the same.

"Don't get too comfortable, Jericho. We'll talk, but you're going back to school."

He rolled his eyes. "But—"

Trevor held up a hand in a surprising turn. "Don't talk back to your aunt, man. Eat your food."

That was a switch. Usually Trev would have found something like that funny.

"I can drop him back at school if you want. I know you're not driving yet."

"I've driven a little, but I'd rather not fight the lunch traffic." With only one main strip through town with all the fast food joints, the noon rush could be a real nightmare.

"No problem."

"Thanks, Trevor. I do appreciate that. Let me just talk to this kid and then I'll—"

He dropped his gaze. "Can he wait? I really need to share something with you."

I sighed. No way out. At least Jericho was here, in case things got ugly. "Okay." I dropped onto the sofa. He remained standing. "Shoot."

"I just wanted to let you know…I've found the Lord."

I rolled my eyes. "I never knew He was lost."

Trevor wagged a finger at me, laughing. "I knew you would be like this. I knew it. But you know what?" He paused as if I'd answer. I didn't. "It's okay…because He loves me."

The glee of a child on his father's lap radiated from Trevor's face. My jaw tightened. How dare he throw this in my face? Was I supposed to believe that he found God just like that?

*I did it for you.*

Well, anything was possible, I guess. If it wasn't possible, nobody had bothered to tell Trev. He looked downright giddy. And this from a man who used to practice his sneer in the mirror. "Girl, I know that not too long ago I was sweet-talking you. Truth be told, I was scheming on getting with you even after marrying Dahlia—"

I gasped.

He laughed. "See what I'm saying? I was a dog. Wretched."

Was? How was I supposed to believe he was anything else now? I'd heard all this before. Sure, change was possible, but this brothah would have to show me something—walk it out, just like I did. Then, I'd give him some props.

"I know you'll be watching me. And you should. But the cool thing is, God sees me as good right now! I don't know why people sit up in church all miserable and hateful. This is good stuff! The hustler I was wishes I could sell it."

He stared up at the station, where Jericho had paused the TV on a man with a booming voice and big hair boasting Jesus coffee mugs and Jerusalem rocks for a specified donation.

"Well," he said, "I guess folks have already beat me to the selling part, but I'm going to sell it anyway by telling folks. People been telling this thing all wrong. Even you, Dane."

My neck thrust forward. Me? When did I tell him anything?

He nodded as if answering my mental question. "Yes, you. Before we broke up, you were going to church and you always tried to put the heavy on me—stop drinking, stop smoking and stop acting a fool. But I was just doing all that to drown out being messed up. I mean everybody knows they're messed up. You left out the best part—the switcheroo."

"I didn't really understand things then myself. I was just echoing what I'd been told by others." Sort of like you're doing now. "What's this switcherwho business?" Was that the cousin of who-moos?

He raised his hands and waved as if dancing to a song. "The switcheroo. All my mess, my foolishness, my mistakes? All on him on the cross. He lived right, did it all good, was a straight-A guy, but when He did, He became me. My sins."

I tried to smile at his enthusiasm. What was happening to me? Not so long ago I had been this hyped about the cross, too.

"Uh-huh. I know that look. I ain't finished. Listen." He pulled up a chair from the kitchen table. "Not only did He become my sin, but check this out—I became His righteousness." He paused for effect.

I paused, too. I'd heard it. I knew it. Why then did it suddenly make sense coming from the newest and most unlikely Christian in my life? My head bobbed in agreement.

Trevor made a little "umph" sound and clenched his fists. "All His goodness, all His perfection, like about how you think Tracey and Chelle were perfect?"

I blinked. "I didn't think that."

"You did. Probably still do. You was so busy trying to live up to their righteousness that you never realized you had His. It's a trip. I have to prove myself to y'all, but not to Him. He sees me clean." He slapped his hands together. "Good."

A sigh escaped my lips. After that psuedo-sermon it was all I could muster. "Well, what does all this righteousness mean for you and my sister?" Talk was cheap.

His face tightened a little, but the smile remained. "It means that I get your name off my arm, for one thing. And that I move out while we take the New Foundations class and go through premarital counseling."

Whoa. "And how does Dahlia feel about all this?"

"She's excited. She's knows this is what we need."

"I hope that works out for you." I bit my lip. This was all so hard to swallow. It was if he'd taken a Jesus pill. But wasn't salvation supposed to be this powerful, this dramatic? Was my anger because my own life lacked this power? "I'm just glad that I'm not a point of contention anymore. That wasn't fun."

"Right." He hung his head. "I'm sorry about any hurt I caused you with that. And the hurt I caused Dahlia. It wasn't you I loved—no offense—but it was what you represented."

I didn't know whether to be offended or not. "And what exactly do I represent?"

He shrugged. "Family. Faithfulness. Hard work. All of that. I think what got me is how Sierra connected with you. Neither Dahlia or I had clicked with her on that level. You just see what people need and try and provide it."

"Ah. So I'm the poster child for the hard-working black woman, huh? I guess I can live with that."

He laughed. "Ah, you thought I was gonna say your hips right?"

I looked away. He might have found Jesus's righteousness, but the man was still dangerous.

"No, Dane, it's not just that, although you do know how to hold it down. It's love, too."

"Love?" What was this man talking about? The way I'd loved him perhaps?

"Yes, love. It's what drew me to you in the first place. When I saw the effect you had on Adrian at his own wedding, I knew you had to be a powerful woman."

"I think you're confused, Trev."

He shook his head. "There's two things I know—music and women. Adrian held Sandy's hand, but part of his heart was with you. When you two spoke before they left for the honeymoon? Man, I'd never seen anything like that."

I flicked a tear from my eye. How could such a silly memory spark such pain in me? "What do you mean? We hardly looked at each another."

Trevor stood. "Exactly. It was too painful. That pain stirred something in me and as is my fashion, I pursued you. And not that you aren't beautiful and kind, but that kind of fire didn't stick with us."

"I guess not." Though there were plenty of sparks.

"So it was the feelings between Adrian and me that made you want me?"

"Basically. And it was the same thing that drew Dahlia to Adrian."

I stiffened. "You know about that?"

He snorted. "Of course. I knew the first time I saw them at our place together. Reading people is part of my nature."

"Why didn't you say anything?"

"It wasn't my place. I considered it a few times to get Adrian out of play since I knew you still loved him—"

"That's not fair! I never talked to him at all."

"Nope. You just talked about him."

He had me there. I stretched my neck. It was time for Trev to go. "Well, I'm thrilled about you turning your life over to Christ. We've all had a bumpy ride, but like you said He's traded out the bad for the good. I wish you and Dahlia all the best. Tell Pastor he really hit big with you."

"Pastor Galveston?"

"Yeah, isn't that who you talked all this through with?"

He shook his head. "Nope. It was Adrian. And his friend, Joshua, that little news chick's husband? Pastor's doing the counseling though."

I should have known. Switcheroo didn't sound like anything Pastor would say.

"Well, turns out those two guys have been praying for me for a while. Then we started doing the lunch thing. They tolerated my questions and just talked to me about whatever. Adrian broke things down yesterday and about three hours later—I was all new, baby!" He raised his hands to the sky.

He started for the door. "Anyway, I'll see you. Get with Adrian. Talk to him." He winked. "God's got plans for y'all."

# Chapter Sixteen

I had to lock myself in the bathroom and read Psalm 139 again. I was fearfully and wonderfully made all right, but made of what? This year, these weddings, my health—it all showed me what I was really made of. And it wasn't anything pretty.

If Trevor's little testimony hadn't rocked me enough, my nephew's proclamation that he wanted to skip college and get married threw both Trevor and me for a whirl. When I heard Adrian pull up—weeks in bed train you to identify cars by sound—I shut myself in the bathroom for some quick prayer time rather than run to the door. The last visitors had probably left it unlocked anyway.

"Anybody home?" His voice rang clear and sweet.

"I'm in here. Just a minute." I read the last two lines of the Psalm, tossed up a quick prayer, cleaned myself up and came out of the bathroom.

"Hey, you." He smiled, putting a stack of papers on the table. He held one up, a sales page for the shop with a wedding dress floating in a pool of bubbles. In swirling script below the image read, Wonderfully Made. Make everyday your wedding day. My eyes misted over. It looked like something straight out of the mall. And very expensive.

"How?"

"Tracey redid the logo. My ad guy is on retainer so I didn't pay extra for him to do this. The printing wasn't much—"

"Tracey? But I've been talking to her every day. She didn't say a word."

He nodded. "That was the plan." He sat down and pulled out the seat next to him. "So seriously. What do you think? Colors? Tagline? Concept?"

"The flyers haven't gone out yet?"

"Of course not. It's your shop, Dane. I would never do that." He checked his watch. "I probably need to call and check on Trevor—"

Trevor! "No. He came by. He got saved—"

"I know. Isn't it amazing? As much as I hate that you got sick, God really used it to heal a lot of relationships—namely him and me. He and Josh really vibe, too. They want to do a record together. R&B with some Jewish worship samples. Isn't that a trip?"

I just stared at him. Suddenly I felt so left out. So out of the loop.

He dropped the ad and reached for me. "Did I say something wrong?"

Mopping my eyes with the back of my hand, I straightened. "No. In fact, you've said and done everything right." Well, not everything. "I just feel so...out of it. I mean it's nice being home and slowing down. The Lord and I have been having a grand time, but—"

"But you want your store back?"

I took a deep breath. "Not exactly. I'm seeing that it can't be just my store. You, Dahlia, Austin, even the cousins and Aunt Cheryl coming to help. Tracey on the computer. Renee and Rochelle's word of mouth. Your marketing and management. It all works together." Another sniff. "I just want to get back into it somehow. A few hours a day maybe. And I want to exercise my faith again. Listening to Trevor talk today…"

"That new fire is something, isn't it?"

I nodded. Why did Adrian seem to still have that fire, even if it was a little more contained? "It's like I've burned out completely."

He shook his head. "No way. Sometimes God just has to stoke the embers some. He's been doing that for me for the past few years we've been apart. You and I both skipped from sinner to superservant because of the expectations of others. There are a lot more pieces to the journey. Just let Him carry you right now."

He sure knew what to say. My head dropped onto his chest. "Thanks. I needed that."

I needed you.

His chest rose sharply at my touch. "Thank you for being you. For being real. This is the Dana that I've missed."

Me, too.

With that my head popped up and I lifted the ad to eye level. "Now about this wedding dress logo…"

Adrian shook his head. "I told her you'd say that. Before you say anything more, read this." He reached for the next glossy in the stack, a beautiful sistah with an afro and pink lip gloss sat in a bathtub with a tiara, a veil and pink sundress. She held an opened umbrella over her head with Wonderfully Made across it.

I smiled in approval and read on:

Tired of buying wedding gifts for your friends while waiting for Mr. Right? Wondering what it'll take for you to be showered with gifts? Enter now. And bring your umbrella.

My mouth dropped open as I read the details of the Sell-a-brate Yourself contest, where the winner got a shower of bath blessings for herself and six friends—facials, makeovers and a weekend in Chicago. The occasion? Life itself.

The final sentence took my breath away. "So if being a bridesmaid is getting you down, shower yourself with love—you're worth it."

"Who wrote this?" My fingers trembled.

Adrian smiled, the line in his forehead filling in. Had it meant so much to him that I like it? "I wrote it, but Tracey and Rochelle edited it. It started out as a 'Marry your Maker' contest, but they thought that was a bit much."

I didn't. "Tell me more."

He crossed his arms. "Well, the concept was for single Christian women to win actual dedication ceremonies—to Jesus. A re-affirmation of her faith and commitment. A renewed understanding of his intimate love toward her."

Where did he get this stuff? I squeezed his biceps. Definitely real.

He pretended to scowl. "Hey!"

"You scare me sometimes."

He leaned in closer. "I steal all my ideas from you, remember?"

I cringed and moved away. "Okay. I'm sold. But what about Kick!? You're putting all this energy into my stuff…."

He sobered. "About that… It doesn't make much sense for me to run back and forth across the street. We've really got the same customer base. Why not put both shops together?"

Breathe. "To-gether?"

How on earth would this work? Being across the street from him was bad enough. And the cost? "I can't afford that. And your stuff is so well known. You need your name. I need mine. It wouldn't work."

He massaged his temples. I realized now that the ad and contest was meant to sell me ahead of time. "Money isn't an issue—"

"It *is!*"

"It isn't. I own the whole strip next to you already. I was going to give it to you as a gift."

I stared at him as though he were speaking an alien language. "You can't buy people real estate, Adrian." My heart thudded. Was he trying to send me back to the hospital?

"Why not? Some jewelry costs more than those units. And real estate is a gift that keeps on giving. Not romantic I know, but it's how my brain works."

And I like it.

"But the names—"

"Not an issue. I just signed for national distribution. My candles will be in lots of stores, in addition to the Kick! stores around here. The warehouse will keep churning them out and I'll commission some special edition just for your lines."

"That's too much. I've got so much stuff. Too many scents."

He smiled. "I've got most of the scents duped at my home lab in case you wanted to branch out into candles later. What'd you think I bought all that stuff for?"

I just stared at him. "You've been working on this all that time?"

Adrian nodded. "I want to simplify my life. Smell the roses." He took my hand and sniffed it. "One in particular."

"Made of Honor, it is. I wasn't thrilled about the name at first, but you're right, I need to just embrace this wedding thing. It's what God has given me. And I love the new logo Tracey whipped up. She is amazing." The words came easy and so did Adrian's response, a soft kiss on the top of my hand. I smiled at how frequent his affections were becoming. And this time it came easy. I really did love the name.

The name combined the essence of Adrian and me, all that we wanted to be but weren't—valiant and courageous. The logo brought it all together. Just to make me laugh, I'm sure, there was a candlestick and a long-stemmed rose faded into the background. That Tracey was something else.

Perhaps this shop would help me and Adrian deal with our own altar issues. Perhaps not. At any rate, the name, logo and blended colors of teal, fuchsia and tangerine told it all. It was all about the two of us.

People flooded the place on the grand reopening like ants at a picnic. They stampeded up and down in their bare feet, slushing through the newly installed shag, sniffing, sniffing and sniffing.

Austin's hair brushed my shoulder, her entire face in a Vanilla Smella jar candle. She inhaled in disbelief. Adrian had stayed up two nights straight to formulate that particular scent into his soy wax. From the look on my friend's face, he'd hit the right note.

"It's heavenly," she whispered in a husky voice, clamping the lid and balancing the stack of bottles and jars under her arm. "But I can't smell anymore. It all smells so good…."

I nodded and guided her to a crystal bowl full of Colombian coffee beans, where she buried her head once more.

Rising, she smiled, then snorted. "Ah, there's my nose. That's amazing." She picked up the bowl and eyed it closely. "Nice touch. Your idea?"

"Nope."

She patted my hand. "That man is a business genius." She looked over at Dahlia, whose infraction I had finally shared with Austin. "Not so smart in other departments, but a business mastermind. You just keep coming up with the wonders. He knows how to make them sparkle."

I could only nod. She had me there. Adrian and Dahlia moved about the new, enlarged double unit like flickering diamonds, shining and smiling, while I sat behind the counter with a fake grin of my own.

Usually, I'd be dishing up facials or twittering with something, but Mr. Biz had assigned a unit price per cup and packaged up the facials fresh this morning with the new labels and a "Don't starve your skin" sticker with the day's date. With the smaller quantity, we sold more for the same price and less would be thrown out at the end of the day. Down to the alternating instrumental jazz and gospel tracks, he'd thought of everything.

*Why am I even here?*

As if he'd read my mind, Adrian crisscrossed the store, pointing someone to the bathroom and politely taking her bag to the counter. "For your convenience," I heard him say. I looked down at the new security cameras under the counter in time to see the slight nod of his head at the woman's frustrated look.

He lifted it into my waiting hands.

"So what do you think?" He asked, sounding deep in thought. Was he really that concerned about my opinion? For the past week, he'd made all of the decisions. Did he really care what I thought now? Oh, sure, I'd approved them, but it wasn't quite the same.

"It's great. The customers seem to love it."

He nodded, then took one of my hands. "Can you see everything? On the monitors, I mean? I tried to move everything so there'd be open space—"

"It's fine." I mustered a reassuring smile to clear the doubt from his voice. "What's with all the nervousness, Mr. Illinois Businessman? You could pull this off in your sleep. Besides, they love it."

His grip tightened on mine. "But do you love it?"

*I'm not sure.*

"I like it. The love will come."

He stopped then and looked at me in a way that almost made me turn away. I didn't though. He came closer. "I hope the love will come. In fact, I'm banking everything on it." A lopsided smile eased across his face. Adrian released my hand and reached for bag of the customer who'd gone to the bathroom. He paused to thank her for shopping with us.

Warmth rushed to my face and I stared down at the new computer screen on the cash register. When I looked up Dahlia, wedged into a pair of tight jeans and a tube top covered with daisies, stepped between us. Her hand rested on Adrian's shoulder. Was she squeezing?

Now see…this is how people end up on the news.

"Can I borrow you for a minute, Adrian? A customer needs an explanation about the ingredients in the foaming bath gel," she asked him, without meeting my eyes.

Hadn't she already borrowed him?

Adrian gave me an apologetic glance. "Be right back."

I shook my head, moving around the front of the register. "That's okay, Dahlia. You stay here. I've got this." I looked over my shoulder at Adrian. "Come on."

This was my store, and recovery or no recovery, I wasn't handing it—or anything else—over to my little sister.

Adrian's Birkenstocks clipped behind my clogs. *"Umph,"* he said. "Did love show up just then?"

Sometimes love shows up only to find its seat taken.

Why was I tripping like this? What woman had a man buying her real estate? I'd loved this fool most of my life and even with all that had happened, I couldn't stop loving him. Me learning to love me was the problem. Dahlia's hand on his shoulder a few minutes ago played again in my mind. Could I be brave enough to love both of them, my sister and my man—that's what he was whether I was willing to admit it or not—even though they'd hurt me? Why couldn't I just be a good Christian like Rochelle and have all the answers?

Because you're you.

Yeah. Me. Without losing my customer service smile or smudging the stay-on lip gloss adorning it, I turned to Adrian and kissed him full on the mouth. "Love's here, baby. I just have to find a place inside me big enough for her to live."

Bibb lettuce, crisp turkey bacon, red grapes, fat-free Italian dressing…and Adrian. Add a glass of water with a twist of lemon and that concludes the menu for my lunch with Austin. Like only girlfriends can, we skewered the guy into every forkful. It'd been almost a year since Chelle, Tracey and I had bonded this way, at the time serving Ryan up to a basket of riblets at Applebee's. I missed the two of them, but I was grateful for this new friendship, too.

"So," Austin paused to take a sip of water. "Can you get over it? This thing with Dahlia? It's a tall order, I know. If someone told me the story, I'd say forget the bum, but you can't let him get away. Not again. He's too fine."

I looked around her sunny solarium and down at my blue-and-white china plate, looking for answers. "Listen to you, calling folks fine. What would your husband think of that?"

She picked a bit of bacon out of her pearly whites. "Nothing. I call Josh fine, too. I call 'em like I see 'em. And in you two, I see a couple of people who are destined to be together—"

"And you invited me over today to make me to understand that?"

She giggled, then cleared her throat. "Not exactly. I've been wanting to get you all to myself for a while. I love Dahlia and your other friends, but they don't seem to like me too much."

"What gives you that impression?"

"Rochelle, for one. I've bought some pumps and a pair of mules from her since you turned me on to her place, but she didn't seem too happy to get my money."

It was my turn to laugh. "She just looks like that."

Austin shook her head. "I'm in journalism, Dana. I know when someone dislikes me. Besides, someone else came in right after me and she lit up like a bulb...and the other woman was white, so it wasn't a white-black thing. It's personal."

I blew out a breath. She went there, didn't she? Austin should fit right in. "Okay, so maybe Rochelle's got a problem, but it's not with you, it's with me. Same as the thing between me and Adrian. Issues, girl. Issues." I pulled the top off one of the lemon ices heaped next to my plate. The yellow slush oozed down my throat, swallowing my thoughts with icy sweetness.

Austin grabbed one and attacked it with her spoon. "Issues? C'mon. You don't have to give me details, but I've learned these last few months that you are a resilient woman. Whatever else it is, God can handle it. Just put it out there, you know?" She licked her spoon. "Aren't these good?"

I nodded.

*My God is my shield and my salvation. Whom shall I fear?*

What was I afraid of? Why not just clear things up with Adrian, Chelle and whoever else and let the chips fall where they may? "I don't know if my sister can continue to work for me."

Austin nodded. "She's insecure, Dana. I've been around those types of women all my life. What you and Adrian have is so obvious and what she has with Trevor is tenuous. Pray for her and stand your ground." She sipped her mineral water between spoonfuls of lemon ice. "And give her a good recommendation."

A long, lost laugh came up from my belly. The big kind, the kind that made milk come out your nose in grade school. It seemed like forever since I'd laughed like that. "You crack me up, you know that?"

She nodded. "So you've told me. I do hope things work out for your sister and The Fonz—"

My head fell back at her nickname for Trevor. The Black Fonzarelli. That was him for sure. "Girl, you are about to make me holler to the top of my lungs. That is too funny."

Austin looked blank that time. "That's funny? I call him that all the time. He comes to the study at Nehemiah."

I held my throat. "You call Trevor that to his face?"

She nodded, wide-eyed. "Is something wrong with that?"

He's for real saved.

I shook my head. "I guess not. So he comes over there, too? His car is at our church like he works there or something. I guess he's taking this pretty seriously."

"Yep. Dahlia comes too, most times brings the baby. Such a cutie, that one. The last time they came, Josh's mother didn't stop nudging me the whole night. She's on the hunt for a grandchild."

I bit my lip. "Must be nice to have things fall into place so neat like that. Rich husband—" I waved my hand over the room "—beautiful home. I guess a baby would be next." I tried not to think about Shemika and her growing belly. She and Jericho showed up at my house more and more. The fun had worn off and the reality had set in. It would be a long haul for all of us.

Austin's spoon thudded against the linen tablecloth. She smiled in contradiction to the tear running down her face. "Dana, I can't have children." She flipped the tear away. "My mother-in-law, she doesn't know."

I reached across the table for her hand. "I'm so sorry." Her salad plate fell and broke as she pulled back. My hand slid across the empty space.

Austin closed her eyes for a moment. "Forgive me. I've asked so much of you today, while guarding myself at the same time. If we're going to be friends, real friends, I guess that won't work, will it?"

Shaking my head, I thought about how easy Tracey, Rochelle and I had it in our friendship. We'd grown up together, knew most everything about each other. It was easy. Comfortable. This would require more. So I closed my eyes and leaned forward, listening as Austin began her story.

"I came from nothing. And wanted everything. In between, I lost it all…."

Somewhere between the stories of our pasts, the lowfat fudge bars and the brisk walk to work them off, Austin and I gave one another a precious gift—grace. There were no commentaries or explanations, no defenses or placement of blame, only tears and laughter in all the right places. In the end, we'd parted ways with the strength to confront those we'd hurt and those who'd hurt us.

Knowing my recalcitrant nature, I dropped by Rochelle's shop and left a note on the way home, followed by several unanswered phone calls. As the clock struck midnight, I lost my nerve for any more peacekeeping and decided to tackle Dahlia and Adrian the following morning at work. Both posed a great problem, since my claim against one involved the other. I'd forgiven Dahlia—again—that day at the shower, but somehow her wrong had grown wings from the altar where I'd left it and dropped disease all over my spirit. It was time to bring all my "issues" down to earth.

When I arrived the next morning though, and saw Adrian and Dahlia, laughing together, looking so beautiful, so perfect, my well-planned words escaped me. I returned their waves, but slid behind the protection of the computer at the back of the store, checking for Tracey's devotion to bolster myself. As I clicked on it, I remembered something—it was Rochelle's week. Too late. The words filled the screen.

Therefore, if you are offering your gift at the altar and there remember that your brother has something against you, leave your gift there in front of the altar. First go and be reconciled to your brother; then come and offer your gift.

I stared at the computer screen, blinking through my tears, afraid to scroll down and read the words that followed. The heading, Urgent Grace, had almost escaped me. Though it was copied to the loop, it was my name alone that came next.

Dana,
I write asking your forgiveness and to say that this year has been more difficult than I could ever have imagined. Somehow you've been tangled up in the middle of it all. I tried to spend some time with the Lord today. The Lord met me there and took my hand, leading me to this verse in the Word. And so I come, cowardly I admit, writing an e-mail instead of calling or coming over, but it's all that I have today.

Will you please forgive me? And not just for what's been going on lately, but for the last few years. I've been a controlling maniac over you since you became a Christian. I've so wanted to protect you that I put you under rules and systems that I couldn't even keep myself. And now I fear you'll become as confused and bitter as I have.

Don't. You're a wonderful, beautiful woman. Your own woman. I release you, Dana, from everything that I've placed over you. May only the good things remain. I pray our next meeting will be better than our last.

In Him,

Rochelle

P.S. You were right about Shawn. It didn't work out.

Stunned, I read the message again and yet another time before writing off a quick reply. I wanted to leave it, to write back tomorrow when I wasn't crying so hard that my contacts were about to pop out, when the words weren't so true. But I knew how big a step this had been for Rochelle and how I'd be waiting by my monitor for a response if it had been me. So I typed.

Rochelle,

I forgive you.

And thank you.

You wanted me to live a sincere life for God. A life like yours. Though I can say many things about you, I would never say that you don't do things with both purpose and passion. As much as you've tried to change me. I've tried to change you, too. Now that you are changing, I miss the old Rochelle that I once ridiculed.

Also, anything that I fell bondage to was my own doing as well. I have a house full of Bibles. You have been my schoolmaster. Without you, who knows what might have become of me. Let us both now be free of the law, free of expectation to conform into each other's likeness, free to be wonderfully made in the image of Christ. Let's not speak of it again.

Hush now,

Dana

If only it could be this simple with Dahlia.

Not that the three years of pushing and pulling and praying that had led up to those two e-mails had been easy. Whatever the case, I felt lighter. A weight I hadn't known I was carrying lifted from my heart, though I still felt a little weepy.

I clicked off my Web browser and spun in the chair, staring at the door, where women prowled outside waiting to get in.

I smiled, now intimate with the morning rhythms of Leverhill's Mothers of the Brides. Coffee across the street at The Bean Counter, which now occupied Adrian's old space, and then shopping on my shelves and chatting with friends, old and new. It was hard to believe I owned all the units on this side of the street.

In an uncharacteristic move, I spun my chair around and slipped off my shoes. I walked from the computer at the back of the store to the front where Adrian was on a ladder, lighting the sconces, and Dahlia was counting off the register. Once on the carpet, I dragged my feet through the teal shag one toe at a time. They both stared at me in disbelief.

I was just as surprised, but the simple act of forgiving Rochelle had opened something up in me, the vulnerable part of me that I'd been trying to guard for so long. The seed of who I am. Though I hadn't realized it, protecting this part of myself had kept others from wounding it, but it had also kept me from accessing it. As a holy stillness settled over the room, I saw Dahlia as God might see her, a little girl with a handful of daisies, walking through the house trying to give them away. Everyone she offered them to declined. Each already had a rose. My rose.

It was an obscure memory, like film on top of a pot of tea, forming then fading, but it was real. Yellow roses. For Mama, Daddy, Jordan and me.

"What about me?" she'd said, crying through her words.

"They're all gone, but you can have mine if you want it."

And she'd taken it, both then and now.

"Are you all right?" Adrian was down the ladder and at my side.

He looked like a boy to me again, with a cropped afro and a pocket calculator in his Levi's. "Want to hang?" I could hear him say, as he so often did back then.

"No. I'm going to ride. You can't stay up under me all the time. Go and find somebody who'll be with you all the time. A new friend."

And he did. He'd married her, in fact.

"I'm fine," I said, allowing the tears to flow freely down my face, blurring the past into the present. I opened my mouth to try and explain, but a scent strong enough to awake my numb nose and smooth enough to soothe my broken heart penetrated my senses.

A Jesus breeze. I sat down on the floor and rolled onto my stomach.

Adrian pitched onto his knees beside me. "What is it?" he asked, though his eyes told me he knew that God was working, healing.

My fingers closed around his. He kissed them all together, even his own, then cleared his throat as though he'd forgotten himself. Dahlia didn't say a word.

I took both our hands and pointed upwards toward the candle above us. "What is that?"

He dropped back onto his heels. Though he knew I loved his candles, I rarely spoke of them and hadn't commented on a scent since I'd been there. "Island Wedding," he said, lowering his head closer to mine. "My pineapple with a splash of your jasmine."

A fat, crazy laugh escaped my lips. Dahlia froze at the sound of my joy. Our happiness seemed to accuse her, assault her. I kept laughing and sniffing until she braved a giggle herself.

"Island Wedding, huh?" What a man, this guy. Though jasmine was my favorite, it wasn't a great seller. Too sweet. I didn't make much of it except for myself and I hadn't been doing much for myself of late.

"A little bit of both of us," I said, drinking in the words.

Adrian nodded. He looked so pleased that I was pleased. I hadn't seen him smile like that in a while. "I didn't plan on it. Just started mixing something for myself and you fell into it." He shrugged and kissed my forehead. "Like always."

The bionic music started in my head. There were many things I wanted to say to him, but we had thirty minutes before opening and we weren't alone. I kissed his forehead, too, leaving a heart-shaped print of coral lipstick behind. He wore it like a crown. I waved toward my sister. "Dahlia, take a load off and come and sit with us real quick before we open."

She moved cautiously, reaching us just as the candle's aroma reached full swell. Daddy's triple-thick pineapple shakes with warm berries and whipped cream and a drizzle of orange juice slid across my mind. My sister's favorite. I hugged her with my free arm. "I appreciate everything you've done here."

"But it's time for me to go, huh?"

Adrian answered before I could say a word. "Basically. I hired you at Kick! to help you out, but it's become—"

"Confusing?" she offered.

He laughed a little. "Yeah, that."

Here I was all ready to love up on my sister instead of firing her, like I wanted to for so long, and she decides to leave on her own. God was funny like that. Sometimes He just needs to know you're willing.

Dahlia started for the door. "Funny, I was going to quit today and I didn't know how to tell you two. I was praying about it all morning. I have an idea of my own for a business. I'm going to go for it."

I sighed, this time in a good way. "You do that."

"We're here for you," Adrian said. "We'll miss your skills."

He'd better not miss anything else. As my sister let herself out and the new customers in—who'd seen the whole exchange but seemed to be growing used to our weirdness—I turned to Adrian and took another sniff. "Rename that. Island Wedding just doesn't do it justice. That stuff smells like peace, pure and simple."

Adrian smiled. "Peace it is. For them anyway. It'll always be Island Wedding to me. It's what my dreams smell like."

By noon, I'd come up with a whole new line of peace products—body gloss, bath milk and scented eye pillows. Maybe I'd even have Tracey design some scented drawer liners... Anything to keep my mind off what I would say to Adrian, who gave me the puppy dog look every few minutes. It was going to be a long lunch.

Unable to wait that long, Adrian assisted the last morning customer, flipping the closed sign behind her and pulling down the blinds.

"What are you doing?" In all the time he'd been here, I'd never seen him close during business hours even if nobody came through. He believed a business should be open during its scheduled hours. Period.

The next blind fluttered down. "I'm conducting real business. Something I should have done a long time ago."

I swallowed hard, trying to sort through the determination and regret battling in his voice. Before I could sort out my thoughts, he snuffed all the candles but one, which he grabbed before dragging me to the back room.

He pulled out my chair and set a tall white pillar with gold chunks on a pewter saucer between us. He trimmed the wick to almost a nub and lit the flame, his eyes focused on the flickering light and then on me. "I need to tell you something."

"Wait. I—"

"Please." His voice was firm. "Let me get it out."

Realizing that he needed to receive forgiveness as much as I needed to give it, I sank back into my chair for the second time in one week and listened to a tale of seduction, sin and sorrow. Only this time, it was much harder to hear. Adrian hung his head as he told of his baby Christian pride and how he'd allowed himself to be alone with Dahlia in hopes of "ministering" to her. And that's just what she had done, but to him instead.

"Why didn't you just tell me?"

"Yeah, right."

I nodded. God had really helped me restrain my emotions in the past few years—a little anyway—but back then? Who knows what I might have done? And he had been a snob about his spirituality. I'd considered myself a Christian and he'd gotten on my nerves. Jesus makes all the difference. "But Sandy? Why get married?"

He dropped into the chair and leaned over, his elbows gouging his thighs. His head rolled into his palms. "When I got up from that bed with Dahlia, it was like I'd killed somebody. Murdered something. How could I face you? Face your mother? Your father?" He stiffened. "I could barely face myself."

His hands slid to his ears as though he were holding his head on his body. "So I stayed away—from your family, from our church family, from everything that I knew. And Sandy, well, she filled the gap. Eventually, I told her everything and she convinced me that marrying her was a way out."

My head rolled in a circle the way it had during the cool downs for my workouts at the hospital.

He touched my shoulder. "Don't hate her. I think she believed that."

Okay. Maybe Dahlia as the villain was easier than dealing with the first wife thing. "I don't hate Sandy, Adrian. How could I? She loved you. You loved her."

He shrugged. "She was a good wife, Dana. She helped me a lot, especially with my mother. I don't know why things happened the way they did, but we were happy together."

A chuckle cracked the tension, surprising us both—especially me, since it came from my mouth. "I have to hand it to her. She wanted you bad."

He didn't laugh. "I guess. I grew to love Sandy and I mean no disrespect to her memory. I forgave her for some of the things she said and did without my knowledge and I asked her forgiveness for using her as a way out, though I grew to love her. I would have liked to never revisit all this, but I needed to come clean with you. Especially about your sister."

My head moved up and down a bit. Not quite a nod, but close enough. "Dahlia told me anyway. At Tracey's shower."

He froze. "All this time? You knew? Is that what—"

"No. It probably didn't help, but the stroke was the result of many things." I rolled my shoulders back. "You know what? We've both done some shaky stuff. I never should have left your wedding with Trevor. The real questions we have to answer are about right now."

A knock on the glass interrupted.

We ignored it. The customers would have to heed the sign today.

Adrian rotated the candle plate, watching the pool of wax widen around the wick, now curled over like a bent reed. "Can you forgive me—can you love me—knowing, well, everything?"

I smiled. "I do forgive you." I paused. "And I couldn't stop loving you if I tried."

A relieved look passed over his face.

"Building a relationship though is going to take some time and effort, on both our parts."

Adrian nodded and kissed my hand. "And a lot more candles, huh?"

I laughed and opened my arms to him for a brief, sweet hug. Hand in hand, we walked to the front door, to find Dahlia, crying.

As Adrian clicked the lock and pulled back the glass, my sister tumbled into his arms and wadded his shirt into her fists. "It's over. Trevor's called off the wedding. What am I going to do?"

"What? Why?" Adrian pulled his cell from his pocket and flipped it open, dialing furiously.

I clicked it shut. "What happened, Dahlia?"

A fury of microbraids streaked with blond tumbled over her fingers. "He overreacted. He—he came by the house and I had a friend over. It was innocent—"

Adrian threw up his hands. "Who was it?"

Not that I wasn't curious myself, but why did he care?

Don't go there.

She bit her lip. "Bob."

Adrian pinched the bridge of his nose. "The Visa guy?"

I shook my head. "You didn't." And what was up with Bob? He was better than that, though evidently he didn't know it yet.

She paced back and forth in front of the door. "No, I didn't. It was just a kiss. I was lonely. Upset. Confused. I kept trying to talk to Trevor, but he's so scared of doing something wrong that he wouldn't even be alone with me…." Her voice broke up. "He says maybe we're not ready to get married if I'm kissing somebody. That maybe we should get rooted in Jesus first. How long does that take?"

Adrian and I grabbed hands, trying not to count how much time we'd spent apart. I touched my sister's hair. "You don't want to know."

"Looks like that karate is doing some good."

I shoved the leftover salad into the refrigerator, then dumped the leftover red velvet cake into a disposable container and slid it across the counter. Dad would have to take that home with him. I popped another cube of honeydew into my mouth. "It's kickboxing, Dad. And thanks. I think so, too."

My father came closer, smelling of figs and fried potatoes, a refreshing change from the years of beer and Old Spice imprinted on my memory. Caught up in memories, I tread on our moot subject. "Would you like to go back to church this evening?"

He stroked his beard.

"It's a singing."

Dad's salt-and-pepper eyebrows bushed upward. Sermons were one thing, but singings were quite another. He dumped the fried chicken grease into a coffee can, replaced the lid and dumped it into the trash. He seemed to have made the healthy transition on most things, but he still thought anything fried with olive oil was healthy eating. He frowned at the can for a second as though saying goodbye to an old friend.

I shook my head.

"I'll tell you what, moppet. If you and your sister sing a duet for me tonight, I'll come."

The refrigerator door slammed on my finger. "I don't even know if she's going tonight—" Since Trevor had called off the wedding two weeks ago, Dahlia's church attendance had been scarce.

Dahlia's perfume entered the kitchen ahead of her. "I'm going to church tonight," she said. "And I'll sing if Dana will."

Now you've done it.

Daddy did a little jig. His laughter filled the kitchen as the scent of his dinner had an hour earlier—fried chicken, baked pork chops with an apple-onion sauce, au gratin potatoes, snap beans, red velvet cake, and my dessert, a wedge of the biggest honeydew melons I'd seen in many a summer. He tugged his beard once more. "Be sure and sing it a capella now. No music. I want the real thing."

I took a deep breath and nodded in agreement as my sister's eyes met mine. She smiled. I tried to, but she'd hopped on

Adrian's lap after church. He pretty much pushed her on to the floor like she was a giant bug, but I still wanted to knock the taste out of her mouth. Instead, she'd knocked the taste out of mine. I hadn't been able to eat a thing until this melon. Now I was starving, but we were out the door and at the church before I could think about eating more. I didn't like to sing on a full stomach anyway.

For some reason, the church was packed. I wonder now if Daddy didn't call everyone in the church directory. Pastor certainly didn't seem surprised when the Minister of Music asked if anyone would like to share a song. We hadn't done that since the old days, when evening services were a loosely stitched patchwork of prayers and praise. Today's modern programs didn't allow leeway for such sharing. But tonight was different. For the first time since in years, I sang with my sister. My mother's missing alto echoed in the shadows.

Dahlia started first, both in the procession to the front and in the song. I sighed, thinking she was grandstanding, but I followed anyway, urged on by Daddy's pleading eyes.

"I'd rather have Je-sus…" Dahlia lifted the mic to her mouth, singing in a haunting key.

I followed, trailing up and down the scale, both with my voice and my emotions. "Than silver or gold——" I brought the other microphone closer to my mouth, then farther away. "I'd rather be His…than to have riches unto-oold." My cornrows tickled my neck. I looked over at Dahlia for the next note, but she wasn't singing, she was just standing there. Crying.

The preacher started clapping. "Yes, sir. Yes, sir. Better than gold."

Tears blurred my vision, but my ears worked just fine, though I couldn't believe what I heard next. A deep gut voice, Mama's note, came out of my sister's mouth. She sang the next verse, but refused to relinquish the song, going on to Christ's nail-pierced hands and beyond. It was as if she'd found her ten-year-old self, tucked away all these years waiting to be reclaimed. Like a master, she pulled the room in until most everyone was singing. At "sin's dread sway," she waved for me to join in.

I gave myself to the song, too, remembering what my sister and I had once had. What my family had once had. In the corner of my tear-soaked eyes, I saw a trail of people heading for the altar. We sang on, Dahlia and I, losing our shoes and our pain as Trevor led the pack. Daddy, Rochelle, Jericho, Shemika and Adrian followed close behind. The pastor and his wife came next, sinking between the mountains of brown skin and tailored suits.

When my sobs choked back the song, another voice, a clear tenor rang out between us.

"I'd rather have Je-sus…"

Jordan. I came unglued.

Mother Holly met us down front. The pastor stood and waved to the seated congregation. "Come on. This is some good ground down here. Holy ground. Take off your shoes and bring somebody you love."

I sang on, even as the last creak of my voice slipped away. The revival that Rochelle, Tracey and I had prayed three years for, had come. Only not in the way we'd expected. Had all the pain of this last year led up to this?

I watched as daughters crossed the church to hug their mothers and sons took their father's hands. Jericho climbed the stage and stood next to Jordan, adding a son's voice to a father's. They didn't hold hands, but they stood so close their shoes touched. When they finished, the quiet was so strong that no one spoke for what seemed eternity.

Finally, Trevor broke the silence. "Y'all know me here now."

"We do," Pastor said.

"I'm happy to say that I only love one woman now. Sorry for that confusion."

Laughter rippled through the sanctuary.

"We were supposed to get married…."

"Come on," the pastor nodded, urging him on.

"And we will. But not right now. God has been made real to me since I started coming here, but I realize there's a lot I don't know about being a man, about treating a woman the way she should be treated, especially a woman as fine as Dahlia."

Strained laughter flowed into the aisle.

Trevor, however, took a more serious tone. "We're not ready, but we're not giving up. Even though we went about this thing backwards, God gave us a beautiful baby. We're asking everyone to pray for us as we study with the Pastor and his wife and try to prepare the foundation for a marriage that will last a lifetime. In the meantime, we need to parent this baby girl and learn more about Jesus." He lifted Sierra up on his shoulder.

"Amen to that."

Trevor slid a wad of bills out of his pocket. "Pastor, we had a lot of money tied up in this wedding, but I know that flowers and cake won't make things the way they need to be. Take this for the church."

Pastor waved for two deacons to come and take the money to the back. "Thank you, brother. We're going to use that to start a daycare for your baby and all the others coming up behind her." He stared up at Jericho. "We'll all make it through...together."

I wiped my face and headed off the stage. I'd have to sit down for this.

Trevor raised a hand. "Wait, Dana. Your sister has something for you." He handed up another wad of money to Dahlia, who stepped toward the mike, speaking once again with her own high voice.

She waved for me to come back and held my hand. "Church, this is my sister. I've done her wrong many times, but she keeps forgiving me. Tonight, I want to make a new start for her and for me."

I stared down at Adrian, now seated on the front pew. He shrugged. Daddy swiped at his face with a handkerchief. I stared at the ground as she continued.

"Dana, you've been through it this year. You've almost lost your life and your business, but you never stopped trying to help others. This time, Dana, it's your turn." She motioned to Trevor, who slid yet another envelope from his breast pocket. "Here are our honeymoon tickets to Jamaica and a little change, just enough for a nice wedding of your own." She pressed the envelope with the tickets and the money into my hand.

I blinked in disbelief as the pastor jerked up Adrian's hand as though he'd won a boxing match.

"Do you hear that, church?" the preacher shouted. "I think we're going to have a wedding after all."

# Chapter Seventeen

My arms stuck to my sides, I looked around the church in sweaty horror. Spring would do her damage to me after all. Disappointed by the whole impromptu engagement party at the altar when I hadn't even been proposed to, I left the stage. My sister had given me something for once and everyone was already taking it away. Not that there was anyone else on earth I wanted to spend my life with besides Adrian... But at this moment, I'd rather have Jesus.

After trying to get the microphone from Pastor with no success and trying to shout over the clapping without being heard, Adrian lifted me off my feet and carried me to the car to the cheers of the congregation. "Sorry about all this," he whispered into my hair.

"Me, too." Amazing how a handful of money and some plane tickets made us couple of the year.

Daddy, who somehow managed to beat us to the car, hummed "Victory is Mine" all the way home, where he disappeared into the back bedroom while Adrian and I dropped onto my sectional, exhausted and confused.

I smoothed my hand against his neck, shiny with perspiration after the long service. The cool metal of a ring, laced through a chain, met my touch. His wedding ring again? And they were marrying us off already.

He shook his head at my questioning glance. "It's new. Something between me and the Lord. Something to remind me—" He looked away. "That if I never have the earthly relationships I long for, I will always be joined to God."

I cocked my head to one side. "I guess I never thought about that, guys and Jesus."

He rubbed his chin. "I tried to stop Pastor. I saw it in his eyes before he said it. You know how he is when he gets something in his mind...."

I nodded. "Especially something that's been in his mind a long time."

We both laughed. The refrigerator slammed shut in the kitchen. More humming. Daddy probably had the whole congregation on a conference call.

"So what are you really going to do with the money?"

"How do you know we're not getting married?" I hadn't meant to say it aloud.

He tugged a hangnail off the side of my pinky and lifted my finger to his lips. "Because I haven't asked you yet, let alone gotten a 'yes' out of you."

I love this man.

Adrian looped the chain off his neck and closed his eyes. He clutched the ring, then my hand. He pulled me close, cradling my head on his chest. Hope surged through me. Through us. He took a long breath as if trying to inhale me. He slipped onto one knee.

The room began to spin. "Adrian, don't. Please." Why did I always say that when we got to this strange new place? This was what I'd longed for, so why didn't I feel ready? Is it even possible to be ready? For everything to be just right?

He tugged me down beside him. "Don't you think we've waited long enough?" He ran a hand down my back. "I just need to know...."

A contented sigh escaped my lips. "I want to marry you, Adrian, if that's what you're wondering."

Blowing out a breath, he closed his eyes. "You don't know how bad I've wanted to hear you say that." He swatted my arm. "Hey, you didn't let me ask you!"

I swallowed back my tears. "You asked me a long time ago, remember?" Suddenly, the rest of what had transpired that day on the stoop when Adrian's store had been born came to my mind. A Life Saver ring that I couldn't even get my pinky into and a sincere proposal....

And acceptance.

He looked away. "I thought you forgot that."

"I guess I did, until now."

As if released from a cage, he reached for my face with both hands and brought it to his. His kiss, though gentle, forced back my every fear, reinforced my every hope and threatened my decision not to use Dahlia's money to marry him.

He pushed himself away from me and licked his lips. "You know I'm down with the island wedding thing, but I'm not sure if I can handle another man footing the bill."

I pulled him back. "Ah. Control issues. I knew there was something wrong with you. What do you think about a small ceremony in the pastor's office at the end of the month? Surprise me with the details."

Adrian cocked his headways and let a crooked grin rip across his face. "Now that sounds like a plan. I think I'll die if we go on like this much longer. I have my water heater set to freezing as it is."

"I want to laugh, but mine is probably set lower." Working with Adrian every day hadn't been easy.

His Adam's apple bobbed in his throat. He chuckled uneasily, leaning toward me again. "Don't be mistaken though. If you want to do the island thing, I'll have to set my pride aside. I'll marry you in a minute. Anytime. Anywhere." He patted his suit pocket. "I keep my Altoids ready."

I tried not to cry. How did God take all the broken pieces of my life and somehow make them into something, someone, so beautiful?

His lips brushed my cheek. "Just tell me again that you want to be my wife. When I get home tonight, I'll have this all messed up."

That made me giggle some. I had always been the one wondering, hoping, trying to figure out what was going on…. There was no more time for confusion or fear.

"Let me show you." I let all my fears go and leaned forward, tilting his chin down so as not to miss one inch of the mouth I'd been missing all this time. I laid a kiss on that man the likes of which I'd never felt. It wasn't long—I was too chicken—but it was long enough to convince him that I wasn't looking to be his buddy.

A silly grin stared back at me. "See, that's what I'm talking about. End of the month, you say?"

I nodded. He could be so funny sometimes.

Adrian wasn't laughing. "I know there's lots of water under our bridge, but I'm willing to swim through it to make a future for us." He grabbed my wrist, then let go. "Let's not go back, okay? Let's just be here, Dane. Right now."

I propped up on my elbows, considering his words. Not go forward or back? Be all here? What a concept. If only I could duct-tape my mind to the present. I mustered a smile. "My lipstick looks good on you."

It didn't deter him. "I hope so. I plan to wear it every day. So, what will you do with the money?"

"I have an idea, but it seems selfish."

He shook his head. "Dana, you feel guilty for going to bed at night. You almost died, okay? Don't be afraid to love yourself. Please don't, as you would say. How can you love me, if you don't love you?"

Daddy's fake snoring spewed into the hall. I ignored it. This was too taxing for me to divide my attention. Did I know how to love myself? It sounded so…wrong. "Isn't that un-Christian? We're supposed to die to ourselves and all that…."

Adrian nodded, setting me upright and pulling me to him. "Yes, we must die to self, Dane. But don't literally die. You've spent your life celebrating others. It's okay to do something special between you and the Lord. Why not take your girlfriends on a Sassy Sistah getaway?"

It was a great idea, but I had something else in mind. I squirmed, searching for a way to explain.

Understanding filled Adrian's eyes. "I'm doing it again, aren't I? Okay, I'm going to hush, as you ladies like to say. Tell me what you want and if you want me to help in any way."

I trembled with excitement and not only about my plans. Though we weren't married yet, Adrian's little power bursts had been on my prayer lists each day after work—alongside his prayers for my mood swings and wishy-washiness, I'm sure. "Okay, don't laugh, but… I think I want to do that 'Marry Your Maker' thing you came up with for the sales event. Like a wedding, but to Jesus—a sort of rededication. Do you think a cake would be too much?"

Adrian laughed. "Not if you want one. But don't get me started or I'll open that phone and order one. I'm staying out of this. I'll help with the errands, but the choices are up to you. I think I've done enough with the shop."

I frowned. "Well, I do appreciate what you've done with the shop, but…"

"It's too much, huh?" He looked like a building was about to fall on him.

What fool tells a man he's giving her too much? It seemed ridiculous, but if this marriage was going to work, we both had to be honest. "It's a little too much maybe. I know this is all old hat to you, but this is my first shot at a business. While I appreciate your help…"

He took off his glasses and set them on the table, then draped his arm around me. "I get it and I apologize. The marketing fever, it gets to me. But it is your shop. I mean that."

"I almost believe you." I ducked, but he caught me and kissed me. This getting married stuff was all right.

"Just think about what you like, what's fun for you. Remember how you used to send yourself roses for Valentine's and everyone thought they were from me?"

Now why did he have to go there? I punched his arm. "That was middle school! I just wanted some flowers, okay?"

He kissed my nose. "Yes, it *is* okay. That's what I'm saying."

Plans for my celebration flitted across my mind. "What if I just took the money and paid everyone's way to Jamaica and had a simple ceremony on the beach?"

He closed his eyes, then opened them adding a toothy grin. "I think that—would be awesome. I have only one request."

My head inched upward as if trying to avoid a hook punch. Did he want to pick my dress? "What?"

"Can I be your man of honor? You'd have to promise not to hit me with the flowers of course—"

I kissed him silent. "No promises about the flowers, but I'd be blessed to have you stand up for me, first as my man of honor and then as my husband."

He kissed me back. "Promise?"

I dragged him to the door by his tie. "Promise."

As I padded down the hall to my room, my father's voice stabbed into the hall. "Well, Nella, you didn't live to see it, but I think those two are finally getting married. The pastor's office ain't the way I would go, but we'll take it, won't we? Yes. We'll take it."

With a chuckle, I dove into my bed, fully dressed on the outside and my heart bare within.

* * *

"This is so exciting. Just like that logo I drew."

"Pretty much." Tracey was such a hoot with her associations, though this one wasn't too off base. "So can you two make it? I know it's short notice."

Her voice changed. "Both of us? Ryan, too? I was thinking just the girls. I'd love to get to know Austin better. I'm loving having her on the loop now. She's sweet."

I agreed, but sensed something else afoot.

Tracey continued. "Besides, I need to get away, maybe stay in Jamaica for the week? I can pay the extra—"

Find another scapegoat.

"What's wrong now? I thought things were better between you and Ryan. Did he do something?"

I could imagine her squirming , shifting the phone from ear to ear. "Did he do something? He's done nothing." She paused. "And everything! He shaves his face and leaves these hunks of hair everywhere. He washed his car with my face towels—"

Oh, no. "Not the pink ones?" I'd once used her yellow set to wipe up some spaghetti sauce and seen a side of Tracey I'd never known existed. One of my ears still pointed east as a result of the cuffing she gave me, with an oven mitt, no less.

"Yes. The pink towels…and the new yellows, too. He used those on his tires!" She half sobbed, half screamed the last part, while I felt for a seat. Rochelle had Jericho and Tracey had her towels. I knew better than to mess with either. Somehow Ryan hadn't picked up on his wife's affinity for linens. Should we have written him a memo about the untouchables?

"I, uh, well…I'm so sorry. But he's a guy, Tracey. They don't always think about these things."

"Oh, no, he's not a guy. Adrian is a guy. Ryan is a pig! You know what he did on our little 'light the fire' weekend, the one that was going to make everything better? Watched NASCAR and worked! We went to the beach one day. Then the cell phone

that he promised not to bring suddenly appeared and started ringing. I was too ashamed to tell you guys."

I nodded my head, silently remembering the phone's promi-
nent display on the few outings I'd had with Ryan. It was as if
he'd been saying, "You're nice and all, but this phone here? She's
my real woman. Didn't want there to be any confusion." And
there wasn't. I'd figured out very quickly that neither Ryan nor
his phone were the next big thing in my life. Why had Tracey
taken until now to figure it out? Probably that whole not waiting till the wedding thing she'd divulged at her baby shower. Hard
to believe that I was the sensible one for once. "Well, Tracey, you'll
get used to it."

Somehow.

"I thought I would get used to it, but I can see now that I let
that diamond and…other things cloud my judgment. I feel like
I'm waking up from months of sleeping."

What a word picture. The phrase "I told you so" bounced
around in my head, but I squelched it like the evil it was. That
was the last thing she needed to hear. "Hey, it's not so bad. This
is how it is for everybody at first."

Her voice perked up a bit. "Really?"

"Really." I hoped not. Until this conversation, I'd really been
considering skipping my little dedication ceremony and getting
married instead. We had all the paperwork done. The end of the
month seemed years away. But listening to Tracey, I realized how
difficult marriage could be if I tried to do it without being
grounded in God. Adrian was a good man, but he was still a
man. And God knows I can be a real piece of work myself. "It'll
just take some getting used to. It's like Rochelle said in that devo
yesterday—"

"That's the problem."

"What? Chelle?"

"No—me. I've been deleting the devotionals, skipping my
turn, not reading my Bible. It's like I'm having a showdown with

Ryan…and God. I try to pray, but I just can't. I know He's going to tell me to let go of my anger and I don't want to! My husband is wrong!"

I took a long breath and ran my tongue over my lips, which still went numb from time to time. What a price anger had exacted in my life. Tracey's words made me cringe at first, but only because they could have once come from my own mouth. Even worse than her, I'd kept doing my "Jesus stuff"—church, Bible study, devotionals—and kept my anger, too.

"Tracey, believe it or not, I understand the angry frustrated thing. I do. But we both know that we can't stay here." When had *she* become *we?* "God doesn't want us to hold on to this stuff. It's poison. Go back in there and talk to your husband. Tell him calmly what you told me and pray on the rest. Let's just see what the Lord is going to do."

The Tracey I knew and loved responded from the other side of the receiver. "I love him. I really do. I just didn't figure it would be like this. I guess I haven't been exactly praying for him, either…"

"See? There you go. Just take a step. Sow a seed to righteousness. The next one might be easier to toss."

"*Umph, umph, umph.* Girl, you always know just what to say."

Sure do. Except to myself.

I stayed silent, knowing she'd talk it through. This listening thing was really cool if you could get the hang of it.

"I guess a trip to Jamaica won't hurt. I know I'm nearing the end of my pregnancy and I'm all crazy, too."

Nearing the end? Had it been that long? "Will you be okay to fly?"

"Sure. I've got a few weeks yet. My only problem was flying with him."

"You're too much. Now scoot, before Ryan thinks the phone has swallowed you." I really wanted to get off the phone so I could call Adrian. We talked a lot, now that we'd allowed ourselves to relax a little. Very little. It didn't take much to get us going. Still, I was starting to wish I hadn't invited everyone to Jamaica. More and more, I wanted to spend time with just Adrian. But without being married, he and I being alone on a beautiful beach pretty much wasn't going to happen. I closed my eyes. Maybe we could get married before we went and have that as a honeymoon. The phone beeped. "Tracey, you still there? I think that's Adrian."

She giggled. "I'm going. Pray for me, okay?"

I'd been praying since the day they announced their engagement. "Will do."

I pressed the button and listened for Adrian's voice. There it was, real and smooth. Strong. He bid me good-night, told me he loved me and said a short prayer. He was exhausted, I could tell. I prayed, too, and we said our goodbyes. It was a simple thing, those few minutes at night, but they meant a lot. I pulled the headset off my ears and let it dangle around my shoulders, before dragging myself to the back bedroom to grab some bath fizzies just for me—pineapple, coconut and orange with a few drops of Vanilla Smella added in. And of course, one candle.

Island Wedding.

Peace.

It was a hard sell at first, especially since I could only pay for a few people and the whole church was still convinced I was going to marry Adrian anyway, but didn't want them to be there. Once I explained about my "Marrying My Maker" ceremony, my plans were being discussed and duplicated all over town.

And that was okay. Most women I knew had spent their lives caring for other people and never so much as lit a candle for themselves. I certainly wasn't any expert in this allowing-God-to-love-on-me thing, but it was time to learn, especially if Adrian's planning was anything near what he kept hinting at for our wedding. Rochelle thought I was unwise to let him plan it, but just doing this ceremony was driving me mad. He wanted to give me something and for once, I was going to allow myself to receive. For now, I had Jesus to get ready for.

I prepped myself with small wonders at first, fresh roses for my dinner table, tea with Austin on Mama's china, taking out my hair extensions and getting my own hair braided, with cowrie shells in unexpected places.

Though I only had two weeks to plan, my ceremony of redemption and renewal came together so smooth even I couldn't believe it. All those travelogues from Adrian with notes in the margin didn't hurt, either. The sight of Seven Mile Beach took my breath away and from the looks of its dog-eared page, Adrian liked it, too. Some days I got overwhelmed with it all and considering canceling. How could I do such a frivolous thing? Whenever I doubted my worthiness, I heard the Holy Spirit whisper, *You are bought with a price...a daughter of the King.*

And so, I pressed on, sending out jasmine-scented linen notes written in Daddy's calligraphy to remind travelers where to be, and to remind Adrian that I loved him. The travel agency, familiar with vacation weddings, picked up the flowers and decorations, leaving me only with a dress to choose. I took my array of pastel sheaths on the rounds for my friends and family to see.

My sister picked pink. Rochelle, lime. Tracey used Photoshop to change the lemondrop-colored dress into a multicolored rose print. "Dana's Garden," she'd named the file. Adrian smiled, but said nothing. When we were alone, I asked him why he hadn't expressed a preference.

"They're all nice, but it's your choice."

"Uh-huh." He couldn't fool me that easily.

He shrugged. "Why not white?"

I raised an eyebrow. "I think you know exactly why not."

He shook his head. "See, that's your flesh talking. You're forgetting who you are. Who God is. It's your decision, but when you go back, consider trying on the white."

Though I'd decided against it, on a whim before I left the store empty-handed, I did try on something white. Adrian might have heard me screaming six blocks away. Forty pounds slimmer than I'd been in years, I still hadn't braved so much as a white towel, much less a straight dress. But this one with a gauzy jacket and bows at the hem was perfect. Just perfect.

It occurred to me that on the day I got saved, I'd found Trevor and Dahlia together and now I'd recommit again on a happy day, but one that found the two of them apart. I'd invited them both to the ceremony, even offered to pay their way—with their own money, don't you just love that? Though still in pastoral counseling and spending more time apart these days than together, they agreed, admitting that they wanted to reconnect with Jesus and makeover that day, as well. They only had one stipulation.

"Invite us to your wedding, too. And we'll do likewise."

I smiled, excited at the thought of keeping both promises.

The seating on the plane worked out with me next to Austin, her hubby across the way and Rochelle on the other side of him. I could see Adrian's head if I leaned down and to the right. We switched seats so Austin and Josh could be together, but Adrian let Rochelle stay next to me. He knew both of us all too well. She needed some girl time. Jericho, Daddy and Shemika were two rows in front of us discussing the Bradley birthing method or some such foolishness. Dad kept emphasizing that it was also known as the husband-coaching method of birth. I have to give it to him. He never lets up. Dahlia, Trevor and my niece were all together in first class, looking too good for us to be mad at 'em. To my surprise, Jordan had showed up at the send-off with a packed bag and now sat three rows behind us. He'd insisted on coming to escort Rochelle down the aisle with the rest of Christ-maids or whatever they were. I was thankful to them both, knowing the tension between them.

I turned to face Rochelle. "So what does this mean? You and Jordan being here?"

"It means that we love you. Very much. Nothing more."

"But where's his girlfriend? She wasn't at the church. I haven't seen her since—"

"They're getting married. Next spring."

I gulped back a mouthful of stale airplane air. And a few tears, both of regret and relief. What a weird feeling. Not that I was too hot on the idea of Jordan marrying that woman, especially if she insisted on dressing like Elvira, but for some reason I was glad that Rochelle would be moving on. My face sobered. Or would she move on to another weirdo from the singles group? Even worse, would she move on from our family? From being my friend? "How do you feel about all this?"

She stared over at Jericho, smiling in oblivion next at Shemika. "I really don't know. I've got bigger things to worry about than your brother now. Shemika and Jericho will make it through the school year, but next year will be harder. Mother Holly can only do so much. Shemika may end up moving in and Jericho moving in with Jordan for a few months. I don't know."

I nodded. This year, this trip, was a turning point for us all.

I laced my fingers between hers, trying to ignore the rising voices of Tracey and Ryan behind us. "Well, whatever happens, know that I'm here for you. And I support you."

"I really hope you mean that." Rochelle smiled a tight smile. She eased back on her pillow and closed her eyes.

I stared out of the airplane window into the clouds, trying to interpret my friend's last words. Pineapple scent wafted back to me from the seat ahead. "We'll have our time soon," he mouthed when no one was looking. We planned to announce our wedding plans after my ceremony, but everyone, including our pastor, seemed confident that we wouldn't make it back to the States without being wed.

One of Adrian's wide, brown hands reached back and clutched mine. My mind ceased pondering Rochelle's puzzles. I had mysteries of my own to figure out.

# Chapter Eighteen

"Is it really that blue?"

My father stared doubtfully at the sequined gown of turquoise lapping against Negril's white sand.

Jordan walked in tandem with Rochelle and Jericho to the right of us. "It's real, Dad."

I was with my father. The view was incredible. Even the occasional gusts of wind felt good, though the sand shifting between my feet and the sandals Rochelle had made me was a little distracting at first. We marched silently, as the waves rushed to the shore, then eased back, like somebody getting up from a table after a good meal. Across the beach under a rose-covered arch, I could see the waiting minister, bent and brown with graying dreadlocks. Strains of the accompaniment band whispered in the mist of the ocean, so salty against my lips. I'd picked the right place and the coordinator had done an excellent job. Everything seemed too good to be true. Especially Adrian.

I smiled at our little crowd, made bigger by the surprise arrival of my aunt Cheryl and my two cousins last night. Only Renee, who'd been too deep in Fingerhut bills to attend, was missing. One never knew when people would come through for you. That's what I'd like to think anyway. In truth, they were here to go home and give a full report to the gossip mill, but hey, the more the merrier.

We ambled toward the ceremony location, taking time to appreciate the surroundings and God, who had created them. A few feet separated Adrian and me. He shielded his brow from the sun with one hand, taking in the view. "You picked well, Dana. This place is unbelievable."

We reached for each other's hands at the same time. Adrian's grip was sure. He was trying to be let my family have me, I could tell, but more and more, I wished we had this beautiful scene all to ourselves. "Thanks for your help. It made all the difference." Jamaica was nice, but it was Adrian who was unbelievable. More so every day since I'd told him I'd marry him. Walking on this beach, I couldn't remember exactly why I wasn't marrying him today.

Adrian kissed my hand. That dull ache that always gripped me when I picked the wrong answer on tests, hit my midsection. Suddenly, I wanted nothing more than to run to the makeshift altar across the sand, though it wouldn't do us a bit of good. My desire must have shown of my face.

"There'll be time for that," he whispered. "Though I have to admit, this is so beautiful, I've got honeymooning on my mind, too."

Yes, there would be time. For now, all I had to do was enjoy this day with my family, my friends, my man and God. How hard could that be? Real hard, when a big fine man, smelling like pineapples and cherry wood—must be something from the hotel— is holding my hand. I can almost hear my mother's voice in my head, "You should have married that boy last week!" And as always, she'd be right.

I flashed a look at Austin, who was snuggling with her husband a few paces ahead. As if she felt my glance, my new friend looked back and smiled. She knew what I was thinking, I could tell by the curl of her mouth and her wistful stare. "Do it," she whispered.

Do it? Do what? Marry Adrian? If only I could. The file with our marriage license and birth certificates was back on my desk in Illinois. Though it would have been nice to have a ceremony here and get married later, that wasn't going to work, not the way Adrian was looking in that suit. It was the gray one I'd spilled punch on at Tracey's wedding. I felt just as breathless seeing him in it today as then.

Tracey walked up and took my left hand, trying to gain balance for her bulging belly. Ryan lagged behind her, chatting with Trevor about his latest album. She smiled, but sadness flashed in her eyes. "This is so beautiful. I'm so proud of you. For waiting. For holding out."

The underlying tone in Tracey's voice left me speechless. Was that…jealousy? "Well, I've only been holding out for four years, but I'm thankful for God's grace to keep me. It was only Him."

Tracey snorted, then looked back at her husband. "Yeah, well, be thankful." She hung her head a little. "I'm ashamed to say it, but I envy you a little."

So there it was. No need to wonder. I just nodded, understanding totally. Too bad I hadn't been woman enough to admit the same thing at her wedding. Tracey's hand dropped from mine, but her smile stayed fixed. "It's okay. You know what? On your day, I envied you a little, too, Tracey. I was happy for you, but a little jealous. I didn't realize it then. So forget it. I understand."

She nodded and let out a long breath. "Yes, that's it. Happy and hurt at the same time. I feel like I'm losing you all over again."

"She's not married yet," Adrian whispered across us the way the waves played against the beach.

I winked at him, forgetting for a moment that Tracey was there.

Tracey patted my hand a final time then let go and waved toward her husband. "Come on, Ryan. Walk with me."

"Sure-sure babe." My friend's husband bounded towards us with a reluctant grin, one he'd worn in my presence since their wedding day. He knew that Tracey and I discussed him often and didn't think I liked him anymore.

I flashed all thirty-two teeth to prove him wrong. "Thanks for coming, Ryan."

He forced a smile. "Thanks for inviting me, Dana. And for-for being such a good friend to Tracey."

As we closed in on our destination, the minister motioned for us to come closer. His eyes, though brown, sparkled like the bright blue water of Seven Mile Beach. The band, clad in ochre, crimson and a crisp, happy green moved little, but released a gentle thunder of steel drums and other instruments I couldn't identify. Dahlia, who'd been somber through most of the trip, broke out in a round of giggles, then stepped across the sand toward me.

I eyed the minister for a rebuke on how long we were taking, but he merely smiled. The band continued to play.

My sister moved tentatively at first, and then with purpose. "I know there's not a lot of time but I feel like I really need to say this, I'm just going to say it."

"Go ahead." Even Dahlia couldn't dim this moment.

"I'm embarrassed about how I've acted. I don't know why I try so hard to outdo you, Dana. Maybe because Mama always loved you better—"

"Now you're talking crazy, Dahlia," my father spoke softly.

"Maybe, but that was how it seemed. Anyway, I just wanted you to know that whenever you and Adrian do get married, you don't have to worry about me."

Adrian kissed my temple. I found my voice. "I'll always be concerned about you, Dahlia. We both will. Thanks for coming."

My father cleared his throat again, this time sounding like a radar siren. "Yes, thank all of you for bringing me to this beautiful place. Just make sure the next time it's for a wedding. This marrying Jesus business is a good thing, but we could have done this at the Holiday Inn for what it cost."

The truth of his words stung a little, but I kept silent. Adrian kissed my cheek.

Daddy smoothed his worn Stacey Adams shoes over the white sand. "By the time y'all get around to getting married, I might not be anymore for this world—"

"Daddy, please." I tried to make the words sound frivolous, but they choked in my throat. I hadn't expected my stroke or Mama's death. Though Daddy seemed healthy, he was getting older. And what about me? Just because I'd made a good recovery and some lifestyle changes, every day was a gift. An urgency washed through me. Adrian and I would marry as soon as the plane touched down in Illinois.

"Seriously, moppet. All our days are numbered. Who would have ever thought that your brother and sister would be here like this? That you and Adrian would end up together after all? Just don't be foolish and wait too long. That's all I'm saying."

"We won't, Dad. We hear you," Adrian spoke before I could find my voice. I waited to see if he'd tell about our plans at the end of the month...well, as far as Adrian knew. I'd be marrying that brothah at the airport if I could swing it.

I stroked Dad's wrinkled hand, extending from the cuff of his favorite suit, one Mama had picked out for him for Jordan's graduation. After all this time, he wore it well. "We're getting married soon, Daddy. We hear you."

The minister nodded, but didn't say a word. Maybe those "Jamaica, no problem" commercials were accurate. In the States, the preacher would have been long gone by now.

My father nodded back at the older man, stopping short at the rose-covered arbor. "I hope God hears me, too." He turned his face to the sky. "Lord, they're all here. All my children. I thank you for bringing us together and for saving my baby's life. And whenever these two get married, whether I'm there or not, I give my blessing and acknowledge Adrian as what he's always been to me…my son."

Adrian released my hand, took a few steps and gathered my father's frail body into his arms. His wet eyes were fixed on me as he spoke to my father. "Thank you, Dad, for those words. And for…" Jordan, Rochelle, Tracey and I closed a circle around them.

"For being a father to me when my father died, and even before, for opening your house to me, for feeding me, for loving me and most of all for forgiving me."

The music played on softly. The minister nodded as though it was this that we'd come for and his job was only to watch.

Tears played down my face. Forgiveness? Had Adrian gone to my father and told him about what had happened with him and Dahlia? Or worse, with him and me? I bristled at the thought of it, but knowing Adrian, that was exactly what he'd done.

My father pulled away and straightened his tie. "You hurt me, son, I can't lie. I promised Nella I'd take care of these girls, you know? But I can't hold a thing against you, knowing all that God has forgiven me. Welcome to the family."

God? Daddy had slipped back into my life at the worst time. All my tracts had been thrown away and my witnessing tools long forgotten. I'd stopped trying to convert him and just loved him like before. Had God, in His lavish grace, seen fit to save my father while I was out to lunch? Though I prayed it was true, I knew it probably wasn't that simple. But we had a place to start. Dad's last statement alone was worth this trip.

Adrian took his place at my side, making no effort to wipe his tears. Tears that I'd seldom seen. Tears I longed to kiss away. Tracey sobbed softly. Rochelle and Jordan stood shoulder-to-shoulder, both wiping their eyes.

A stem of one of the roses from the arbor pressed into my side. I took a breath and waited for the pain, but there was none. I was dressed in satin again, but this time there were no thorns. Warmth blew in off the water, tugging the tulle off my shoulders.

"Are we ready?" The minister finally spoke with an echo much the same as the steel drum.

I nodded. Adrian stepped back. My heart broke. Suddenly, I wanted more than me and Jesus. I wanted Adrian by my side, too. "Stay," I whispered to him. He pivoted quickly, retaking his spot.

At my nod, the minister produced the anointing oil I'd prepared and broke open the seal. He smiled at the pineapple-jasmine scent that escaped the bottle. The best of me and the best of Adrian. Peace.

He touched it to my forehead. "Do you, Dana Ann Rose—"

A voice I later recognized as my own broke the moment. "Wait!" An awkward pause slipped between us as I gathered my resolve. I bit my lip. "Can you do it again, only for me and him?" My thumb pointed to Adrian. "Maybe we can make it legal when we get back." Waiting weeks for a honeymoon wouldn't be easy, but this was torture.

Adrian closed his eyes as if saying a silent prayer. He turned to Ryan, who waved a folder—had he had that in his suit or what?—in the air. He traced my eyebrow with his finger. "I know I said I'd stay out of it, but I meddled a little, just in case."

I smiled. I knew his nerdiness would come in handy sometime. "What did you do?"

He made a cute face. "Since you got the Wedding Moon package, I went ahead and submitted our marriage license and birth certificates to the travel agent. She set up everything for a valid wedding in case you changed your mind. You'd paid for it already, after all."

My father clapped his hands together and looked up at the sky. "I knew the boy had some sense."

"It's all here," Ryan said. "And I checked with the travel agency and government here. I'm a notary public and can sign the Illinois paperwork, as well. You'll be legally married after the ceremony."

The minister smiled as though he dealt with such crazy people every day. "What do you say, young man? Is this what you want?"

"I say Hallelujah. Let's do this thing." A beautiful, crooked smile danced across Adrian's lips.

I was still back on him bringing the marriage license. "How did you know?" I whispered.

He kissed my forehead to the applause of the crowd. "I didn't know, but I hoped." He reached into his pocket again, this time for two rings, mine a diamond cluster with a middle stone as big as a sugar cube. He'd lost his mind, but I wasn't complaining. The inscription drained any shred of resolve I had left. Thank God for my big fingers. I needed every word.

For Dana, Made of Honor, Bride of Christ and Wife of Mine.

The words blurred before me. I pressed my face into his shirt. This was my family, but he was going to make me cry like a baby in front of them. So many times, I'd passed the ball, but not today. This was my shot.

"All right, preacher." It was Daddy's voice, overflowing with contentment. "Don't pay these two any mind. Let's get on with it."

Adrian nodded, taking my hand.

My husband-to-be gave me a little wink. Ryan stood near the minister with his seal—had he hid that in his shoe? Adrian pulled a napkin from the plane out of his pocket and handed it to the pastor.

The old man unfolded it and began to read. "Do you, Dana Ann Rose and Adrian Luke Norrell take this Jesus to be the God of your lives, the Love of your souls and the Head of your marriage, whether sick or well, poor or rich, distressed or blessed, for as long as you both shall live?"

They were my vows, the ones for my service with God, adapted to include both of us.

Adrian tucked my arm under his and stared into my eyes. Our voices flowed together like a melody. "We do."

The preacher took hold his makeshift pulpit. "Do all those here pledge as witnesses, commit to pray for Dana and Adrian, to encourage them in times of despair, to correct them in love when needed and to forgive them when they fail?"

"We do." The voices rang out stronger than the numbers. Daddy's and Jordan's deep voices formed the foundation. Shemika took the high top note, with my aunt and cousins mixing in. How beautiful their voices sounded.

"I now pronounce you man, maidservant and maker. Married to each other and to an Almighty Husband who'll return soon for a church without wrinkle—and has His own iron to get things straight. Delight in Him always. You may kiss the bride." The old man smiled in satisfaction.

The reggae band struck an upbeat rendition of "Holy, Holy, Holy" as Adrian took my face in his hands and kissed me until my toes curled in my sandals. Austin and Tracey's laughter and Josh and Trevor's whistles melted into the background as I accepted my husband's loving kiss. I smoothed his bald head, returning his kiss. The truth of the moment crashed against my mind. Adrian was my husband.

As we broke our lip-lock, a white bird settled on the top of the arbor. The dove I'd paid an extra fifty dollars to have released during the ceremony and forgotten about. My eyes again blurred with tears. The waters of my heart had finally receded. It was time to emerge from where I'd hidden for so long. It was time for peace. For love.

I released my husband's hand and sank to the sand, arms outstretched to heaven. "Thank you. For everything." When I gathered my hands into my lap, unable to rise, just as he had that day at Tracey's wedding, Adrian gathered me into his arms, stopping only to pluck a rose from the arch. He slipped the stem into my hair then bent down for my bouquet, a circular braid of pink roses and baby's breath—I didn't want to injure anyone. He hurled it over his shoulder.

I struggled to look around his muscular arms. He turned in time for me to see Dahlia miss the catch and the ring of flowers hit Rochelle square in the forehead. I laughed through my tears.

Ryan ran behind us with his notary stamp and a pen. Adrian hurriedly signed his name. I scribbled mine just as quickly.

Adrian handed the paper back. "Is that it? Are we legal? I almost forgot that part."

Already walking away, Ryan laughed. "Yes, that's it. I'll fax it now and file the original at the courthouse. I've got to get back, the next ceremony is starting."

I poked my head up from the crook of Adrian's arm. "The next ceremony?"

Ryan nodded. "Yeah. Dahlia's going to do that commitment to Jesus thing since you didn't. She wanted to, evidently, but didn't want you to think she was trying to push in on your thing. The minister is down with it, so…" His voice faded into the wind.

Funny, when we planned all this, I had it backward. This was supposed to be Dahlia's honeymoon and it turned out to be mine. It was going to be the memorial of my commitment to Christ and it ended up being Dahlia's fresh start with God instead. When God says that His thoughts are not our thoughts, believe it. This is how it should be.

"Thanks, man!" Adrian shouted, then waved to Ryan as he rejoined the others. As much as Adrian loved my family, he didn't even discuss the option of sticking around. In fact, he broke into a jog towards the vans we'd rode over in. He kissed me again before depositing me into the passenger's seat of the first one we came to and bent over, feeling for the key under the mat.

I swallowed. "Now what?"

He looked up with an intensity that made me shiver. "Now, dear wife, I take you home. And this time, I'm coming in to stay."

## ACKNOWLEDGMENTS

Writing a book is never the work of one woman.
The fingerprints upon these pages are many. My apologies
if someone is not mentioned by name as space is limited.
My gratitude, however, is not, I thank you all, with all
my heart. That said, special thanks to:

Christ, for helping me tell this story. As always,
You brought me through.

Ashlie, Michelle, Fill Jr., Ben, James, John and Isaiah,
thanks for eating all that Chunky soup without complaining
and for tolerating all the soap and candles I made
instead of dinner. I love you all.

Fill, for your unflinching belief in me, for proofreading my
proposal, keeping my computer running, making graphics
when I need them yesterday and tolerating my mania in
general. You are my hero. Your love makes me strong.

My mother, Donna, and all the Freeman clan, thanks for being
so funny, even when life was serious. I'm honored to be
part of such a gifted family.

Kent and Debbie Nottingham and the family of
Calvary Chapel Tallahassee, thanks for loving my family
and teaching us the Word for the past ten years.
Thanks for being a place of refreshing.

My editor, Diane Dietz, for laughing in all the right places
and for being a pleasure even amidst her losses; executive
editor Joan Marlow Golan, thanks for giving me a chance
and for your hard work for our line.

Dave Robie, for his diligence in finding a home for my work.

Jessica Ferguson, thanks for being my best critic and
my cheerleader in hard times. I never could
have done this without you.

To the many people who gave input on this book at varying stages: Lisa Samson, Sharon Ewell Foster, Laura Jensen Walker, Linda Baldwin, Beth Ziarnik, Tracey Bateman, Lynn Bulock, Rachel Hauck, Stacey Hawkins Adams, LaShaunda Hoffman, Vanessa Davis Griggs, Stephanie Perry Moore, Dr. Gail Hayes, Cyndy Salzmann, Kristin Billerbeck, Colleen Coble and everyone I'm forgetting to name.

Angela, Jackie, Vicki, Donna, Rosemary and the other godly single women in my life. You inspire me.

My friends, Joy, Melissa, Gail and Claudia, thanks for tolerating my silences and disappearances. Each of you is a gift to me.

The ladies of The Threshing Floor: Amy, Jennifer and Staci, thanks for your great feedback and support. You mentored the mentor.

Yolanda Callegari Brooks, for your friendship and support. I love you. Sisterly.

My Faithchick.com sisters. Blogging with you and getting to know you has been a pleasure. I'm honored to know you all.

To Heather, Claudia, Bobbie, Paula and all my friends in the blogosphere. Thanks for being there. It means a lot.

To the Word Praize family, thanks for your support and friendship and for hanging around despite all my absences. I believe in each of you.

# DISCUSSION QUESTIONS

1. As the book opens, Dana has mixed feelings about her best friend's wedding. When her instincts turn out to be correct, she prays for Tracey and tries to help her sort out her feelings but realizes she wants her own marriage to be different. Have you ever known ahead of time that a relationship might not be the best idea for you or for a friend? Did you go through with it anyway? What happened?

2. Dana, Tracey and Rochelle are some of the last members of the Sassy Sistahood e-mail list. If you had a chance to join a group like this, would you? If so, which of the three friends would you probably be closest to? Whom did you identity with most?

3. Dana's sister has done some hurtful things to her, but now Dahlia's trying to live for Christ. Would you struggle with having someone like her back in your life or would you freely forgive Dahlia, knowing that God will transform her as she grows as a Christian? Did Dana do well in how she handled this situation? If not, what could she have done better?

4. Austin, the local news reporter who visits Dana's shop, becomes a new and unexpected friend. Though the two women seem to have little in common at first, as they spend more time together, they realize they have much to share. Have you ever made an "instant friend" like Austin? Are you still friends with that person today?

5. Dana spends a lot of time thinking about the past with Adrian and struggles at first to consider a future with him. Though her memory of him stealing her business idea turns out to be false, something much worse turns out to be true. Have you ever reached a turning point when you had to let go of the past to grab on to the future? What did you decide? Do you think that Dana made the right decision with Adrian?

6. Dana's relationships with her father and brother start out rocky at best. Yet, in the end, Jordan and her dad are there for her and support her. Have you ever had to rethink your feelings on someone in our family? Has someone you know made a great turn around in their life? Did you find their new life hard to accept?

7. Though Dana's goal is to make products to help women relax, she stresses herself out to do it, to the point of endangering her own health. Have you ever been so concerned for others that you couldn't find time to take care of yourself? Do you struggle to balance work, family and faith? If so, what is one thing you can do this week to relieve some stress?

8. Throughout the story, Dana struggles with her weight, although she ends the story at the same weight she started at. At the end of the tale, however, she is healthier and feels better about herself. What do you think made the difference in her attitude?

9. Dana's business started out as a hobby. Is there something you've always wanted to try or learn about, but you've never had the time? If your resources were unlimited, what kind of craft or hobby wold you try? If the funds for a business start-up were at your disposal, what kind of business would you be interested in?

10. The verse at the front of this book is Psalms 139:14 "I praise You because I am fearfully and wonderfully made..." The return of her brother and old boyfriend, starting a new business and almost losing her life certainly showed Dana what she was made of. In the end, she was both stronger and weaker than she'd thought. Have circumstances in your life revealed what's in your heart? Were you surprised by what you saw? If not, what do you think made the difference?

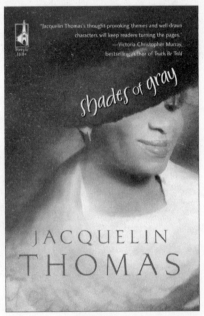

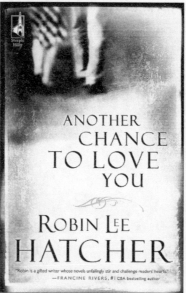